The Library of Scandinavian Literature

THE LOST MUSICIANS

This work is the 26th
in the series of translations published under the auspices of the
Council of Europe in order to make available to a wider public
literary works written in the lesser-known European languages.

THE LOST
MUSICIANS

William Heinesen

TRANSLATED FROM THE DANISH BY
ERIK J. FRIIS
INTRODUCTION BY
HEDIN BRØNNER

TWAYNE PUBLISHERS, INC., NEW YORK
&
THE AMERICAN-SCANDINAVIAN FOUNDATION

The Library of Scandinavian Literature

Erik J. Friis, *General Editor*

Volume 12

The Lost Musicians, by William Heinesen

Introduction

To many American readers this book will represent a literary voyage of discovery, because Faroese fiction has remained unknown on the western shore of the Atlantic until very recently. William Heinesen, whose work epitomizes a fascinating duality in Faroese literature—insular simplicity woven through with European refinement—has only once before appeared in English, and then only in Great Britain. This neglect of an area rich in literary tradition and independent thinking cannot be due entirely to language hurdles, for many of the works in question were originally written in Danish rather than in the rare and difficult Faroese tongue. Have English-speaking readers been assuming that a tiny dot in the ocean cannot have anything to contribute to modern thought? If so, perhaps it is time for a reassessment of values. Perhaps a chastened world can turn to microcosms like this for spiritual rejuvenation.

The Faroes are a jumble of eighteen craggy islands that tower over the swirling currents and raging surfs of the North Atlantic, about halfway between the Shetland Islands and Iceland. They are better known as the Faroe Islands, though this is redundant because the Danish name *Færøer* (Faroese *Føroyar*, pronounced "Furr'yar") means Sheep Islands.[1] The population of roughly 40,000 subsists mainly on

---

[1] The derivation of *Fær-* (*Før-*) is in dispute, but at least *-øer* (*-oyar*) means "islands."

1

fishing and fish processing; sheep raising; home crafts (particularly knitting); and seamanship. There are no forests on the islands, and the unpredictable gales and short summers make normal forms of agriculture well-nigh impossible. But like all other North Atlantic islands, they are overgrown with grasses and other meadow plants, which achieve prodigal lushness in the constantly moist climate. The Gulf Stream keeps the surrounding waters open the year round and prevents the thermometer from going to extremes, so that the islanders can say—to use an Icelandic expression—that they have no summer and no winter, or that they have no climate —only weather. The resulting hazards and uncertainties in Faroese life have a profound effect on the national character and on literary style. In a land where some communities may be suddenly cut off from the rest because of freakish tides and currents—where a village may lose its entire adult male population when its boats are struck by a sudden squall—in such a land people do not raise their voices or waste their words on nonessentials.

The early history of the islands is only sparsely chronicled, but according to the sagas they were first settled about 825 A.D. by Norwegians, who carried their tradition of political organization with them, establishing chieftainships with representation in a central parliament or *Thing*, the site of which has given its name to the promontory Tinganes[2] in Tórshavn. The Icelandic *Færeyingasaga* tells how the chieftain Sigmund Brestisson, about the year 1000 A.D., was struggling against his rival, Thránd í Götu, in an effort to Christianize the islands and bring them under the Norwegian crown. Sigmund failed, but after his death the forces of the new time eventually gained the upper hand, the Faroes were Christianized, and in 1035 they became a fiefdom of Norway.

[2] Heinesen gives it the name *Skindholmen*—Skin Islet—in this story.

2

Barren of trees and tillable soil, the islands became economically and politically dependent on the mainland. As part of Norway they passed into a union with Denmark in 1380—coming at the same time under a strict trade monopoly that was to be managed from Copenhagen for nearly five hundred years. When Norway broke away from the Danish crown in 1814, the Faroes were left with Denmark, but they soon began to achieve greater self-determination. This tendency was accelerated after the mid-1800s, when the tide of liberalism swept into many remote corners of Europe.

Today the Faroese people enjoy a unique kind of self-government under the Danish crown. They have all the rights and privileges of the home counties and send two representatives to the Folketing in Copenhagen. In addition, they have their own parliament or *Løgting* in the capital city of Tórshavn, which now numbers about 10,000 inhabitants. They manage almost all their own internal affairs, choosing for convenience and economy to leave certain matters such as the postal and monetary systems to the Danes.

Through their centuries of relative isolation in the North Atlantic the Faroes, like Iceland, preserved many elements of the old Norwegian language while great changes were taking place on the mainland. For various reasons, however, they were not able to maintain a continuous written tradition through this long period. Officials of church, government, and trade were all Danes, and the business of the land was conducted in the Danish language. By the time the impulse to write in their own language came to the Faroese people with their national awakening, certain elements of Danish had penetrated into the vernacular, though it retained its over-all distinctive character. It is today far more different from Danish than is either Norwegian or Swedish, and it can be understood by no one from the three mainland countries without study. It is closest to modern Icelandic,

3

though it is much simpler as regards inflectional forms. Faroese and Icelandic fishermen who come to each others' shores are said to require two or three months' practice before they can communicate easily.

Regular publication of Faroese works did not begin until the second half of the nineteenth century, but there already existed at that time a mature body of literary material that had been handed down by oral tradition—sometimes in fairly refined form—since earliest times. The islanders had found entertainment through the centuries by developing and reciting sagas, folk tales, rimes, and ballads that recounted the exploits not only of the best known Northern heroes—Olaf Tryggvason, Olaf the Saint, and Sigmund Brestisson—but also of the Volsungs, the Crusaders, Charlemagne, Roland and Oliver, and many others. No area has afforded collectors of the medieval popular ballad greater treasure than have the Faroes; the ballad, or *kvæði*, has continued in use into modern time as an accompaniment for the heavy-rhythmed chain- or ring-dance that has brought the Faroese people together and restored their spirits in times of trouble. It has been steadily augmented by later additions of both known and unknown authorship. Even today the man of the Faroes seems to grow bigger than life as he chants and steps the beat of a *kvæði*. And the commitment of hundreds of stanzas to memory is considered no singular feat.

The late appearance of a Faroese written language was naturally attended by a correspondingly late development of fiction as a literary form. Writers of the late nineteenth and early twentieth centuries devoted themselves to political, social, and pedagogical matters, and to folk tales, ballads, and national lyrics. The first novel, *Babilstornið (The Tower of Babel)*, published in 1909, was written in the vernacular by Rasmus Rasmussen, an educator who had adopted Grundtvigian ideas in the course of his studies in Denmark

4

and who founded the Faroese Folk High School. He used the pen name Regin í Lið. In the ensuing decades several others published novels and short stories in Faroese, but a true breakthrough in fiction was not achieved until William Heinesen, using the Danish language, published his first novel, *Blæsende Gry* (*Stormy Dawning*), in 1934. Like his subsequent works it was published in Copenhagen and thus reached a Danish and, to some extent, a Norwegian as well as Faroese reading public. His *Noatun*, appearing in 1938, was the first Faroese novel to reach readers beyond Scandinavia; an English translation was published in London under the title *Niels Peter* in 1939.

Meanwhile, other Faroese novelists were appearing on the scene—some writing in Faroese, some in Danish. Hans J. Jacobsen, under the pen name Heðin Brú, published the novel *Lognbrá* (*Mirage*) in Faroese in 1930. It dealt with the problem of a young man seeking reality but failing to realize that he is, in fact, only pursuing a mirage. The sequel, *Fastatøkur* (*Firm Grip*), came in 1935; it is a salty as well as thoughtful work, rugged and terse as only the Faroese language can be. In the following years, Heðin Brú produced a number of novels and collections of short stories, and he is still writing at the age of seventy. His novel *Feðgar á Ferð* (literally *Father and Sons on a Journey*), published in 1940, is a kindly reflection on the generation gap of yesterday. Not until it was translated into Danish in 1963, under the title *Fattigmandsære* (*Poor-man's Pride*) did it attract the attention it deserved in the North. An excellent translation by the Englishman John F. West, published in New York in 1970 under the title *The Old Man and his Sons*, brought it the distinction of being the first Faroese-language novel ever to appear in English. A few of Heðin Brú's short stories had been translated in *The American-Scandinavian Review* between 1966 and 1970.

Still another Faroese author who began writing in the

thirties was Jørgen-Frantz Jacobsen, whose Danish-language novel *Barbara* (1939) has been a little favorite in Scandinavia through the years. This spicy but sensitive story of a warm-blooded widow in the Faroes of the 1700s has been reprinted several times, was translated in England in 1938, and was the subject of a German "on location" film in the early 1960s. Jørgen-Frantz Jacobsen, who was a distant cousin of William Heinesen, died quite young, leaving this single work of fiction as a monolithic study in feminine psychology—but much more important, as a vivid and lusty portrayal of Faroese life in bygone days.

But back to William Heinesen—who, by the way, polished up the last, half-finished chapters of *Barbara* after Jørgen-Frantz Jacobsen's death. This Proteus among Scandinavian artists is endowed with a background that affords him matchless historical and geographical perspective in his interpretation of the "native heath." He was born in Tórshavn in 1900, a time when—as he remarks in one of his writings— "the extraordinarily persistent Faroese medievalism" was "blossoming wildly and anachronistically." Oars and sails were plying side by side with steam engines and steel hulls; social life and the national economy were poised for innovations. Heinesen's family was one of many that nurtured the Danish language along with the Faroese—though as a matter of tradition rather than from a feeling of cultural dependence. In autobiographic sketches he mentions with affection and admiration "min Københavnske Bedstemoder" —his grandmother from Copenhagen—whose home appears to have been an oasis of world culture. And he mentions his uncles on the isle of Vágoy, where Faroese life was less influenced by the cultural and social traffic of the capital. His early childhood alternated between free and fanciful adventures with playmates on the steep meadows and dizzy cliffs around Tórshavn and on Vágoy, and frequent visits to the colorful world of his grandmother's home—to her books and pictures and music.

6

In his mid-teens he was sent to a commercial school in Copenhagen, and his eyes were opened by such marvels as paved streets, streetcars, bicycles, trains, block-long buildings, and horses "of hitherto unseen dimensions, with eyes like ponds and pasterns like women in blessed circumstances." His artistic instinct told young Heinesen that he was learning more in the streets and parks, the museums and cafés of Copenhagen than he was in the stuffy classrooms. Together with a chum he played truant with increasing overtness until he received a friendly suggestion from the schoolmaster that he might as well terminate his studies altogether. He then turned to private studies in music and writing, living somewhat from hand to mouth until he finally joined a Ringsted newspaper as an apprentice journalist. Meanwhile, he was writing poetry. When he was twenty-one he had enough to publish a collection under the title *Arktiske Elegier (Arctic Elegies)*.

At this time Heinesen moved back to Tórshavn to commence a life devoted to creative work in a multitude of art forms. One cannot examine any aspect of Faroese cultural life—which is rich and varied—without encountering something either directly created by him, or else brought about with his encouragement or participation. Strewn about the islands like fruits from a cornucopia are oil paintings, illustrations, cover designs, musical compositions, articles, and introductions bearing his signature. None of them shows the hand of an amateur; none is mediocre. His poetry fills several volumes. He is one of the many Faroe Islanders who play instruments alone or with friends for personal pleasure. He has been the leading spirit in musical, literary, and art societies, and co-editor of the cultural periodical *Varðin*. All of this merely by-the-by, of course, for his main activity has been the writing of fiction.

Although William Heinesen writes in Danish, his themes and settings are Faroese. His works are peopled—as are the islands themselves—with rugged individualists, children of a whimsical terrain and freakish weather. Some are eccentrics. In the few instances in which a conformist is found, he will as likely as not be the very source of conflict, stirring up friction between nonconformists who otherwise would have lived on in tolerance of each others' idiosyncrasies. He may at times represent the world beyond the Faroes, or he may be a conformist within the framework of a social group that itself is eccentric. Frequently he is a revivalist whose missionary zeal brings tragedy into the lives of others.

The action in most of Heinesen's work is set in the early part of the twentieth century, but there are two notable exceptions. *Den Sorte Gryde* (*The Black Cauldron*, 1949) is a story of profiteering and human inconstancy during the Second World War; and *Det Gode Håb* (*The Good Hope*, 1964) is a high-spirited historical novel based on the life of Lucas Debes, the rebellious Danish clergyman in Tórshavn who defied the corrupt and tyrannous commandant of the Faroe garrison, a Holsteiner who had been visited upon the helpless islanders by Frederik III's privy councillor, Christoph von Gabel.

In 1965, a year after publication of *Det Gode Håb*, William Heinesen shared the annual literary prize of the Nordic Council with the Swedish author Olof Lagercrantz.

The present work speaks best for itself and needs little by way of introduction. Its Danish title is *De fortabte Spillemænd*, and it first appeared in Cophenhagen in 1950. The setting is Tórshavn in the years immediately preceding the First World War—a time, of course, that Heinesen can well remember. The colorful and tragicomic characters are first and foremost the product of his vivid imagination, but they no doubt also represent a synthesis of eccentrics and other people who were known about town at the time. There must have been a Sirius, Moritz, or Little-Kornelius in recent Tórshavn history—simple but sensitive souls who have been inclined to accept and enjoy whatever the moment offers, to

8

give thanks and demand no more. And there have no doubt been bank-manager Ankersens and Ole Brandys and others. Several of the minor characters reappear in Heinesen's short stories, giving the reader an additional illusion of historical authenticity. But one should guard against taking Heinesen's historical or scholarly trappings too seriously because—as the Scandinavian says—he frequently has a "fox behind his ear"—he has a roguish humor and loves to play a joke on his reader.

The versatility of Heinesen's style cannot, of course, be appreciated through the reading of just this single work. It would be a mistake to think, for example, that the exaggerated formality found in certain passages represents the one and only Heinesen. Wherever he draws out his sentences, crowds his phrases, or steps out on the proscenium to comment on a character, he does so with a special purpose. His Fieldingian effects are quite deliberate. And the attentive reader will see that in many cases this affectation disappears —notably in the dialogue and in accelerating action. At such times the characters seem to walk through the pages on their own feet, just as they do in *Blæsende Gry*, in *Noatun*, and in *Det Gode Håb*.

De fortabte Spillemænd contains situations that are familiar from other novels by William Heinesen. The treacherous foreigner or outsider makes his appearance (i.e. the self-exiled Matte-Gok); the revivalists exercise their subtle tyranny on the community; women are fickle or faithless—but not always without good reason; superstition leads to fateful action at a decisive point; but the tangled web of human affairs is kept intact by a thread of human kindness and generosity—not sanctimonious or bombastic, but quietly woven. Despite the humorous framework of the novel—the waggish chapter headings, the mock solemnity, the satirical asides, the surprising twists and turns of action like "Presto's!" of a magician—there is a constant undercurrent of

9

thoughtfulness—a wistful turn, a reflective air, a lyric strain, a note of longing, a nostalgia that reaches beyond life itself —beyond earthly existence—finding no rest short of the starry firmament.

HEDIN BRØNNER

Heidelberg

Part I

*In which the musicians, their family, and their circle of
friends are introduced*

CHAPTER 1

About Kornelius, the aeolian-harp maker, and his sons

Far out in an ocean that gleams and glitters like quicksilver
may be found a small leaden-colored land. In proportion to
the immense ocean the size of the tiny mountainous land is
like a grain of sand to a ballroom floor. But viewed through
a magnifying glass this grain of sand is an entire world, with
mountains and valleys, inlets and fjords, and houses with
tiny human beings. At one place there is even a complete
little old town, with jetties and piers, warehouses, streets,
crooked lanes and steep alleyways, gardens and market-
places and cemeteries. There is also an old church, situated
high above the town; from its steeple there is a view out
over the roofs of the houses and beyond—far out over the
almighty ocean.

On a windy afternoon many years ago, a man and three
boys were sitting in the steeple, listening to the unpredictable music emanating from an aeolian harp. It was Sexton
Kornelius Isaksen and his three sons, Moritz, Sirius, and
Little Kornelius. The aeolian harp to which they were listening was the very first in a long series to have been built by
the sexton; this remarkable man in time became an aeolian-
harp builder on a very exceptional scale. At one time there
were no fewer than seventeen aeolian harps hanging in the
steeple, and they must have produced music that pierced
the listener right to the marrow of his bones.

But we will revert to the day that the magical music from
an aeolian harp for the first time reached the ears of the

three boys and awakened a strange and ravenous longing in their young souls. Until that time they had not heard any other music than that produced by the old asthmatic organ upon which Lamm the organist was fumbling every Sunday.

"Father, who is playing the aeolian harp?" asked Little Kornelius, who was six years old at the time.

"It's the wind, of course," answered the oldest brother.

"No, it's the cherubs, isn't it, father?" asked Sirius, who, wide-eyed, tried to catch his father's glance.

The sexton absentmindedly nodded in agreement, and the three boys listened even more breathlessly and with greater abandon. Sitting there, they stared out through the shutters up to the sky and the solitary wind-driven clouds that seemed to have put on an attentive mien, as if they also were listening to the distant music. The three brothers never forgot that strange afternoon, and when Sirius grew up he immortalized it in his poem "Cherubs Were Passing By."

As already mentioned, the building of aeolian harps later got somewhat out of hand. Indeed, Kornelius Isaksen was on the whole an immoderate man; he would always get too enthusiastic about some fad or craze and often set himself impossible tasks. And when he did not succeed, he took it very hard, succumbed to melancholy, and not infrequently hit the bottle.

Nevertheless, he was a good and considerate father to his sons. It was his doing, for example, that their musical talents came under the diligent care and supervision of Kaspar Boman.

Kornelius became a widower early in life; as for himself, he attained to an age of a mere thirty-four. Therefore, his three sons were left to their own devices early in life and had to manage as well as they could. But the restless spirit of the builder of aeolian harps lived on in them, and, among other things, manifested itself in their immoderate love of music.

14

CHAPTER 2

About a wedding, a funeral, and an angry man, and also about the name Orfeus

Moritz, the oldest son of the sexton, was only twenty-two years old when he married Eliana, an eighteen-year-old bottle-washer, whom he had gotten to know in Boman's singing society, and who had been courted by many for quite a long time. It was about this girl Eliana that Sirius wrote his poem entitled "Sunshine in a Cellar," which later became so treasured, and in which he depicts a blonde girl rinsing out bottles in the greenish twilight, soaked and somewhat disheveled, but nevertheless young and happy like Aphrodite just come up on land. And this is the way Eliana was in reality—as if created out of lighter material than other mortals. Indeed, she had that divine light in her eye that is peculiar to certain particularly blessed female beings—a glance that seems to look straight through everything in the most cheery and matter-of-course way. In addition, there was something light and airy about her whole being, an innate feeling for graceful movements—which, indeed, had not escaped the attention of Lindenskov, the dance instructor, and during his lessons he would point out Eliana as a very paragon of natural grace and plastic art.

It goes without saying that Eliana made a beautiful bride. Moritz, too, looked fine; a tanned and nicely got up young seaman, erect and confident and with the lifesaving medal gleaming on his lapel. Everything considered, there was

15

about the young bridal couple the carefree aura of innocent happiness that is capable of making other people strangely bitter and suspicious. And gossips soon got busy, for the wedding itself gave cause for anxiety and headshaking; indeed, there is no denying that this wedding that had commenced so beautifully ended up in an equally horrible manner.

It started when a male choir, in which the bridegroom himself sang first tenor, treated the assemblage to "At the Wondrous Moment of Dawn," written for this solemn occasion by Sirius to a melody by Little Kornelius, who here made his debut as a composer. Next, a string quartet played, with the bridegroom himself playing first violin, Haydn's well-known Andante Cantabile for solo violin and pizzicato. This time too the performers scored a success, and the soloist was enthusiastically applauded. Thereupon everyone ate and drank, this being followed by dancing; in many respects it was a rough party, although hardly any rougher than other celebrations in those circles, but unhappily, the festivity caused some one's death, in that an old shoemaker by the name of Esau—a seventy-seven-year-old worthy, who had merely one fault, being incorrigibly attached to liquid refreshments—towards morning was found drowned in the inlet known as Kelp Inlet, only a few yards from the house in which the celebration took place.

The wedding celebration was supposed to have lasted at least two days, but as might be expected it came to an abrupt end; the guests wended their way homeward, and every one thought that what had transpired was very sad and extremely deplorable.

The old shoemaker was buried a few days later, the male choir singing beautifully and movingly at the graveside. In the evening Moritz gathered his friends for a sort of funeral feast. All that was left over from the interrupted wedding celebration was now consumed, but spirits were subdued and the entire proceedings were carried out with decorum.

Even so, Mr. Ankersen, the manager of the savings bank, felt that the occasion called for his interference. He put in an appearance at the height of the festivities, red-faced and fuming as usual, and spoke about blasphemy, retribution, and damnation. The little group listened dutifully to his fierce reprimand. Ankersen looked horrible, he had no control at all over his blotchy bearded face with its irate-looking spectacles, his voice broke several times because of his rage, and his double shadow danced on the wall and looked like the devil incarnate. There were two lighted candles on the table, they flickered in the breeze emanating from his mouth, and one of them was completely blown out.

He finally seized a nearly full keg of gin that was standing on the table, took it outside, and emptied it in the gutter. Not even then did Moritz and his friends utter a single word in the semi-darkness.

But when the manager at last had left them Moritz got out another crock of Dutch gin and opened it. With his face turned away and with a sigh he said: "It was of course an awful thing that Esau, that poor old fellow, should drown like that, so it was. But how can any one put the entire blame on me? I hadn't even invited Esau, he just crashed the party, but naturally I didn't throw him out. On the other hand, I couldn't be expected to act as his nursemaid. But what's done is done, and an old and lonesome man he was anyway. Skoal!"

Even though Moritz was merely engaged in the lowly trade of a ferryman, he was, as already indicated, a man who to a rare degree lived and breathed for music only. He had an excellent singing voice and never had to be begged to sing at weddings and funerals; in addition, he also played at dances when the opportunity presented itself. He played the violin, the viola, the French horn, the flute, and the clarinet. This is not the same as saying that he mastered any of these instruments to the extent that he could be called a real musician. But when he played, he was magnificent, especially when playing the violin.

Yes, Moritz had a musical talent given only to a few, and about a year after the wedding when he became the father of a boy, he wanted to give him a really musical name. He consulted a few people on this matter—people who were better acquainted with the history of music than he was. Kaspar Boman, the gardener and music instructor, who was bedridden at the time, compiled a long list of musical names for him. Moritz kept this list, which lies about somewhere even today; it was indeed composed with touching meticulousness and reads as follows:

> Franz (Schubert)
> Christoff Willibald (Gluck)
> Wolfgang Amadeus
> Amadeus or Amadé
> Wolfgang
> Franz
> Felix (Mendelssohn)
> Ole Bull
> Paganini (not a good name)
> Papageno (not so good, either)
> Johan Sebastian Bach
> Corelli
> Giovanni Battista Viotti?—No
> Franz (Schubert)
> Orfeus (crossed out)
> August Södermann
> Louis (dull)
> J.P.E. Hartmann
> Carl Maria von Weber
> Franz Schubert

Why Moritz from among all these names selected Orfeus, a name that had even been crossed out, has remained a mystery, but the boy was christened Orfeus.

Many years later Orfeus found a faded letter from old Boman next to the list of names which we have copied above and which Moritz had kept on the bottom of his sea chest. The letter read as follows:

"Dear Moritz,

I am genuinely sorry that I cannot come to the christening party, as I still feel too weak, but I did put together a small speech in honor of my godson; it had better wait until his confirmation, if the Lord will allow me to live that long, something that he perhaps certainly will not do; but do not refuse the little present I enclose, and do not go overboard in the matter of liquids, Moritz, promise me that, and remember the beautiful words of Ibsen:

> Orfeus by his perfect tones
> gave souls to beasts and fire to stones.
> Play, so that stones will sparks emit!
> Play, so that the animals' hides will split!"

CHAPTER 3

About a nocturnal trip to the Desert Isles

Poor Sirius! In time he became a respected poet, but not until many years after his untimely death, as so very often happens. While he was living, he was thought to be a lazy fellow and rather stupid.

But Sirius did entertain many peculiar ideas and had many seemingly crazy habits; among the latter was his habit of walking about in the middle of the night, especially during the light summer nights, and then he would show no consideration at all when it came to disturbing his sleeping fellow creatures.

Once, in the middle of a balmy night in August he took it into his head that it would be wonderful to set out on a trip to the Desert Isles and admire the sunrise. With this in mind he first awakened Little Kornelius and also the young couple living in the house next to Kelp Inlet. They all naturally wanted to come along, for such was the nature of these people—ever since the early innocent beginning of time. Even the little Orfeus, fast asleep and at that time only three years old, was taken along, carefully wrapped in woolen blankets and placed in a big basket. The Desert Isles that we are referring to, were not, of course, the well-known group of islands off Scotland of practically the same name,* but were merely a small rocky reef at the

* A play upon words: the similarity of the Danish name for the Orkney Islands (Orknöerne) and the Desert Isles (Örkenöerne). Tr. note.

20

entrance to the harbor. It was Sirius who had thought of this odd name.

While Eliana made coffee and buttered sandwiches and crackers, Sirius and Little Kornelius were sitting in the parlor, busily engaged in composing a morning song, a matin. That is the way they were, these sons of the aeolian-harp maker—there was always something they had to cele-brate. The tall and thin Sirius sat with his hat pushed back on his head, writing in his dog-eared poetry notebook with a chewed-up pencil stump; and Kornelius was peering over his shoulder through his pince-nez and humming the while. There was something perfectly helpless about Kornelius's pince-nez. The reason might be that it was too small and fit too loosely or perhaps it was because he had no idea of how to wear it with the correct dignified nonchalance. Be-sides, a pince-nez, which was fashionable in those days, does not go with a plain honest face with a protruding lower jaw and ears that stick out. No one could call Little Kornelius handsome, that would have been a deviation from the truth; he also squinted a bit, and stuttered to boot.

When the poet and the composer had completed their work, they discovered that the "Crab King" was also among those present in the parlor. He was sitting in a rocking chair, staring dejectedly into thin air, as was his habit. He is the dwarf that Sirius has immortalized in his soul-stirring poem "The Man from the Moon."

Moritz returned, accompanied by Ole Brandy, the ship's mate. Ole Brandy was rather inebriated; Moritz had found him sitting half asleep in a boat that had been pulled up on shore. Ole had half a bottle of brandy in his pocket and eagerly offered to rush home and get some more.

At long last the little group boarded the boat. It was an unusually quiet night. Ole Brandy's bottle went from mouth to mouth. Only the Crab King did not drink anything; this curious shadow of a man seemed completely unapproach-able, as always.

21

Kornelius gave him an encouraging pat on the shoulder, and the dwarf looked at him with an expression of loyalty and faithfulness. Kornelius was the only living being for whom the Crab King is known to have felt any affection.

The ocean sighed and heaved; the waves were gleaming, and numerous silent eiderducks were sitting on the surface of the water. The descending full moon had had the happy inspiration to appear in the west, between motionless clouds. It gave the landscape, suffused by darkness, a reddish tinge, which seemed to have been produced by a sort of spectral trumpet call.

When the little party had arrived at the Desert Isles and had sat down, Moritz got out his violin, and while Eliana was placing the sandwiches and the coffee on the clean and bare rock, he played with verve and difficult double stops the singularly joyful Andante of Pergolesi's Concertino in F Minor.

The bottle kept on circulating, but the menfolks remained silent. Only the Crab King cleared his throat moaningly, as was his habit, and looked out across the sea, his careworn face seeming as if it once and for all had drunk its fill of somber and superior knowledge. In the meanwhile, the moon was down, and the eastern sky had been given a colorful touch by the sun, which was still below the horizon, like a sunken fairy-tale castle. When the coffee had been drunk and the bread and crackers consumed, the first blushing traces of dawn began to trickle forth between the long, straight cloud formations and to ignite the roof made up of gay fleecy clouds.

Sirius then came forth and recited his morning song in a voice quivering with emotion, a sort of matin in praise of the sun and of life. The Crab King doffed his cap and folded his hands. Moritz was sitting down, the bottle resting on his left knee, and with his right arm he was holding his young wife in a tight grip. Ole Brandy had stretched out on a flat rock and was sending aloft clouds of smoke from his old meerschaum pipe. The rays of the morning sun made his red broken nose look twice as red and were reflected in his golden earrings. But suddenly Sirius stopped declaiming, pointed out across the water, and shouted: "Look!"

Every one got up to see better. Out on the rippled surface of the sea, which had taken on a bronze-like glimmer, could be seen a flock of dolphins. They beat the water with their tails and made somersaults as if filled with unbounded joy, while rushing along with the current and disappearing in the far distance.

Little Orfeus had awakened in his basket, just in time to enjoy the sight; he stretched his arms upward and shouted, beside himself from a delight mingled with fear, and the picture of gloriously happy dolphins below a rising sun was to be forever imprinted on his mind.

Sirius completed the reading of his poem. Ole Brandy lit his pipe again and grabbed for the bottle. Now Kornelius had the melody all done, and he handed the piece of paper with the scribbled notes to Moritz, who played the melody through a few times on his violin. He nodded approvingly and began to sing the new tune. Kornelius and Sirius added harmony, Ole Brandy tooted on an empty bottle, and thus that beautiful morning song had been created about which the literary historian Magnus Skæling, in his very fine essay about Sirius Isaksen, says that because of its powerful and naivistic depiction of nature it reminds us of the great Thomas Kingo.

When the song had come to an end, the dawn broke and things got really lively. Ole Brandy smashed the bottle against the rock and commenced to sing a strange song about the rough and tough men of the sea. Ole saw things as through a mist, and Moritz too felt somewhat inebriated; he went over and grabbed Ole's hand and listened patiently to the latter's loud and disjointed account of life at sea during his youth, of unforgettable voyages to distant lands with the bark *Albatross,* and of the Indian girl Ubukoshara, who bit part of the ear off the fine Norwegian sailor known as the Moster Man! °

Sirius had caught sight of an anemone floating in the water; he carefully climbed down in order to have a better look at it. The fleshy flower seemed to stretch, with feeble, enamored movements, up toward the faint sunlight, as if it were filled with a longing tinged with sadness.

A fresh breeze was now blowing from the south; Eliana wrapped the blankets around the infant, almost shivering while she collected cups and jars. But suddenly there was heard a cry and a splash. Sirius was gone! Eliana cried out, a loud and ominous double echo came from the opposite shore, and the Crab King, again feeling hopelessly aggrieved, made a wry face. But Moritz immediately threw off his jacket and jumped into the water, and after a little while he reappeared with Sirius, the latter blindly floundering and flapping his arms and legs the while emitting gurgling sounds. Ole Brandy managed to haul him ashore, where he remained lying on his stomach, moaning and with water streaming off his threadbare clothing. Eliana bent down and with a sigh of relief kissed him on the cheek. She began to wring the water out of his hair and comforted him as if he were a little child. Ole Brandy took off his grubby and brandy-scented peajacket and put it on Sirius. Moritz got the boat ready for departure, and the little group embarked in a hurry.

Sirius was shaking and shivering, and his teeth chattered. Little Orfeus was crying and was inconsolable, but he quieted down when his mother took him on her lap and reminded him of the big wonderful fishes that had been cavorting just for him far out on the ocean. He looked into his mother's reassuring eyes and became quiet, lost in remembrance of the sight.

° Literally, "Uncle" or "Aunt's Husband." Tr. note.

24

CHAPTER 4

*Incidents from the life in the basement of the Bastille, and
on Skin Islet*

During his adolescence and early youth Moritz had sailed
on the great oceans, but at the present time he made his
living by ferrying travelers and seamen from shore out to
the large steamers. This was the time before the harbor and
the quays had been constructed, so a ferryman was very
essential. Once in a while he also conducted a sort of passenger and freight service as far as Seal Island and to other
small villages not too far from the capital. It mostly entailed
sailing in sheltered waters, but Moritz's trade was far from
being unhazardous. The ferrying often demanded considerable courage and resourcefulness, especially in wintertime,
and when misfortune struck, it might even become a game
in which the stakes were life and death.

Moritz enjoyed a deservedly high reputation as a seaman;
he was both experienced and bold, and the rescue that he
had effected the year he was twenty-one, by singlehandedly
bringing seven men and one woman safe ashore from the
foundered Finnish schooner *Karelia*, served forever after to
lend luster to his name.

During a pitch-dark night around Christmas 1904, however, Moritz had the misfortune of being shipwrecked
himself. He was on the way back from one of the big ocean-
going liners, which because of the strong onshore wind had
cast anchor far out; onboard ship and in the company of

25

a much too hospitable agent he had downed a few unusually strong greenish-looking drinks, which the agent jokingly had called "Certain Death."

Moritz did escape death, almost miraculously, but his boat, which drifted ashore at Stake Spit, was smashed to bits—and it had not been insured.

For some time Moritz went around feeling ashamed, albeit secretly happy, for he had come out of it alive, and that means quite a lot to a young man who looks to the future with confidence. After some consultations with his wife he decided to sell the small but well-kept house at Kelp Inlet and use the money to buy a new and bigger boat. The family, which incidentally had increased in size, with the addition of the two lovely frizzy-haired twin girls, Franziska and Amadea, thereupon had to rent rooms in the Bastille, the large, ramshackle house on the eastern side of the Skin Islet.

This house had at one time been the domicile of the rich Consul Sebastian Hansen, "Old Bastian," as he was called. The basement flat had just become vacant, following the death of its recent tenant, Sundholm the photographer. Sundholm had been a melancholy and lonesome man of indeterminate background. But even though he was dead and gone, there was nevertheless no way of finally disposing of him; the rooms still smelled from Sundholm's tobacco and photographic fluids, despite thorough washing and cleansing; and during the first few nights after the new tenants had moved in, little Orfeus dreamed on and on about the dead photographer. He dreamed that Sundholm was sitting on the side of his bed, heavy and with a brooding mien, dressed in his threadbare shiny jacket, from the lapel of which his pince-nez was dangling and reflecting the light. Sometimes the boy would awake in the middle of the night, with the peculiar, rather abominable smell of the dead man's photographic fluids in his nostrils. One night he dreamed that

Sundholm's spirit opened a trapdoor in the floor and guided him around a hidden apartment down below, an endless suite of rooms, all of which were dimly lighted by sinister-looking lamps, and in one of these eerie rooms the ship's figurehead Tarira was sitting, her pale eyes staring at him. This figure was in actuality placed below the bowsprit of the old bark *Albatross*. It was supposed to be a pale and imperturbable angel staring straight ahead. But at times it would visit him in his dreams, and these occasions were the most horrifying that he knew of. Not because it wasn't in itself quite beautiful and friendly—that it certainly was, yes, it even reminded him a bit of his own mother. Still, she was a frightful apparition, indeed, and to make matters worse one had to keep up good appearances and mention it by name and make believe that one was very fond of it.

Aside from that, the Bastille was not a dreary place to live in. It was a large house with space for several families. In the basement lived, besides the people from Kelp Inlet, the gay and cheerful fellow Fribert and his old toothless dog Pan. Fribert was a coal-heaver and worked for the firm Sebastian Hansen & Son; he always had black rings around his eyes, making them look penetratingly bright, and he had the jolly habit of every evening lulling himself to sleep by singing old ballads, most often the one called "Ole Morske Lies Shriveled in the Loft."

On the second floor of the Bastille there were two apartments. The Adventist family Samsonsen, father, mother, daughter, and the latter's son, lived in one of the apartments; they ran a sort of laundry and clothes-pressing service and observed Saturdays by playing on a reed organ and singing very loudly. In the other apartment, the one that faced east and was very small, lived Josef the carpenter, who was known as the "Corpse Crower," because he was a willing

27

and frequently hired singer at funerals. Josef was also an active member of the male choir, in which he acquitted himself very well in the tenor section. His hair and skin had a peculiar, colorless hue, and his eyes were reddish and reminded one of port-holes behind which a faint light is smoldering. His wife Sarina had been a maid at the hotel The Dolphin, and it was common knowledge that she had married the Corpse Crower because she had been seduced by a traveling salesman who thereupon had disappeared in foreign parts without so much as a trace. Josef, however, was delighted with his wife and daughter and toiled and slaved to make them comfortable.

Up above, in the "towers" as they were called, there were also two small apartments. Little Kornelius lived in one of them; he was always very particular of stressing his independence of others. The other tower apartment was the domicile of Magister Mortensen, a man who had seen better days and whom everybody pitied; nevertheless, he gave the impression of being stiff and pigheaded and was also something of a pompous ass. He was a widower and had a daughter who was not right in the head.

Orfeus loved to stand by his uncle's window in the tower and look out. It felt almost like flying, for the Bastille was not only a tall building but was also situated on the edge of a rocky slope. From it one had a fine view of the ocean and Skin Islet with its crooked lanes, tiny garden patches and multitude of roofs, some of which were covered with turf and inhabited by chickens and hens.

Skin Islet, which really was no islet at all but an elongated and rocky promontory, was the town's oldest section, and here lived old Boman, Ole Brandy, and the Crab King along with many other odd persons, such as the rose-painter Pontus, whose windows were decorated with a profusion of roses and lilies; on his door he had placed a showcase which featured gay pictures of girls and ladies. There lived also

Ura on the Cliff, the fortune-teller whom the entire town secretly feared and who could not be persuaded to leave her little rickety house on Cliff Hill, even though it was almost freely floating in the air, and actually one fine day it did crash into the abyss. There lived also the three old maids Schibbye, who owned the world's smallest milliner's shop and looked like three skeletons. Here was also the old inn, Olsen's hotel or The Curious Duck, where King Frederik the Seventh had lived when he was a young prince, and farther out on the naze lay a larger hotel, The Dolphin, which did not have a very good reputation either.

All the way out on the most southerly point of Skin Islet could be seen the Höje warehouse and other old buildings and stalls from the time of the Danish trade monopoly. They were now owned by Sebastian Hansen & Son and were used to store lumber, salt, and coal.

In the days of Old Bastian the Bastille had been a stately building, but as the town grew, Skin Islet became a curiously outmoded and impoverished area, a place from which nice and decent people moved away. The close proximity of the houses made for unsanitary conditions and increased the danger of fire, and all the cellars were filled with moisture and rats; Skin Islet had indeed gone downhill, and the new parts of town, with their larger and more airy houses and gardens, were now the town proper.

The large room that had served as Sundholm's photographic studio and in a part of which, facing the courtyard, there was an opening letting in the daylight, was made into a sitting room by Moritz and Eliana, but the frugal furniture that they had brought with them from Kelp Inlet looked lost in the large room. The room seemed resoundingly empty, depressing, and chilly; the wintry pale harbor sighed and seethed outside, its black ships riding at anchor, with masts stripped bare and seemingly agape, and letting themselves be hopelessly tossed back and forth.

29

But the former studio was very useful in one way: it was just right for the playing of music. It did not take Moritz long to discover this, and in the course of the winter the string quartet, others who played string and wind instruments, and some days even Boman's choir would practice here.

The string quartet, which at times could be enlarged to a quintet and at one time had numbered all of eight musicians (playing the minuet from Schubert's Octet), was, just like the choir, the result of the efforts of old Kaspar Boman. It consisted at that time of Moritz, who played first violin; Sirius, second violin; Magister Mortensen, viola; and Little Kornelius, cello. Most often the old music teacher would be present and would do the conducting. Besides the people living in the building, the audience was composed of friends and acquaintances of the musicians, all coming and going as they pleased: Ole Brandy; the one-legged sailmaker Olivarius; the rose-painter Pontus; the dance instructor Lindenskov; at times also the smith, Janniksen, and master painter Mac Bett, and on special occasions Count Oldendorp and Judge Pommerencke, both of whom were lovers of good music.

Orfeus relished these evenings. He would sit in a corner and enjoy himself. The stove was red hot, there was a reddish light from the big brass lamp in the ceiling, the musicians grew red in their faces, and even the music itself took on a reddish tinge. At such times it seemed as if the memory of photographer Sundholm had been completely blown away. Old Boman would scurry about, pointing with his finger, ever full of zeal and enthusiasm, or would sit listening attentively, stroking his gray goatee with his small veined hands. At times a peculiarly happy smile would light up his face; then, in spite of beard and wrinkles, he would look like a boy, a small, shy boy who attends a birthday party. On the whole, there was something childlike about these men when playing, especially so when a certain composition had gotten off to a good start and everything went smoothly. They would sit with a relaxed expression on their faces and a sentimental, attentive look in their eyes. The strict and suspicious Magister Mortensen looked like virtue incarnate. Kornelius was pale and sweaty from the excitement of it all; he sat with his lower lip pursed forward, his tousled hair hiding his forehead and his pince-nez. Sirius was sitting with his head bent over to one side and was fondling his violin. He was actually only a mediocre violinist and was often the butt of impatient remarks on the part of the other musicians.

But Moritz, the first violinist, sat up straight as a ramrod, and the music that poured from his instrument seemed like joyous reflections of the sun.

Outside, the dark waters were sighing, and whenever one looked out through the window one could discern the outlines of the ships rocking to and fro in the dark. But they also seemed to be suffused by a touch of red and to have a mien of longing and listening, as if they were avidly looking forward to escape the imprisonment of their anchor chains and give themselves over to the wonderful freedom found on the stormy ocean.

CHAPTER 5

About the tender-hearted and contented composer Little Kornelius and his secret project

If these musicians, about whom more will be told in the following pages, had minded their mundane business and had not been as eccentric and heaven-defying as they were, they would perhaps have made out quite a lot better in this most petty of all known worlds. But that is not the way things were. Each in his own way, they were obsessed, just like real musicians are so by nature.

This was not least so in the case of Little Kornelius. He was known to be a person one did not have to worry about, since he was always happy and in a good mood and rarely said anything that made real sense to other people.

This last-named quality had something to do with the fact that he stuttered. His lamentable stuttering would especially afflict him when he waxed enthusiastic about something, and it could get the upper hand to such an extent that he had to stop talking completely and had to try to make himself understood with the help of gestures and facial expressions.

In everyday life Kornelius was compositor for the newspaper *The Messenger*. The job provided him with a small but steady monthly wage, one that barely kept him on a subsistence level and would not lead to anything better in the future; in addition, it was dull and unhealthful work. The fact that Kornelius nevertheless was a young man with very few worries may be ascribed in part to music, to which he devoted himself with heart and soul, but also in part to an inborn ability to liberate himself from the pompous but trivial cobweb of the daily grind and to lose himself completely in strange and extraordinary vistas, to behold the mysterious and to await the unexpected.

Today you might walk around as a plain compositor and musician, but who knows if you are not the one who is going to find the *hidden treasure?* It lies deeply buried some place or other here on Skin Islet, according to an old tradition that will not die, and whoever seeketh, he shall find. Why couldn't this old treasure just as well be hidden in the old cemetery as in any other place?

A wise man by the name of Sansirana or Sansarasena lived here on Skin Islet in days of long ago; he was a buccaneer and lived the dissolute and hazardous life of the affluent and the prominent; but then came the day of retribution for him too, pirates landed and captured his robber's castle, invaded his houses and buildings, killed him and his retainers and sailed away with all that they could lay their hands on. But it was not much that they got hold of, for Sansarasena was a prudent man, and he had put away his money and his precious objects before the robbers had managed to get ashore. Since that time these treasures have not seen the light of day, but they still *do exist,* wherever they are located. And one thing is certain: no one but *you* is thinking about this treasure and is making any effort to track it down, and if you are fortunate enough to find it you at least don't have to wear yourself out as a typesetter for the world's smallest and—in the opinion of many—also the world's most foolish newspaper. And what happiness and blessings you would be able to spread around you if it should so happen that you suddenly became a prosperous man? Kornelius was not merely thinking of his own welfare;

he was also thinking of his brothers and of the sweet and hospitable Eliana and her children, and also of old Boman and the unhappy and destitute Magister Mortensen, and also, of course, of Ole Brandy and other friends, not to forget the Crab King.

In brief: It may take all of a man's life to find this treasure, but if one has any kind of luck one is just as apt to find it tomorrow as any other day, and, in any case one has a chance that other mortals don't have.

And Kornelius had indeed made a beginning. From Sebastian Hansen & Son he had leased the old cemetery that had been abandoned long ago and was located on the western side of Skin Islet; as a pretext he had said that he wanted to have his own vegetable garden. He had rooted out the entire wilderness consisting of angelica and sour dock that had been flourishing here for centuries, and he had collected all the mouldering dead men's bones and placed them in a common grave, for which the Corpse Crower had made a beautiful wooden cross with the words "Rest in Peace." And at the same time he had secretly been searching for the treasure.

But it wasn't there. Now at least he knew *that* much.

But the attempt had not been entirely fruitless. During his work in the garden he had not only got the inspiration for a string quartet in three movements and in his head had sketched out the first two: *an allegro ma non troppo* and an *andante con moto,* but the kitchen garden also produced some welcome extra money for the enterprising treasure hunter. This money he put aside. He was saving to buy a diving outfit, for his plan was now to search for the treasure on the bottom of the little bay known as the Commandant's Hollow, adjacent to the little cemetery.

He had come to the conclusion that the treasure most likely was located just in that spot. But this likelihood had now become a certainty, thanks to Ura on the Cliff. For this woman had second sight. Whenever any one was missing a valuable he would steal up Cliff Hill to speak to Ura, and if it suited her and if the spirit moved her, he would be told where to look, and in an astonishing number of cases her predictions would prove correct.

But Ura was not one of those who would oblige each and every one. Many had come to her in vain, others had received no more than a hint and it would then be up to them how they were to interpret it. Whenever any one brought gifts he was well received, and she promised to do something for him. But otherwise she was an unpredictable person, feared and hated by many people, partly because of her witchcraft and also because in her youth she had led a sinful and scandalous life.

One evening, the night before Christmas Eve, Kornelius decided to visit this strange woman and to present her with a fattened and nicely plucked duck and two heads of red cabbage. Ura seemed quite overwhelmed at the sight of these gifts, but when she heard what it was that Kornelius expected of her, she shook her head vehemently and, sniffing, turned her face away and looked up toward the attic.

"No, no, such a thing goes far beyond my powers," she said. "Remember that I am an old woman. If I had been my old self, it would have been an entirely different matter. But since the time Doctor Manicus took away my spleen, it seems as if everything has come to a standstill for me. No, it's better that you take back with you your blessed gift, Kornelius, I don't think that there is anything I can do for you, as much as I would like to."

Ura started to laugh, as she often did; she used to burst out laughing when least expected to do so; this would serve to confuse and even to some extent alarm those with whom she was talking.

"But—you are going to keep the duck in any case," Kornelius said.

35

Ura laughed once more and gave in. "Come inside at least and have a drop of coffee, Kornelius!"

The expression on Ura's big reddish face with its prominent cheekbones indicated that she was quite moved. Her black hair did not have even a touch of gray.

"Ah, what I wouldn't like to do for you, Kornelius," she said plaintively. "You are a wonderful person, kindness is written all over your face; and I wish I was able to help you find this treasure, for you certainly deserve it. But it is quite a difficult thing you are asking of me."

"Are we alone?" Kornelius asked warily. "I mean . . . I think . . . for it must be kept in strict secrecy, that thing about . . . that matter about. . . ."

"Of course," Ura reassured him, "and you don't have to worry about Kornelia over there, for she does not associate with any one but me, and she is as loyal as can be."

Kornelius looked about him in the little shabby kitchen, his pince-nez became misty, and it was a while before he discovered Kornelia, the young granddaughter of Ura's sister; she was sitting by the fire with a black cat in her lap. He suddenly remembered that the poor girl was blind. Perhaps he ought to go over and say hello to her.

He walked over and caught hold of her hand. Kornelia bashfully got to her feet and put the cat down. A very young girl, not bad looking, not at all. A great pity that she was so hopelessly blind. Actually, her eyes did not seem to have anything wrong with them at all, they were big and wide open, yes, it even seemed to him as if she met his glance—it made him feel rather strange.

"He is one of the young men who play such beautiful music," Ura explained. She added, as if speaking very confidentially: "Kornelia, you know, is so very fond of music. She often stands outside listening when you are playing in the Bastille. The poor thing doesn't have much to amuse her."

Kornelia blushed and sank down on her bench. Kornelius was intensely sorry for her. He felt a pang that she should love music, this blind creature whose name was almost the same as his. Stuttering and groping for words, he said: "But . . . why don't you instead come inside and join us? Tell her that she is heartily welcome . . . then she will hear so much better and can sit down in a warm room instead of standing outside freezing!"

"No, we will never be able to make her do that," Ura said with a smile, "for she is so terribly shy!"

She began to make coffee, and Kornelius sat down by the kitchen table. While they had their coffee Ura was silent and seemed distracted, but the good-humored expression did not quite disappear from her face. Then suddenly she began to stare at him excitedly and said with an eager little smile: "I can tell you this much, Kornelius, that your treasure *does exist,* and it lies, it lies, it lies in a moist place where there grows a whole lot of something or other!"

"Yes, seaweed!" Kornelius affirmed, feeling overjoyed.

A shadow passed over Ura's face, she rose and spoke rapidly: "It lies right here, Kornelius, yes, perhaps I can even point right at it, but . . . I can't do it after all!"

"But this is almost all I need," Kornelius said animatedly, "for now I understand that it lies under water, isn't that so: at the bottom of Commandant's Hollow! I have always had a feeling that it does, and even had a dream about it one night!"

Kornelius felt a powerful urge to squeeze the hand of the old woman, but Ura suddenly got up, and there was such a sharp and evil gleam in her eyes that he almost began to shiver.

The old woman stood by the window looking out. "We are getting a damnable visit!" she said.

Kornelius too had got up in order to look out the window. Three persons of fairly advanced age were struggling up

37

Cliff Hill; they were Mr. Ankersen, the savings-bank man-ager, and Mrs. Nillegaard, the midwife, and her husband. All three of them looked very serious.

"It is the welfare committee of the Christian temperance society Ydun," Kornelius said with some surprise, without even stuttering. "What do *they* want here? Of course, it doesn't concern me, and I'll say good-by, Ura, and a thousand thanks for your help!"

The welfare committee was standing outside on the slope. Out of breath, the nearsighted savings-bank manager pointed with his walking stick at one of the four rusty iron anchors that kept Ura's little cottage attached to the naked rock, while Mrs. Nillegaard energetically shook her head as if in protest. Ankersen lifted his stick and hit the anchor with some force—and it cracked! It was corroded right through from rust.

"I call on you to testify!" Ankersen cried, and in his righteous wrath he grabbed Kornelius by the sleeve, but relinquished his grasp when he discovered who it was: "Oh, you are not one of us, young man, not at all, walk with the Lord!"

Feeling quite confused and walking away backwards, Kornelius made a slight bow and stammered forth: "Thank you, Mr. Manager, many thanks!"

CHAPTER 6

*More about that phenomenon, Ankersen, and his strange
engagement in charity and revivals*

The welfare committee of the Christian temperance society
had a busy time of it that day before Christmas Eve. The
three representatives had just come from the rose-painter
Pontus, with whom they had been remonstrating because of
some obscene publications that had been exhibited in his
display cabinet, and they were now on the way to Captain
Öström no less, the proprietor of the infamous inn The
Dolphin. But en route they were also to speak a word of
admonition to the obdurate woman on Cliff Hill. As Ankersen said, it was a question of life and death.

"Get up in the attic!" Ura said and gave her sister's granddaughter a shove. "I want to be alone with them!"

Kornelia disappeared without a sound up through the
trap-door, and Ura received the three visitors; she smiled
at them but did not display any real warmth as she asked
them to sit down, while she herself assumed a reserved and
expectant pose.

Ankersen sat down heavily at the kitchen table, puffing
frightfully from the climb. Mrs. Nillegaard, who was dressed
in an old dark-green plush coat, also sat down. Her husband
remained standing by the door. Adjunct teacher Nillegaard
was a cautious and reserved man.

Ankersen's spacious chest heaved up and down; he sniffed

the air in through his hairy nostrils. "Phew!" he said and began to stare at Ura through his thick glasses. "It is like climbing a mountain to get up here! And on top of that, your house is actually floating on air, Ura, yes, things are worse now than the last time I was here, for the iron anchors are completely eaten through by rust. The next storm will topple you into the abyss, Ura. Yes, yes. Even when I came here as a young man, Ura, your house was in a tumble-down condition."

He then turned toward the Nillegaards and said with stifled self-accusation tinging his voice: "Yes, it is quite on purpose that I mention it now, that I came here when I was young, for I have decided to make use of this opportunity to once more ask Ura Anthoniussen to answer a question which it is becoming ever more urgent for me to be fully informed of, and I would very much like that you, my dear friends, act as witnesses."

He wiped his spectacles with his handkerchief and put them back on his pudgy nose.

"Let us handle this in all friendliness," he said in a muffled voice, "yes, in mutual love. I do not wish to tear down, but rather to reconcile and to build up. I have not come here in order to reproach you, Ura, for having trod the path of sin and immorality in your youth. And I have a perfect *right* to mention this to you, Ura, since I am giving myself away at the same time. Isn't that so? I am not sparing myself."

Ankersen lowered his head and said in a voice that was charged with brooding self-accusation: "*I* was among those who together with you trod that horrible path of sin. Even though it only happened two times!"

He slowly removed his spectacles. The expression on his face alternated between tears and laughter: "It happened when I was drunk. Drunk! And how it has constantly tormented me, by day and by night, for these many years."

40

With a distorted face Ankersen turned toward Mrs. Nillegaard and, unable to see clearly, pointed a finger at Ura: "That is why I have looked her up so often, in secret, and alone! But she has not wanted to answer my question and thus give my conscience the relief that it so sorely needs and longs for."

Groaning, Ankersen now turned and faced Ura: "Whether it *is* I or it is *not* I who am the father of your unhappy lost son Matte-Gok, Ura, the whole truth will lift a much too heavy burden from my breast."

Ankersen caught his breath; he put his spectacles back on his nose and his face took on a beatific expression: "And that is why today I confide fully and completely in my friends the Nillegaards and have brought them up here to have them serve as witnesses when I now once more and for the last time ask you, Ura Anthoniussen: In the name of the Lord, am I the father of your unhappy child, who was begotten in most heinous sin and later on may have gone to rack and ruin?"

A curiously sly glint appeared in the savings-bank manager's eye, and there was an almost unnoticeable smile on his lips: "You don't have to answer, Ura, I don't insist at all that you do. Because, if you remain silent, Ura, I will this time consider that to be an affirmative answer! And I will ask not only these two people to be witnesses, but the Lord also, who is of eternity! Do you understand, Ura?"

Mrs. Nillegaard quickly got out her handkerchief and dried her eyes and nose. Her husband over by the door had turned almost the other way.

Ura remained silent. She just stood there, with head held high and with slightly raised eyebrows; but her eyes were closed and a tiny stubborn smile hovered on her lips.

A few minutes passed. Ankersen looked at his watch. Then he snorted and breathed heavily. At long last he spoke, saying in a low voice: "Let us pray."

41

He made an impatient motion to the Nillegaards, as if wanting to embrace them both, and all three kneeled down by the kitchen table. Ura remained standing in the same spot. Ankersen's prayer took the form of a profound self-indictment, during which he begged for mercy and with a quivering voice made a solemn vow to do anything within the power of a human being to find the lost son, poor Mathias Georg Anthoniussen, and help confer on him the blessings of faith and salvation.

Mrs. Nillegaard was greatly touched; her heaving shoulders showed that she was sobbing.

At last the prayer came to an end. Ankersen rose with some difficulty; his thick lips were parted, and wisps of his thick wolf-gray hair were hanging down over his forehead. Bewildered, he tried to catch Ura's eye, sat down again on the bench, and said: "And then, Ura, there is another thing! We've also come here with a very practical proposition to you. The Christian temperance society Ydun has been offered the little house by the brook that belonged to the late Mangling-Marie, and we will let you have it, if you would like to move in." He added, in an ever stronger and firmer voice: "You know, our welfare committee wants to help in any way it can. The town council, of course, does not mind having people live in houses that are a hazard to life and limb; they are indifferent to that as to everything else. And the Church! Well, I wager that you have never had one visit from Pastor Lindemann? Isn't that so, Ura? And your old father Anthonius, the time he tumbled down the slope in his seventy-ninth year and was almost drowned—that was no concern of the minister, either, was it? He didn't even take the trouble to come and administer the sacrament to the old man when he died at the age of ninety-two! But we, on the other hand, Ura, we want to help. We want to do our best for you. Not from pride, Ura, but in remorse, in faith, and in justice. Do you accept our offer?"

Ura seemed to be flattered, but she said in a firm voice: "This is very nice of you, Ankersen, but I would like to stay here where I have lived all my life and where I have had my joys and sorrows; that's the way it must be."

Ankersen exchanged glances with Mrs. Nillegaard, as if both were shaking their heads. He nodded and fidgeted, then continued in a more subdued voice: "And then there was another thing. H'm, yes, we also wanted to help you in another way, too, Ura Anthoniussen, in such a way that you don't . . . . that you don't have to make a living from these strange predictions and prophecies of yours. Our society wants very much to help you get away from all that. You recall what it says in Holy Writ: 'Thou shalt not perform black magic!' You will no doubt say that that is not what you are doing, Ura. But wouldn't it in any case be much better if you could have a nice and respectable job, a small mangling room, for example, and then you might join us and repent and fully accept our Lord Jesus Christ?"

"There's no reason for all this fuss," Ura replied. She turned towards Mrs. Nillegaard, as if trying to bypass Ankersen: "I take care of what's mine, and you just worry about your own business, in the name of God! I have never been a burden to any one, and I never wish to be one."

"Yes, but just listen, dear woman. . . !" Mrs. Nillegaard attempted to continue, but Ankersen brushed her gently aside.

"Fuss did you say, Ura? *Fuss?*"

His voice rose to a falsetto, it trembled from seemingly unbounded tenderness and compassion: "But it doesn't come about without a certain amount of fuss, when God calls human souls! For we blind sinners, we fight against it, because we do not know what is good for us and do not seize the opportunity! That we don't, Ura! We fight against it! Until the day things can't *go on* like that any longer. Then we submit . . . then we become small and weak,

43

sinners imploring for forgiveness!" Ankersen's voice became normal again, he raised his head and puckered his forehead imperiously: "Your time is coming, too, Ura. Think about what I have said and about what has happened here today! I believe and hope to God that there soon will occur great things, also of concern to you, Ura. But we shall in any case not forget about you. We shall be back, Ura, we shall be back!"

CHAPTER 7

*The poet Sirius makes a new attempt to secure firmer ground
under his feet*

Sirius made a living from playing, together with his brothers, dance music at The Dolphin; in addition he wrote occasional poems. Since none of these occupations yielded much of an income he also worked as a painter and paper-hanger and lived in the house of his master, Mac Bett. He had previously worked in an office, but he had not been able to handle that job in spite of his unusually beautiful handwriting and his having received good marks when he graduated from high school. For a short time he had also been assistant teacher in Miss Lamm's primary school.

Although Sirius was not particularly fascinated by working as a painter and paper-hanger, he had nevertheless gained considerable skill in putting up wallpaper. He took a certain fancy to wallpapers, he was almost fond of them, at least the ones with flower motifs; with their constant repetition they sometimes inspired reflection in the same way that did the sight of extensive grassy fields, endless gardens in the bud, mystical seaweed forests, fallen snow, yes, at times as the distant and lonely majesty of the starry sky itself. But in spite of this and the fact that Master Mac Bett, otherwise very particular and demanding, had to admit that Sirius had an obvious talent for paper-hanging, the poet daily felt an ever-increasing distaste for this trade. Mac

45

Bett, for his part, would often wish he could get rid of his assistant, especially so whenever he had overslept, something that Sirius did rather frequently, since he would read in bed half the night.

As is also evident from Magnus Skæling's beautiful essay, Sirius was quite well read, and it was not the popular literature of the day with which he occupied himself; thus, he was the owner of Dante's *Divine Comedy* in a Swedish translation. Besides that, Sirius's reading consisted chiefly of biographies and books in the field of cultural history, as is shown by the loan records of the public library.*

On a sunny afternoon in May, when all the town's gardens had turned green, Sirius went up to see Mac Bett and told him that his paper-hanging days were over. The master painter, who was of Scottish descent and could be terribly quick-tempered, began to thrash his apprentice with a ruler, and when the poet climbed up on a table and tried to defend himself with a roll of wallpaper, the angry master threw a pair of scissors at him. It grazed his cheek and he started to bleed a little.

"Merciful God!" Mac Bett cried, terror-stricken. "It might have hit you in the eye, and then both of us would have been unhappy for the rest of our lives!"

He helped Sirius to get down from the table and, still shaking from agitation, he examined the cheek.

"It's only a superficial scratch," he noted with much relief and sat down on the floor, completely exhausted. He stroked his silvery whiskers and sighed: "Good heavens! Yes, of course, it is best that you leave me, Sirius, for I would sooner or later have beaten you to a pulp, and you never fight back. I'll give you credit for that. But what are you going to do

---

* The books borrowed included: *The Life of Johannes Ewald; Victor Hugo and the New France,* by Ahlberg; *The Christian Preaching of Sören Kierkegaard,* by F. Petersen; *Miscellaneous Studies,* by H. S. Vodskov; *W. A. Mozart,* by Nissen; and *Notes of Ben Jonson's Conversations with W. Drummond.*

46

now, you rascal? Since you are poor and have always been lazy, there's nothing else that you can do!"

Sirius smiled and said softly: "I write, Mac Bett, I'm a poet!"

To this the old master painter could make no comment. He stared at Sirius with a perplexed expression on his face, revealing mixed feelings of scorn and pity.

But Sirius had a plan. He wanted to establish a primary school on the pattern of Miss Lamm's. Three full days he nosed about in the town partly for the purpose of procuring pupils, and partly in order to obtain suitable premises. Both of these desiderata proved to be harder to get than he had thought. During his vain roaming around the town in the spring weather he met Mac Bett, who with a sigh took him by the collar and offered him a chance to get back his old job. Sirius declined the master painter's offer with thanks, and divulged his plan to him.

"Come home with me and get something to eat," said Mac Bett, "I think I can make you a good proposition."

This proposition was to the effect that Sirius was to teach school in the back room of Mac Bett's little picture-framing shop. He would have no rent to pay, but Sirius was in return to wait on the customers in the shop during forenoons.

"Thus we will save the wages I've paid to that slattern of a girl who has been taking care of the store," Mac Bett said. He added encouragingly: "And it won't be difficult at all, because for one thing we don't have many customers unfortunately, and for another you already know the trade."

Sirius gratefully accepted his offer. In a week's time he succeeded in recruiting four pupils, namely, his nephew Orfeus; Peter, the son of the gravedigger; Emanuel Samsonsen, the son of the Adventists; and Julia Janniksen. Julia was fifteen years old and was the daughter of Janniksen the blacksmith. She was exceptionally big for her age and was slightly retarded as regards her mental faculties.

The window of Mac Bett's back room faced blacksmith

47

Janniksen's garden. It was a beautiful view, especially now when the leaves were sprouting; but it was soon to be evident that the proximity to the blacksmith's had an unfortunate effect on the instruction. All went well the first two schooldays; the three boys were eager and learned quickly; the girl was slow, but thanks to her more advanced age she was able to keep up; and the customers of the frame store were no trouble at all. The view of the blacksmith's flowering currant bushes was refreshing.

The third schoolday, which was a Saturday, also started out with sunshine and bird song, and every one was in a happy mood. The smithy was quiet; the blacksmith had a visitor, namely Lindenskov, the dance instructor. The two were fast friends and frequently bowled behind the house. But at noon the blacksmith suddenly appeared in the garden, with a bottle in one hand, followed by the dance instructor. Both of them were already quite inebriated. With a thoughtlessness fit to tear one's heart they seated themselves right in the middle of a bed of purple crocuses and began to drink to each other. Soon the blacksmith began to sing. Sirius forbade his pupils to look out the window and by using a loud voice and rattling his ruler he attempted to drown out the blacksmith's singing, which assumed an increasingly ribald character.

Neither teacher nor pupils, however, could resist the temptation to look out. Blacksmith Janniksen was a large, rawboned, and hairy fellow. He had a beard of the type worn by Emperor Francis Joseph, and had a large dent in the middle of his forehead. The dance instructor was small and wizened, with protruding fish-eyes and front teeth and a drooping mustache.

Julia sighed. She even seemed to be on the verge of tears. "Look!" she said suddenly. "Father is dancing!"

Sirius stepped over to the window. Yes, the blacksmith was indeed dancing. The huge fellow made some absurd and clumsy jumps, pirouetted, gesticulated with his enormous arms, stamped his feet, and bellowed. It was the so-called "solo dance"; Sirius had seen it performed quite often when people had a merry time at The Dolphin; it was a kind of feat of strength that the blacksmith would always attempt at a certain stage of his intoxication. The dance instructor sat next to him, striking one empty bottle against another—it was supposed to be the accompanying music. But what is going on now? The blacksmith bends over Lindenskov and lifts him up, rocks him in his arms as if he were a newborn babe and . . . suddenly throws him into one of the big currant bushes!

"Oh no!" Sirius exclaimed. "Now they are ruining the entire garden!"

"The blacksmith *is* that way," Gravedigger Peter said matter-of-factly. "He smashes everything when he is drunk."

"Look, Mother is coming!" Julia cried, and bit her nails.

Sirius sighed. Mrs. Janniksen *had* arrived. She was large and swarthy just like her husband; in her protruding eyes there was an expression of self-control and somber singleness of purpose.

"Listen, Julia," Sirius said sternly, "you are going to stop peeking; sit down and mind your business!"

Sirius too walked away from the window and stood by the wallpaper-covered packing-case that served as his lectern. Julia sat down, laughing nervously. A few customers came into the store, and Sirius had to go out to them. When he returned, it was no more than to be expected that the children were standing over by the window. Julia was sobbing uncontrollably.

"Get back in your seats!" Sirius commanded them. But the children made no move.

"She has killed the blacksmith," Gravedigger Peter informed him in a muffled voice.

"What has she done?" Sirius cried excitedly.

49

Well, that wasn't quite correct. It is true that the black-smith was lying on his back in the flower-bed, but he wasn't dead; he was just lying there, howling a little, either from pain or from joy or merely on account of being so drunk. His wife was busy trying to rescue the dance instructor out from among the currant bushes and the multitudes of red flowers and small round innocent leaves. Lindenskov had a few scratches in his face and a bleeding cut on one side of his mouth.

"This is going much too far!" Sirius said and clucked his tongue. He held the hefty Julia close to him and stroked her cheek with his skinny hand: "Please stop crying, my girl, it won't help any!"

A little while later he was down in the garden. The black-smith was still lying there, howling. Lindenskov, too, was moaning. There were currant blossoms in his clothes and in his hair, blood was dripping from his mustache, and he was humming in a cracked voice:

> Of all the small flowers of spring,
> the fine and the fair,
> there's specially one
> that's close to my heart. . . .

Mrs. Janniksen brought a piece of cloth and wiped Lindenskov's face. Then Sirius took him by the arm, led him out of the garden, and took him home.

As usual, Lindenskov's house was full of women; he had seven daughters, but the Misses Schibbye and other ladies were also present, and there were porcelain cups on the table—it seemed to be quite a get-together with hot choco-late being served. Lindenskov clung to Sirius and wanted him to go in with him; but the ladies scolded them and were almost frenzied in their ire and feeling of having been offended; they called Sirius a drunkard and a seducer, and his attempt to clear himself was all in vain. Reluctantly, the little dance instructor disappeared in among a multitude of skirts and puffed sleeves, and the door was slammed shut with a meaningful bang.

Sirius let the children go home. The boys ran off immediately, but Julia stayed behind; she had stopped crying but, in fits and starts, she seemed to be gasping for breath.

"You'd rather not go home, isn't that so?" Sirius asked with an air of concern. "Well, you just sit down and wait until Mac Bett returns."

Sirius sat down by the lectern. He had taken a pencil out of his pocket and was working on a poem. Once in a while he would get up and pace the floor and walk into the shop. It was a poem whose theme had been running through his mind for a long time. Now it seemed that the lines were emerging ready-made. It was a poem about spring and the budding of leaves, about the multitudes of flowers, about the sunshine that almost miraculously liberates one's soul from its threadbare raiment of sorrow and longing and prepares for it a refreshing bath. It was strange, indeed, that the words should come to him now, in the middle of this mess.

Julia was sitting on her chair and just stared at him, feeling completely lost. Mac Bett returned, and loud grumbling was heard as he paced up and down inside his shop. Sirius had completed his poem. He took Julia by the hand, and together they walked out to the Bastille. Sirius got hold of Eliana and said, his voice very serious: "We must look after this girl a bit; she is not very sharp, but she has a good heart, and her home is not very inspiring, as you know."

Eliana made coffee for Sirius and Julia. The girl kept on staring at her and looked so pathetic that Eliana just had to kiss her on the forehead. But right then the blacksmith's wife arrived. The big woman's face was swollen and grimy. She didn't say a word but seized Julia firmly by the arm and marched off with her.

That afternoon Sirius made a clean copy of his poem. He

read it through several times, until he knew it by heart. It was a good poem, perhaps the best he had ever written. Filled with enthusiasm he went to see the editor of *The News*. Here at last was a poem that deserved to be printed!*

Editor Olsen skimmed through the poem, shook his head, and handed it back.

"You don't like it?" asked the poet.

The editor took off one of his brown canvas shoes and started to examine its interior. Then he fetched a hammer from the composing room.

Disheartened, Sirius watched the big man struggling to pull a small nail out of his sole with the aid of the claw of the hammer. The editor at last abandoned the experiment and drove the nail into the sole. Thereupon he absent-mindedly walked back to the composing room and disappeared.

Sirius folded the sheet of paper and put it in his pocket; but he had still not given up the hope of seeing the poem in print. He went to editor Jacobsen at *The Messenger*, the radical paper. Jacobsen gave the impression of being very busy, but he took time out to scan the poem very rapidly. He laughed, peered at Sirius over the rim of his glasses, and for a few moments sat back in his American rocking chair.

"This is for the birds," he said. "What's the use of such romantic nonsense? We're living in a realistic time, not in a golden age, dear sir! We have no use for idylls, Sirius Isaksen, keep that in mind, if only for your own sake. Write a satirical poem about the conditions here, about the duck pond, about the reactionary forces that are gaining ground, about teacher Nillegaard and savings-bank manager Ankersen and their hysterical Christian temperance tom-

* Vide Sirius Isaksen, *Posthumous Poems*, "Spring," pg. 57. Dr. Chr. Matras in his literary history says about this poem that it reveals a very fine touch and is filled with ecstatic music to such a high degree that one is reminded of a no lesser poet than H. A. Brorson and his poem "Here we're silent, here we'll wait."

foolery! Teach them a lesson, all of them, and then you'll be doing something useful! Sunshine and chirping is something that you can amuse yourself with all by yourself if you're so inclined and have the time."

He gave the sheet of paper back to Sirius and relit his cigar butt. The editor was unshaven, and there was a trace of yellowish foam in the corners of his mouth. Puffing sedulously, he added: "But, by God, you're talented, Sirius! Of course, you're *balmy* just like your brothers and your father with his aeolian harps. But you *can* do it, all of you, when you just pull yourselves together! That song you wrote on the occasion of Captain Öström's silver wedding, that was not bad at all, at least you covered everything. But then it was directly taken from my editorial in *The Messenger*, he, he! You did a good job, though. But, as I said, romantic springtime—the Lord save me from that. Write something that has a kick in it, something biting!"

He emphasized these last words by shaking his head so vehemently that his fat and sagging cheeks quivered.

Sirius, feeling discouraged, walked aimlessly up and down the streets for about an hour. Then he went up to see Kornelius, who had just come home from work and was having tea with hardtack.

Kornelius read the poem, nodded, while chewing calmly, and said that he would set it to music that very evening, as soon as he had shaved and changed clothes. Sirius also had a cup of tea. Kornelius took his cello and began to strum it and to hum along with the music.

In the evening the weather was unusually lovely. Kornelius and Sirius got their brother and his wife to go with them for a walk. Moritz brought his horn. They walked along the beach to Stake Spit and sat down far out on its seaweed-scented point. Moritz played Kornelius's new melody through several times and then made some jolly improvisations on the entire theme.

CHAPTER 8

About old Boman and his godson

Orfeus had long since begun to play the violin, under the tutelage of his godfather, Kaspar Boman, and he was making good progress.

It was obvious that he had inherited his father's natural talent. The old music teacher was strict and rather caustic throughout the instruction period, but outside the lessons he would sink into a certain mood of boundless and sad friendliness and he would talk to his pupil about music and the great masters, or he would lose himself in his own memories.

Boman was born on the little island Hveen,* the son of a gardener and virtuoso on the mouth organ; he had left home at an early age and had for years traveled about, earning a living as gardener or musician. At one time he had been the pupil of a well-known teacher in Copenhagen, and he might possibly have amounted to something in the field of music, but Fate had ordained otherwise; now he was, worse luck, a lonely old childless widower. But he didn't feel lonely at all, for he had his pupils and friends and his flowers; and music, of course, had also been a good companion, and as long as one had that, why, then one possessed everything that one's heart might desire!

Boman's little cottage resembled a garden. On the win-

* Located in the Sound, between Denmark and Sweden. Tr. note.

dowsill and any other place where there was room, luxuriant potted plants stood or hung, and vine leaves covered almost the entire ceiling. Faded portraits and engravings of composers and musicians hung round about the walls. All the faces had that kind and attentive expression that also characterized Boman; but they, too, seemed capable of being gruff and firm whenever necessary. They were all famous and distinguished men, but almost all of them had begun at the bottom, as poor boys who often might have had a hard time of it. Boman spoke about them as one does about old friends one has known in childhood and has observed growing up, blossoming out in brilliance and splendor, and thereupon dying—leaving everything behind; for most of them died young—some of them, perhaps the best of them, dying as mere boys.

One day when Orfeus came for his lesson he found Boman lying down on his threadbare sofa. The old man lay with his eyes tightly closed and had a strange, suffering expression about his mouth.

"Is it you, Orfeus?" he asked in a whisper. "Sit down, my boy. It will soon go over, I hope, it is only a minor attack."

For a quarter of an hour Orfeus suffered great inward agitation, for he couldn't stand to see his amiable old teacher lie there suffering. All the plants, the pictures on the walls, and the big double bass, which stood under its hood of oilcloth looking like a human being—in their own mute and expectant manner, they all shared in Boman's suffering. The composers looked as if they were thinking: This is very bad, but what must be, must be.

At last the old man began to breathe more easily. He sighed and stretched out the length of the sofa; he opened his eyes, raised his head, and smiled: "Well, now I feel much better."

A little while later he was his old self again. He pointed at the portrait of Weber hanging on the wall: "Well, think

55

of that now! I am an old man, a dotard pretty soon, but that one over there was a sick and decrepit man all his life. Not to speak of the one over there, Beethoven, the greatest of them all, he even became stone deaf, yes, what do you think of that? While still in the prime of life!"

Boman fell silent and shook his head, and for a moment he looked completely distracted, but suddenly his face took on a firm mien and he commenced with the lesson.

Orfeus had gradually gotten to know quite well the many faces on Boman's walls; he would imagine that they appeared before him, and at times they would show up in his dreams, sometimes singly, at other times in large groups, at times accompanied by Boman but at other times in the company of photographer Sundholm or Tarira, the ship's figurehead. It wasn't always pleasant—especially when Tarira was among them. Things became downright bad one day when Orfeus came down with the measles and a high fever. Then there was a tremendous influx in the Bastille basement of men with wigs or with long, womanish hair; they smiled at him and winked sarcastically and ambiguously—there was one especially who was a mean one, a thin fellow with a slender nose, with the daintiest-looking spectacles, and a large fur collar. He remained standing in the semi-darkness over in the corner, blinked his eyes, and made the most peculiar grimaces.

Having been told by Moritz about his godson's strange visions, Boman that evening came out to the Bastille and sat by the boy's bed a long time.

"I do believe that the ghost he talks so much about is none other than Carl Maria von Weber!" Boman whispered, smiling uneasily. "Don't you think it will help, Moritz, if you play a piece on your violin? Something by Weber, perhaps? Of course, I am not sure. It might be a very silly idea!"

"No, not at all!" Moritz said, taking heart.

He went to get his violin, and Orfeus heard the music as

through a drowsy mist; it came from deep down below and went up on high; suddenly everything became bright all around him, and the strangers, the guests brought by his fever, crowded together at the door and rushed to make their exit.

In the end, only Tarira remained. But in her pale eyes there was now a kind and attentive look, and she walked over to his bed and obligingly straightened his pillow.

"Don't you recognize me at all, my little boy?" she asked reproachfully, smiling the while; oh yes, now Orfeus could very well see who it was—it wasn't Tarira at all, it was only his mother!

Part II

In which strange things begin to happen

CHAPTER 1

*Moritz is swallowed up by the ocean, while a singing count
and his sweetheart are left behind on a desolate island*

Boman's choir would give concerts once in a while for
charity; at such times it was no more than natural that
Moritz and the other musicians from the Bastille would take
part. Now there was to be a concert to raise money for a new
organ; it was to be held in the church, with a bazaar, tom-
bola, and a wheel of fortune. It was the new minister, Pastor
Fruelund, who had conceived the idea, and one day he came
out to the Bastille and asked Moritz to perform.

"But of course we can use only fine—in fact, only the
finest music," he added with some emphasis. "Do you follow
me?"

Pastor Fruelund was a tall man with an air of authority
about him; he had a beautiful, sonorous voice, and he used
to speak clearly and with some force as if he suspected
people of being a little hard of hearing.

"What does the pastor think of Mozart's Quartet in D Flat
—you know—the one that goes. . . ?" Moritz was about to
hum the beginning of the andante, but the minister shook
his head: "Well, no, I had in mind a beautiful little piece
called 'Nazareth.' Do you know it? I can't for the moment
remember who composed it, but my wife has the music, and
you, who are known to be so musical—you will learn it very
fast. I would like to have it played on trombone and organ."

61

"I know that piece very well, it's one of Gounod's," Moritz said. He felt like adding: "It's a deadly dull and slow waltz; Mrs. Fähse, the apothecary's wife, used to sing it in her time; it was awful!" But he let it go.

The minister nodded, adding in a didactic tone: "A trombone, you see, is all right to use in church, but it is not a piece for a quartet, not at all. Well—and then we ought to have a few hymns sung by the male choir; I might want to conduct the choir myself, if you on the other hand could get them together and have them practice the hymns, just roughly."

"For three years I was a member of the students' male choir in Copenhagen," he added.

Nodding his handsome, curly-haired head, he continued: "The rest of the program will mainly consist of organ playing. Then I will recite a religious poem by Paludan-Müller, and then the daughter of Lamm, the organist, will sing 'The Daughter of Jairus,' and Count Oldendorp will sing "Among His Brothers Known as the Little One."

"Lamm?" Moritz said. He would have liked to say: "Lamm the organist can't play anything but Thorvaldsen's funeral march, and he does it in such a way that people think there's something wrong with the organ."

"Yes, *Lamm!*" said the minister, shooting the ferryman a glance that discouraged humorous remarks.

When the great day dawned, the weather was fair and flags were flying briskly in the wind.

At noon Moritz set out with his boat for Österöre; among his passengers was Count Oldendorp, who was fetching his sweetheart, the daughter of Pastor Schmerling at Österöre. The count was in a jolly mood; he was trying to memorize the hymn that he was to sing at the concert. "For it looks more impressive if one doesn't have to sing with a book in front of him," he said. "Moritz, please look at this and listen to me to see if I know it!"

He handed the book to Moritz. Then he pulled a half bottle of cognac out of his back pocket. "We both need some added strength," he said, looking very serious. With a sigh he took a big swig and handed Moritz the bottle.

The two men were sitting in the stern of the boat, which was gaily dancing over the crested waves. The count was a fairly young man but of quite unusual dimensions; his powerful, somewhat tremulous voice drowned out the noise from the motor and the roar of the sea.

Happy and feeling refreshed, the count stepped ashore at Österöre. His sweetheart, Anna-Iris, was a girl of around thirty who had a motherly, worried, and searching look in her eyes; she was waiting at the landing, wrapped in shawls and kerchiefs. He took her in his giant arms and lifted her into the boat and then attended to a basket with carefully wrapped bottles.

"Oh, do be very careful, Karl Erik!" Anna-Iris said. "It's currant wine from our garden. It's a little present to the bailiff from Father!"

The pastor at Österöre, who was confined to his bed because of sciatica, was waving enthusiastically from his bedroom window, and the two lovers waved back. The boat left the pier. The count handed the book to his fiancée so that she could see if he knew the song by heart. He lifted up his jolly, ruddy face and sang in a voice that drowned out everything else:

> Pensively I walked and fingered,
> Deft, a lyre I had found;
> And my song within it lingered,
> Like a harp, with organ-sound.

The boat started to pitch when they passed Mermaid Islet; they had the current with them, but the wind blew the other way. Anna-Iris, with a worried look, clung to her sweetheart's arm; he patted her reassuringly on the cheek and sang the while. But suddenly the motor came to a full stop.

Moritz turned the tiller over to the count and began to examine the motor. The boat was drifting sideways in the direction of the northern point of Seal Island; Anna-Iris moved even closer to her sweetheart and placed a corner of her shawl over his knees.

"There's nothing to worry about," the count said reassuringly and continued singing.

Moritz struggled to get the motor going again—he was sweating and there were black splotches and streaks in his face. The boat was drifting at a good rate of speed. The wind was stronger than it had been during the trip out. In the middle of the sound, where the wind and the current were battling each other, veritable mounds of angry water had formed, gleaming in the sun. Moritz stood up and held the tiller for a moment. "We'll have to stay away from the maelstrom," he said.

The count continued with his singing. He had closed his book and had put it in his pocket. "Get that infernal engine going again!" he shouted between two verses and threw his sweetheart an exaggeratedly reassuring glance. Moritz tackled the motor once more. A few irregular chugging sounds were heard, the boat made a jerk and turned its snout in the right direction.

"Bravo!" the count shouted and pulled the book out of his pocket.

But a moment later the motor stopped again.

Moritz shook his head. Anna-Iris began to whimper and looked worried. The count laughed and yawned as if nothing had happened. He went over and stuck his head and the upper part of his body into the little engine house and said to Moritz: "This calls for something to strengthen us, doesn't it?" Moritz felt the neck of a bottle against his chin. The count sat down again next to his sweetheart and resumed his singing.

The wind became stronger, and the foaming water was

64

seething merrily but mercilessly about the scudding craft. Moritz once more succeeded in getting the motor to show signs of life; they steered in toward land, under the shelter of Mermaid Islet, and Moritz jumped ashore and secured the painter around a piece of rock that was jutting up. The count laughingly helped his sweetheart onto dry ground; they seated themselves where they were protected by a ledge, and he got his book out again. Moritz, who was lying with the upper part of his body inside the engine house, could hear the count's boisterous song through the sighing and seething of the waves:

Pensively I walked and fingered. . .

It was now blowing hard, a white border had appeared around Seal Island, and the air above the heaving banks of water in the sound was filled with foam and spray.

"You could at least stop that foolish singing!" Anna-Iris said scoldingly. "I don't think this is the time and place for it. And besides, it's the same stanza you're singing over and again!"

"Yes, but it's such a beautiful stanza," the count replied, "you know—the passage where he is strumming. That's something for me—pensively strumming away."

He got up to see how Moritz was making out with the motor, but he couldn't see the boat anywhere.

"What the devil . . . !" he roared and burst out laughing as he peered out over the sea. Anna-Iris had also risen. Pointing out across the rushing waves, she said in a tearful voice: "Oh no, look! over there! He's sailing all the way out there!"

Now the count too could see the boat—a black dot in the far distance, visible against the white background.

"It's broken loose!" Anna-Iris wailed.

"Oh, that's not at all sure," he countered. He wildly

65

slapped his thigh as if in a transport of delight: "Yes, by God it has; a piece of the painter is right over there!"

"But is that anything to be so gleeful about?" Anna-Iris exclaimed, looking at him in dismay. "Now we've been left all alone on this desolate islet! We might not even get back alive, Karl Erik!"

"Oh won't we now!" yelled the count. He climbed up to the highest point of the little island, and Anna-Iris followed him, sobbing. The wind and the spray stung their faces. The count got out his handkerchief and waved, but there was no living thing to be seen on the wind-swept opposite shore.

"Come on down!" Anna-Iris shouted. "Where are you taking us? Let's at least get down to a place where there is some shelter from the wind!"

"Yes, right away! Right away!" the count said reassuringly. He bent down behind a projecting ledge and took a long, lingering swig from his flask. Thereupon, beaming with joy and singing at the top of his voice, he walked back to his sweetheart.

Anna-Iris just stared at him. In her eyes there was a trace of fear, but there was also contempt, chilly despair, and a certain resoluteness.

"I have never in my born days experienced anything so stupid and so awful!" she said.

He put both his hands on her shoulders and answered her by singing, with great composure and with emphasis on each word:

> Pensively I walked and fingered,
> Deft, a lyre I had found . . .

"Oh, why don't you stop it!" she complained. "You're driving me crazy with that nonsense!" She added, a threatening note in her voice: "I don't *trust* you, Karl Erik! I have no *faith* in you!"

66

Very calmly he answered her, with great intensity and with emphasis on each word:

> And my song within it lingered,
> Like a harp, with organ-sound.

"Like a harp!" he repeated, stressing each syllable: *"Like a harp!"*

Even though Moritz had been busy with the motor he did notice that the boat had broken adrift, but he didn't do anything about it; there was no use raising a hue and cry, for the count couldn't be of any help anyway. The boat was scudding in an easterly direction toward the sound, where the waves were running high. He had to grasp the tiller and try to steer around the maelstrom. In this he succeeded to a certain extent. The boat entered waters that felt bumpy and hard like a frozen road, and at a great speed it was taken eastwards and into the open sea. It was like being swept away down a torrential and rock-filled river. At last, however, it glided out of the current, and the immense ocean received it with a broad and friendly indifference, lifting it up on its huge billows, where the wind blew hard and the spray rained down—then pulling it down again into the troughs, where there was a moment's shelter.

Moritz proceeded to consider the situation. True, there was a strong wind, but it was not a question of a real storm. Fortunately, the count and his sweetheart had been brought to a safe place. At least people don't perish on Mermaid Islet, so close to human habitation. At worst, they might experience some frigid temperatures, but they did have their woolen blankets and could also stay on the lee side of the island.

But he was drifting ever eastward and into the open sea; there was no other boat to be seen anywhere, not even a small fishing smack.

The hours passed. The late-summer afternoon was slowly waning. The sun-dappled streaks in the water became darker; the sea became greener in color. It wasn't particularly pleasant—this limitless mass of water, to whose whims he was now completely subjected.

The concert! It was supposed to start at six o'clock. Oh, well! It was probable that he would be missed; so would—not least—the count and his sweetheart. And a search for them would be instituted. Probably with Consul Hansen's big motorboat *Triton*, perhaps also with the small steamer *Neptunus*, which was just lying in the harbor. The count and his sweetheart would be located first, and the rescuers would be told the direction in which the boat had disappeared. All that was needed was patience.

Moritz got to his feet and beat his arms against his body in order to keep warm. The basket with the wine bottles was still there in the stern.

Contrary to expectations and to all likelihood, the wind got stronger toward sunset. The sun broke through for a moment and suffused the billowy landscape with a copper-brown tinge. The hump-backed top of Seal Island appeared dark violet against the sky. At worst, it would be a few hours before *that* would pass from sight.

Moritz once again tried to fix the motor. But it all seemed rather hopeless. It was slowly getting dark. The soughing of the waves turned into an angry whipping sound. Stars appeared in the sky here and there. The stark horizon began to fade and the huge cave of endless darkness opened hospitably before him. Quite so. But it still seemed unthinkable that the end was drawing near. It was just a question of being patient.

He rose and swung his arms, felt warm again, and banished all melancholy thoughts. Various musical compositions went through his mind. A massive and sort of sunlit largo by Haydn. He heard the individual instruments, the little

68

hesitant, chromatic solo of the cello, during which the piece, so to speak, darkens, as if a cloud obliterates the sun, and then surges out into the friendly, warm light. Yes, there was something very nice about that largo—sunshine and happy days.

More string music. A solo for horn, marches. The three military marches by Schubert. While the wind whistled and bounded past the boat, and night began to fall.

Humming, Moritz once again began to busy himself with the motor, but in a rather haphazard manner. It *might* just be that through some miracle it would start up again, in spite of everything. But the clammy, greasy metal contraption did not give any sign of life.

He turned his back on the engine, and once more stood face to face with desolate darkness. Indeed, a man was but a speck of dust in the night. He suddenly thought of the Bible verse: In the beginning God created heaven and earth, and there was darkness over the abyss, and so on. This passage made him again think of his father and his peculiar doings in the church steeple, where he had had his aeolian harps. When the wind howled in the dry sheep-gut in those harps, it sounded as if supernatural forces were at play. It was a music fit for the departed and those that were mouldering. They could surely hear it in their graves. He shuddered.

Then he again happened to think of "The Dance of the Blessed Spirits" by Gluck, and in that connection he also thought of Eliana, who used to hum this melody. Yes, being so musically inclined, she had hummed it at Orfeus's cradle. She had used it as a kind of cradle song. Not only that song but also the charming little minuet from Schubert's Octet!

Death and damnation! Moritz once again turned his back on the darkness hovering over the abyss. He was deliberating with himself whether he should have a taste of Pastor Schmerling's wine and arrived at the conclusion that this

69

might be justified under such unusual circumstances. The wine was sweet and heavy, it tasted like a liqueur. The quiet, flushed pastor certainly knew how to make a good brew.

Moritz was hungry, he could feel the effect of the wine, and the music began once more to bubble forth within him. He intentionally made use of it to put to flight all the sad thoughts. Eliana . . . what would happen to her and the children, if he perished out here? Oh what nonsense! Here came Söderman's "Wedding Feast at Ulvshög"! It was one of Boman's favorite compositions; it made one think of summer and sunshine and a carefree life without end.

But then "The Dance of the Blessed Spirits" again intrudes itself, and the thought of Eliana surges forward and will not let him push it out of his mind; against his own wishes her face reappears, he can see her right in front of him, the way she looked during those early days when he had been infatuated to the point of madness, when she was still working as a maid at The Dolphin and sparkled—sparkled in close competition with the glittering water below the windows, a blonde revelation, admired and sought-after by every one, but quite beyond one's reach. To him it still seemed somewhat unreasonable that he turned out to be the one who won her, he, the poor sailor, and not, for instance, the elegant Storm, the office manager, or the prosperous attorney Wenningstedt, who also had been very persistent in courting her; the elderly clown had even written her several letters proposing marriage.

It was music that had come to the aid of Moritz. Eliana and he had met in a common love of music. And when all was said and done, it was Boman they could thank for everything.

Ah, how many things old Boman deserved thanks for!

Moritz took another swig from the bottle, then suddenly emptied it completely. He was still alive in spite of everything. He sat there holding on to the wet tiller. He was

70

chilled and wet, and alive. And there was a whole basketful of bottles left. And tomorrow was Monday.

It was Monday. So it was, no matter how one looked at it. A Monday at sea. A Monday of loneliness. A Monday of cold and hunger and sleepiness. A Monday of distress at sea, true enough, but it was, at any rate, Monday. And as for the rest, it was for the time being rather unimportant.

And thank God for that.

It took more than four hours for help to reach Count Oldendorp and his sweetheart at Mermaid Islet—this despite the fact that from the very beginning a living being who was sitting on the opposite shore had seen the excited waving of the two lovers.

But this being was the Crab King. He was sitting by a small puddle of brackish water, which he visited once in a while in order to inspect some hermit crabs that he kept there.

It is possible that it never occurred to the inscrutable dwarf that the people opposite, doing so much shouting and waving, were shipwrecked and had to be rescued. Perhaps their constant waving, now with kerchiefs and now with shawls flapping in the wind, merely had the effect of sending the little man off into a reverie. At any rate, his only visible reaction was to shift into a better sitting position and to give himself over to surveying his surroundings with the greatest interest.

The wind would at times carry to his ears the sounds of singing, laughter, and ludicrous words and sentences, and he listened with rapt attention: "You hopeless idiot! You baboon! Yes, that's what I said! I'll never forget this, mark my words! You just wait!"

The Crab King emitted a deep sigh and stroked his black, silver-streaked beard. To the end of time it will be unknown whether his shocking passivity was grounded in malice, in-

71

difference, or foolishness. Even Manicus, the county medical officer, who was an excellent physician and a keen judge of character, could never fully grasp just what exactly lay concealed within the Crab King, this acondroplastic dwarf with his small flipper-like arms and legs and his lined face with its almost unnaturally worldly-wise and pensive look.

CHAPTER 2

*Concerning that which later happened to Moritz and the
excesses of Ankersen, the savings-bank manager*

The humdrum life in a little town and the everyday repetition of events and small frictions make people stupid and
irritable, envious and petty-minded. It may therefore be
somewhat edifying to observe the great change for the better
that sets in occasionally when the unusual occurs and gives
a jolt to the sour and crabbed balance of things. It was as if
the town for just one moment became fully conscious of the
fact that it was located on the very edge of the enormous
abyss of the ocean.

A man, a fellow human being, whom we are used to seeing about us every day—who might indeed have been any
one of us—is suddenly swallowed up by the great unknown
that surrounds us—has disappeared in an all-powerful and
insensate waste which perhaps is not as irrevocable as death
but nevertheless is as merciless as the ocean. There is still
hope that the man may be saved, and this hope spreads like
wildfire and fires up young and old; all the townspeople
flock down to the pier to have a look at the docked boat
Triton and the little steamer *Neptunus* setting out in an
effort to wrest another prey from death.

They'll no doubt find him, the spectators think and nod
encouragingly to one another. And they call Moritz a
splendid human being, a musical talent, a good father and

73

husband, and in addition a *hero,* yes, they lose themselves in proud and painful memories of Moritz Isaksen's spectacular deed, that November day in 1899 when he singlehandedly rescued seven seamen and a lady from the schooner *Karelia.* That was a heroic deed, if anything ever was. That winter Moritz had been the most talked-about man in the islands, and he had also, of course, been awarded the life-saving medal.

Yes, Moritz was fine fellow through and through.

Still, there are always some people who don't think the way others do. There is, for instance, Ankersen, the savings-bank manager. He declares point blank that what is now happening to Moritz Isaksen has been sent from on high as punishment for his worldly and intemperate life.

"Yes, but it would be a shame if . . ." Fat Alfred, Ankersen's clerk, objects.

"Shame?" snarls Ankersen, getting up from his chair, fuming. "Yes, a shame and a *sin,* too! Exactly that! Sin brings sorrow and unhappiness in its wake! The wages of sin is death!"

Ankersen is in a terrible state of agitation. He walks back and forth and sputters like burning pitch. Fat Alfred sits quietly observing his employer with a mien of deferential apprehension, thinking: "After all, Ankersen is at bottom a good man. Ankersen does want the best for every one. But he is just horrible when this comes over him!"

Ankersen was indeed horrible. Noisily he put on his galoshes and went straight out to the Bastille, where he executed a veritable attack on Moritz's wife and the little group of friends who had gathered to comfort the poor woman.

"It just *had* to turn out this way!" he thundered. "It's God's finger, God's chastising finger! Don't ever believe that you can escape this finger pointing at you! Don't ever believe that, all ye who think it does not matter how ye conduct your life on earth, ye who make light of the Life to

74

come, which in fact is the only life that should be of real interest to any one!"

His eyes bloodshot, he looked around the circle of pale, bewildered faces. There were four women: Magister Mortensen's housekeeper Atlanta; Sarina, the wife of the Corpse Crower; the Wailing Woman, and her daughter Mira, along with a few men like the Corpse Crower and the old coalman Fribert, and that good-for-nothing Sirius. The Wailing Woman was weeping steadily and drying her eyes incessantly. Moritz's son, Orfeus, was also crying, and hiding his face in his sleeves. But what about Eliana herself! She did not look remorseful at all; on the contrary, she looked at Ankersen with a friendly and cheerful expression in her eyes and made some remark to the effect that everything would probably turn out all right.

"I am not afraid," she said. "I am certain that Moritz will be back with us soon."

"Be back!" Ankersen murmured ominously. "He won't come back under his own power! Don't you ever believe it, you poor frivolous and proud woman! You must change your ways, you must humble yourself, you must pray and confess! Come, let us all join in silent prayer. . . !"

Ankersen motioned with his arms as if to embrace them all, but suddenly the door opened and Magister Mortensen, as tall and skinny as ever, stepped inside. He placed his pince-nez on his nose and addressed Ankersen in a low but sharp tone of voice: "Listen here, what the devil does this mean, Mr. Ankersen? What kind of conduct is this? What business do you have out here anyway, if I may ask?"

Ankersen involuntarily made a motion as if to defend himself with his big fists, and he smiled in a curiously ambiguous manner. It took some time before he collected himself sufficiently to be able to retort, but then it came like a ferocious and merciless torrent: "So, this is what *you* think you can permit yourself! An atheist like you! A . . . .

75

er . . . spawn of the devil, yea! That's what I said! Spawn of the devil! Yes, for you are an apostate, that's what you are, you who even studied to become a minister once! Are you really coming here to thwart me in joining these poor anxious people in prayer for . . . for . . . . the rescue of the lost one?"

He reached out and said, his voice filled with emotion: "Is it not so, O people? We will pray to the Almighty to help us avoid sin and punishment and the evil designs of Satan. . . !"

And now suddenly Ankersen falls down on his knees, closes his eyes, and folds his fat and flabby hands under his chin.

"The man is crazy," says the Magister, regarding him with a shake of his head. "But you might come up to our place, if. . . . ?"

"I was thinking the same thing," his housekeeper says, looking questioningly at Eliana.

But now Ankersen suddenly gets up from his kneeling position. His face is swollen, his nostrils are quivering and he groans without any self-control whatsoever: "You . . . . you generation of vipers! You *vipers!*"

"Yes, well and good, Ankersen," says Magister Mortensen, wearily. "But you could have minded your own business. No one sent for you."

Then suddenly a curious change comes over Ankersen. He clears his throat, coughs, takes off his spectacles, wipes the perspiration from his forehead, becoming at the same time quite friendly and subdued, almost polite.

"No," he says imploringly, "No, that must never happen. Now please listen to me and try to understand me. You must not leave. It must not come to such a pass that I drive you out. Please do sit down again and have a little patience; do give me a chance to explain!"

Turning to Magister Mortensen, he continues: "H'm. . . .

76

I'm a bit excitable, am I not? But my intention was good. But now I'll be so . . . calm. For you see, Mortensen, you who are a wise man, you who are even a theologian, you must surely understand me? When one is a believer, don't you know, and feels this urge . . . this *duty* to . . . as it is written: go ye therefore and teach all nations! Well, perhaps you do not understand me, but let us be good friends just the same, that I beg of you."

He sighs deeply and looks around with a gentle and fatherly mien: "Now, now, it's much better, if I may say so."

Every one in the little gathering now looked calm again; Magister Mortensen too sat down and became amenable and placid. A tiny smile seemed to be reflected in his pince-nez: "Yes, indeed, Mr. Ankersen, I have no doubt that basically you meant well. But to be quite honest, I can't say that I think you are suited to this kind of business."

"Perhaps not." Ankersen nodded, hanging his head. "Perhaps not."

For a moment his face flushed deeply, and his nostrils flared. But then he quieted down again and nodded his head silently. He got to his feet with a sigh, walked over and patted Orfeus and little Franziska on the head, nodded again and looked sorely distressed. A trace of foam was still to be seen in his beard. Then he reached out his hand to say good-by, walked around the room and shook hands with every one, nodding his head all the while but not saying a word.

In the entrance hall he snorted and rummaged around for his rubbers. Once more he came back into the room, nodded silently, and made the sign of the cross. A faint, rattling sound emanated from his nostrils.

The Wailing Woman stopped crying and just sat there staring and snuffling. A pearly drop was quivering below the tip of her nose.

"He is such a good man, so good, the savings-bank manager," she moaned. "He does so much for people, and he does it in secret."

At dusk, when the two little girls had fallen asleep, Eliana took Orfeus by the hand, and they set out for a walk along the beach. It was windy, and the ocean looked desolate and even sinister. Orfeus felt like crying; he intermittently had to swallow the feeling down and after a while was unable to stop a hopeless and ridiculous hiccoughing. And he wondered at his mother's calm and her constant assurances that everything would no doubt come out right.

"I just have the feeling," she said, "that he will come back."

Out at Stake Spit they sat down in the shelter of a protruding rock formation. There was a lovely smell of kelp and sea water, and the wind piped through a little tuft of dried flowers.

Eliana hugged her son tightly and pressed her cheek to his. "I'll tell you what," she whispered. "I am so calm and so certain of everything because Ura on the Cliff has told my fortune twice, and each time she said that I would die before your father. And Ura never makes a mistake!"

"Oh, you mustn't die!" Orfeus sobbed, brimming over with a new, indeterminate sorrow. He tugged at his mother's hand. She replied with a deep, calm little laugh: "No, certainly not . . . we'll worry about that when the time comes."

The hours passed.

It was early morning. The wind was slackening. The sun appeared for a moment between the clouds that were racing by in such an indifferent manner. There is nothing in the world so indifferent as a drifting cloud; it is not interested in anything, not even in itself.

Moritz sat there nodding, dozing, and feeling cold; woke

up, took a drink from his last bottle, listened to the music passing through his mind. The wind was still blowing, and the boat was tossed hither and yon between the dirty-gray waves. Spindrift and spray deposited beads on his face and his clothing, he was wet through and through, but he had long ago fallen into a calm state of dull and obstinate indifference. Once in a while, however, he started as if awakened by distant trumpet calls from the abyss. But just as soon as he came round and shook off the sleep and the dream, everything was as before. One can get used to anything, even to drifting around on the ocean in a boat without oars.

To be sure, he was still among the living, and the darkness was gone. It had been a confused and an awful night, filled with misunderstandings and stupidities that it pained him to think of. For the motor had actually been running, however that had come about, but while he had been sitting there, holding the boat into the wind, he had fallen asleep, into a relentless, deathlike sleep, caused, of course, by the minister's wine, and when he had awakened, the motor was once more cold as ice and the boat was half filled with water. But again . . . he was still here, he *existed*, he was breathing and shivering and freezing.

But suddenly he jumped to his feet: he could see smoke on the horizon. A little while later a fishing trawler appeared. Was it getting closer? His heart hammering in his chest, Moritz attempted to make his presence known. He took off his jacket and waved it. Then he took off his shirt—perhaps it could more easily be seen at a great distance. However, the steamer did not seem to have noticed anything. The distance between him and the ship increased. Then he poured some gasoline on an oily rag and made a little fire. That was not noticed either, not even when he sacrificed his shirt to the flames. The steamer continued on its course, deaf and blind, and disappeared in the great watery desert.

It began to rain hard. There was still a half bottle of

wine left. Moritz emptied it at one gulp and immediately regretted his greediness. He could hardly see a thing around him. It was like being locked inside a room.

As the hours passed, it became ever more difficult for him to keep even half awake, even though he was now distressingly sober. Although he resisted heroically, he fell into a tormented trance-like sleep, filled with absurd and cheerless dreams. He dreamed that he was sitting in the church steeple with his father and was listening to the many-voiced howling of the aeolian harps. But then he suddenly becomes an aeolian harp himself, the wind rushes in between his ribs and makes his nearly dried-up intestines give off music. . . .

He woke up, shaking from the cold, but pulled himself together once more, got to his feet and began to bail water out of the boat. Otherwise, everything was just the same: it was Monday and the ocean was a desolate ocean, there were clouds and empty bottles.

A little while later he once more fell into a reverie. The boat was just allowed to take care of itself; he was fully aware that it was shipping water, but he didn't do anything about it. The music in his mind behaved in a curious manner; there was no longer any continuity to it, it broadened into a large orchestra, an exceedingly boundless and seething orchestra in which trumpets, as big as the smokestacks of a steamship, played somber and meaningless solos.

There was especially one of these heavenly trumpets that sounded distressingly fateful; it was a monotonous bass part, and after a while it became the persistent pedal point about which the other voices gathered like a whirlpool, all of them soon to fade out, for now the piece had just about come to an end. Through his slumbers he could indeed hear that the end was drawing near. But then suddenly things took another turn: the enormous trombone persisted in playing

80

on, entirely on its own, long after the other instruments had emitted their last sounds, and smoke and fire and a greasy smell poured out of its mouth.

Suddenly Moritz awakened with a start: there was a steamship nearby, he had both heard and smelled it—true enough, it was up close, and it was the *Neptunus!* It looked so shabby and good-natured, so blessedly ordinary and sensible, homelike and wonderfully commonplace. And for all that, as wonderful as a vision!

A dinghy was lowered. And in that dinghy sat among others Ole Brandy. Ole Brandy, with his wispy mustache, broken nose, and golden earrings. Ole Brandy, old and new at the very same time. He was smiling blissfully like an apostle who steps down from a descended cloud. Kornelius was there too, as well as Olivarius and many other good men; it passed all belief how cheered and peaceful he felt just at the sight of them again—the hale and the hearty, the young and the old.

Moritz stepped up on the deck of the steamer. His boat was taken in tow. Once again he was homeward bound.

The thought that something sacred had occurred would not leave Moritz's mind. He was sitting in the ship's mess, drinking coffee and brandy, and men with good and familiar faces were sitting and standing around him in a circle. They all looked so exceedingly gentle and merciful. The bright forenoon sun had broken through the clouds and was shining on the worn oilcloth on the table.

"Look here, you should lie down on this bench and get some sleep," the skipper suggested. "You must try to make a nice impression when you walk ashore, for there will be many spectators."

Moritz fell asleep almost immediately. Once in a while he would start up, dreaming that he was still sitting in the boat, surrounded by the rattling aeolian harps of death, on

81

the way to the abyss. But then it was true, after all, that he had been rescued and was lying here by the edge of the sacred oilcloth.

In the evening there was a celebration in the basement of the Bastille. It came about all by itself. Members of the male choir sang jolly songs, Kornelius and Moritz played duets for the horn, there was dancing, and coffee punch was served. The wine was flowing copiously, no one knew just where it was coming from; later it became known that Count Oldendorp, who had put in an appearance for a short while, had contributed a generous share.

But what about Ankersen, the savings-bank manager?

This amazing man naturally did not miss such a heaven-sent opportunity. Through his spy, Fat Alfred, he had learned what was happening in the basement of the Bastille: there were not only drunken men but also women present, not only drunkards like Ole Brandy and Janniksen, the blacksmith, but many others.

"Well, who?" asked Ankersen, deeply stirred. "Magister Mortensen?"

No, Alfred had not noticed him. But . . . dancing instructor Lindenskov, the Corpse Crower, Olivarius, Lukas Gravedigger, the rose-painter Pontus, Fribert Collier, Atlanta, and Black Mira, and many others. . . .

Ankersen shuddered and closed his eyes. A little while later he put on his galoshes and stealthily walked out to Skin Islet in order to ascertain whether Alfred had spoken the truth. Through one of the windows in a wing of the house he could see everything. Ankersen tossed his head so that his cheeks and his double chin quivered. In his excitement he grasped Fat Alfred's hand, as if he were a small boy, and said breathlessly: "Horrible! Horrible! You know where we'll go? We'll go and get the new minister. This will give him his opportunity. Now he will get his

82

baptism of fire. And then we will clear out the dive! In the name of the Lord! Come!"

"Janniksen the blacksmith will kill us!" Alfred objected, with a nervous laugh.

"Don't laugh!" Ankersen admonished him. "For what you say may very well be right. But we'll do as I have said. Nothing ventured, nothing gained!"

Pastor Fruelund regarded the excited Ankersen with a mixture of curiosity and astonishment, since he seemed more than any others to have had one too many. The manager had immediately gone right to the heart of the matter and had completely forgotten to introduce himself; breathing hard, he now made up for the omission.

"Please, sit down and rest a while," said the minister, placing a chair in front of him; but Ankersen did not want to sit down, he just stood there shaking like a motor, his small nearsighted boar's eyes blinked incessantly behind his spectacles, and there was a trace of foam in the beard next to the corners of his mouth.

"These people are on the road leading straight to perdition!" he said.

The minister had to suppress a smile, and this gave him an especially serious expression. Ankersen lifted up his arms in ecstasy and shouted: "I can already see that you understand me! You are on my side! Your predecessor, Lindemann, was a good-for-nothing, he didn't have the energy to get out of his rocking chair, he became my enemy, my bitter enemy! Never, never did I become reconciled with him!"

Ankersen lowered his arms.

"He drank port wine!" he hissed in a confidential manner. "Yes! he used to drink port wine together with apothecary Fähse!"

"Well, did he really?" said the minister absentmindedly.

"Yes!" Ankersen shouted jubilantly. The savings-bank manager's voice had suddenly turned into a falsetto, and he continued speaking in a state of subtle exaltation: "He tried to hide it from me, but I had my net out! I had my net out, I tell you!"

The minister just stood there, rocking on his toes as if giving the matter some thought. With a certain infatuation, Ankersen regarded the slim young man with the elegant wavy hair.

"Come with me!" he said. "Come!"

"Now, now—just a moment!" the minister said in a loud clear voice; "I practically don't know these people you are talking about, don't you see, since I am a complete newcomer here. They are intoxicated and will of course dislike having us come. We won't be able to achieve anything that way, will we? Doesn't it make more sense to talk to them when they are sober? We might, for example, . . ."

Ankersen interrupted him with a low, ominous roar: "Dislike it? Dislike it, you say? Are you afraid of being disliked? You? A minister? A disciple?"

He turned his back on the minister and gave himself over to blubbering woefully.

The minister felt ill at ease. This whole thing began to get on his nerves. Was he dealing with an inmate from an insane asylum? He made a deprecating and somewhat irritated sign to his wife who, with a look of astonishment, had appeared in the doorway to his study.

"No, of course not, I am not *afraid*, Mr. Ankersen," he said icily, "the more so as I am able to defend myself bodily too, if need be. No, but as I was saying. . . ."

"Yes, you are young and strong," Ankersen said and sank down into a chair. "You are young and strong. I am only a defenseless old man. But in spite of that I am never afraid. Oh no, not in the slightest! The only infirmity that I don't know the meaning of is fear!"

Ankersen's voice once more rose to a twittering, imploring treble: "Do not forsake me! Just now I was having such a

84

high opinion of you! Come! Follow me! Help me! I believe in you, young Pastor Fruelund, I have faith in you! You are young and strong, you possess the fervor of faith!"

"Wait just a moment," the minister said. He walked into the other parlor and telephoned Bærentsen, the parish clerk and head-teacher. Yes, Bærentsen knew Ankersen very well. He was a real gentleman. A man of note. Capable administrator and financier, who had done great and unselfish work for the Christian temperance movement. A dedicated man!

The minister returned. His forehead was flushed. "Let us go, then," he said.

Ankersen felt humble with joy, he rubbed his shoulder against the minister's arm, speechless and silent with gratitude.

It took a while for the celebrants in the basement of the Bastille to realize who it was that was paying them a visit. Ole Brandy poured schnaps into two glasses and shoved one of them over toward Ankersen, who nodded affably, and Black Mira drew nearer to the minister, dancing the while and smiling prettily. An exceptionally shapely girl, Pastor Fruelund noted to himself, moving into shelter behind Ankersen. The situation was quite beyond endurance. The savings-bank manager took a seat and began toying with the glass of schnaps as if he looked forward to emptying it. But suddenly he got up and screamed: "Alas, you fools! Woe unto you, generation of vipers! This gathering, which ought to have been a feast of thanksgiving because a human soul, through no doing of its own, has been given back to this accursed vale of sorrows . . . because a Lazarus quite undeservedly has been raised from the dead . . . you have made it into a ball for Satan himself! Think better of it, before it is too late! Turn about, you poor deluded souls, on your path leading straight down into the bottomless morass of perdition. . . !"

Pastor Fruelund turned away in shame. He was not used

85

to this tone, which he only knew from the asinine street meetings that the Salvation Army held in the big cities. Ankersen's exclamations, however, were quickly drowned out by the general uproar, by the shouting and the singing.

Suddenly the minister felt a hard shove in his side. Quick as lightning he turned around, prepared for the worst, and met—Ankersen's indignant glance! The manager's eyes were bloodshot, he roared at the top of his voice: "You're not saying anything? You're just standing here and . . . keeping silent and approving everything, what? You're not supporting me in my struggle, which, as you can see, is in full swing?"

The minister was boiling with anger and shame. He actually had to make a violent effort not to give this stupid and impudent man a well-deserved dressing-down. The insolent fellow! Many of the onlookers were laughing heartily at the spectacle. And suddenly Ankersen also burst out in loud, derisive laughter!

His face drawn, Pastor Fruelund made his way over toward the exit. He remained standing in the doorway. "Ankersen!" he shouted in a stern voice.

But Ankersen had disappeared in the crowd, he was not to be seen anywhere . . . but, yes, he was on his knees over there, in front of a music stand . . . stammering forth a prayer! A group of listeners had formed around him. His red nose with its quivering nostrils was all shiny from sweat or tears.

The minister turned away in disgust. He walked out to the entrance hall. But could he in all decency go away and leave the crazy fellow in the lurch? Now the sound of hymn singing reached him from the parlor. Hymn singing! It was one of the hymns that Pastor Fruelund had personally selected for that church concert that so sadly had come to naught: "Now rejoice, all ye Christians!"

He opened the door and shouted, in a shrill, commanding tone of voice: "Savings-bank manager Ankersen!"

But Ankersen heard him not at all. He was standing there, broad and thickset, with unseeing eyes behind his spectacles, singing to his heart's content the last verse of the hymn.

The minister felt somewhat confused. The thought crossed his mind that Ankersen perhaps had been right in a way and had been—victorious. For obviously the entire assemblage was participating in the hymn singing. What kind of hocus pocus was actually going on here?

When the last verse of the hymn had been sung, he made a quick decision and reentered the parlor. Ankersen spied him and rushed over towards him. The manager's face was distorted from pain and anger, and he wailingly denounced the minister: "You! You ran away! Ran away! You, who ought to have raised the sword of the spirit against them, stricken them with the lightning of the word, these despairing and lost lambs! You, who ought to have guided them back into the fold! You ran away like a dastardly coward . . . afraid for your . . . for your *beautiful hide!*"

For a moment Ankersen laughed out loud, but stopped just as suddenly, stepped right in front of the minister, then spat him in the face with all his might and bellowed: "I spit on you! You are not my friend, you are my enemy! Get thee hence, thou Levite, thou Pharisee!"

The minister bit his lip and left the house. He was very pale.

Ankersen was standing in the doorway shaking his upraised fists at him: "Dare not to cross my path again, thou wretched hypocrite!"

CHAPTER 3

*A peculiar self-contradictory fate in the matter of love
pursues the young poet Sirius*

The so-called "Leonora Poems" are a beautiful and significant portion of Sirius Isaksen's lyrical production. They are, as Dr. Matras has expressed it, "love poems of a curiously transcendental and serene type, which at times almost make one think of Shelley himself."

Within literary circles it has long been assumed that the Leonora with whom these poems deal was a pure abstraction, something on the order of the "poet's muse," but subsequent investigations have shown that this supposition is not correct, since the Leonora of the poems has actually existed and is identical with Leonora Maria Pommerencke, daughter of Ib Thorlacius Pommerencke, a rural judge who later became high-court judge, and of his wife Elisabeth, née Paludan-Müller.

About the poet's relationship with this lady we will now relate further.

Success had attended Sirius's school for small children. During the year and a half that it had been in operation it had obtained thirteen new pupils. Three old ones had left, namely, Peter and Orfeus, who had enrolled in the public school, and the smith's daughter, Julia, who had grown up.

But Julia had not left school completely; she had obtained

a position in Mac Bett's picture-frame workshop and at the same time she kept the schoolroom neat and tidy. It was Sirius who had arranged it, feeling sorry for this big, slow-witted girl. She did not have a very pleasant home and besides, it seemed, she had begun to be pursued by certain louts who hardly had any good intentions. Julia, for her part, was very fond of her former teacher, never letting an opportunity go by to show her high regard for him; yes, Sirius rather suspected that she actually was in love with him, in her own quiet and doltish way.

But at this time Sirius had thoughts only for Leonora.

Leonora looked like a nun, a saint; she was very blonde, very dainty, but there was a certain pensiveness about her young and fresh features. Sirius knew that she read a great deal and that she had a marked preference for lyrical poetry.

Alas! *She* was the daughter of a high-ranking official, *he* was a poor schoolteacher. There was a great gulf drawn between them. But then strangely it was to come to pass that fate—hesitantly and uncertainly to be sure—would build a bridge across this gulf.

It started with his writing her a poem in which he declared his love for her point-blank. This poem never got further than his table drawer. But he sent her another one, entitled "Marsyas," which he himself thought contained something that was exactly right.

For Sirius had read about this unusual mythical personage in *The History of Music*. His heart had been pounding with indignation over and tenderness toward this great musician who with his flute had made even Apollo so madly envious that he had had him flayed alive and hung up to be dried in a windy cave. For a time the young poet had been downright haunted by the thought of the poor human hide that was hanging all by itself in its cave, writhing in the darkness whenever music sounded; and to obtain peace of mind he had let Psyche, in his poem, take pity on it, cut it into strips and then twist them to make strings for an aeolian harp, from which there emanated divine music until the end of time.

To this poem Sirius appended a few humble words, expressing his hope that Leonora would not reject this modest attempt. He sent the letter off in a state of exuberance, and when the envelope had disappeared into the mailbox he felt thoroughly ashamed of himself and regretted bitterly what he had let himself in for.

But the next day, just when the schoolchildren were about to leave for home, Leonora showed up in person in the picture-frame shop, not to purchase anything but to meet Sirius and thank him for his poem.

"It shows promise," she said, "definite promise. There is *passion* in it!"

Sirius was speechless, but collected himself sufficiently to ask Leonora to come into the classroom. He took her umbrella and placed it respectfully over in a corner, pulled his desk chair into the middle of the floor, asked her to sit down, and seated himself meekly at one of the children's desks.

"If you have any other poems," Leonora said, "then do let me see them!"

Sirius had many, many poems lying in his table drawer. With the air of a sleep-walker he poked through the batch of papers, but his head was swimming so strangely, and before he really knew what he was doing he had shoved all the sheets down into the drawer again and closed it.

"But, but . . . . if you would allow me to send you some poems later on . . . . some of the best ones!" he said, stirred to the bottom of his heart.

Miss Leonora smiled. "I believe that you are a real poet," she said in a kind voice.

Leonora had a beauty spot on one cheek. She was blonde, but she had brown eyes and long eyelashes that were darker than her hair. She continued with a smile: "*Sirius,* that is

90

a beautiful name, even though it is odd. It is the name of the brightest star in the heavens, isn't it?"

"I was named for my mother, her name was Sira," he replied almost apologetically.

Leonora regarded him warmly and said: "By the way, do you know whom you remind me of? Well—of Lord Byron! Yes, it's really true. There is something about your eyes and your profile and your hair. Do you know Byron?"

Sirius knew next to nothing about that famous poet. None of his works were available at the library. Leonora promised to send him Byron's *Don Juan* in Drachmann's translation.

Sirius once more proffered his most heartfelt thanks and fetched Leonora's umbrella, which he handed to her with a deep bow.

Following Leonora's unexpected visit, some time passed before he felt like his old self again. He sat at his desk a long time, absorbed in thought. Just what was it that had happened? Leonora! *Leonora* had come and paid him a visit!

He bent forward and, feeling quite overcome, hid his face in his hands.

When he looked up, Julia was standing there, staring at him. The large, red-cheeked girl looked completely lost, she was nearly crying.

"What seems to be the trouble, Julia?" he asked in a kindly voice. But he knew full well what the trouble was: she was jealous! He smiled and stroked her arm: "There, there, Julia! I'm leaving, so you may start cleaning up the room now."

She gave him an inconsolable look, he had to stroke her arm once more, she leaned close to him, he felt her hair touching his cheek, a faint trembling passed through her body.

"What is wrong, my dear?" Sirius asked, and patted her soothingly on the back.

"Nothing," Julia said, but in that very instant threw her

91

arms around his neck. He was conscious of her firm and swelling bosom, and without really knowing what he was doing he held her head in his hands and kissed her tenderly on cheeks and mouth . . . once . . . several times. The end was that he placed her on his lap. Passionately she snuggled up to him.

Sirius sent a selection of his poems to Leonora and a little later they were returned to him with a brief letter in which she thanked him and asked him to send her more. He kissed the little scented letter with her dainty handwriting, and during the whole evening and night he gave himself over to his immense and despairing yearning.

But the following day after school he once again enjoyed some tender moments with Julia. The big, clumsy, and plodding Julia—she had actually grown into a beautiful young lady. It had not been noticeable until now. She had become an entirely different person, she had blossomed out and had become a rose, yes, in her own way she was almost enchanting, a new and plump sparkling rose! True enough, Sirius had been enamored of young girls before, but things had never gotten so far that he had been close to any one of the fair sex. Julia was the first one that he had kissed and held in his arms.

Still, it was Leonora that he loved, of course. She and no one else.

He despised himself for this double-dealing. But it had been downright forced on him. For a long time he was at a complete loss as to what he should do. He worshiped the distant and exalted Leonora and wrote poems to her and about her. But at the very same time his passion was fulfilled by the ever-near and warm Julia. It all happened rather against his own will, and nevertheless as something that was inevitable.

Leonora, of course, was now and always unattainable. She was not meant for him, she most probably already belonged to some one else. Rumor had it that she spent much time in the company of one of the officers on the coast-guard vessel *Poseidon*.

Spring came, the bushes in the blacksmith's garden burst into leaf, and one day Sirius read in the *News* that Miss Leonora Marie Pommerencke had become engaged to First Lieutenant Rasmussen. Even though this piece of news did not come as a surprise to him, he was nevertheless heart-broken and furtively shed his manly tears. But in the after-noon he assuaged his grief at Julia's breast.

During the following days he wrote passionate and des-perate poems to Leonora, one after the other, and in his strange sort of infatuation he sent several of them in a letter to her, not caring that her name was mentioned several times.

One day he received an unexpected visit from Miss Leonora and her sweetheart.

"This is my fiancé," she said, introducing him. "And here is my poet! Can you see that he resembles Lord Byron?"

The officer laughed to be polite, and Leonora and Sirius laughed also; everything went along very nicely. The young stranger, who incidentally was a short and freckled fellow with thin red hair, complimented Sirius on his poems and purchased a few boxes of thumbtacks.

That afternoon Sirius decided to announce his engage-ment to Julia.

This made Julia very unhappy, and she was firmly op-posed to his going to speak to the blacksmith about it.

"He'll kill you!" she said anxiously.

"But . . . but, why in the world should he. . . ?" Sirius asked, greatly surprised.

"Because they want me to marry Jartvard, Consul Hansen's warehouseman!" Julia said, hiding her face be-tween her white and shapely arms, as if she were afraid of being beaten.

"But that's out of the question!" Sirius said, vehemently.

"I am afraid there's no way out," Julia moaned, kneeling down in front of Sirius and stroking his hands in desperation: "It has almost been decided in a way. . . !"

"Decided?" Sirius asked, now becoming quite breathless with emotion. "They just can't decide about you in that way! You'll say no, that you don't *want* to. You're a grown woman! And that's the end of that!"

"Oh, I don't know," sobbed Julia and rubbed her eyes.

Sirius chose to look at the humorous side of the matter. He laughed out loud, heartily and indulgently: "You don't know, you say? But you aren't fond of this Jartvard, are you?"

Julia sobbed more loudly; she replied in a choked voice: "Yes, I almost believe . . . I almost believe . . . and besides, *he* thinks so too . . . and has spoken with father and mother!"

"Now listen to me!" Sirius said. "This is the most stupid thing I've ever heard of! Don't you love me at all, then, Julia?"

"Yes!" she replied, trembling violently.

Sirius continued in a shrill voice: "But perhaps you love *him*, too, the other fellow?"

Julia's answer was indistinct, but it was yes.

Sirius stood up and walked over to the window. The big flowering bushes stood partly in the shade, partly in the sunlight. In the sunlight they appeared red, in the shade, blue. He whirled around and asked her, imploringly: "Do you love *him* more than you love *me?* Please answer, Julia."

"I almost think I do," Julia whispered.

"I didn't have the slightest idea," Sirius murmured in a tearful voice. "I didn't have the slightest idea. This is a complete surprise to me."

Julia had sat down on one of the benches. Her young and ample body was trembling; her sobbing abated. A little

94

while later she said in a low but clear voice: "We are to be married in the autumn, he and I."

"You two have actually been engaged, I take it!" Sirius said dully.

Julia nodded.

"So that's it," Sirius said and closed his eyes. "So that's it, Julia. Why haven't you told me before?"

"I thought you knew it," Julia sighed. She added as a kind of explanation: "I also thought that you . . . that you loved her, the other one. . . !"

Shaking his head, Sirius took his hat, glanced over at Julia, who was still sitting on the bench—big and healthy and ripe and with her shock of brown bangs all tangled and wet from tears.

He sauntered about aimlessly that whole afternoon. It was an exceptionally fine day with light clouds in the sky, budding bushes and trees and the fragrance of new grass. Everything glittered, windowpanes and roofs and the water in the harbor, and the big coastal steamer *Mjölner,* that was lying at anchor out there, was surrounded by gleaming white seagulls. At the bridge leading across the brook Sirius met Leonora and her fiancé. He saluted them respectfully and they both returned his greeting pleasantly.

After dusk he met Ole Brandy down by the beach; he was sitting in a boat that had been pulled ashore. Sirius noticed that Ole was drunk and wanted to steal past him without being noticed. But Ole called him in an imperious voice and made a great commotion in the boat. The upshot was that he seated himself next to Ole and drank a little of his rum.

"Yes, I'm treating rum tonight," Ole Brandy said. "I'm treating rum tonight, and do you know why? Because today is a red-letter day in my life."

"You see," he continued with a serious mien, "fifty years

ago today it was that the person addressing you now for the first time set foot upon the soil of the great outside world, namely, the quay at Constitution Dock in the English city of Hull, and when evening comes it will be exactly half a century since he had the first foreign girl sitting on this here knee of his!"

Ole Brandy patted his knee elatedly, took a nip of rum, and continued in a familiar tone: "Her name was Mary, I can still remember her exactly the way she was, she was the worst slut!"

He sighed and started to sing an old ballad, and Sirius listened with pain to its sad words.

> Seaman on the ocean billow,
> Quick thy happy days will flee;
> Drain thy glass, thou hapless fellow,
> Ere thy bitter fate thou see.
>
> Soon the whirling Maelstrom wildly
> Will embrace thee in its breast;
> On the ocean's bottom mildly
> Shalt thou seek thy final rest.
>
> She who had thy heart's protection
> Scarce remembers now thy name—
> Faithless seeks thy foe's affection,
> Dancing, smiling, lacking shame.

It was now getting quite dark, the waves of summer were lapping softly at the beach. Completely still, like cigar smoke in a parlor, light, horizontal strips and dainty rings of fog and mist hovered above the harbor.

Sirius felt as if there were a deep chasm within his heart and mind. The liquor made wild flowers of sadness and sorrow and immense longing glow within his breast.

Ole Brandy had put his arm around his shoulder. Joyfully inebriated, he sang in a muffled voice:

> But from Death's dark cave ascending,
> Thou shalt rise again 'ere long;
> Blesséd now thy voice is blending
> With the sacred angels' song.

CHAPTER 4

*Magister Mortensen has an unexpected and not very
welcome visitor*

"Of course I won't outright oppose your paying a call on
this Magister Mortensen. I don't know him personally and
only go by what I've heard from others. And of course he
may be better than his reputation."

Provincial Governor Effersöe smiled as he looked at his
brother-in-law, the Minister of Church and Education, who
returned this somewhat ironic smile with a distant nod sug-
gestive of understanding and forgiveness. The Minister had
spent his summer vacation with the Governor. He had several
times expressed a desire to visit Mortensen, but he had
gathered from his brother-in-law that the idea did not greatly
appeal to him. But now, when the day of his departure was
drawing near, the Minister had once more, with a gentle
stubbornness peculiar to him, touched on the idea of calling
on Mortensen just before leaving. Minister of Church and
Education Östermann and Magister Mortensen had known
each other slightly during their years at the university, and
the Minister had rather profited from reading the little study
of Sören Kierkegaard that Mortensen had written during his
youth. It was an interesting though somewhat immature little
book. Östermann had even quoted a few passages from it in
his dissertation on Kierkegaard for the doctorate in theology.
He was saddened to hear that things had gone downhill for
this really quite promising man Kristen Mortensen.

The Provincial Governor stared into space with raised eyebrows: "You see—if it was just a matter of Mortensen being a bohemian, then . . .—but in addition, he has been behaving like a *hooligan*. I refer to his assault on school principal Berg some years ago. That was the scandal that forced him to leave the school. Assault and battery, yes, that's really something for a so-called *scholar* to have perpetrated, isn't it? There must be other ways to settle a controversy, and one doesn't need to be a rowdy just because one is hot-tempered."

"No, of course not," Östermann nodded in assent, "of course not."

The Provincial Governor cleared his throat, a bit impatiently, and continued: "And then there's another thing, and I'll come right out with it: Mortensen lives in . . . what shall I call it . . . in promiscuity with certain loose female characters, from what I've heard. But as I said, this is all something that I'm telling you so that you won't be too *unprepared!*"

Östermann kept nodding and regarded his brother-in-law with a look of forbearance in his bright eyes; the Governor added with a laugh: "You might perhaps bring the *count* along with you! I mean, in case something unpleasant should happen to you. For Count Oldendorp is strong as a bear! And besides, he knows how to get there. He does have some odd friends and connections in this town. It is because of this . . . 'ethnological interest' of his, as he calls it."

The Governor and the Minister smiled, indulgently and without malice, even approvingly—in short, the way one is wont to smile at a dissolute nobleman.

The count was indeed willing to accompany the Minister out to the Bastille. During the walk he related in his lighthearted way this, that, and the other about Mortensen, whom he knew personally, and with whom, as he expressed it, he had had many an amusing argument. For Mortensen

99

was a marvelously gifted man, and his misfortune in life had not at all made him hang his head.

"Does he drink very much?" Östermann asked with a sad mien.

"Well . . . ," the count hesitated. "He takes a drink once in a while, as one is apt to do in these latitudes. But you mustn't think that he is a rowdy and a drunkard, far from it. And this business about his living with *Atlanta* . . . Lord help me, Atlanta is in many respects a thumping good woman, she doesn't look bad at all, and it is in a way wonderful how she is so attached to Mortensen and takes such good care of both him and his poor feebleminded daughter. One certainly must take one's hat off to her. For if Mortensen didn't have her . . .!"

Östermann stopped short and cleared his throat, seeming a bit distressed: "But my dear sir . . . Mortensen doesn't actually live off this woman? Or how. . . ?"

"Good Lord," the count said, laughing out loud. "Mortensen is not a pimp, is that what you thought? No, by heaven, he is just as decent a man as you and I! He makes his living very properly, by tutoring and as a librarian. And then he is something of an astronomer. At least, he has a curious-looking telescope standing in the attic. Besides, he is musically inclined. And he is writing a great *work*."

"What kind of work might that be?" Östermann asked, lowering his voice to a confidential tone.

"Well now, that is something that Mortensen doesn't want to divulge. But it is supposed to be a work on philosophy— on the philosophy of religion."

Östermann nodded, with a guarded look in his eyes. "Well, well. Yes, you see," he added, "as I've said before, I knew Mortensen somewhat during our student days. For a short time we both lived at Regensen.* He was a tall, fine-looking

* A venerable old building in the center of Copenhagen used as a student dormitory. Tr. note.

fellow. Of peasant stock, I think. A Jutlander. He rolled his
r's. And then a little boisterous. But quite a gentleman just
the same, and very fond of the ladies, from what I understand."

Östermann spoke hesitantly and in a muffled voice, blink-
ing his eyes and continuously clearing his throat: "And
Mortensen was for a time engaged to an exceptionally
lovely girl. From a very fine family. A real lady. Of Jewish
descent, I believe. But then it went to pot. It was she, it
seems, who . . . became fond of another, as they say. Well,
and then . . . yes, then one day Mortensen had completely
disappeared. And then I found out to my great astonishment that he had ended up *here*. Tell me, what was his
wife like?"

His wife? Well, Oldendorp had never actually talked to
Mortensen about her. It had never occurred to him.

"And about how old might this feebleminded daughter
of his be?"

"Oh, seven or eight years or so."

Östermann's eyes became big and round. "That is very,
very sad for Mortensen," he said. "Very, very sad."

It took a while for Mortensen to thaw out. Minister of
Church and Education Östermann's call was too much of a
surprise. True, he had figured on the possibility that Östermann would call on him while spending his summer vacation
on the island. He had in fact pictured such a meeting and
thought of what he would say. But since then such a long
time had passed that he actually thought the Minister had
departed.

And then suddenly one afternoon Östermann sits here
on the sofa and has, in fact, not departed at all. Doctor of
Theology Chr. Fr. Östermann, the former pastor in charge
of several parishes, the Minister of Church and Education,
the budding bishop. Right in the middle of this mess! Yes,
there was a terrible mess in the little room in the tower. . . .

101

Vibeke's matches and cardboard boxes were spread all over the floor. Atlanta's sewing machine, surrounded by pieces of cloth and patches, was enthroned on the writing desk next to two empty coffee cups, one of which even had no handle, and there still lingered a faint odor of fish cakes in the room.

In the midst of all this mess he had been playing his viola, standing in front of the old broken-down music stand that was held together with twine, when the visitors had entered. Of course, the room didn't usually look as awful as now, for Atlanta was not slovenly. On the contrary. But this was Saturday afternoon—and one thing or another.

But there sat Doctor of Theology Östermann himself, the cabinet minister, the town's most famous summer visitor.

Well, what of it! Actually he was the very incarnation of theological circumspection and an inane careerist and climber! The famous man had supposedly at the very last moment brought himself to look in on the reputedly seedy former fellow student. Brought himself to? No, he had probably not been able to control his old-womanish curiosity!

"Yes, you just go right ahead and stare," Mortensen thought to himself, while for the first time in ages he noticed the big ink splotch on the wallpaper above the battered old sofa. It had gotten there once, when in a fit of rage, he had thrown an inkwell against the wall. Fortunately, one could not tell how it had happened. Or perhaps one could after all?

And what a sight he was, the way he was dressed: the patched dressing-gown and the worn-out slippers. He had hung his shirt front and collar on the bookcase so that he could be rid of it while he was playing! And then, what was it that he had been playing! He who otherwise detested cheap music and this very afternoon had been practicing for two full hours the devilishly difficult passage in the "Der Tod und das Mädchen" quartet! For Atlanta's sake he had finished up by playing a Swedish fishermen's waltz that she was so very fond of. He had been standing there, reeling off this horrible music, just when the distinguished visitors had entered.

So here sat this Östermann, this so-and-so. The devil with Count Oldendorp. But Östermann—! This blasted theologian. This budding bishop. This political and ecclesiastical climber. This out-and-out mediocrity, who had even had the gall to write about Sören Kierkegaard. A typical piece of theological quackery, by the way: this old priest-hater is accepted in spite of everything, because he is after all a theologian and, with a little adroitness, in spite of his sharp edges, can be pressed into the system! And because it makes an impression on people to be seen in the company of this inaccessible celebrity! Like a good housewife one mixes a little sugar and sentimentality into his gall and puts the main emphasis on his patent conservatism: but he was a *believer*, the old stick-in-the-mud. We can therefore use him in furthering our political aims.

Kierkegaard!

Mortensen had of course read Östermann's little oh-so-circumspectly-written dissertation and had made poisonous notes in the margins of the book. "Positive Aspects of Sören Kierkegaard's Concept of God"! Ugh! Mediocrity through and through! What is it that Kierkegaard says in a certain passage: "Mediocrity . . . . the most extreme kind of perdition is mediocrity, O, all crimes are much to be preferred to this self-satisfied, smiling, happy demoralization: mediocrity!" He, he!

Enough of that. But since this wretched Östermann was the very incarnation of mediocrity, why should any one be so petty as to be ashamed of the way he is dressed, and so forth? An inconsistent and petty bourgeois notion!

Up to now the magister had entrenched himself behind a mask of gloom and gruffness, and had only absently taken part in the conversation that Östermann and the

103

count had been trying to get going about this and that. Then suddenly he sat up straight, as if awakening from a great preoccupation, and said in a tone that he himself thought sounded a little affectedly carefree-chivalresque: "Oh say, what might I offer you, gentlemen? Unfortunately, I don't have any cigars in my home. But . . . . a small glass of cognac?"

Östermann neither smoked nor drank. Naturally. But Mortensen fetched two glasses and filled them for the count and for himself. It was two beer glasses. Never mind, damn it all. The drink seemed to bring him back to his real self. He took a long breath and felt ready for battle.

Here you come, you cheap little spiritual snob, to satisfy yourself by direct observation how deep Kristen Mortensen has sunk in the quagmire! he thought. And he saw in his mind's eye how Östermann following his return to Copenhagen would get together with the now greatly flourishing acquaintances from his years at the university . . . and say with that concerned air characteristic of the clergy: "Incidentally, do you know whom I met up there? Mortensen. Yes, the one who was interested in Kierkegaard." And so on and on!

But you just wait, you mediocre worm! Magister Mortensen thought to himself with suppressed anger.

Secretly he was aching for the conversation to turn to Kierkegaard. And so it had to do sooner or later. It even occurred rather quickly, and it was Östermann himself who began: ". . . . Your thought-provoking and perspicacious little treatise about Kierkegaard. . . . !"

"Thank you," Magister Mortensen said with a tight little smile and added, sounding a bit more eager than he actually intended: "But it can hardly be said that that scribbling was thought-provoking or perspicacious! For it was written by a young student who idolized this man Kierkegaard. Actually, it's enough to make a person vomit, thinking about it now!"

104

Östermann cleared his throat and said with a smile indicating a bit of concern: "Now, now, don't say that!"

"Now we are going to hear something!" The count winked and was in great good humor.

"Yes, I am referring to Kierkegaard as a thinker and a human being," Mortensen continued and, ready for battle, seated himself in the battered old wicker chair underneath the bookshelf: "As artist, as stylist, as spirited writer of aphorisms and analyzer of the self, he is, of course, praiseworthy. But besides that—this everlasting, this petty self-absorption that he is wallowing in. This miserable, sterile megalomania of his!"

Magister Mortensen had not intended to express himself with so little self-control, but the words just flew out of his mouth. It was the sight of Östermann, sitting on the sofa, that did it. He continued: "As for instance, where he talks about his divine qualifications . . . how does it go now. . . ."

"But dear Magister Mortensen," Östermann objected in a gentle voice, "disregarding the exact way in which he expresses it—Kierkegaard *is* right: he was a unique human being!"

Magister Mortensen stroked his lean face, pretending to be perfectly calm: "Yes, he was at any rate very eager to assert himself as a unique human being and to collect pieces of evidence showing that it was so—in order to be arrogant toward others!"

Östermann smiled and shook his head. Mortensen rose from his chair and excitedly threw out his hands: "Yes, for that is what Kierkegaard is forever doing! He is waging war against a small handful of petty theological windbags, all he ever does is intended to convince these mental midgets that he is always right and is absolutely unique and number one and the cock of the walk! He knows which weapons are most effective against those idiots! And he is without mercy, because his innermost being consists of hatred and malice!"

Magister Mortensen leaned back and chortled derisively. "But, do not misunderstand me," he continued, "the pastors and the professors of theology deserve full well the lesson that Kierkegaard is teaching them!"

Mortensen sat down again in his wicker chair and said with a sigh: "But this basilisk Kierkegaard will of course lose out in the end, for he will at last be swallowed down in spite of everything . . . . yes, *swallowed,* for he will end up in the belly of his worst enemy, the clergy . . . . as a big, indigestible lump, but that's where it actually is to be found, even though it may feel heavy and a bit painful. There are as you know certain boa constrictors that are able to swallow a whole lion, skin and all! Mediocrity . . . mediocrity will always have the last word, esteemed sir! Kierkegaard perished miserably in his own gall, but mediocrity extends far and wide, it even dominates the institutions of higher learning and holds down the fattest positions. . . !"

The count burst into loud, somewhat uncertain, laughter. Mortensen once again filled the glasses. He looked spitefully at Östermann out of the corner of his eye. The cabinet minister smiled in a cordial manner. Of course. What else could one expect. Smiling indulgently, he shook his incorrigibly dense and conceited pate.

"Well . . . yes," he said with a little sigh. "I understand that you have changed your opinion of Kierkegaard since you wrote that beautiful little treatise!"

"Skoal!" said Mortensen. It can't be denied that he felt a little embarrassed at having been so excited.

During the succeeding somewhat awkward lull in the conversation the count remarked in a conciliatory manner: "Yes, you philosophers, you know a lot! As far as I myself am concerned, I never got beyond Kant's *Kritik der Urquellskraft* . . . actually it was difficult enough, he, he."

Östermann cleared his throat and asked in a friendly manner: "Does your new *work* also deal with Kierkegaard, Mortensen?"

106

Magister Mortensen looked him right in the eye and said sternly: "No, your excellency, it deals with *Satan!*"

"With Satan!" the count repeated and once more burst out in exuberant laughter.

"What the hell are you laughing about?" Mortensen flared up. "My work deals with evil. With the evil in Man and fault-finding and coarseness and pettymindedness and shrewishness and overweening ambition which are inextricably intertwined with and form the basis for all theology, for the entire priesthood down through the ages! With that scourge of humankind that is known as confessional religion!"

Östermann's face had flushed. At last he had come out with it!

The count pulled out his handkerchief and noisily blew his nose. He said: "By the way—what was I going to say—how goes it with your star-gazing, Mortensen?"

"Yes, . . . you also take an interest in astronomy, I have been told," Östermann said with a smile, a little nervously.

"Yes, and also in music," the count added. "Mortensen is very musically inclined. He is quite a virtuoso on the viola. He is a member of Boman's little orchestra that practices in the basement."

Östermann nodded and looked at his watch. His hand was shaking, and he said: "Oh, it's late! I'm afraid I have to pack three big suitcases, so. . . ."

He shook Mortensen's hand: "Well, I'll say good-by and wish you all the best, Mortensen. It was nice to see you again."

"I was the one who felt *jolly*," Magister Mortensen replied derisively. The Minister gave a slight start, as if he was afraid of being hit or pushed. A stiff little smile played on his lips.

"Well, good-by, old fellow, and thank you for the treat!" the count said. "We'll meet again soon and have a little chat!"

"Oh, you keep your stupid mouth shut, you imbecilic hippopotamus!" Magister Mortensen snarled at him.

The count gave him a heavy slap on the shoulder, saying: "Now, now, take it easy, old fellow!"

Minister Östermann opened the door quickly and slipped out, glancing uneasily about him . . . . it seemed to him that some one might get clipped.

Mortensen stepped out on the landing, he was deathly pale and shouted in a shrill voice after Östermann, who was hurrying down the steps: "I don't give a damn for your religion. It lacks both seriousness and reality! An old whore who helps an old beggar get up from the gutter is worth more than all you theological windbags and 'fraidycats put together!"

The cabinet minister was now out of sight. Mortensen shouted so loudly that it reverberated up through the empty stairway: "*Goodness,* damn it to hell, is something real! But hypocritical climbers and eunuchs like you will never in all eternity know anything about that!"

"Well, what do you think of—the beast?" the Governor asked his brother-in-law. They were just sitting down to eat.

The cabinet minister smiled uneasily. "Poor Mortensen," he said absentmindedly. He added, nodding his head and searching for the right words: "He has become a very bitter man, and it may be for obvious reasons. He talked at some length about Sören Kierkegaard. But it was the curiously spiteful speech of a down-and-out human being. He has become quite a nasty old fellow, our Kristen Mortensen. He doesn't hesitate to use the most vulgar expressions. It's too bad, but that man has changed considerably, very considerably, since the time he wrote his excellent dissertation. But perhaps there was nothing else that one could expect. . . ."

Östermann unfolded his napkin and stuck a corner of it between his collar and his chin: "Truly, Mortensen is an extremely unhappy and unfortunate man."

CHAPTER 5

An important and joyous event, which unhappily is followed by a funeral feast

Orfeus continued to make progress on the violin.

Old Boman did not coddle him at all; on the contrary, he was often unreasonably gruff with him, but that happened to be his way of teaching, and it had borne fruit. Both Moritz and Kornelius were very able when it came to music. Of course, one could not call them real musicians, but they were at any rate excellent instrumentalists. Yes, they were quite a bit more than mere instrumentalists, for they both had their hearts and ears in the right place.

But Orfeus was something much more; the boy was musical through and through, he had an incredibly good ear for music and he learned rapidly, he was musical to his fingertips—he could play Schubert's *Ständchen* like a little angel. Greatly touched, Boman would strum the accompaniment on his cello. It was beyond description.

"That was superb, my boy," the old teacher said, clasping Orfeus's hand. "You are by far the best pupil I've ever had, and I'll tell you something: you have a future ahead of you! You are not going to stay forever in this god-forsaken place, it is pleasant enough, it isn't that . . . you must get *out in the world*, Orfeus, you must get a chance to spread your wings, you are going to be something *great*, my boy, you are going to *experience* what we here have only been dreaming about and messed around with; you are going to be a real musician, a real conqueror!"

Boman's old and wrinkled cheeks flushed; elatedly he stared into space and said: "You will prove to be *the meaning of it all!*"

Laughingly he shook his head and gave his godson a little slap on his behind: "Well, we'll see what you will amount to, if you apply yourself with all your might and stick to your music, for it will cost you much, it will cost perseverance and steadfastness; you don't rise to greatness by sleeping, Orfeus, and you must work like a horse, you must feel an obsession, you must be raving mad and fully believe that you are Paganini, even when things look more hopeless than ever!"

Boman's face had again taken on its gruff expression, he met the boy's glance and said severely: "Are you going to promise me that, then, you rascal? Do you realize that the name Orfeus puts you under an obligation? And so also does the fact that you have had old Kaspar Boman as your teacher?"

The old man's face turned into one big, sad smile.

"Well, run along now!"

During the summer, Boman started to keep to his bed. Lately the energetic old man had begun to show his age, and the painful heart attacks occurred with greater frequency.

A crowd would assemble in Boman's quarters every Sunday afternoon; in all justice one must admit that his friends did not leave him in the lurch. The string quartet would at times meet in his parlor and play his favorite pieces.

But at the beginning of August there occurred a rather unique musical event, something that completely pulled Boman and his musicians out of their closed little world and exposed them to a musical gust of wind from the outside that almost took their breath away.

The great day began like any ordinary Saturday with cloudy weather and a slight haze. Before lunch time Moritz came home and breathlessly demanded that his wife and children should put on their Sunday best and be ready, for onboard the steamer just arrived from Iceland there was nothing less than a *symphony orchestra,* and this orchestra would in all probability give a concert on shore, while the ship was unloading. It was the Hamburg Philharmonic, all well-known, first-rate musicians.

Moritz hurried on over to Boman in order to tell him the big news and talk him into going with him to the concert. The old man's emaciated cheeks flushed like those of a young girl, and in his excitement he sat bolt upright in his bed.

"Yes, I must go with you and hear that, no matter what will happen to me afterwards, yes, even if you have to carry me there!"

Moritz felt elated and happy like a young boy, and he warmly shook Boman's hand: "That is agreed! We'll come to get you!"

It was shortly after noon that Moritz ferried the visiting musicians ashore with their instruments in boxes and cases. The men were dressed for travel, they were sunburned and weather-beaten from the long voyage, they looked like ordinary people and were dressed like any one else. Many of them were older men, bald and with a worn-out look, and some of them had big mustaches. They were puffing on pipes—some short, others long; one of them cut himself a piece of chewing tobacco. No one could understand what they were saying, but they carried on a lively conversation. They seemed to be regular fellows.

The concert had to be given in one of Consul Hansen's warehouses; that was the only place large enough for such a big crowd. Accompanied by Kornelius, Sirius, and dancing instructor Lindenskov, Moritz had called for Boman in good time before the performance and had made sure that he got a good seat. The old man sat there hunching himself up in-

111

side his big overcoat, his entire expression indicating a feeling of happy anticipation; Moritz and Eliana sat next to him. Orfeus and his friend Gravedigger Peter were standing in one corner, on top of a couple of coils of new rope. From there they could survey the entire crowded room.

The sun had burst through the clouds, and rays of sunlight entered obliquely in through the small dusty windows. A sputtering gas lamp was burning above the orchestra, bathing it in a whitish and shimmering sea of light. It was the count who had arranged everything; red-faced and perspiring, he walked around putting the finishing touches to his handiwork.

It almost took Orfeus's breath away to look at all those instruments. Down in front the violinists were sitting in two rows, behind them the cello and viola players, then the woodwinds and the horns. In the very rear sat the drummer with his kettle-drums; he was a small, fat, nearsighted man; he reminded one in a curious way of a chef busying himself with his pots and pans.

Merely to listen to all these men tune their instruments was a strangely stunning experience. The orchestra sounded like an immense henhouse in which there were no hens but all kinds of strange and curious birds. The clarinets warbled long, low notes, like the singing of supernatural snipes; the sound from the bassoons seemed to emanate from a joyful abyss, gurgling wildly from mirthful throats; and the double-basses were even further down the scale, like doomsday music. And yet it was the violins that were most clearly heard; the familiar festive five-note harmony, so touchingly homey and familiar.

Then the conductor mounted the flag-bedecked box. He was a fairly young man. He had a piece of adhesive tape on his neck. For a moment there was a deep silence. Then the music burst forth! It was Gluck's *Iphigenia* Overture. The music began high up among the violins, wistfully and fate-

112

fully, but then the basses leaped to the fore, like large and coarse growths, angular and rough, obstinate, trembling with rage, but nevertheless curiously gay, as if the whole thing were a joke after all. And now the music was *gliding* along, like a tremendous well-oiled machine . . . . like a mad colossus, moving on nimble feet eager for the dance.

And then came the basses again, threatening and ominous in their masculine self-assurance—angry—almost ferocious. And once again they flowed together in a springy harmony with the gentler voices and lifted themselves up in noble and joyous dance to the conductor's baton, which moved with ineffable softness and feeling, like the antennae of a butterfly.

When the piece was over the tumultuous applause broke loose like a huge landslide. Then once more the voluptuous strumming and tuning was heard—the hurried crowing of the clarinets, flutes, and oboes—the bright and ringing notes of the horns—and the rugged and contented rumbling of the basses.

The count stepped forward and announced the next number on the program: Schubert's Eighth Symphony.

Orfeus completely forgot to look at the instruments—the muffled complaint of the basses made his throat contract, and he had to screw up his eyes. The jolly, good-natured theme, which at times would rise on high, would then be mercilessly subdued by the powers of darkness and not allowed to sound forth. It was like a little cluster of red and luminous flowers struggling against a wildly sweeping storm —a storm which, though not chilly and stinging, was nonetheless uncompromising in its dark greed. Orfeus had to think of Boman's potted plants, which always stood there listening to music . . . yes, they almost sang! He felt happy on Boman's behalf and looked for the back of the old man's white bald head somewhere in the multitude.

It was almost a relief when the gay avalanches of applause

began to roll again, and he greedily drank in the silhouettes of all the familiar everyday shapes and figures among the auditors: Governor Effersöe with his white lion's mane, young Consul Hansen with his big face and perpetually offended expression, Bailiff Kronfeldt with his neat gray Vandyke, apothecary Fähse and his enormous parrot-like wife, Justice Pommerencke and his daughter Leonora, physician Manicus with his kindly face underneath the silk skullcap . . . savings-bank manager Ankersen, eagerly bent forward, with quivering nose, housepainter Mac Bett with white sideburns and embroidered vest . . . smith Janniksen, editor Berg, Captain Öström, the midwife, Mrs. Nillegaard, and her husband, the rose-painter Pontus, Magister Mortensen, and all the others. Farther back in the room were dancing instructor Lindenskov with all his daughters, the Misses Schibbye, Sirius and Kornelius, Jakob Siff, the lady who owned the hotel The Curious Duck . . . and way back in the semidarkness by the far wall, Fribert Collier, Ole Brandy, and sailmaker Olivarius, all three of them in their Sunday best.

The count once more stepped forward and announced the last number on the program, the minuet by Boccherini. Orfeus felt a jolt of rapture when the well-known melody burst forth, borne high by carefree violins, while all the other instruments just sat back and chuckled. This was not a storm that made one tremble—just homey mirth and friendly humming; the many-headed monster gave itself over to a cozy and foolishly goodnatured friendliness that made one run hot and cold. But when the minuet was over, Orfeus felt as if his heart would break.

Gone, gone . . .

Gone—never to come again. Never again, never again.

The orchestra made ready to leave. The instruments were put back in their cases and boxes. The count, on behalf of the listeners, thanked the musicians for this unforgettable

114

occasion and also said a few words in a foreign language. Alas, alas! Never again . . .

Orfeus and Peter remained standing where they were, while the room gradually emptied. One after the other the instruments passed out through the wide warehouse door and disappeared in the desolate afternoon. Finally, there was only the softly singing gas lamp left.

Gone, gone. One could walk down to the quay, though, and observe the members of the orchestra boarding the ship. The two boys hurried down to the pier. Moritz was standing upright in his boat and as they were passed to him he got a good hold of the big double-basses, which in their cases looked like human beings. A strong wind had begun to blow up. The water was full of blue-black choppy waves. The steamer whistled impatiently. The musicians stood about in small groups, chatting, while awaiting their turn to be brought aboard.

It was early evening. The lighthouse on Seal Island was turned on. Against the unfathomable depths of the heavens there were lingering clouds passing silently overhead, illuminated from below by the light of the setting sun. It seemed just like a last, visual echo of the symphony . . . as if it lived on in a ghost-like manner up above in the evening light, pale and distant, but everlasting, while the steamer gave its departing whistle and grew smaller and smaller out on the limitless gray ocean.

Roman felt happy that it had been his lot to attend the great event. He was lying down, smiling, with his eyes closed, and it was clear that he was very tired.

"I hope it wasn't too much of an exertion for him, after all," Moritz remarked.

Kornelius was of the opinion that they ought to ask the doctor to come over and look at the old man, just to make sure.

115

Back in the basement of the Bastille sat the count. He was a bit drunk and had a couple of bottles with him. "Let us drink a toast!" he shouted joyfully to Moritz. "Long live music!"

The count emptied his glass and poured another one, the veins swelling in his temples. He pulled Moritz aside and put his elbow in his ribs: "Try to get hold of Black Mira, ask her to come over! By God, I want to have something nice to look at tonight!"

Several people assembled in the large parlor after a while. Dancing instructor Lindenskov and Magister Mortensen had stopped in to see how Boman was.

"I am afraid that he won't last very long," Lindenskov whispered to Moritz, with a shrug of his shoulders, adding: "But I don't think we should be sorry that we made him come along. . . . !"

Moritz looked in on Boman later in the evening. The old housekeeper plucked nervously at the buttons on his vest, her eyes red. "The doctor was here," she said, "and he looked very grave."

Moritz decided to keep watch by Boman's bed just in case he should get worse. Kornelius, Sirius, Lindenskov, and Mortensen had evidently all had the same thing in mind; they drifted in and took seats in the little parlor, sad and silent. Among the many potted plants there was one that was about to bloom, it was an amaryllis; with its red buds it looked as if it were bursting with a sense of tranquil well-being. The composers on the wall were staring into space, looking as if they were listening to something. Boman's housekeeper rummaged restlessly about in the kitchen; at times she would dab her eyes with a corner of her apron. At midnight or thereabouts she disappeared, and when she returned she had the Wailing Woman along. The two women sounded sad and hoarse as they talked together in the kitchen. The Wailing Woman had brought

116

along a bag of dried pretzels. The visitors were asked if they wanted a cup of coffee, but they just didn't feel like having any. The Wailing Woman was crying silently and whispered reproachfully to Moritz: "How could you ever think of dragging that deathly sick man to that nonsense!"

The sick man woke up toward morning and looked about him with a troubled expression. When he saw Moritz a smile of surprise and admiration lit up his sallow face and he said in a thick voice: "Franz Schubert! Oh, how nice of you to come and see how I am! This is almost too much! But you must sit down and have a cup of coffee, if you please. . . . !"

He looked questioningly at Moritz, who nodded with a helpless expression on his face. Boman leaned back, looking very tired. A little while later he stopped breathing. Everything had come to an end for old Boman.

And thus the first and the oldest of our musicians passes out of the story. Boman was indeed a good man, he was a source of energy, he lived on in his deeds and retained a place in the grateful hearts of his friends.

Moritz and Kornelius and Boman's other friends had decided to do everything in their power to make the old teacher's funeral as dignified as possible. The male choir was called together in order to rehearse hymns and songs, and it was also their intention to have a small brass band play Mendelssohn's funeral march. But nothing came of it, for just as they were fully occupied with the preparations, some one found among Boman's things an envelope on which was written: *Afterword and Last Will*, in which he had written, among other things: "In regard to my funeral, I wish no sermon and no singing. My only wish is that the enclosed serenade by Schubert, which I have been fond of since childhood, and which I have arranged for solo violin and a little bass pizzicato, and which is to be played in a not too

117

slow and not at all in a sad tempo, and to be played by my dear boy Orfeus and by some others among you my old friends, is to be played at my grave, after it has been closed, and not too late in the day, perhaps in the morning or before noon, if that can be done without too much folderol."

Thus it happened that Boman's funeral came to be something completely out of the ordinary. The old musician was laid to rest on a sunny day in late summer, and the hopeful, almost cheerful, notes of the serenade blended in with the sighing of the wind in the bushes and trees of the churchyard.

Orfeus felt very proud that he had given a good account of himself without stumbling at this, his first appearance as a musician. He had been playing almost without thinking of the music at all, he had just been thinking about Boman.

Just as he and his mother were leaving through the cemetery gate, someone behind him put his hands on his head and then patted him on both cheeks. It was Magister Mortensen.

"It sounded lovely," Magister Mortensen said. "Thank you, my boy!"

Following the funeral Boman's friends held a funeral feast that lasted the better part of the day. But everything proceeded in a very seemly way; they exchanged reminiscences about the deceased, and no one forgot for a moment that it was a feast of sorrow.

CHAPTER 6

How Kornelius, treasure hunter and musician, obtained a treasure through his music and brought it home one stormy winter evening

Little Kornelius, the composer, in contrast to his brothers Moritz and Sirius, reached a quite high age. It is only a few years ago that he died, about seventy years old. But the many years did not turn out to be a great blessing. A strange fate decreed that poor Kornelius already as a young man was to turn his back on the light of the world. . . .

But we shall revert to his youth and the good days, when the fact of existence was the most natural thing in the world, and the future beckoned with the most mysterious possibilities and prospects.

As far as Kornelius was concerned, one of these prospects had to do with a certain hidden treasure. The hope of finding this treasure cast an enviably magical and joyful light over a large part of his youth. But following his visit to Ura on the Cliff another secret source of joy had welled forth in Kornelius's breast.

It had begun in a very small way, as a quiet and tender trickle in his mind when he thought about the young, blind girl whose name was so like his own and who had stood listening to the music emanating from the basement of the Bastille . . . . had stood there outside in the dark all by herself. And this trickle soon grew into a strong purling, which after a while filled him to such an extent that the hunt for the treasure was completely shunted to the background.

Some time after his visit to Ura he stopped by again with an invitation to the old woman and Kornelia to come over to the Bastille for a cup of coffee and to listen to some music.

But no—Kornelia did not want to go. She was sitting there, squirming on her bench, quite dismayed at the thought of it, and she was not to be persuaded. Kornelius had to return without having accomplished his mission and with a wound in his heart. But the young girl continued to appear in his mind's eye: her pure and shy face, the large eyes with their somehow supernatural glance, the slight figure and the rich, ash-blond hair. He yearned madly to get to know her better and to bring music close to her, to fill her darkness with tones and harmonies.

And then he got the idea of bringing his cello over to play for her in Ura's house. It was perhaps a foolish thing to do, but he knew no other way out of it.

"I was just passing by," he lied and then stuttered, "and then I thought that perhaps Kornelia . . . since she is so fond of music?"

"Oh, how wonderful of you!" Ura said, deeply touched. "Many, many thanks, but it is too much!" Kornelius sat down and began to tune his instrument. The young girl looked deathly afraid, she hunched herself up, and when Kornelius began to play—it was "The Dance of the Blessed Spirits"—to his great dismay she burst into tears.

Alarmed, he stopped playing and asked: "But . . . but . . . perhaps it was wrong of me . . . to, to force myself on her. . . ?"

Ura looked a bit uncertain, but then laughed it off: "Oh nonsense, you just keep on playing, Kornelius!"

With some despondence he resumed playing. It was all

120

strangely confusing. The girl was sobbing, the black cat darted nervously back and forth and came over to rub itself against his legs, and in the middle of it all he happened to think of the well-known picture of Beethoven playing for a blind girl. For a moment he felt as if he had embarked on something quite blasphemous. He felt most of all like just leaving, but he forced himself to finish the minuet.

Kornelia had stopped crying, but she was intermittently gasping for breath, like a small child who is at its wits' end. Greatly bewildered and disappointed, Kornelius put his cello back in its case and tried to make light of the whole thing: "As I was saying . . . I was just passing by . . . and then I thought . . . just for the fun of it. . . ."

"Now didn't that sound beautiful and nice?" said Ura, turning to Kornelia, with a touch of reproach in her voice.

The young girl did not answer, but heaved a deep sigh.

"But now we will say thank you ever so much," the old woman said and shook his hand warmly. "Shake his hand, Kornelia, and say thank you very much!"

Kornelia's hand felt warm and hesitant in his, and with eyes closed she shook her long hair away from her face. She was red-eyed from weeping. Kornelius felt deeply sorry for her and squeezed her hand between both of his.

Ura accompanied him out on the cliff.

"It was almost as if she just didn't . . . didn't . . ." Kornelius whispered unhappily.

"Sometimes she is a little funny that way," the old woman said, frowning. "But then again, you know, she is hardly more than a child, and one thing and another."

Ura sighed deeply, as if in despair. "And she is a woman too, and . . . sort of infatuated in a way, like all young girls."

"She is what-did-you-say?" Kornelius asked anxiously.

Ura shook her head and answered evasively: "Yes, for you must understand, she doesn't meet any one and she

121

doesn't get to go any place, and then *you* come here, Kornelius, and set the entire house on end. . . !"

She smiled sadly and shrugged: "You see, the little one is most probably crying because she feels that everything is so hopeless for her."

Once again Kornelius felt dizzy, his tongue stuck to the roof of his mouth, and there was some time before he could make himself understood. "Hopeless, oh no!" He burst out in a staccato laughter: "But, but, it is just . . . the exact opposite!"

Most of all he felt like walking back in and taking the girl in his arms, tempestuously pressing her to him. But suddenly it was as if his feet had become stiff, he felt as if he had to pull them up by their roots in order to move away from the spot.

"Hopeless . . . oh no!" he repeated, while convulsively shaking Ura's bony hand. "No, not at all, that she must never believe . . . you must tell her that . . . and tell her that I'll be back and will play for her. . . !"

In his excitement he pressed the cello to him, and drunk with joy he staggered on his way.

Kornelius was flushed with the excitement of it all and with a sense of anticipation; he felt like celebrating the event, and when he met the Crab King on the way, he wept from joy, embraced the little man and pulled him with him inside The Curious Duck, where he ordered dinner for them both. Later on they were joined by Ole Brandy and Olivarius Sailmaker, and the little group ended up out at The Dolphin, where they sang and celebrated until the early morning hours.

From then on Kornelius was a frequent guest in the House on the Cliff, and it did not take long for Kornelia to thaw out.

Kornelius had now reached the summit of his happiness.

As the days passed he felt ever more intoxicated, and often he could not fall asleep at night from the sheer joy of it all.

During all this the quartet had virtually grown within him all by itself; two movements were almost completely finished in his head, the third one, which he was going to call *allegro vivace,* he had under full control. It was to be his and Kornelia's wedding march. And the entire composition was to be dedicated to the memory of old Boman, yes, the quartet was to be known as the "Boman Quartet."

As the days grew shorter and bad and windy weather set in, Ura's little house became an evermore unsafe and uncomfortable place; all its joints creaked, just like a sailing ship, and far below, at the foot of the precipice the sea was churning and boiling.

"It is quite senseless for you to continue to live here," said Kornelius. "Now we'll get married, Kornelia and I, and then we'll all three move out to the Bastille!"

"Yes, you just get married, children, that is the way it should be," Ura said, "and you go ahead and move over to the Bastille and set up your own home. But you'll never get me to leave this house, not until I'm carried out of here in a coffin!"

"But then again, maybe I won't!" she added, and then she had one of those fits of laughter for which there seemed to be no reason, and which Kornelius did not like at all.

"But why not?" he asked, quite perplexed, pressing Ura's hand.

"Why not what, then?" Ura laughed noisily, and to that he had no reply either. Ura would at times speak vaguely and in riddles, and there was nothing any one could do about it.

The church was completely filled on that dark and stormy

December afternoon when Kornelius led his young bride up to the altar. For the entire town wanted to go and have a look at the odd couple that according to public opinion had been joined together by Ura, perhaps not without the aid of supernatural powers. For whoever would marry a blind girl, right in his best years—a girl who was poor as a church mouse to boot, and perhaps not even right in her head? Certainly nobody but Kornelius—a mad, stuttering musician.

Kornelius's wedding was long thought of and talked about, especially because it occurred on one of the stormiest nights any one could remember.

The storm was already approaching while the wedding ceremony was being performed in the overcrowded church; the singing of the male chorus competed with the howling of the wind, while children and young people shouted with joy and the Wailing Woman wept. But during the evening the force of the storm increased tremendously, the gale headed in from the southeast, and the heavy surf and sea spray streamed in wild and salty curtains over Skin Islet. The bridal couple and the wedding guests almost did not make it out to the Bastille unharmed, and some of the guests decided to go back, especially since it was rumored that the Adventist family Samsonsen had made a headlong flight from the raging elements, and also that Ole Brandy had been found battered and bruised and with a broken arm in the vicinity of the Höje warehouse; he had wanted to visit his friend Olivarius, but right outside the entrance door he had been thrown to the ground by a barrel that had been washed ashore and that the wind was playing ball with.

But the few courageous ones, those who forced their way through the inundated narrow alley and in a more or less dry condition were pulled in through the entrance to the Bastille, also found the wedding feast to be a mixed pleasure.

124

Like whistling fountains the salt water was pouring in through the chinks in window casings and there was no question of being able to keep warm in the drafty rooms.

There was an especially bad state of affairs down in the studio, where the party was supposed to have taken place; here the floor was covered with water, and bulbs and lights flickered and threatened to go out. It was just like being onboard a ship in distress. The entire celebration that Eliana and Moritz had arranged together with Atlanta and Sarina, inexorably broke down, and the little party, which now consisted almost entirely of the building's own tenants, huddled up in Kornelius's small parlor.

With wine and song, Moritz, Kornelius, Mortensen, and the Corpse Crower tried to put every one in the right mood, but that was not an easy task, and for a while it looked completely hopeless. Especially Sarina, the Corpse Crower's wife, was on the point of collapse; she insisted that every one should leave the house, just as the Adventists had done, and there was hardly anything they could do to keep the terror-stricken woman under control. Finally, they had to let her have her way. Through foam and darkness the woman was carried across the flooded alley and brought to safety out at The Dolphin.

After that, the others felt more at ease. Moritz and Kornelius got out their horns and played a few duets, and Magister Mortensen, who gradually had become very drunk, sang an old South Jutland love ballad, of which no one could understand a word; nevertheless, because of the melody and Mortensen's emotion-laden voice it went right to every one's heart and brought tears to the eyes of both the bride and the groom.

But . . . *now* what—? Suddenly there is a sound of hurried footsteps and a clatter of weapons out in the stairway, someone bangs on the door, and a bearded man in oilcloth and sou'wester sticks his head in. It is Debes, the constable! For a moment he stands still, then waves Kornelius over to him.

Kornelius jumps up from his chair, and in doing so inadvertently gives the table a shove, so that glasses and bottles topple over and fall clattering to the floor.

"What's up, Debes?"

"Don't get excited," says the policeman, who now has caught his breath. He pulls Kornelius out into the hallway and closes the door behind him; thereupon he unbuttons his overcoat so that his sabre comes into full view. "There's been an accident," he says, "an accident that may have cost a human life—yes, it is Ura on the Cliff. Her house has been blown off its foundations and has fallen over the edge of the cliff!"

Kornelius is struck dumb. The constable continues in a calm voice: "Ura has been saved and has been brought to the hospital. But she is unconscious."

Kornelius is still unable to say a word, he utters some stammering and incoherent sounds, but he cannot help thinking to himself: "But it was her own fault, the foolish old woman, she could just as well have moved over to us here —she could at least have joined the party here tonight, but even *that* we couldn't persuade her to do, she wanted to stay home, all by herself, that impossible woman. . . . !"

"I'll be coming with you," he managed to say at last. "I'll only . . . my overcoat . . . the boots. . . !"

"There's really nothing you can do," says the constable reassuringly. "The house, as I said, *has* fallen down, and Ura is unconscious, and the weather is terrible, so it is just as well that you stay where you are. It was only my duty to come and report what had happened."

But Kornelius has already put on his overcoat. He opens the door to the parlor to tell Kornelia and the others the horrible news, but once more his voice completely fails him, and Debes has to come to his aid: "Yes, it concerns the House on the Cliff, it's blown down," he says calmly, "but Ura is, at least so far, all right!"

The wind is blowing just as hard the following day, and the thundering surf fills the air with a muffled sound. Curious people flock out to Cliff Hill in order to stare at the place where Ura's house had stood and at the pitiful pieces of wreckage that are being tossed back and forth by the foaming waves underneath the cliff and by and by are washed ashore in the form of splinters and driftwood on the flat rocks inside the bay.

About Ura herself the word goes round that she is still hovering between life and death.

About the catastrophe itself the strangest stories are being told; they spread from house to house, people shake their heads, cower and shudder at the thought of it, or smile deprecatingly, all according to the way they feel. Ura must have been up to some of her tricks, some people stubbornly contend, there was much smoke coming from her chimney the night of the accident; sparks had also been seen flying about, and a neighbor woman who had passed the House on the Cliff about midnight had clearly heard that Ura was quarreling with some one, and it is not too hard to imagine who that was, it was hardly the cat, rather a certain sinister personage, the same one who had conferred on her the ability to ferret out lost objects, know the future, link two people together and thereby cause their ruin, and inflict sickness and other troubles on her enemies. Now they had probably begun to quarrel, the two of them, perhaps about the soul of the poor fool Kornelius, who knows? And the devil, of course, had turned out to be the stronger and had given her a warning.

Savings-bank manager Ankersen's housekeeper, Mrs. Midiord, who was Ura's half-sister, was heartbroken when

127

she entered the manager's office and sobbingly confided in him what the rumor-mongers had made up.

Ankersen listened attentively. He nodded: "Well, yes, Mrs. Midiord. But suppose there really is something to it?"

He looked at his watch: "At three o'clock they have visiting hours at the hospital. Let us both go over there and talk to her, if it is possible. But let us at least *pray* for her."

CHAPTER 7

Orfeus encounters the sad remains of his grandfather's
aeolian harps, entertains troublesome thoughts and
evil visions, but is somewhat comforted by the
phantom Tarira

The fierce southeast wind that began to blow on Kornelius's
wedding night did not seem as if it wanted to abate; it
lasted for days and weeks, and the little town by the sea
was wrapped in a raging sea foam which made all the
windowpanes quite opaque on account of the salt deposited
on them, and the incessant roar of the surf pressed against
the ear like a deafness.

Christmas Eve began just as wet and windy as all other
days, but at noon the weather suddenly cleared up and the
wind began to slacken. Eliana had decorated the Christmas
tree, and Orfeus had been given permission to bring his
friend Gravedigger Peter and his sisters home with him that
evening. Lukas Gravedigger's wife was sick and he himself
was drunk, and thus the children would not have a very
pleasant time at home.

Orfeus met Peter in the church tower; he was sitting up
there in the company of Poul the sexton, who was busy
putting new hinges on a trapdoor. Orfeus and Peter were
inside the dark church loft. Here was a heap of strange
objects, something that seemed to be alive and to emit curious
and sickly sighs whenever a draft passed over it. Orfeus

jumped back in alarm, but Peter shouted: It's only your grandfather's aeolian harps! Isn't that right, Poul?"

"Yes, it's his grandfather's aeolian harps," the sexton confirmed and mumbled something about "Kornelius at Kelp Inlet, the foolish dolt."

"Yes, your grandfather was a real *crazy fool*," Peter explained in a friendly tone of voice, while the two boys descended down the tower staircase. "He made aeolian harps, and that's a thing one does only when one is crazy. And your father and his brothers are all of them a little daft. But you mustn't worry about that, Orfeus," he added encouragingly.

Peter could not come along and see the Christmas tree at the Bastille, and he secretly confided to Orfeus why he couldn't: he had his own Christmas tree. "Come on up with me and look at it!" he coaxed.

Orfeus was cold. The strange sound made by the draft in the old aeolian harps in the church loft kept resounding in his ears. In great suspense he followed after Peter. They walked in a northerly direction out of the city; the fields were gleaming with hoar-frost and the stars were shivering from the cold.

"Look how they're moving about up there!" Peter said. "That's because the angels are playing with them and making them explode!"

The northern lights flared above the hills to the north, then quickly spread and billowed like frenzied sails across the entire sky.

"Watch out that you don't look around too much," Peter warned him in a whisper. "There are swarms of ghosts around here!"

They passed a frozen brook across which there was a rickety old wooden bridge. Peter stopped and said in a hollow voice: "Look, Orfeus, this place next to the bridge is especially horribly haunted; here an old ghost usually comes walking with a stick in his hand and a long file of

130

geese in front of him. They are spook geese! They shine brightly in the dark! Look, there are some of them right now! No, it wasn't them. But you'll probably see them a little later. But look over there!"

Peter was pointing at a tumbled-down haybarn and said: "You've never noticed that one before, have you?"

Orfeus could not recall whether he had or not.

"That's just what I thought," Peter said, "for it stands here only on Christmas Eve. At other times it's not there. It belongs in heaven. For it is really the stable in which the child Jesus was born!"

Orfeus was overcome with amazement and stopped short in order to take a closer look at the barn. Of course, he did not believe what Peter had told him, since Peter was always full of boasts and tall stories. But still, the old dilapidated building was standing right there and looked so queer: pale and frozen the gable jutted up into the clear air, which was shining with a silvery gray sheen as if it were faded by the northern lights and the starlight.

"Come and see!" Peter whispered. "For this is the place where I keep my Christmas tree."

He walked over and opened a creaking door. Orfeus stepped inside; he felt stunned from the suspense of it all, there was a pungent, moldy smell in the place, and in the half-darkness he could hear a subdued tittering. Peter's sisters were sitting there waiting for him. Peter lit a match, and then they all could see the little Christmas tree that was standing in a barrel, sparkling with tinsel and angel's hair.

"Now you've seen it," Peter said when the match went out. "We're not going to light it until later."

"Where have you got it from?" Orfeus asked.

"It's always standing here," Peter whispered, "for it is a real Christmas tree from Bethlehem!"

"No, he's chopped it down himself," was heard with a giggle out of the darkness.

"Now *you* just sit quiet and keep your mouth shut, Grethe," Peter admonished in, a gloomy tone of voice, "otherwise I'll lock up the ghosts and the devil, and then the whole thing will be spoiled!"

Once again he lit a match and hurriedly showed Orfeus a few colored objects inside a carton. There were Christmas candles, tinsel, and some round cakes and crackers.

"You can join us if you wish," Peter said in a friendly manner. But Orfeus had to go home to his own Christmas tree.

"But be careful when you leave here," Peter warned him, his voice once again ominous. "As you know, there are spirits lurking about all over!"

There was a delicious smell of food and of spruce in the basement of the Bastille, and the Christmas tree was lit in the big parlor. Sirius, Kornelius and his wife, in addition to Fribert Collier and his dog, were participating in the Christmas dinner, and later on the Corpse Crower and his wife and daughter, Ole Brandy, Olivarius, and the Crab King also arrived. They were treated to beer and aquavit with their food. Sirius read the Christmas story, and they sang and played, but right in the middle of it savings-bank manager Ankersen turned up, dressed as Santa Claus, holding a thick stick.

"You're singing hymns?" he said with evident emotion, but discovered in the very same moment the glasses on the table and burst into a lamentation that boded no one well: "Oh, even on this holy evening, Moritz! Even in this most sacred hour of the entire year!"

Ankersen worked himself into a state akin to indignation, but it was quite evident that on this particular evening he had not come to castigate but was rather brimful of the holy gospel of peace. He looked very odd in his red pointed cap. Little Amadea was frightened by him and began to cry.

132

"What is the matter with the little one?" Ankersen asked, removing his spectacles in order to wipe them. "Wait a while, children, it's not your fault that the grownups do not celebrate a church holiday properly and that they besmirch everything that is sacred!"

He sat down, breathing heavily, and waved to Fat Alfred who was standing in the hallway holding a basket. Ankersen placed the basket on the floor between his legs, blew his nose, and pulled a few small tracts out of his pocket: "Look here, read this, you grownups, and study it well! It may be too late before you know it, for as the Good Book says: 'He comes like a thief in the night!' "

It turned into a thundering speech, to which every one listened in silence, but afterward Ankersen thawed out a bit, he patted the children's heads and presented the small ones with gifts and sweets from the basket; and when he learned that Sirius already had read the Christmas gospel aloud he got a gentle look in his eyes and accepted a glass of beer. The little girls were not afraid of him any more, he placed them on his lap and chucked them under their chins.

"But we are very busy tonight; we have to move on," he said to Alfred with a nod and got up. "Let us in parting sing 'In this Sweet Christmastime.' "

The hymn was sung, Moritz, Kornelius, and the Corpse Crower harmonizing. It sounded beautiful, and Ankersen's spectacles moistened. He shook hands with every one present. Fribert's old dog also received a friendly pat from Santa Claus's large hand.

When Orfeus had gone to bed that night he could not get the strange aeolian harps in the church loft out of his mind, and his head filled with fear and with horrible thoughts.

"Your grandfather was a crazy fool," resounded in his ear. "And so are your father and his brothers." Half dozing and on the verge of tears, he dully listened to the noise coming from the studio, where the grownups were still celebrating. Fribert Collier was singing "Ole Morske Lies Shriveled in the Loft," an indefinable song about suffering and distress, fighting, and howling darkness. He wished that it already was morning and that it would be light and everyday-like always, so that the world could be set right again and become *ordinary*. He clung to what was ordinary: to the morning meals, attending school; he could not get his fill of what was ordinary, but always dreaded what was *behind* it, that invisible chasm of dread and horror, death and insanity. When one fell asleep, the gate leading into this chasm was opened wide, and one had to travel about all alone in hidden, extensive realms, to journey in solitude along windy paths in the dusk and through boundless wastes, where departed souls lived their restless lives and all kinds of lunacy had free play.

Still, in this swarm of horrors, there was one ally that never failed him.

Orfeus turned around so that he lay on his stomach and pressed his eyes against his arm; multicolored fire began to fall like snow, gorgeous flowers opened up, and there he saw that which he secretly had been waiting for as well as been afraid of: Tarira's eyes, which stared at him and entrapped him in their smile of awful familiarity.

Tarira was not an evil spirit or a ghost. What was she? One thing was certain: before her all sad thoughts and horrible visions had to yield. But one had to give in to her whims and to follow her on her dizzying journey all through her realm.

"Whew—now we are taking off, like two birds whizzing through the air, Tarira and I, and we fly into a limitless moonlight high above the earth, where everything looms lonely and distant and vast!"

134

CHAPTER 8

*Sirius is once more subjected to an unpleasant twist of fate
but behaves in a way that reflects honor on his character*

During the last few decades Sirius Isaksen's star has slowly
but surely been rising ever higher. In the course of time,
lovers of literature have had their eyes opened to what is
thoroughly original in the work of this long misunderstood
lyricist, and according to *The News* a proposal was recently
made in the city council to rechristen Smiths' Lane, which
has now been modernized, and to call it Sirius Isaksen's
Road. *The News* supports this suggestion and maintains that
we ought to be proud and grateful to have produced in our
midst this famous poet whose life was as brief as it was
unhappy.

Actually, it isn't quite correct to say that Sirius's life was
as unhappy as it was short. On the contrary, deep down in
his soul he was in fact tremendously happy; indeed, in his
inner being he was—despite his impressionable mind—in a
way curiously *invulnerable*.

This had something to do with the fact that as a poet he
was living in two worlds at one time—that of reality and
that of poetry—and had the amazing ability to move
at will from one over to the other, meanwhile making an
occasional stopover at some border station between these
two omnivorous or cannibalistic empires.

Sirius Isaksen was, as Magnus Skæling perspicaciously

135

points out in his monograph, what one in our modern idiom would call an *escapist*. The same was the case—*mutatis mutandis*—with the other musicians dealt with in this book. They evaded the pressures of reality by fleeing into the worlds of music and of imagination, or, in the case of Magister Mortensen, into the realm of religious philosophy.

The reason that Sirius could walk about for days on end in a state which must needs be characterized by the uninitiated as a stupor, was that the poet was lingering near the borderline between spirit and matter and was giving himself over completely to the indescribable sensation of active equilibrium that may be induced by such a state.

This, of course, could not be comprehended by Mac Bett the house painter, and it is therefore easy to understand that there was tension between the young poet and the old painter, who could never think of anything except his trade and his picture-frame shop. It is indeed to the great credit of the hot-tempered old Scotsman that for about two years he allowed Sirius to carry on with his school for children, even though his shop had long needed more space, and that in addition he provided the poet with room and board in his own home for an extremely modest remuneration.

But when Sirius gradually started to take the task of instruction less seriously and when the number of pupils dropped at an alarming rate and the teacher's already fantastically low income was proportionately reduced, it simply became too much for the painter, and on a certain November day that was unusually misty and dark and conducive to irritation, he asked his protégé in a towering rage to pack his things and rely on his own devices.

Sirius for his part felt both relieved and liberated.

The school, as well as his daily association with the painter, whom he always had to help in his spare time by mixing paints or framing pictures, had felt like an intolerable straightjacket. It was therefore with unmixed pleasure that

136

he said good-by to the children and told them not to come back but to explain to their parents that the school did not exist any more. The following days he walked about and completely abandoned himself to his unbounded freedom.

He went for long walks during the night, observed the starry sky and the ocean, and listened to the sound of the surf, and during the day he slept on a sofa in the Bastille. He ate his meals at no fixed time and in various places— with Eliana, with Kornelius, with Ole Brandy or Lindenskov the dance instructor, or on board the fore-and-aft schooner *Lalla Rookh*, whose skipper was an old schoolmate of his.

This free and easy life lasted the whole winter through.

That winter was an unusually mild one, typical for the islands. Green grass was shooting up everywhere already in February, and the chilly and snowy spring that was expected to appear as punishment completely failed to materialize; spring arrived as early as the middle of April, and the big currant bushes in the smith's garden were in full bloom.

Spring jolted Sirius out of his nirvana. All through the winter he had worshiped in solitude his two ladies, Leonora and Julia, or rather, he had nursed his unrequited love for these two beings; and hardly a night had passed without his tarrying by the smith's garden fence to gaze at the reddish light in the window of Julia's bedroom. Leonora was away and was staying in Copenhagen.

But now it so happened that on a mild and foggy evening as he passed by the smith's house, he heard Mrs. Janniksen scolding her daughter violently, calling her a shameless hussy. There was also the sound of something that fell and was smashed; then Julia appeared in the doorway and disappeared into the garden. Sirius heard the smith's wife muttering angrily and using savings-bank manager Ankersen's name as a threat; a little while later he thought he could detect a faint sobbing inside the garden. He

137

climbed warily over the fence and whispered: "Julia! Don't be afraid—it's only me!"

It was some time before he found the girl. She had hidden herself in one of the fragrant bushes, she was weeping violently and was very unhappy. He stroked her hair and kissed her moist cheek.

"But what's the reason for all this, Julia?" he whispered urgently.

It took a long time for Julia to be able to utter a word because of her wretchedness and weeping, and when at long last she got her voice back, some one in the smith's house called sharply: "Julia!" It sounded like a fateful stroke on a cracked bell.

"It's mother!" Julia whispered, trembling in fear. "I have to go in!"

She disengaged herself from his embrace and made her way out of the bush, but then came back and whispered: "Come back tomorrow night, Sirius! I must speak with you!"

Sirius remained sitting underneath the bush the greater part of the night. He could hear scolding and carrying on inside the smith's house. But at last everything quieted down. The acid scent of the currant blossoms was intense in the misty air, and once again he noticed how his heart swelled with earthy, painful compassion and a dull need for affection. It was on this occasion that Sirius conceived his poem "Darkness Speaks to the Blossoming Bush," about which it has been said that it reminds one of the gentle trembling of young leaves in the night wind.

The next day it was raining hard, and toward evening the wind began to blow. Sirius had been sitting in the smith's garden for almost three hours before Julia finally came. He was drenched from the profuse, constant dripping of the twigs of the currant bush. Julia took off her raincoat, and they both crawled underneath it for shelter.

"You're freezing, you poor fellow!" Julia whispered and tenderly nestled close to him. A refreshing warmth exuded from the body of the plump young girl, and the passionate kisses that she planted on his cheek and on his mouth felt like blissful fiery flowers. But after they had been sitting like this for a while, Julia too became soaked and began to shiver.

"It's really no fun sitting here," she said and shook herself. And suddenly she began to sob.

"What is it?" whispered Sirius unhappily.

"Oh, everything is so terrible!" Julia answered, her mouth close to his ear.

Bit by bit he learned of the misfortune that had been the lot of the poor girl. Her sweetheart Jartvard had gone away, and no one knew where. The unscrupulous fellow had broken off with her and left her, but that was nothing to worry about, Jartvard being a wicked fellow, one whom it would have been miserable to get for a husband.

"Yes, there's no doubt about that!" Sirius said.

He stroked her thick, long hair which had become wet from the rain: "But you'll get over it, my dear, you're young and healthy. It could have turned out much worse."

Julia swallowed her tears and replied eagerly: "It *has* turned out much worse, Sirius, it's as bad as it can possibly be. We were supposed to be married in the spring. And now I'm being left alone with the shame of it all. And what will life be like for the poor child. . . ?"

"You're expecting a—child?" Sirius asked, with a sinking heart.

Little by little it had stopped raining. The wind tugged at the bushes and trees in the garden. Julia was crying, silently, her body shaking. Suddenly she made a start. "Didn't some one call me?" she asked, holding her breath and listening.

"No, it was nothing," Sirius said.

They were both silent for a while. Julia had stopped crying, but now and then spasms would shake her body. When Sirius at last spoke there was an ardent and firm resoluteness in his voice: "But we could get married, the two of us, Julia!"

"No, that we could never do," she answered, pressing him close to her.

"But why not, my dear?"

"That would be more than I could possibly ask of you, Sirius. And besides—besides, what would we live on? Have you thought of *that*, Sirius?"

"These things will always take care of themselves," Sirius asserted. "And that's one thing you can leave to *me*. So, cheer up, Julia, you just rely on me, I won't leave you in the lurch! Do you think I ought to go inside and speak with your father right now?"

"No, no," Julia replied, clutching him anxiously.

"Then we'll wait until tomorrow," Sirius said, feeling elated. "You'll see, everything will be all right, Julia! You just rely on me!"

"You want to marry Julia?"

Blacksmith Janniksen ran his hands through his huge ash-colored mane, staring at Sirius with bloodshot eyes that seemed a part of the series of red bags and folds underneath. When he had stared to his heart's content, he turned and grasped a piece of iron from the forge and began to belabor it on the anvil. Now and again he would look at Sirius out of the corner of his eye through all the smoke and sparks, and Sirius looked back at him with an air of courtesy and frankness. The blacksmith put the iron into the live coals.

"Come over here, come along with me for a moment!" He beckoned, walking over to a door with peeling paint at the back of the smithy. He opened it, and Sirius followed him into the dim little room. There was a box with a round

140

opening in the lid, and through the hole rose the loud noise of a purling and babbling brook that ran underneath the floor.

"What in the world is all this about?" asked Sirius. But the blacksmith slapped him reassuringly on the back and said with great warmth: "Sirius, my poor boy. It is best that you and I talk about this thing in complete privacy. You are aware then, that the girl has let herself be tricked and that the scoundrel has run away?"

"Yes, I am," Sirius assured him.

The blacksmith continued: "It is in order to help the girl out of her difficulty, then, that you—?"

"I do feel sorry for her," Sirius answered, "and she is my old pupil. But I am also very fond of Julia, that I am, I know that she is a fine girl. And she is also fond of me."

The blacksmith sighed and spat into the babbling water.

Sirius continued: "There is only one awkward thing about it, just now, I don't have steady work, but that. . . ."

"Never mind *that*," the blacksmith said thoughtfully. "That is one thing that can be worked out."

Suddenly blacksmith Janniksen displayed his worn black teeth in an absentminded smile: "But there's something else that makes this damned difficult. You know what that is—it's my wife."

He leaned against the wall and explained, one thumb pointing up in the air: "You see, it is her habit to make a mess of everything, for she is a bungling fool in every way. Now she has gotten the absolutely insane idea of taking the girl to Ankersen to confide in him! And that, of course, I would not permit . . . but what good is that when that mad *loonipermoonia* is upon her?"

The blacksmith spat passionately into the hole and continued: "You see, now she and Ankersen are putting their heads together and deciding that Julia is to suffer all the torment possible and is going to show up in the religious society and confess her sin. In every one's presence, damn

141

it! What good can come of that kind of *crapidoopery?* Won't it just be something for people to gloat about?"

"That is not going to happen!" Sirius said with emotion.

"Well, that is easy for us two to stand here and say," said the blacksmith, shrugging his shoulders. "You don't know Rosa, you don't know how she is when this damned *obstreperation* rides her. If we could only make her turn around and run the other way. Yes, if we could make her run the other way!"

The blacksmith stared longingly down into the opening and continued, in a low voice as if imparting a confidence: "You see, it is not actually Julia the whole row is about. No, I am the one that's to be strung up to hang and squirm on the tree! *I'm* the one that's to be put into the *choppacka-topper*, don't you see? My taking a little drink once in a while and getting a little tipsy—that is now to be blown up, you see, as the real down-to-earth reason for this terrible occurrence. 'The drunkard's daughter!' And so on! And you know how Ankersen is, he is capable of anything when that sanctimoniousness of his rides him!"

The blacksmith made a violent jerking motion with his entire body and clenched both his quicksilver-gray fists: "I could break every bone in his body, I hope you believe that and don't doubt it? But Rosa—that one I can't manage, her meanness and her *tricknicks*—there is no limit to them . . . well, you people only know a little bit of that, but I, Sirius, I'm leading an awful life, an awful life."

The blacksmith groaned and ran his fingers through his hair.

"I think we should be able to straighten out this situation when I have had another talk with Julia," Sirius said in a comforting tone.

"Hush," whispered the blacksmith, opening the door a little. His face took on a slyly expectant and at the same time strangely helpless expression: "By God, they are here

142

already! They are rummaging around in the apartment and calling for Julia!"

"Wait a minute!" said Sirius and ran through the smithy and out into the garden where Julia was waiting for him behind the large bush. She rose to her feet, trembling all over.

"I knew they would!" she said, paralyzed with terror. "They have thrown you out! I knew it would happen!"

"No, of course not!" Sirius whispered reassuringly, placing his arm around the girl's waist. He told her how matters stood. "Yes, that is the situation," he concluded, "and now there is only one thing for us to do, and that is that you tell everybody that the child is mine, and that I say it's true, and then everything is in order. We are engaged, Julia, and we'll get married as soon as possible. Your father is on our side!"

"Julia!" was heard from inside the house.

"You go in," Sirius whispered. "I'll be back in a little while."

Savings-bank manager Ankersen had seated himself in a rocking-chair in the parlor in the blacksmith's house. He sat there as if brooding over something, breathing hard through hairy nostrils. His hands, which were clasped on his stomach, moved slowly, ominously, up and down with every breath. He did not change his position when Julia stepped into the room.

"Well, here is the poor child," the blacksmith's wife sighed. "Sit down, Julia."

Ankersen remained silent. Mrs. Janniksen continued, in a gloomy voice: "Yes, Julia, manager Ankersen knows everything, and he has promised to help you rise from out of the mire! We have decided to enter upon the only path that is still open to us. Isn't that so, Ankersen. . . But you are not saying anything?"

Ankersen nodded. He cleared his throat, making a muffled sound, and his voice seemed to come from way down at the bottom of a well: "The wages of sin are death, but whoever repents his sin and confesses it, for him a door still stands ajar, leading to God's incomprehensible gift of mercy."

Julia sat with her head bent, staring down at her feet. She listened to Ankersen's pounding sentences as if through a heavy daze. He spoke about the woman who was taken in adultery, about the accursed consequences of drunkenness that made for broken homes and led the children into the impassable wilderness of sin.

"What am I supposed to say?" Julia thought, perplexed. For no questions were being asked of her. Ankersen's words added up to one thumping indictment: You must start life anew, woman, you must set out on the path of the repentant sinners. You must confess your sin to your fellow Christian sisters and brothers, so that it will serve them first as a warning, and later as edification and spiritual liberation. . . .

Julia tried to fight back her tears. At last she could no longer hold them back, but gave herself over to her despair and began to sob out loud. She heard Ankersen say: "It is a good thing! It is only to the good that repentance comes in full force, with all its power! That is the first step!"

But now a tentative knocking was heard at the door, and Sirius entered. She heard his voice explaining things. It sounded so strangely thin and small, he stammered and coughed: "As I said, Julia and I are engaged to be married, and the child is mine—and then the matter should be settled, shouldn't it?"

He was seized with a violent fit of coughing.

"What is it this young man is saying?" Ankersen asked with an ominous tinge of laughter in his voice. "Is the child his? And the girl has been engaged to some one else? She has in other words. . . ? No, no, the whole thing is just too incredible! In that case she has indeed lived the life of a

144

harlot, worse so than any one suspected. She has given herself to two men? No, no, that is too repulsive for words!"

He got to his feet and tried to seize Julia's hand: "My child, my poor lost lamb! What can we do? You've really gotten that far away from the fold?"

"I'm going to marry her!" Sirius said, his coughing fit having come to an end. "I have her father's permission! We're going to get married as soon as possible!"

"But why have you been silent about all this, Julia?" Mrs. Janniksen asked. "Why haven't you at least confided in your own mother? So *that* was the reason that Jartvard went away? Now it's an entirely different story! If only I had known. . ."

"But that doesn't make the situation any better!" the infuriated Ankersen wailed, turning in the direction of the blacksmith's wife. "This makes it doubly shameful! For the girl has . . . the woman has very obviously committed *adultery!*"

"Yes, that is true," her mother confirmed gloomily and stepped over to Ankersen, facing her daughter.

Ankersen took Sirius by the arm and forced him to stand next to Julia.

"Of course, it's nothing but a good thing that the truth is revealed in all its atrociousness," he said in a hollow-sounding voice. "And whether you get married or not, you must both enter upon the path of repentance and atonement and confession. You must shoulder the blame for your horrible behavior, and I will then do everything in human power, yes, more than that, to help you rise again! I will spare no effort, so help me God! But then you both will have to humble yourselves before your Christian sisters and brothers. Is that agreed? And that which is to be, let it be soon! Let it be this very evening! Let us all together. . ."

Ankersen was suddenly interrupted by the door opening

wide, and the blacksmith entered. His face was dark red, and his eyes glowed excitedly within their series of bags.

"You stay away!" his wife cautioned him hoarsely.

The blacksmith stepped over to the table and pounded it so hard with his fist that it resounded throughout the crowded room.

"I am the master of this house!" he shouted threateningly. "I have given my consent to Julia's marriage to this man, and that should be the end of this damned shit-chat!"

"You get out!" his wife shrieked, gasping for breath.

"*He* get out, that damn meddler! That twaddling ape!" the blacksmith thundered.

He grabbed Ankersen from behind and shook him so hard that his starched shirt-front bulged out from under his vest.

"Oh, he's killing him!" Mrs. Janniksen wailed, sinking down on a chair.

"Oh nonsense," said the blacksmith, seeming a bit frightened when he loosened his hold on the savings-bank manager. "I only ask that he leave this house quietly!"

Ankersen's knees failed him and he remained sitting on the floor, with his short legs stretched out. He groped for his spectacles, breathing heavily.

"Well," muttered the blacksmith. "Will you get off with you!"

"My spectacles!" Ankersen said in a demanding voice.

His spectacles were lying next to him on the floor. Sirius picked them up and gave them to him. Ankersen remained sitting there, with the spectacles in his hand. He was breathing heavily, but otherwise seemed to be strangely calm. He lifted his big face toward the blacksmith, saying in a low and long-suffering voice, while gesticulating with the spectacles: "You don't have to carry on like that, smith Janniksen, I haven't forced my way into your house like a

146

thief or a robber, but because your wife asked me to come, and because I thought it was my duty to come. A duty that was anything but pleasant. I only wish to help! To help! I will certainly not oppose these two young people being joined in the bonds of honest matrimony. But let us also give some thought to the *spiritual* aspect of the matter!"

He got up with difficulty and continued speaking, still addressing the blacksmith: "Or isn't sin always sin? And doesn't sin always carry with it its own punishment? Do repentance and mercy have no meaning for us small helpless grains of humanity? What's going to be the end of it all, Janniksen? Well, perhaps *you* have a better suggestion?"

Ankersen put out his hand to the blacksmith, as a token of reconciliation. Janniksen grasped it hesitantly. "Yes, but leave now," he said, "and then we can forget the whole thing, let us agree on that."

"Don't ever think that I consider myself free from sin!" Ankersen continued, looking the blacksmith right in the eye. "No, on the contrary, I have been a slave of sin, just as bad as any one, Janniksen! Perhaps—perhaps worse than. . ."

"Than *me?*" said the blacksmith and laughed out loud. "Stop it now, Ankersen. And take your leave now while the going is good, as we just agreed. Isn't that right, Rosa? For now everything is settled in a way, isn't it? Yes, by God it is! You agree, Rosa? Be sensible for once! For we can have a cozy time together, we two, once in a while, isn't that right?"

He winked at his wife and nudged her with his elbow.

"Well, what do *you* think?" Ankersen too turned toward the blacksmith's wife.

Sirius stared anxiously at the large woman.

"It was first and foremost in order to give *you* support that I came," Ankersen said impatiently, looking at his watch.

"And it shall not have been in vain," Mrs. Janniksen said

147

with great fervor, turning her back on her husband. "It certainly shall not! For we won't give an inch, Ankersen! Not an inch!"

Ankersen placed his spectacles back on his nose and gave her his hand.

"God bless you!" he said with a sigh of relief.

He turned to the two young people: "Now, my young woman and young man! It is now up to you whether you will do your simple Christian duty and open the door which stands ajar for you! It is always standing ajar! God is inexpressibly forbearing. However, not—not without limits, no, there is a limit, and woe to the one who does not know the time of his visitation!"

He shook hands with both of them. The blacksmith nudged his shoulder as if reminding him to leave. He accompanied the savings-bank manager into the entrance hall and gave him his overcoat and his stick, and then he returned to the smithy.

When Sirius a little while later came in to say good-by, the blacksmith was standing next to his anvil. He winked merrily and punched Sirius playfully in the stomach: "Well, it turned out pretty well after all, didn't it? At least you did very well, I'll give you credit for that. And if only you and I stick together, then we'll surely be able to get their" —he gave the anvil a resounding blow—"*snivel-drivel* taken down a notch or two! Then we can, devil take me, make their"—once again a powerful blow with his hammer— "*smidgeon-pigeons* fly through the air!"

148

CHAPTER 9

The return of the prodigal son

Johan Wenzeslaus Ankersen, this lay preacher and manager
of a savings bank—in whose nature pettiness and greatness
every day waged an embittered but hopeless battle at close
range—quite naturally appeared to his contemporaries as
something of an enigma: a kind of split personality or
centaur—up above a blameless and quiet office worker who
headed ably, zealously and punctiliously the financial institution that had been entrusted to him, but down below a
snorting and merciless being, whose unpredictable whims
were feared by all.

One of the other unusual and surprising things about
Ankersen was the fact that he got worse with the years.
People who have known him in his younger days describe
him as a reserved and courteous man, rather a shy young
fellow who only reluctantly would intrude himself into other
people's affairs; also, every one knew that, like Jacob
wrestling with the angel, he was carrying on a never-ending
struggle, in his case against a weakness for alcoholic bev-
erages inherited from his father, Captain Napoleon
Ankersen. It was only on very rare occasions, such as the
great church holidays, that Johan Wenzeslaus gave in to this
tragic inclination, and even when he let himself go, it would
not at all happen in a violent and provocative manner—on
the contrary. He might be seen of an evening ambling

149

along the streets, all by himself and loaded to the gunwales, or standing in a dark corner at The Dolphin; and during the next few days he would withdraw completely from the world, and in profound loneliness behind rolled-down curtains he would give himself over to his contrition, which was known to be unusually pernicious.

Actually, it was not until he reached the age of forty and some—that is, just the age when other people usually quiet down and become sedate—that Ankersen all of a sudden began to show signs of that impetuous behavior that was to characterize him for the rest of his life. As far as is known, this sudden change in his manner was not caused by external events of the dramatic kind that one will often observe as causing a psychic eruption in a human being, such as unrequited love and so on. To make a long story short—one fine day the savings-bank manager came to see Pastor Lindemann, a very proper and good-natured clergyman of the old school, and wanted him to embark on a new way of preaching the gospel; when Lindemann showed himself disinclined to do so, then Ankersen set out for himself and began to play the role of a preacher, calling for repentance and atonement; at times he would preach on the street corners, at other times—on various and often far-fetched pretexts—he would intrude in other people's meetings or would visit families or individuals in their homes.

At first people would shake their heads at this new self-appointed spiritual adviser. But it wasn't very long before people had to recognize him as a spiritual force of some consequence. He gained followers and established his own congregation. In the beginning they would conduct open-air meetings, especially on Sunday afternoons on the Shoemaker Flats. Later on they obtained a permanent assembly room, and in the course of the next few years Ankersen's odd little congregation grew slowly but surely. Ankersen got his first real breakthrough, however, when he allied himself with the Christian temperance society Ydun and placed total abstinence on his program. From then on his star kept rising ever higher, his activities became quite considerable in extent—indeed, he became, as every one knows, a man of great power and influence.

Ankersen scored the biggest triumph of his life the day that he could welcome back his prodigal son Matte-Gok in the presence of a large crowd of spectators.

It was common knowledge that Ankersen for many years and with unflagging energy had endeavored to trace his lost son—in truth, practically the whole town had followed his unremitting efforts with great suspense and sympathy, and on the day the rumor spread that the savings-bank manager now at last, through the Salvation Army, had made contact with his son, this development became the dominant topic of conversation.

Have you heard it? He has received a letter from Matte-Gok! He expects him home from South America in April! Yes, it is true, he has announced it himself in Ydun, and Mrs. Nillegaard has confirmed it, he's arriving with the *Mjölner* on the eleventh of April!

Thank God! Thank God! people would sigh, and they smiled and shed tears, and the number of Ankersen's followers rose, the assembly hall of the Ydun Society became crowded, every one had to go there to see the savings-bank manager—he was, as never before, the man of the hour.

Even Ankersen's bitterest enemies felt it best to keep quiet, or at least to get out of his way for the time being. "Yes, let's just see now," editor Jacobsen said. "Let us see how it will end. Let us have a closer look at this prodigal son. I remember the rascal well."

"Oh, yes?" said Captain Öström and with every sign of enjoyment opened a bottle of port wine.

"Yes, I remember him quite well," the editor repeated.

151

"A no-good fellow. A miserable lout. His nose always dripping."

Captain Öström looked a bit disappointed. He had been prepared for something really sensational. "Skoal," he said, rubbing his little waxed and bristling mustache.

The editor felt a great desire to say: "And he was a *thief*. That is why he went away." But it was probably best not to say anything and just wait. First, because he *was* the editor of *The Messenger*, which politically was a very liberal newspaper, one of whose tasks was not to attack people of the lower classes. Secondly—h'm. As a young man he had himself known Ura on the Cliff, the mother of the rascal. And suppose it was neither Ankersen, as he himself claimed, nor the old Consul Hansen, as rumor would have it, who was the father of this Matte-Gok?

The editor emptied his glass and, in order not to disappoint Öström, began to talk about Ura. For Öström was not born or raised in the town; he was a new arrival and originally Swedish, and he had not known Ura on the Cliff in his youth.

"Ura comes from a very fine family," Jacobsen informed him.

"I'll be damned!" Öström said, brightening up.

"Ura is as a matter of fact the daughter of old Trade Commissioner Trampe, and it would be ridiculous to assert that he did not belong to an illustrious family," the editor explained in a low voice. "And *her* mother, on the other hand, was the daughter of Commander Zenthner-Wättermann himself!"

"The devil take me!" Öström laughed. He laughed loud and long, ending with a chuckling cough.

"One could see it on the girl, when she was young," Jacobsen continued, "she looked *distinguished*, that she did, slender and agile as a. . ."

"A jellied eel?" Öström suggested and suffered another attack of his chuckling cough.

"Exactly!" Jacobsen said. "Devilishly seductive she was, no one could resist her, and she set her cap at people in exclusive circles, yes, she adhered to a certain high standard. There was nothing there for admirers of the Ole Brandy type! Yes, even the rose-painter Pontus, who also is the son of old Trampe. . ."

"But then—then he is her half-brother!" Öström said with a cough and weakly raised his glass.

"That's right, but I am telling you that there was nothing there for him!" Jacobsen said and slightly averted his face in order to get out of the way of the shower from the captain's coughing laughter, now seeming to approach the stage of a serious spasm . . . the big man's eyes had a glassy, rigid look as if they were crying for help—he resembled a drowning man who was struggling against a huge breaker.

"Well, well . . . . in that case this Matte-Gok is a man with the finest pedigree!" he summed up, completely exhausted.

"Yes, he is, dammit all," the editor confirmed absent-mindedly.

"And then there is this heart-rending aspect to it all," said apothecary Fähse, rising from the bridge table to proffer every one another cigar. "There is this heart-rending aspect to the matter, that this Matte-Gok is not Ankersen's son at all. Not so at all. And not of old Consul Hansen either, as some people think."

He ducked his head a bit and lowered his voice: "No, the whole thing is much more serious and complicated, for his progenitor was none less than old Royal Trade Commissioner Trampe!"

"Come now!" said Mr. Berg, the school principal, who was in high spirits. "If that is so, won't that make him the son of his grandfather? Or how else can you explain it?"

Bailiff Kronfeldt and Springer, the provincial secretary,

both had an expression of open-mouthed watchfulness. The pharmacist nodded affirmatively and with a long sniff. He added, in a regretful tone: "The old libertine was over seventy at that time."

"Oh, don't you ever believe it!" Janniksen the blacksmith playfully punched dancing instructor Lindenskov in the stomach. "By God, he is neither the son of Ankersen nor old Bastian nor attorney Wenningstedt, no one knows that better than I, for Ura has told me herself! Of course, she hated to admit it, but I tickled her until she was half dead, until she had to give in! No, you see, you old gossip: they were no less than seven of them involved, but it was apothecary Fähse, though, who nailed the pigeon to the tree!"

Then the great day dawns.

It is a busy Saturday, but every one seems to have taken off from work; there is a large crowd on the pier, and faces may be seen in the windows of all the adjacent houses— some people have even climbed up on the rooftops.

In apothecary Fähse's large and stately home fronting on the harbor, all the windows have been opened wide, and one can make out the faces of various notables inside, such as Count Oldendorp, the young Consul Hansens, Berg the school principal, the Kronfeldts, even the Manicuses. There is a large crowd in the Bastille also, and blacksmith Janniksen and master painter Mac Bett are actually coming to blows about using Magister Mortensen's telescope in the tower. As for Mortensen, he has, according to Atlanta, gone out for a walk. That sourface doesn't even want to stay home and use his wonderful telescope on a great day like this.

Ole Brandy's boat has stationed itself next to the place of disembarkation; in it editor Jacobsen and Captain Öström have reserved for themselves the best seats in the whole assembly, verily the first row in the orchestra, and Ole Brandy and Olivarius Sailmaker, who is at the oars, keep the other boats away with their angry glances and shouts, one of these boats being the one in which editor Olsen of *The News* is seated with his camera.

Now everything is ready. The curtain has gone up. The performance can begin.

Ankersen stands by himself, he has wiped his glasses and puts them back on his nose, adjusts his clothing, pushes his cuffs up into his sleeves, lets his stick dangle from one wrist, folds his hands, lifts his head, snorts solemnly, puts on a serious and reserved expression, he is really a good-looking man, having grayed with dignity, not at all unlike Gambetta, and there is also something about him that reminds one of Henrik Ibsen. A person of note. An idealist, who is stopped by neither fire nor water when he believes in something, never fearing to make himself look ridiculous in the eyes of the common people as long as it is for the good cause.

Who else could face a situation like this so to speak without flinching? A mighty wave of sympathy engulfs Ankersen as he stands there, waiting for his lost son, whom he has called home from lean and miserable years abroad. One forgets about the centaur, forgets his excesses and the roaring madman. Something unusual is about to happen, something great, something that will purify the mind.

And the great moment has come. The ferryboat comes alongside, and the passengers get up and walk ashore—it is deathly quiet, every one holds his breath. There are no less than three young men on board, besides a few ladies and one older man. Two of the young men are nicely dressed, one is small, the other one is big, they are dressed in checked ulsters, the big one wears a derby, has a beard and uses a pince-nez; the little one is thin and with red, blotchy skin. They are immediately identified as being commercial assistant Egholm and post-office clerk Hjort. Then there is the third

155

one, he also has got up from his seat, but then he sits down again—or falls . . . yes, it looked as if he fell, he certainly fell, and he is lying in an awkward slanting position across the thwart. The ferryman helps the ladies and the old man ashore, then he waves to Ankersen and walks over to the fallen man and shakes him, shouting something or other at him to make him sit up.

And suddenly the stranger comes to life, he swings his arms and crawls ashore. Yes, crawls! He crawls over to Ankersen and puts his arms around one of his legs.

It is *he*, Matte-Gok, the prodigal son. He is very evidently drunk to the gills. A compassionate and subdued murmur is heard throughout the assembled populace. The suspense becomes almost unbearable. The insolent lout has made Ankersen topple over! No, that wasn't exactly it either. Ankersen had just bent down, sat on his haunches, and took his son's head in his hands.

And now comes Little Kornelius and helps him get the drunken man to his feet. Ankersen and Kornelius each grab an arm. A wide avenue opens up in front of them. Many of the male spectators doff their hats and caps, as if they were attending a funeral. The Wailing Woman and others among the women are weeping. Matte-Gok is bareheaded, and his blue suit is full of mud. Good God, the way he looks! His jacket is rumpled and soiled, his patched trousers are frayed at the cuffs, the heel of one shoe is coming loose—yes, he does look like what he indeed is: a lost and miserable sinner!

Ankersen has left his stick by the gangway, but Mrs. Nillegaard, the midwife, walks over and picks it up. She is red-eyed from weeping and is holding a handkerchief pressed against her mouth and nose. A few young people can't help laughing at her. But suddenly she removes the handkerchief, raises her swollen face and shouts in a piercing voice: "It was a *great thing!* It could not have been greater!"

"Great! Great!" she repeats as if in ecstasy, and with the

156

stick lifted high she hurries up the street and joins Ankersen. Her husband, adjunct teacher Nillegaard, follows her a bit hesitantly.

Everything had been made ready for his son's reception in Ankersen's spartan but well-kept little house in the new section of town. Mrs. Midiord, his old housekeeper, was standing in the doorway, dressed in black with a white fancy apron and cap. The pungent aroma of fried potatoes emanated from the kitchen. Matte-Gok was placed in a velvet-upholstered rocking chair. He sank back in the chair, with his eyes closed and with a weak smile on his lips.

"Just let him sit like that a while," Ankersen said in a low voice, "and he'll be his old self again. And you others—you too sit down, my dear friends, you too, Kornelius, if you wish. Then you will have a bit of veal with us."

But teacher Nillegaard, unfortunately, could not stay, he had to go to a teachers' meeting, and a little later the midwife was urgently sent for. Kornelius was considering whether he too ought to leave. But he decided to stay. He felt it in a way to be his duty, for he was a kind of brother-in-law of Matte-Gok's.

Ankersen paced the floor with his hands on his back. He felt elated and happy, it seemed. Matte-Gok sat with his eyes closed. Kornelius looked at him closely. Matte-Gok was a tall, muscular fellow with a prominent nose and chin. He looked weatherbeaten and fit, but he had not shaved for some time. Down along his left cheek he had a long white scar. His reddish hair was mussed up, but aside from that he had a fine head of hair. There were blue and red tattoos on the backs of his hairy hands. Matte-Gok was a lean and well-built, fine-looking young fellow, about thirty years old. "Actually, he doesn't look very prodigal at all," Kornelius thought, "yes, indeed, he looks almost sober now. . ."

At last he opened his eyes and looked about him with an

air of wonder and amazement. Ankersen places himself right in front of him. He stands there with his stomach jutting out and with his thumbs in the armholes of his vest. A satisfied, kindly, downright enamored smile plays in his beard. He resembles his own self playing the role of Father Christmas.

"Well?" he says encouragingly. "Do you feel better now?"

Matte-Gok looks at him as if he is terrified by something and clutches the armrest of his chair.

"Where—where am I?" he groans.

"You're with your father!" Ankersen says with great warmth, nodding his head.

Kornelius has to turn away in order to hide his emotion. A scene like that is just too much for him. He hears Matte-Gok beg for forgiveness, and Ankersen responds with prayers and passages from Holy Scripture. It takes a long time. Kornelius feels so strangely superfluous and is conscious of the fact that he has no father. Dimly, very dimly, he can recall his own father . . . two sad eyes, a humble, stubbly chin.

Once more Kornelius was about to be overcome by emotion and tearfulness; he tried to brace himself by staring intensely at the smooth-looking, white kitchen door. It had not been completely shut to, and in the chink he caught a glimpse of the watchful eyes of the old housekeeper.

The attentive reader will probably already now harbor a certain suspicion that Matte-Gok was not the prodigal son that he pretended to be, but was a swindler and a cheat with a considerable dramatic talent. It is in no way a pleasant task to recount the dirty tricks that this monster succeeded in perpetrating in the ensuing time, to the irreparable harm to other people.

The only thing one might say in the defense of Matte-Gok is that his progenitors had been no good, neither on the maternal nor the paternal side of the family. Neither the coarse and fiercely energetic Consul Sebastian Hansen nor the cheating and bigoted Royal Trade Commissioner Trampe, any more than the farcically pompous and martially hot-headed Commander Zenthner-Wättermann could have claimed to be blameless in this respect, if they had still been alive.

It is perhaps possible that the undoubted ability of Mathias Georg Anthoniussen would have come to fruition in another and more widely recognized direction if he had grown up in more favorable circumstances. Who knows? A smart and audacious businessman, an outstanding attorney or diplomat was perhaps lost to the world when Ura on the Cliff's dissolute son left home at the age of seventeen and entered upon the motley and checkered career of a vaga-bond.

Now, however, Matte-Gok has returned to his point of departure and shows himself to be a seemingly guileless young man, friendly, with courteous mien and modest behavior, pious and repentant, yes, there is actually something poignant about his whole appearance. Matte-Gok is in reality a good-looking young man with pleasant features, with a Roman nose and a cleft chin, he resembles to a very high degree his great-grandfather the Commander. And he very ably plays the role of the son who had been lost and found again; and he very effortlessly becomes a member of the Ydun Society, just slowly and reluctantly enough, but one evening he has permitted himself to be fired with emotion, to get down on his knees and with much loud sobbing he has confessed his sins and his past lack of faith.

And now he becomes—all according to his dastardly plan —a staunch pillar of support for the simple-minded people belonging to the Christian temperance society. He tells, simply and unostentatiously, and without placing himself in the foreground, about the wild life in the strange jungles of America, where idol worship is still rampant among the uneducated populace and murder and robbery are the order of the day, and also about the self-sacrificing and hazardous work done by tireless missionaries in conducting revival meetings among crocodiles and other poisonous vermin.

Matte-Gok's fame spread quickly and in wide circles, and there would often be a veritable crush of people at the evening meetings of the Ydun Society.

This last was not solely due to Matte-Gok, however. We are now on the whole approaching that curiously fateful time when savings-bank manager Ankersen and his comrades in arms could in earnest feel that they were making progress and could dimly see the realization of the great goal of their lives: total prohibition. It was a time of pamphlets, of mass meetings, and newspaper debates, and Ankersen gained at this time a whole flock of new adherents among so to speak all classes of the population. Ankersen eventually became a kind of symbol of unity for all right-thinking people, and the general public also began to be aware of the dangers that one would be exposed to if one tried to put a spoke in the wheels of his onrushing triumphal chariot.

For Jacobsen, the editor of *The Messenger,* things could not have gone worse. First, he became the defendant in legal proceedings because he had permitted himself in an editorial to cast doubt on Ankersen's motives and had called the savings-bank manager an unscrupulous and vain tyrant, who completely trod all human dignity underfoot and with the aid of boorish methods even attempted to obstruct the exercise of the freedom of the individual.

Despite these unfair remarks, Ankersen was instrumental in obtaining for Jacobsen an amicable settlement of the case if he wanted it, but when the editor refused to come down from his high horse and take back the word "boorish," and his newspaper at the very same time printed another editorial with the provocative title "Religious Rowdies Riot," his fate was sealed. He was sentenced to pay a fine, which he thereupon flatly refused to pay, and he therefore had to serve time. Because of this *The Messenger*, too, suffered an irreparable blow; its subscribers fell away, first one by one, but later in droves, and then one day the newspaper ceased publication.

However, it was not very long before *The Messenger* was resurrected in just about the same format and appearance as before, but on the inside it had been changed and was completely unrecognizable, and Ankersen was the editor. The Ydun Society had simply purchased the newspaper and made it into its own mouthpiece.

Yes, Ankersen had indeed brought home another victory, one that really sparkled. It is understandable that editor Jacobsen's towering rage knew no limits. The old man forced his way into his former composing room and, using the walking stick, he destroyed with his own hands an entire edition of the new paper.

During the wild scuffle that took place in connection with this outrage, a curious thing happened, namely, that Kornelius took Jacobsen's side, the consequences being that the young typesetter immediately was dismissed from his job with the newspaper. When he later was to explain his strange behavior to the court, he merely sighed and said: "Well, I don't know, but I really felt so sorry for Jacobsen."

This remark was the cause of unrestrained hilarity in the court and later became a byword in the town.

CHAPTER 10

Kornelius is taunted by Ole Brandy for his treasure seeking, but he is supported by Matte-Gok

Kornelius had no regrets, however, when he said farewell forever to the little dark and unhealthy composing room with its drab atmosphere, its dirty hands, and niggling work. He could always busy himself with his gardening, and in addition there was his music; it would always provide him with some extra change; for some time he had given music lessons to a few of Boman's former pupils, and that activity might possibly be expanded. In addition to that there were the evening dances.

And then, finally, there was the great project. He was constantly thinking of it, and because of it he enjoyed many sweet hours of quiet ecstasy. But not at all times did it force itself upon him and make itself insistent. Sometimes it was felt merely as a faint longing. But it *was* there always, and at times it would flare up tremendously and make him hot and sleepless. It was a good thing to have around, and it would perhaps turn into something even better, it might become big and unmanageable and turn everything topsy-turvy. And now that the foolish drudgery at the type cases was over for good, one might really get down to more important things and concentrate on one's own plans and speculations.

He had never, of course, been able to buy that diving gear

—that alternative had to be left out of account. But one might be able to get along with less expensive methods, if one were sufficiently inventive, persistent, and patient.

One might, for instance, use a weight or some other heavy object, which then would be fastened to a line. With the aid of a so-called sounding lead one might possibly be able to follow the sounds, if one were to let the lead drag along, just touching the bottom, at least if one had the right ear for it. Such an attempt requires one boat and two men, with one of the men rowing, while the other one watches the lead line and listens. The Crab King knew how to row. The work has to be done at night and when the weather is so calm and quiet that every sound can be distinctly heard. An ordinary piece of rock will produce a certain sound, which one will get to know and recognize after a while. A copper chest, on the other hand, will produce a sound of its own, a sound that is not to be mistaken.

When the spot has been found, one throws out a small buoy. So far everything is easy. But the next step in this endeavor must be carried out in daylight: one has to peer down and try to see something. Well and good, it is possible to do that, and one can distinguish the outline of a square, rusty object. Then one has to fish it up, and that is undeniably going to be the most difficult part of the job. Here one will need expert assistance, it can't be done with the help of only the Crab King. But then there are fellows about like Moritz and Ole Brandy. Of those two Kornelius prefers Ole, for the reason that the whole thing should rather come as a pleasant surprise to Moritz; he and Sirius are not to suspect anything until it all has come true.

If he could get Ole Brandy interested in this, he would have come a long way.

"No."

Ole Brandy is not interested at all.

"No, no, I'm not going to fall for that one, Kornelius!" he says, brushing the matter aside, and adding somewhat uneasily: "And I would never have believed such a thing about you. I thought you were a real friend of mine."

"But that I certainly am!" says Kornelius, taken aback.

Ole turns his face away, munching on something. "Well, it's possible," he admits at last. "But then there is some one or other who's playing a trick on you and also wants to tempt me to join in. But he will be disappointed."

Kornelius says with a broad smile: "No, no, Ole, believe me! It's me, I'm the only one who's thought it up!"

Ole Brandy fills his pipe and grunts disapprovingly. Finally, he turns toward Kornelius, punches him playfully in the stomach, and says: "Well, that may be so, Kornelius. For it's all the same to me. But what you're talking about, just between us, is nothing but old women's prattle. For even though that chest existed some time ago, it just isn't there any more. It was eaten up by the fishes and the vermin long ago."

Kornelius is about to remonstrate but Ole cuts him off impatiently: "You are going to tell me that fishes can't eat through copper? Well, if you do, it is just because you are nothing but a landlubber and don't know anything about the sea and the accursed living things in it. Doesn't a catfish have good teeth? Don't you give me that nonsense, but just answer this one: doesn't a catfish have stronger teeth than both you and me? Well, there you see. And I only mentioned the catfish, which is one of the more gentle creatures in the sea. What do you say about sting-rays? And what about sharks? Don't tell me! And have you never seen a ship-worm?"

"Yes, but that eats only poles and ship's timbers!" Kornelius objects with a tinge of timid hope in his voice.

On that point Ole Brandy must admit that he is right. But then he starts in again from another direction: "That

164

may be well and good, Kornelius, but then you are not acquainted with the *power of the ocean*. Isn't the surf able to fling an entire ship up on shore and slice it into sawdust? Well! No, my fine-feathered friend, the ocean, which can grind even the largest rock down to a round boulder even smaller than one of the cheeks of your own rump, such an ocean will be sure to take good care of a miserable treasure box, of that you can be sure!"

"Yes, perhaps it will," Kornelius has to admit. He takes his pince-nez off his nose and succumbs to his gloom and his brooding. "Well, if you say so, Ole, you know the sea."

But then he suddenly thinks of Ura. Ura is never wrong. She has said that the treasure *is* there. That it is lying in a moist spot. And she sticks to what she said. Of course, this moist spot . . . strictly speaking, it doesn't necessarily have to be the Commandant's Hollow. There are other moist spots. That's for sure.

He gets up, his face all flushed; "Very well, Ole. I'm going to think over what you said. And then we can discuss it again later on."

"Yes, do think about it, Kornelius," Ole says in a fatherly manner. "And then just forget about the whole thing and don't make yourself look ridiculous. I once knew a man who thought that he could spin a golden thread from the red matter in a common mussel! And I tell you that man ended his days as a good-for-nothing who went around doing foolish things and ended up a nobody. And otherwise he was a very gifted fellow. But if one sets out on such a course, instead of using one's brains and perceiving God's own nature as it is revealed to a right-thinking human being. . . !"

"Yes, of course," Kornelius nodded in assent, with a contrite air.

He was not at all convinced, however. Far from it. But it was clear to him that Ole was the wrong man to be asked to join him in this venture.

165

But this is how strange the turn of events may be; Kornelius's unsuccessful attempt to get Ole Brandy involved was not to be a fruitless one after all, but only after some curious detours.

One afternoon Ole is having a chat with Matte-Gok. Matte-Gok is always busy talking to some one or other, there are so many old acquaintanceships to be renewed, and he is in general very well liked. And now he has run into Ole Brandy; as a boy he had collected mussels for him and at times he had fished with him in his rowboat. Kornelius happens to pass by, and Ole greets him and says: "Look, there goes the treasure hunter!"

Kornelius turns red and brushes aside the allegation and is almost in tears because he is cruelly disappointed that Ole so suddenly has made him the butt of a joke.

Ole's remark, however, does not seem to have made any impression on Matte-Gok, thank God. He seems to think that it is just the usual banter that the old man indulges in. And he does not ask what treasure hunt he was alluding to. The conversation turns to digging for gold in general.

"You ask what one should do to find out whether there is gold hidden in the earth?" Matte-Gok says. "That is really an easy matter: you just get hold of a divining rod. It only needs to be a regular twig, shaped like a fork. But you see, Ole, it is not every Tom, Dick, and Harry that has the ability to use it. We were tested, in several groups, many hundreds of us! And then they found out to my great surprise, that *I* have the gift! And I'm telling you they made good use of me, Ole! I didn't even have to lift a finger on the job, so to speak, but nevertheless I got my generous share as a finder of the gold. Yes, those were the days!"

"But why didn't you stay where you were then, when you had it so good?" Ole asks brusquely.

Matte-Gok does not answer him immediately. He stares right in front of him with a remorseful expression and for a moment he looks both sad and tired.

166

"I couldn't take my good fortune," he answers at last. "I fell in with bad company, I turned to drinking and gambling and bad women, sank deeper and deeper in the mire, and if I hadn't. . ."

Ole Brandy suddenly begins to laugh derisively and spitefully, turns his back on Matte-Gok and knocks the ashes out of his pipe. "You're a darn liar, Matte-Gok!" he says. "From beginning to end, the divining rod and everything! Don't you come here and tell me stuff like that!"

Matte-Gok and Kornelius exchange glances, the meaning of which is just about this: "Ole Brandy, yes, he knows how to use his tongue, everyone knows that."

Matte-Gok does not look surprised, much less insulted, he is merely full of kindly indulgence. Ole Brandy punches him playfully in the stomach and says in a conciliatory manner: "But you may have been a gold digger just the same! And a pall-bearer! And a bootblack for the queen of Brazil! But what you're saying about that twig, that I won't swallow."

He lights up his pipe and ambles along the pier, excitedly puffing on his pipe. His earrings flash gaily in the afternoon sunlight.

Matte-Gok regards Kornelius steadily with a friendly expression and says: "But what I said about the divining rod, that *is* the honest truth. Ole won't believe it because he is an old liar and teller of tall tales."

"Yes, that he certainly is!" Kornelius agrees with a smile.

"But what was it that he said about you?" Matte-Gok continued, with a yawn. "Are you searching for a treasure, Kornelius?"

Kornelius blushes and looks down. The question has taken him so completely by surprise. What should he answer? Should he just brush it away as stuff and nonsense? Or—oughtn't he rather confide in Matte-Gok and hear more about his divining rod?

He grasps Matte-Gok by the arm and says in a low voice: "Can you keep a secret, Matte-Gok?"

167

"Yes, of course, Kornelius!" Matte-Gok replies. "You know me."

Thus begins this shameful affair. Kornelius relates and Matte-Gok listens. He doesn't seem too eager, or to think this is something completely unheard of. On the contrary, he nods absentmindedly, he has of course heard the story about the lost treasure, but he is not tremendously interested in it. But that, of course, is no more than what one might have expected when such a widely traveled and experienced man is concerned. Kornelius feels downright ashamed that he has shown himself to be so eager.

"Of course . . . looking at it that way," he stammers forth, "it is clear to me that even if . . . that he who finds the treasure . . . that he can't just go ahead and keep it for himself, but will have to . . . to give it up and be satisfied with the finder's reward?"

Matte-Gok shakes his head and says: "There you're wrong, Kornelius. The treasure belongs to the one who digs it up. No power on this earth can wrest it from him, neither by force nor by legal means."

Matte-Gok hides a slight yawn and looks at his watch: "Oh dear! I should have been in the Ydun Society at seven o'clock!"

He pats Kornelius on the back: "But it would be interesting to try the divining rod, you know. It's such a long time since I used it. I wonder if I'm still able to do it. But why don't we meet again tomorrow night and talk some more about it?"

To that they agree. Matte-Gok hurries on his way. Kornelius remains standing on the pier. He feels so strangely bewildered, but a feeling of sweet suspense seethes within him. At last, at last! But one mustn't rejoice ahead of time. Things may still go wrong. But to give up? Never.

The next evening.

At first Matte-Gok merely fiddles with the divining rod, which they have gotten from the blacksmith's garden. He

168

pretends that he has forgotten the art or has permanently lost his wondrous talent. But there is something there after all . . . yes, by heaven. It quivers and stirs, just as it did in times past when there was gold near by.

"It looks promising, Kornelius!"

The twig points in a northeasterly direction. They walk in that direction, while anxiously observing the movements of the forked twig. It is a cloudy, windy evening, with a greenish light above the horizon in the north. Several times it seems as if the divining rod is going to make the decisive downward motion, but nothing comes of it after all. Meanwhile, they continue walking out of town in a northeasterly direction.

"You see, Kornelius, we'll soon be at the spot, no mistake about that! Here, way up in the fields, is where the old scoundrel buried his treasure. Of course! Don't you think so, too?"

"Yes, of course," Kornelius agrees.

"The old smithy is around here some place," says Matte-Gok.

"No, it isn't here any more," Kornelius informs him, "it was blown down, there is only some rubble left of it."

"Look, now it's not telling us anything. Let's go back a bit," Matte-Gok sighs. It sounds as if he has become tired and might even think of giving up the whole search.

"It's strenuous work." He smiles. "It drains away one's brainpower."

But suddenly the divining rod becomes frisky as never before, and Matte-Gok is about to swear out loud: "I'll be. . . ! Look here, Kornelius!"

Kornelius's heart starts pounding violently.

They have come to an isolated, marshy and moss-green spot, not far from the tumble-down smith.

This is it. This is the place. The divining rod points straight down and can't be budged.

"This is a very strange thing!" says Matte-Gok. "I was

always of the opinion, just between you and me, that the story of the treasure . . . yes, that perhaps it was nothing more than a pack of lies. But. . . ! Well . . . above all, take it easy, Kornelius! You understand? And don't say a word about it to any one! Do you agree to that?"

"Of course," Kornelius says. He has started to tremble all over.

"Hey, what was that?"

"What was what?"

Matte-Gok stands still and listens for a moment: "No, perhaps it was nothing. But I thought I heard something rustling over by the ruins. I hope there's no one lurking about and watching us."

They walk up to the ruins of the smithy. But they notice nothing unusual.

"Tell me, you're not afraid of ghosts and all that?" Matte-Gok asks jokingly.

"Not a bit," Kornelius stutters forth. "I never have been!"

"You can be glad you aren't. I myself am awfully scared in the dark. It's all a lot of nonsense, isn't it?"

Matte-Gok nudges Kornelius in the ribs as if they were great chums: "But . . . no, I just can't get over my great surprise over actually finding your treasure! That is really something! You are indeed a lucky dog! But, as we've said, we'll take things easy. We'll sleep on it for a while. I have to think this through. We've won the first battle, but there's still a lot of fuss and details to be taken care of. We must be very careful not to spoil it for ourselves."

They set out on the way home. Kornelius walks in such a strange way, as if he is in a daze. His feeling of suspense seems to have left him completely, yes, he feels so strangely cold and listless, as if the whole thing did not concern him any longer. He can hear Matte-Gok continue talking about other treasures that he has helped to detect and dig up. And so on and on. From it all Kornelius gets a strange feeling as if he were about to choke.

"You're so silent, Kornelius?"

"That's because I'm thinking about something. And do you know what it is?"

"No."

Kornelius sighs: "Yes, you see, I can't help thinking that . . . that actually I'm not the one entitled to the treasure."

Kornelius continues: "Because it is not buried in land that belongs to me, but in a piece of property belonging to some one else. That's one thing. Then there's the fact that it was you and not me that have found it. So, in a way, it belongs to you and not to me."

"Oh nonsense," Matte-Gok says, laughing. "I don't need the money. And besides, the treasure belongs to the one who digs it up. Every treasure hunter knows that."

"Do you mean that?"

"Yes, of course. No one knows that better than I. You just dig it up, Kornelius. All by yourself. I don't have to come along at all. So don't walk around spoiling everything for yourself with such silly ideas. Think of everything you can do with the money. Good heavens! Think of it, Kornelius!"

"Yes, of course." Kornelius smiles. "I haven't thought of anything else in several years. But—I have to offer you my most heartfelt thanks, Matte-Gok. For without your help. . ."

"Oh, tommyrot, that's nothing to thank me for. It was only fun to see that I haven't lost my old skill. But before you start digging, there are a number of small details. For example, there has to be a new moon, of course. And the day of the month is also of some significance. You must not do it tomorrow and not the day after tomorrow either. Best not to do anything this whole week, Kornelius. Perhaps not even this month. It is not dark enough. But on the other hand, it need not be pitch dark. Only an impenetrable twilight. And then there is that matter about the stars."

"The stars?"

"Yes, the planets, of course. I have to get hold of an

171

almanac and find out what position they are in. For it is a very old treasure, isn't it?"

Matte-Gok laughs, a jovial and friendly little laugh. "This is a damned interesting thing, isn't it? And to experience it here, in this god-forsaken neck of the woods!"

Suddenly Kornelius feels like laughing, too. They both laugh, each one inwardly taking a special pleasure from it.

"Yes, this is really great fun," Matte-Gok says, nudging Kornelius in the ribs. "The powers on high have helped us. Do you know what I think? I think that God has selected you to be the man to find this treasure. You and none other. And do you know why? Because you have sort of been wishing it. If a man goes around and wishes something for a long time, it is then granted him. You *have* been praying that you would succeed, I suppose?"

Yes, Kornelius has to admit that.

"You see. And then He sent me along to you. Yes, the whole time I felt something like that. God has blessed our undertaking. And let us not neglect to thank Him. But now we'll go back to town, and we must above all keep quiet about it. And we won't discuss it between us until the time comes. And it is important that we purify ourselves and prepare ourselves."

"How do we prepare ourselves?"

Matte-Gok gives Kornelius a warm and firm handshake: "By rejoicing and by being humble! Well, goodnight, my friend, and sleep well. But what's this, Kornelius—are you crying?"

"It feels so strange, all of it," Kornelius stammers forth. "I certainly had not imagined that it would be like this. Everything is just too overwhelming."

"That is a good sign." Matte-Gok sounds as if he is deeply moved. "I mean that you cried! Secretly I had been hoping that you would. It is the very best that could have happened. Now I know for sure that you are the right man!"

172

Kornelius walks home slowly. He is overwhelmed and doesn't seem able to get back on an even keel again. After his evening tea he just sits there as if in a reverie. If he should become a rich man, what then? It is almost too good to be true. Among other things, he will get himself a new, fine cello. He catches himself thinking that he really had had a nice life when he was still working at *The Messenger* and every evening came home tired and hungry, washed and sat down to his meal and played a little for Kornelia and then went to bed and slept like a log. New times are coming—new and strange times.

Kornelia comes over and nestles up to him, sits down gently in his lap and grasps his hand. He squeezes her hand in return, but finds himself being annoyed with the fact that this woman never says a word—as if she were not only blind but deaf and dumb, too. Only these silent childish handclasps. And then this crazy fear every time he wants to hold her in his arms—as if she were not a girl of more than twenty but a child of twelve. Perhaps she never will grow up, perhaps for the rest of her life she will be like a daughter instead of a wife. But immediately he is sorry for having had such thoughts, and kisses her on the cheek. "My very own Kornelia!" he says, with a feeling of remorse.

"Play a little!" she whispers in his ear.

Kornelius gets out his cello. Kornelia sits down on the footstool over by the stove and with lips parted she is thrilled to the point of trembling when he begins to tune the instrument. He has always thought that she looks so sweet when she feels that way. But tonight he does not like seeing her sit like that, shivering and blushing and looking pretty. "It *is* a bit hard to take," he thinks, and he is almost on the verge of tears thinking about it, "it is a bit hard to take—that it is the cello she loves, and not *me*. . .!"

CHAPTER 11

*Magister Mortensen receives an unexpected letter, and for a
while he loses his head completely*

Magister Mortensen's great philosophical work deals not only
with Satan, of course, but also with God: with God as the
principle of goodness in the soul, in human life, in the life
of society, in history. With the way in which this principle
of goodness is ever being adopted by the petty, the smug,
and the wicked, who in the name of religion and brotherly
love feather their own dirty and blood-stained nests of
vanity and ambition. With the way the church and its
careerists and hangers-on down through the ages have tam-
pered with and desecrated and even now neglect and besmirch the very core of Christianity—while at the same time,
plain goodness, honesty, the spirit of self-sacrifice, and
neighborly love are practiced anonymously every blessed
day by human beings—not with any thought of heavenly
profit in the hereafter, but as the most natural and guileless
thing in the world. Every day one encounters veritable gems
of whose existence one perhaps might have been unaware
if a truly benign fortune hadn't dashed one down from the
pompous and self-important pedestals of barren theological
speculations.

Magister Mortensen has been writing all morning and has
felt himself to be in fine form, but now, when he reads
through what he has written—great, merciful God: it is

174

not as good as he had believed it was, it adds up to nothing at all. As usual, he has just been sitting there paddling with a teaspoon in a great ocean!

He gets up, greatly discouraged and full of self-contempt, and with a sigh walks over to the window. It is all dust, dust, and words, words, compared with life, everyday life, which may be gray but nevertheless secretly sparkles like diamonds because of its *action*. True Christianity is not written words, but action. Jesus Christ—did he sit down to write? No, but that was what that monstrous apostle Paul did—the first of the great swindlers!

But hell and damnation! As soon as one decides to act in the true Christian spirit, one plunges right into all that which one wanted to avoid: pettiness, egotism, thirst for revenge, brutality—usually well disguised by Satan behind beautiful phrases. . .

Outside, the sun is shining, the roosters crow from the squalid turf roofs of Skin Islet, and wherever there is a bare spot in all the greenery, a hen will be burrowing into the dry earth as if seized by a sudden insane desire. Just like theologians burrowing in the philosophy of religion in order to rid themselves of their fleas, their conscience!

Damn it all, now who's that coming over there but attorney Wenningstedt, the owner of the building, the landlord. He's coming here, the old swine! "Yes, just let him come," Mortensen says to himself, savagely, "that vulture, that blathermouth, that erotic snooper!"

Magister Mortensen was boiling inside, and it took a while before he succeeded in taking on a fairly pleasant expression. Devil take it! It wouldn't do to be obstinate when one owed the fellow seventy-five crowns and didn't have any idea where they were going to come from.

Mortensen assumed an air of expectancy and stubbornness. Unfortunately, he didn't have the money and would have to ask for another extension.

"Gladly," said Wenningstedt. "Provided we can agree on a certain deadline. Or, if it should so happen that you have something or other that you might want to sell, I shall be glad to be at your service."

Attorney Wenningstedt's face was characterized by joviality and reserve, his thin ears were sticking out and wiggling attentively like a dog's. He took his own good time, he hummed, he tapped his fingers on the arm of his chair, spoke about the bad times and about how it was just impossible to collect the rents, especially here in the Bastille. Here was the ferryman, for instance, living in the big—indeed the rather exclusive—apartment in the basement—"Do you know, he owes me over a hundred crowns, and besides that he has a debt of another hundred down at grocer Siff's! He belongs to the category of impossible tenants, who always promise to turn over a new leaf but never, never keep their promises."

The attorney looked quickly at Magister Mortensen, bent his head forward a bit, and continued with a forced smile: "And then you don't feel like taking stronger measures against him, for he is such a charming fellow, not to speak of his wife. And you also have to bear in mind the beautiful music he plays. I love music. And then there is his brother up in the attic, the one who got married to the blind girl. He too is a splendid fellow, but he's impossible when it comes to money—since he lost his job in the printshop. So you understand, Magister Mortensen, compared with these two tenants that I've just mentioned, you are in a way heaven-sent, he-he, and I have no doubts that we shall be able to settle our little account."

The attorney peeked out through the window: "It really *is* a delightful place to live in, Magister Mortensen, isn't that so? Look, what a view! Here you're actually able to sit and—look at the stars, can't you? It's true what I've heard—that you do have a telescope?"

176

"It's only a common terrestrial telescope," Mortensen informed him.

"But it *is* stars that you are looking at, isn't that so?"

"Yes, it is stars." Mortensen looked up to the ceiling and drew a long breath.

"If it suits your convenience, Magister Mortensen—I would so very much like to take a look at such a huge contraption!" chuckled the attorney.

"Of course, that can be done."

The telescope was located up in the loft, in the "spire." They had to go through the kitchen to get up there, and Wenningstedt took the opportunity to regard Atlanta at close quarters. By Jove, she's quite young, he thought. What can such a spring chicken see in that elderly wreck of a good-for-nothing?

They ascended a ladder, and Magister Mortensen focused the telescope. A jumble of housetops, glimpses of the sea, blue, sun-dappled— yes, there was Seal Island, so sharp and so close that one could see the ducks and the chickens in the alleyways! If one turned the telescope a bit, one had a view of the sea and the inlet. Well and good. Wenningstedt turned it some more, and now the houses of the town that were close by came into view, and suddenly he looked right into an attic, in which a young woman was standing in her negligee, as far as he could see she was in nothing but her slip!

"Well, this is marvelous," he said, feeling a bit agitated. "It is hard to believe how close that island gets and how beautiful it is out there!"

"Yes, it is remarkable," Mortensen agreed in a tired voice.

"Yes, by heaven, that it is, it is unique, quite unique. A glorious sight. One gets—so close to nature. To eternity! It is really wonderful!"

"Would you be interested in taking a look at the moon?" Magister Mortensen asked, hiding a yawn.

177

"No, thank you!" The attorney laughed and made a deprecating gesture. He smiled politely: "The moon? In broad daylight?"

No jest had been intended, the moon was actually in the sky, Magister Mortensen turned the telescope a bit, and something blurred and foggy appeared within the field of vision.

"Well, well, there it is, isn't it?" Wenningstedt said with a smile, although he was furious and tried in vain to turn the telescope back in the direction of the attic window. "Astronomy, you see, I could never understand nor take an interest in. But old houses, on the other hand, I really appreciate—they are so to speak a hobby of mine. It is a wonderful thing, to my mind, that we're living in an old town, a town that is a thousand years old, and not in a—a mushroom..."

The sleepy, sad face of a child suddenly appeared in the stairway leading up to the attic—it must be that imbecile child! The attorney's eyes were popping out of his head.

"No, not this way, my dear!" Magister Mortensen said. Slowly the face disappeared. Well, she did not look so very imbecilic after all, that daughter of his. Wenningstedt had been imagining something along the lines of a grotesque cretin.

"Look here, in case you were to sell it, how much would you want for that telescope?" he asked.

Magister Mortensen's face took on a harassed but at the same time composed expression. The attorney cleared his throat and said: "I have another suggestion. What do you say to my renting the telescope for a shorter or longer time? Couldn't we arrange it so that in this way you paid off some of the money that I have coming to me?"

Yes, Mortensen also thought that that might be a good idea. They dickered about the price for a little while and made a bargain.

"Well, you understand," Wenningstedt said animatedly, "I really got enthused about this! I love, I dare say, the ocean, yes, I never get tired of observing nature and all the life that rustles about out there. And there's a good view from my house also. And perhaps it won't be long before I too will be mad about the stars in the sky. I understand you fully, Mortensen. For it is good for man to raise his sights and dwell on high, isn't that so, and escape the old grind for a while. . ."

The attorney stared straight ahead with a kindly look in his eyes.

Magister Mortensen lit his pipe. "Oh well, what the hell," he said and flicked the burnt-out match into a corner of the room. "It's how one looks at it, Wenningstedt. In reality, things are on the whole the same up there as down here. It is only that the distances are greater up there. The daily grind is about the same."

The attorney smiled, a bit bewildered, and Magister Mortensen continued while he blew peevish little clouds of smoke into the air: "Yes, this talk about the 'eternal stars' and so on, that is a romantic cliché. The stars are not eternal at all, they are born, they live and perish just like you and me, shuffle about for a time and make things difficult for one another and attack one another from behind and all kinds of monkey tricks—until they at last burn themselves out, and then the ball is over."

"Well, do you really think so?" Wenningstedt said with a little deprecatory laugh.

They climbed down the ladder.

Magister Mortensen went back to his desk. But he found it impossible to think of anything sensible, he felt too exhausted to do any more that day. Perhaps it would help to go for a walk. A short, stimulating walk in pleasant weather.

179

He put on his soiled old topcoat and filled his pipe. But in the stairway he met the mailman, who was waving a letter at him.

"A letter for me?" Magister Mortensen asked. "So help me God, that is something that seldom happens."

Quickly he opened the yellow envelope. Attorney Lauridsen, Ribe—who the devil is that? But this is unbelievable! Great God, what news!

He felt faint. For a moment he thought he was dreaming. He ran up the stairs. "Atlanta!" he shouted and did not recognize his own voice at all. Atlanta had not heard him. It was incredible! Holy Messiah!

Mortensen felt so deeply stirred and so confused that he felt nauseated and had to step into his bedroom and drink a glass of water. It was warm and tasted as if it had been standing a long time, he poured in a few drops of cognac, still he was on the point of throwing up. But it was not a nausea caused by sickness and sadness. It was caused by pure joy: it was as if it had a symbolical meaning. "It is— it is your entire past life that you feel a need to spit out," he said under his breath. He felt faint from transports of emotion.

"Vibeke!" he shouted, and the girl entered the room and looked at him questioningly, with head bent back and mouth open.

"Vibeke," whispered her father. He placed the child on the sofa and whispered in her ear: "Oh, Vibeke—we are *rich*—we are *rich*, Vibeke! You don't know what that is, poor little one. But you see—you see—!"

She stared at him with her sad, mist-filled eyes. He pressed the poor, sad head to his breast and kissed her on the forehead. Then he lay down on the sofa, being weak and drowsy with a dizzy feeling of humility. It was strange, though, how sleepy he felt! For a moment he actually struggled to keep awake. But then he suddenly jumped up, ran over to

180

his desk and seized the letter, read it through breathlessly, and began to perspire.

No, it wasn't a lie. Here he saw it in black and white, soberly and matter-of-factly written, that he had inherited one hundred and forty-six thousand crowns. His Uncle Andreas had died at last, at the age of ninety-two, and he was his sole heir.

"People can really get that old, then!" he said to himself in a loud voice and then he had to laugh at such a silly remark. "Of course, they can get to be both ninety-two and one hundred and eleven!" he continued in the same waggish vein. "I had actually given up the idea long ago that he would ever die!" he laughed. "I mean, that I would live longer than he."

"I want to play with my blocks!" Vibeke said.

"Oh, you want to play with your blocks?" her father said with a smile and rummaged around in search of the tin can containing the child's empty match boxes. "You will get new building blocks, Daddy will buy new and fine blocks, and a neighing horse and a rocking horse and—everything!"

"Just imagine, one hundred and forty-six thousand crowns!" he kept on, talking to himself. "And I thought it would be something like four thousand. And even a little bit like that I would have been mighty glad to get! But this here, this is quite ridiculous! Quite ridiculous!"

"Where are new fine blocks?" the girl asked plaintively.

Mortensen shook his head, chuckled, tears coming to his eyes. "What in blazes is there to laugh about?" he scolded himself. But he could not stop that hysterical laughter, it just happened, just like the nausea that had come over him earlier. He glanced nervously at the kitchen door.

"I don't suppose that I've gone crazy?" he thought, and for a moment everything went black. Once again he had to lie down on the sofa. No, no, that was stuff and nonsense, he was not crazy. He would like to see any one, any poor devil or tormented wretch, who in a situation like this would not lose his head completely!

But who would have thought that Uncle Andreas, that old scoundrel, was so rich! In his youth Andreas had been a farmer and later a plantation owner in America. In his fifties he had sold his holdings and had returned home, broken down by sickness, completely bent over from rheumatism, looking almost like a scythe. But he had been tough and tenacious just the same.

At one time certain rumors had been circulating to the effect that Uncle Andreas had an incredibly large fortune. But such rumors, of course, sprout quickly out in the countryside, where people have so few things to talk about. Well—there had been truth behind it after all!

For a brief moment Mortensen saw his uncle in his mind's eye, fully alive, as in a vision: the old man, his grandfather's brother, bent down as if pressed by an evil and weighty burden, with strained, sour, and piercing eyes in his white face. It was almost as if the old man had come to him in order to be remembered and to be fully appreciated. It was a funny thing. Mortensen once again suffered a brief attack of nausea and heaved a long sigh. He had never been able to stand the old fogey and his tight-lipped, pinched smile.

Well, enough of that.

Magister Mortensen made himself more comfortable on the sofa. He did not feel sleepy any longer at all. He merely felt weak. Weak and calm. He remained lying there with his eyes closed, and tried to collect his thoughts into a sensible pattern. But he just didn't succeed. His entire life passed in review before him. All of it was something that now was done with, something now to be said farewell to. Farewell and thanks.

His childhood in Jutland. The silent father, the timid, pietistic mother. His two brothers, both of whom had died young. Alas—it all seemed so distant and irrelevant, and

182

still it all pressed forward and somehow wanted to be remembered for the last time. It was a time filled with a dull longing to see the world and a hunger for something—for something *great*. The seminary, where he had attracted attention because of his superior aptitude for learning. The student years in Copenhagen, the period of near starvation while living at Regensen, the student dormitory. Religious crises. Kierkegaard. Theological studies, later given up as being a lot of rubbish. The first drunken binges and women. Music. Friends. Witty and brilliant company. Silly girls, whom one nevertheless could not leave alone.

Magdalena Herz—the magic sun of his youth! Ugh!

The final exams. The master's degree. More drinking, degradation, dissolution—following Magdalena's shameful infidelity. Black nights and misery and long and hungry days, full of the bright light of spring and of resounding emptiness. And an echo, a relentless, insane echo of Beethoven's Sonata, opus 31, no. 2, the "Midnight Sonata," as Magdalena and he had called it—the midnight sun with its bottomless abysses of passionate tenderness and boundless agony.

The flight! The long journey to the distant country, where in his desperation he had applied for a position as high-school teacher—in a small town where he had thought it might be possible to cultivate loneliness and philosophy and to regain his strength and write his philosophical treatise. My foot! A veritable hell of a school, a hellish small town! The malicious persecution that one was always exposed to as a "freethinker"! The clashes with principal Berg—this half-educated smatterer of knowledge, this stupid and pompous noncommissioned officer—which ended with the foolish fistfight in the school yard that was the cause of his having to resign his position.

Then there was good-hearted and always disheveled little Nikoline, the teacher who was his sole comfort during

183

those grotesque and ignominious days, and whom he married. More poverty, humiliation, soul-destroying private tutoring. The position as librarian that was given him as an act of charity. The cramped, destitute, and dank library with its everlasting smell of the oil stove. The death of Nikoline in childbirth. The sentimental and hectic worship of his daughter, and the terrible blow when she proved to be— to be—!

Well, now he was almost up to date.

No, far from it!

Long years full of suffering. Impetuous plans about once again fleeing it all. They foundered on a complete lack of money, as well as on—

Well, on what?

On Vibeke? Nonsense. The poor weakminded girl you could have taken along and have had her placed in some suitable institution. The treatise? Not that either. You could have puttered with that anywhere on earth. No, the reason must be sought much, much more deeply, my fine-feathered friend. In a certain fateful, damned inertia: a sickness of the soul. Something that had been smashed to pieces. It was this: more and more deeply to enter into a chrysalis, a metaphysical figment of the brain, and then to try to work your way out again without breaking the cocoon. Until one pulled oneself together at last and broke out of it—whereupon one was pitiably reduced to shuffle about in reality, homeless and freezing, and secretly longing to revert to the existence in the cocoon—!

Well! Continue!

His feeling of resignation. The telescope which he bought or partly received as a gift from photographer Sundholm, that upright and noble social outcast. The telescope, philosophy, and music. Serenity and a cool tranquility.

What nonsense—that serenity soon proved to be a silly illusion. Serenity is a wishful state, which is never fully

184

established and least of all in a small-town hell, among rude and tactless people with their gossip and rumors, their conceit and their contempt for things of the spirit, their tireless efforts to mess up a man's meager, dearly-bought peace and tranquility.

His feeling of desperation! His hatred of poverty, which made one dependent on every Tom, Dick, and Harry—on that banal clerk and meat-gorger, Consul Hansen, or that smooth-tongued sneak, attorney Wenningstedt. His hatred of Providence, of Vibeke, of everything. His decision to commit suicide! The lonely boat ride with his little girl. Lord Almighty! The abject capitulation and tearful return to life. And Atlanta horrified when during an attack of self-contempt he confided to her what he had had in mind. Her despair, her surprising tenderness—resembling the glitter of rare, genuine diamonds in an otherwise cheap piece of jewelry!

"Atlanta!" he called.

Atlanta looked greatly surprised: "Why are you lying there? With your overcoat on? You're not sick?"

He felt a suppressed desire to have a good cry in her lap, hug her in a close embrace as tight and as passionate as if it were to be the last one, to tell her what had happened, make her wild with joy. But he remained in a lying position and merely said: "Yes, Atlanta, I don't feel quite right. I don't want anything to eat, and tell the two pupils who are coming this afternoon that I am sick."

Magister Mortensen suddenly got to his feet and made a deprecatory gesture: "On second thought, just let those two lunkheads show up. Actually, I'm not sick at all. It was only a headache. Now I'm all right again!"

. . . Now then! He had put all this behind him. The comedy was ended. Peace and order had been reestablished. Now he wanted to rejoice and be happy. Only be happy. And to look forward to telling Atlanta the big news. Make her wildly happy! To share her joy, find rest and surcease in it, to be fully aware of the pulse beats of life, to live, to *live!*

Now then—everything seemed to have been brought up to date. *Hic Rhodos!*

"Tonight!" he muttered to himself. "Tonight it will be. And we must be alone. Alone and feeling festive, really festive!"

The rest of the day passed in the usual manner, as if nothing had happened. But at dusk, when the last pupil had left, Magister Mortensen, quite against his will, reverted to the strange feverish state of the forenoon. In his mind's eye, like a vision, he saw the enormous, the quite unwieldy fortune, which now contrary to all rhyme and reason had fallen into his turban—bundles of bills, piles on piles, a veritable snowstorm of ten-crown notes, of hundred-crown notes, of five-hundred-crown notes—he felt dizzy and had to lie down on the sofa; he went to sleep, a troubled, dream-filled sleep. He dreamed that he had bought a new telescope, a really large telescope, through which the planet Saturn appeared so close that it filled the entire sky.

When he woke up it was dark. Atlanta was out. He suddenly felt a great fear that she would not return but had left him forever and delivered him to an emptiness that he could not endure. "Atlanta!" he moaned, while he restlessly walked around in the empty apartment.

He walked into the bedroom, where Vibeke was sleeping. The little dimly burning lamp was on the bureau next to her bed. The poor little girl looked almost like a human being when she was asleep. Indeed, she ought to sleep all the time.

He kissed her on the forehead and suddenly burst into tears; sobbing, he lay down on her bed.

A little while later he jumped up, lit the lamp on the

186

writing table and began to read through what he had written during the forenoon, before all this confusion had set in. Before the flood. Before the deluge.

"As a spiritual type in the wide meaning of the term, Kierkegaard belongs in the category of Mephistopheles. Like Goethe's chargé d'affaires of the devil he is in possession of a superior intelligence, which he puts to use with the same supple elegance and indefatigability. They are both irresistible in a manner which is at the same time witty, impudent, and dazzling. Yes, Kierkegaard is in a sense the devil's superior, as he is unrivaled in the art of attacking reason with its own weapons. He is not only Mephistopheles, he is at the same time Mephisto's victim, Man, Faust. He aims his weapons not only at others, in the end he turns it against himself, without mercy; he remains standing there as a mortally wounded torturer of the self, while Mephistopheles dissolves in a haze of brilliant conversation. And Kierkegaard suffers terribly from his own satanism. He is, one might say, the tragic Satan. . ."

Somebody was walking up the stairs. It must be Atlanta coming home.

Magister Mortensen pushed the manuscript away. Yes, it was Atlanta. She was dressed in her Sunday best, but nevertheless looked exceedingly depressed. Hesitantly, she sat down on the sofa. There were pearls of newly fallen raindrops on her coat and in her rumpled dark hair. She looked at him imploringly, as if she were going to tell him something. What could it be that she was going to tell him? Underneath dark eyelashes she squinted at the light. And suddenly her eyes filled with tears, and she turned away and looked down with a disheartened expression on her face.

"What's the matter?" he asked. "What is it, Atlanta? Why are you so sad?"

He went over and sat down beside her, took her hand and said with warmth: "Of course, you are tired of shuffling

187

around here—here in this shabby apartment—together with an elderly fellow—yes, Atlanta, I think that's what's troubling you! That there seems to be no future in it, isn't that so?"

Atlanta nodded, averting her face.

Magister Mortensen emitted a long sigh. Then he said with a faint smile: "But that state of things is now gone, Atlanta. It is all gone, and it will never return."

She stole a glance at him, questioningly.

He continued, while caressing her hand: "Yes,—I know it sounds like a stupid joke—but it is still a fact, today I was told that I am the heir to a large fortune, to no less than one hundred and forty-six thousand crowns. You can read it yourself."

He gave her the letter. She stared at it without reading it.

He rose and tossed his head impatiently. "Well, as you know, I can't stand sentimental scenes. But, in brief, the situation has been immensely improved. We have become rich. We can get a new start in life. We can travel. We can do almost anything we want to."

Magister Mortensen tenderly drank in the picture of the young woman sitting there on the sofa. She looked like something on the order of a neglected Spanish princess, thin and fiery and young and neglected! For this soul so thirsting for life, humdrum existence had suddenly become a real fairy tale—it had burst upon her like a ray of sunshine entering a gloomy back room!

He went over and placed a hand on her shoulder and tried to catch her eye, but she avoided his glance. She did not look at all happy. She was weeping.

"Well, there's going to be a scene after all," he thought. "But never mind. The situation is not a very ordinary one, either. And besides: haven't I been going around myself making all kinds of scenes all day!" But now he felt himself to be on an even keel again. *This* was probably what had been missing. Atlanta—Woman—the connecting link between man and reality. . .

"Atlanta!" he said, attempting to strike as unsentimental a note as possible: "The two of us have by God endured so many hardships together that we actually deserve to live well, don't we?"

She leaned against him, yielding to her innermost feelings, passionately and silently, without meeting his gaze.

For one moment Magister Mortensen experienced a deep and intense peace of mind, a sense of happy and wholesome balance—it almost felt as if he had moved back twenty years in time and was a very young fellow, in his twenties —this ineffable feeling of primitive happiness between man and woman with immense reserves of prospects for the future. . .

And still, in his inmost being, there was a vapid feeling of an incipient bourgeois idyl, of banal satiety, of medioc rity. . .

And incredibly!—also a smouldering sense of longing for the old, a morbid longing for the old miserable existence, the worries, the hatreds, the sense of desperation—the *treatise!* The book about Satan! What about that now? Would he have to give it up? No, by heaven he wouldn't!

And still—hadn't he now in a way disqualified himself from writing such a book?

"Well, well, my little girl!" he said suddenly, giving her a friendly pat. "Isn't it best that we sleep on it, for the time being? I'm dog tired, and you seem to be the same."

Mortensen was indeed tired; he was completely worn out in mind and body, drowsiness stormed in upon him like a dark night filled with squalls, and he blissfully gave himself over to it.

CHAPTER 12

More about Magister Mortensen, who at this particular time certainly encountered unusual happenings, as well as about the Corpse Crower, who also one day saw an abyss open right before him

Magister Mortensen woke up on the sofa, half undressed, and noted that he had overslept two hours. It took some time before he could remember the events of yesterday, but by Jove! It was true—at least it could be. If only it wasn't something that he had been dreaming—?

He jumped up, shivering from the cold and a sickish feeling; he hurriedly opened the drawer of the writing table in which that fateful letter, if real, would have been placed. Yes, there it was. He laughed to himself. . .

Oddly enough, Atlanta had not gotten up, either. It was cold and dank in the kitchen. He knocked on the door to her room and walked back to the parlor. The sun had already risen high in the sky, and the bay and the sea resembled a huge glittering platinum-covered mirror. Two fishing boats were lying in the sound, they were almost completely invisible in the great brilliance, but then they reappeared, tiny and distinct, like pieces of filigree work. On the rim of the horizon he could see the smoke coming from a ship. It was probably the *Mjölner*, the large steamer that had called here yesterday on its way to Copenhagen.

"You could have been on board that steamer, honored

sir!" Magister Mortensen said laughingly to himself. "You could easily have obtained a loan on the strength of the *letter*, yes, they would even have been bowing and scraping to you and wished you all the luck in the world and been deeply impressed!"

The sunlight filled the parlor with its warmth and made his eyes blink. Mortensen yawned and stretched and emitted a long, thoughtful sigh. But what was *that?* He suddenly discovered, on the table right in front of his nose, a sheet of paper on which something had been written in a childish, clumsy handwriting.

It was a letter. He sat down and hurriedly read through it. It was from Atlanta.

"Dear Mortensen! When you read this letter I am no longer here, but far away, I have left on the *Mjölner*, I wanted to tell you long ago, and again last night, but I couldn't say it, but I made up my mind long since that I can't stay with you any longer, since I have become engaged, and now I have to go with him, he is twenty-six years old, I am never coming back, Josef's wife, Sarina, is also leaving, I thank you for everything, now it is over, I am terribly fond of you and of Vibeke also, I shall never forget you, my heart is so sorrowful, but don't be angry, it must be like this, and best of luck with your inheritance. Sincerely yours, Atlanta."

Magister Mortensen rose and let out a short and bitter laugh.

"Go to Hades," he murmured. "And lots of luck!"

"To hell with all that," he consoled himself. "She was, in spite of all, nothing but a streetwalker. Besides, she was much too young for you. And one thing and another."

What now? Lighting the kerosene stove and heating the water for the morning coffee. He got hold of the primus but couldn't find any matches. The box he had in his pocket was empty, and no matches were to be found in the kitchen.

191

Perhaps there was a box in Atlanta's room. He tore the door open. There was her bed—nicely made, with clean sheets.

"Oh you—you faithless bitch!" he groaned, menacingly. "But I don't give a damn. It was a good thing I got rid of you in a painless proper manner!"

There was a faint aura of cheap perfume in the room. It seemed so touching.

Umgiebt mich hier ein Zauberduft. . .

He sat down for a moment on the empty bed, shook his head and noticed that something was stirring in his neck and his chest—as if a string were breaking inside him— one of those romantic harp strings one reads about when everything occurs in a very fine and elevated fashion.

"You little devil, you!" he repeated, pressing his face against the pillow. He could see her standing there before him—her young face with its ardent expression, the full lips, the warm eyes with a somewhat desperate look in them, soulless, of course—and still they contained both goodness and tenderness, yes, a bottomless chasm of pure womanliness, gleaming like a diamond! Her beautiful, thick hair and small, beautifully shaped ears, her neck and shoulders, her skin, which was dull white and smooth all over, yes, without a blemish—the skin of a virgin, he, he! Her well-formed girlish hands, so good and kind, her bosom, so electrically alive—!

"My heart is so sorrowful! Never mind that. That's enough of that nonsense!"

He got up, remained standing by the door for a while, gave himself over to a feeling of dull self-contempt. Ugh! You old fool. What in Hades had you actually expected. She is twenty-four years old, you are forty-seven! You weren't married or anything. She was sick and tired of you.

192

And she didn't give a damn about your money. Which, incidentally, shows what a splendid girl she was! "My heart is so sorrowful!" Those words were undoubtedly true. She had been hesitating, but then at last she had made her decision, like the sensible and wonderful person that she was. . .

While you—you're irresolutely roaming about, feeble and cold, like a sick moth that regrets that it burst its cocoon and longs to go back to its former metaphysical chrysalis existence—!

He went into the kitchen. But there he once again went off into a reverie. An irritating voice inside him was passionately calling: "You *loved* her! You still *love* her! You may call it what you will—but it is unrequited love."

He sat down heavily on the kitchen counter and stared into space with lifted eyebrows. In the parlor the sunlight was flowing in and warming everything. He rose, shook his head, and walked into the other room. He was back *here* again.

And what would happen now? The very first thing to do was to get hold of a box of matches. He rose and said, in a muffled and moaning voice: "Good God, there *must* be some matches around somewhere in the house."

No, there weren't any.

But he could go down to Jakob Siff's store.

Vibeke was now awake and lay there waiting, patiently and hopelessly, for some one to come and take care of her. She never got out of bed by herself.

Mortensen went over to the wastebasket and retrieved the crumpled-up letter, smoothed it out, but then crumpled it once again without looking at it. Hell! it was matches that he wanted!

In Jakob Siff's store the sunlight fell on the smoothly worn counter. Magister Mortensen got his box of matches and

193

hurried back up. The primus stove was lit and the coffee pot put on. Damn it all! There wasn't any coffee any place. Back to Jakob Siff.

"I hear your housekeeper has left?" said the storekeeper, and Mortensen nodded without replying.

"The Corpse Crower is in bad shape," said the storekeeper, "his wife has run away."

Magister Mortensen gave an involuntary start. He recalled that Atlanta had mentioned something like that in her letter.

"He's completely out of his mind," said the storekeeper.

"Well, what the hell," said Magister Mortensen and hurried back with the coffee. Walking up the stairs he encountered the Corpse Crower, who was standing in the doorway to his apartment. Mortensen threw an anxious glance at the albino, who looked completely dispirited, like a sleepwalker.

The primus stove in the kitchen was smoking. How in hell does one make coffee? He reflected for a moment, got a happy inspiration, and went down and knocked on the Corpse Crower's door.

"Listen, Josef, can you make coffee?" he asked.

The Corpse Crower stared at him. "Coffee? Yes, I know how to make it."

"That's good," said Magister Mortensen, "won't you come up to my place for a moment?"

The Corpse Crower listlessly shook his head. "Yes, yes, but—you've probably not heard about the terrible thing that has happened?"

"Yes, certainly," Magister Mortensen said, "I know all about it. But that's no reason why you can't make us a cup of coffee."

"Well, maybe I could," the Corpse Crower conceded and hesitantly followed after Mortensen.

The pot was already boiling.

194

"It was completely unexpected," the Corpse Crower said and began to blubber. "So completely unexpected. We've been married twelve years."

"Yes," Mortensen said. "But we won't talk any more about it. We don't give a hang, Josef. Here's the coffee. Show me what you can do."

"Yes, that's what Eliana is saying, too," the Corpse Crower snuffled. "Namely, that one shouldn't take it so hard. She's wonderful, that Eliana. She's taking care of my Rita, my poor little daughter. How else could I manage, being alone and everything?"

Mortensen got hold of a few cups, and the coffee was poured. Both drank in silence. Magister Mortensen brought Vibeke something warm to drink in bed and lit his pipe.

"I've no idea what I shall do," the Corpse Crower said with a sad little smile. "I was just about to start work on a stand. . ."

"You just go ahead and make that stand, Josef."

"But now I can't do it, for I've completely forgotten what it's going to look like, and what it's to be used for, and I can't remember who's going to get it!"

"Oh, it will come back to you!" Mortensen said, giving him a pat on the back. "Everything will be all right, Josef. Just look at me, I've also become—what shall I say, a bachelor! Atlanta has left too, by God. But I don't give a damn."

"But she wasn't your wife," the Corpse Crower objected.

"True enough." Mortensen took a few vigorous puffs on his pipe. "But, what the hell—there's nothing that's so easy to forget as women, whether one is married to them or not. Wait just a week or two. Then you will clearly see that you were actually sick and tired of her."

"That I was not!" the Corpse Crower protested in a whisper, his pale eyes taking on a fanatical expression.

195

"Then you ought to have been, in any case," Mortensen said. "She was not at all the right one for you. She was nothing but a whore."

Josef suddenly got to his feet and shouted: "She was my wife! We were married! We were man and wife! She left me! She'll never come back!"

"There, there," Magister Mortensen calmed him down.

The Corpse Crower shouted even more loudly, wailing and weeping; "She was my wife! She was my wife!"

"Bife! Bife!" came an echo from the bedroom; it was Vibeke prattling away in bed. "Bife, gife, bife!"

The Corpse Crower listened with a look of fear in his eyes.

"Now, pull yourself together," Magister Mortensen said, clutching his arm in an amicable manner. "Sit down, Josef, and we two will have a little snifter together."

The Corpse Crower sat down. Mortensen fetched two glasses and a bottle.

"Skoal, Josef!"

The Corpse Crower lifted his glass, his hand trembling. The rim rattled against his teeth. Mortensen sat staring at the wall with its big, intricate, geographical ink spot. It was a funny thing about that stain, which in many ways resembled a well executed, carefully designed map, the work of rational beings, while it actually had come about through sheer idiocy.

"It's typical," he thought bitterly. "It's typical of everything in this life, which we fools have such great difficulty in fathoming, because in our delusion we think that its most profound causes are grounded in divine wisdom."

Nonsense! What have the elementary forces of nature to do with wisdom? With meaning and continuity? The world was created at one time in the same manner as this stupid ink splotch: through a foolish and blind eruption.

Magister Mortensen derived some pleasure from that

196

thought. He cozied himself with it, as he lit his extinguished pipe. The Corpse Crower too began to thaw out. He gave Magister Mortensen a trusting look and took another sip from his glass.

"Sing something, Josef!" Mortensen suggested. "You're a good singer."

"Sing?" The Corpse Crower sounded hesitant. "What in the world would I sing?"

"Something gay!" Magister Mortensen nudged him in the ribs. "Something about joy and happiness and freedom and stuff and nonsense! A song for the singing society, a drinking song! 'Find happiness upon the vine!'" He began to hum, drumming the table with his fingers.

The Corpse Crower shook his head and stared straight ahead as if he were searching for something. But suddenly he closed his eyes and raised his high-pitched penitent and funereal voice:

> By worldly sorrows sorely pressed,
> Thou heedest not how unconfessed
> Thou to thy day's end speedest. . . .

Mortensen made a deprecatory gesture, but the Corpse Crower continued undaunted and unctiously gave his all to the somber hymn. Magister Mortensen filled his glass and let him finish. "My heart is so sorrowful," he thought. He walked over to the wastebasket and once again got hold of the crumpled letter. He flattened it out, avidly looking for that particular sentence—yes, there it was, that was correct: "My heart is so sorrowful. . ."

Magister Mortensen managed at the very last moment to keep from bursting out sobbing by seizing a chair by its leg and lifting it up toward the ceiling. He balanced it on his palm, while walking around the room like a member of a balancing act.

197

There was nothing artificial about it, no literary affectation, nothing half-educated, it was merely a poor young girl's ballad-like, plain and sincere expression of her feelings! "My heart is so sorrowful!"

A genuine precious object. It must be treasured and hidden, kept as a priceless jewel.

The Corpse Crower had, thank God, finished his dreary funereal hymn. Magister Mortensen gave him a friendly shove: "Have another drink, Josef, and then we'll sing together this one here: 'The Pure Crystal!' Do you agree? You know it well from the singing society!"

Yes, the Corpse Crower was all for it. The two men lifted their heads and sang with much passion the old Swedish love ballad.

> Thou crystal so fine, like the bright sun thou shinest,
> like stars that are gleaming on high.
> I know a fair maid, in this district the finest,
> A maiden who dwells very nigh.
> My fair, my fair, my love's dear flower,
> Ah if a trysting were in our power,
> And I were thy true love,
> And thou my dearest dove,
> Thou purest rose and treasure trove!

"Yes, and then she up and leaves us, the pure crystal," Magister Mortensen laughed derisively; he was in high spirits and gave the Corpse Crower a slap on the shoulder: "And we two are sitting here like lonely and abandoned tomcats bawling for dear life!"

The Corpse Crower burst into tears.

"Have another drink, damn it," said Mortensen, angrily elbowing him in the ribs. "We've not come here to cry, but to take it like men! To force ourselves to look the truth right in the eye. 'Das Weib, das ewig weibliche—ein bloss

imaginäres Bild, an den allein der Mann denkt!' We idealize
her in order to justify and adorn our coarse lust. We anoint
the whore in our damned exquisite sentimentalizing, yes,
we even beat her to death in order to completely give ourselves over to the perverse delight of repentance and longing
and yearning—just as he does, Kierkegaard. All infatuation,
Josef, all infatuation is disguised self-pity. It is yourself that
you are in love with! The pure crystal—it's yourself,
honored sir!"

The Corpse Crower sat silent, deep in thought. He looked
like an old Chinese sage.

"I'm thinking about my stand," he said.

Magister Mortensen nodded. "It's actually a very interesting thing, this stand," he said. "There's something symbolic
in the fact that you don't know what it's going to look like,
nor what it's going to be used for, nor who's going to have
it. But—you're already feeling much better now, Josef, aren't
you?"

"Yes, now I feel much better," the Corpse Crower con-
firmed, looking up at Mortensen with a grateful little smile.
"But now I think I'll go down and see how my daughter,
Rita, is doing."

"Are you going to leave now? Well—in God's name, Josef,
you do as you please."

"My heart is so sorrowful," Magister Mortensen thought,
stamping his foot on the floor. "My heart is so sorrowful."

He walked into the bedroom. Vibeke had fallen asleep
again. What about her now? What about everything?

One hundred and forty-six thousand crowns. "My heart
is so sorrowful." A craze for money, and the sentimentality
of a farm-hand. The man of reason—is he completely dead
and buried underneath these piles of plain confusion? Isn't
there as much as a drop of human dignity left in you,
honored sir? Weren't you the one who wrote those damned

199

true and correct words: "The heart is always an old hag. The mark of nobility of the honest man is this: that he feels with his reason!"

Magister Mortensen went back into the sitting room. He began to pace up and down the floor, the customary little walk consisting of six or seven paces, rapid turn-around by the door and by the book-case. The wild animal in its cage. Hasn't the tiger discovered yet that the bars have been taken away, that the hour of freedom has struck? Why doesn't it break loose, then?

Wait a minute, wait a minute, there's not such a great rush. And besides, one isn't exactly a tiger, not an aimless, useless tiger, not an old woman, but a grown man who takes his life and himself seriously. And knows so darn well where he stands. Even though a poor devil suddenly may become a prosperous man, he doesn't for that reason do completely away with his sense of decency. He remains faithful to himself and his views.

Or is it a lie, then, that in your inmost self you believe in goodness as the solely relevant aspect of existence? In the absolute primacy of the moral act? Verily, verily, what shall it profit a man if he shall gain the whole world, and lose his own soul?

Magister Mortensen filled his glass, but did not take a sip from it.

"Wait a minute," he said to himself. "Take a trip to Rio de Janeiro, or to Hong Kong or to Honolulu, buy yourself freedom and love and all kinds of pleasures. Or—for you are after all a man of the spirit and something of a connoisseur—travel to Vienna or Milan and listen to the finest symphony orchestras in the world, go to Rome and look at its immortal works of art. But don't think that *that* is freedom and happiness. Freedom and happiness come only from within oneself. Purify your soul, become humble of heart, be good. Go and sell everything that you own and give the money to the poor, then you will have stored up treasures

200

in heaven! And that, by God, doesn't mean that you can thus buy a guarantee of it with bonds of salvation, but that you should clean out the dung stable that is your soul and make it fit for the only happiness there is, the only freedom there is: the peace induced by a good deed. Hell, *that* is exactly what your book on Satan is all about. That is the very sum total of it!"

Mortensen went over to the window and opened it, leaned over the windowsill, and looked out with wide-open but unseeing eyes. "Well, it doesn't work quite that easily," he thought with a tiny smile. "But then that's too much to ask anyway. Things have to proceed at a natural pace. But it is going to be interesting to see which power will emerge victorious in you. God or Satan. Or neither one of them."

He steps quickly away from the window, clenches both his fists, makes a few angry slashes in thin air, and says with a long, drawn-out, savage snarl: "Neither one of them? Just mediocrity? No, then *much* rather Satan—!"

Suddenly he notices some one standing in the door—it is Eliana, the wife of the ferryman.

"What in blazes are you doing here?" he blurts out, but he immediately regrets his hot temper and feels a bit confused: "Oh, is it you, Eliana? You must excuse me—I'm a little—a little. . . !"

Eliana walks over to him and tries to calm him by placing her hand on his, and smiles as if it were the most natural thing in the world that she came here and interfered in his affairs—just like a midwife summoned by the cries of pain of a woman in labor. . . ! He hears her say something about Vibeke. She wants to take Vibeke with her. Some breakfast. Some breakfast and coffee for both of them. Josef had said. . .

Mortensen sits down on the sofa and buries his face in his hands: "Just one moment, Eliana!" he says, "I'm a bit confused."

Eliana walks into Vibeke's bedroom. He can hear her

201

friendly voice—so kind—so unaffected. And the happy prattle of the little girl. He suddenly gets up and walks into the bedroom and puts his arms around Eliana, he takes her hand, kisses it passionately and places it against his cheek.

"It's going to turn out all right, Mortensen," she says with warmth. "It'll be all right. It's only in the beginning. Things will work out, you'll see. Just come with me both of you and get something to eat."

Rumors cover a lot of ground in a small town. Already that very same afternoon, Magister Mortensen has a visit from editor Olsen, who acts like a completely different man because of the awe he feels, and the following day the *News* publishes in a prominent place the sensational news about Magister Mortensen's inheritance. "A Lucky Man!"

The insipid, snobbish news item disgusts Mortensen. And it gets even worse when the *congratulations* begin to pour in. Obviously, people in this town like to send congratulations. It is not only from Count Oldendorp and Captain Öström that congratulations are received—no, they come from the most unexpected quarters, from apothecary Fähse, Pastor Fruelund, Manicus the physician, teacher and Mrs. Nillegaard, the Misses Schibbye! A whole epidemic of congratulations!

And here he has been naively imagining that he was somebody on the order of a friendless Job—no, it was not so at all, he is in reality a popular fellow, surrounded by warmhearted and sympathetic friends. For once what is involved is something that people *understand,* namely money. Money brings with it prestige, friends, absolution for all previous sins, yes, even Berg, the school principal, has sent—it is almost unbelievable: he has sent a bouquet of flowers, a bouquet of white and red roses!

The only thing missing now is a congratulatory telegram from the Minister of Church and Education, Östermann. But it will probably come. Just be patient. Everything will come to pass.

In brief, Magister Mortensen experiences a time that is both absurd and harrowing. It is of no use that he wishes from the bottom of his heart that what has happened had not happened. One has to resign oneself to be the man of the hour. One must put up with sniffing at a bouquet of roses, yes, even submit to placing the bouquet in a pitcher of water—for where the hell else can it be placed? It would be churlish toward the innocent flowers to throw them out of the window or into the stove. One might of course have sent them back with a note saying: Refused! But one doesn't bother to make such great fuss about such a small thing.

And then the worst thing of all: secretly one observes oneself and notes in sorrow and anger that one actually feels so strangely *flattered* by it all! One catches oneself thinking that one really deserves all the applause. In short, one peeps—touched and entranced—into this sanctum of the bourgeois world, to which one suddenly has received an admission ticket. A place in the orchestra, no less!

And then the reaction comes. Lurking. A dull uneasy feeling, something that moves slowly and reluctantly unfolds in an agonizing half-light, just like that seen in old pictures of the Day of Judgment. Or like the largo upbeat in the Midnight Sonata, the one with the roaring abysses and the little lonely, hesitating recitative—this timid and futile declaration of love made in the darkness. . .

"My heart is so sorrowful."

CHAPTER 13

Concerning agonies of the soul, caused by the fact that righteous people have given a helping hand to an errant count

Bailiff Kronfeldt stood there with his eyes wide open and with an expression as if he were staring into a bottomless abyss of stupidity, yes, he even got up on his toes and stretched out his hands signifying his feeling of helplessness, as if he were to take off and soar like a lost booby into this great void of inanity.

But suddenly he clicked his heels together and let out a short, bitter laugh: "Oh no! There *must* be a limit. This is the last straw! *This is the last straw!*"

He turned towards Debes the constable: "Yes, Debes, you may go back to your place. You at least have done a good job. Thank you."

"You're welcome, sir," Debes bowed, in a well-mannered way, and withdrew to the guardroom, his hands resting on the hilt of his sword.

Feeling elated, the bailiff paced up and down the floor, gesticulated angrily, rubbed his chin, and said: "Can you beat it! And we have befriended this monster and catered to him and introduced him to the best people, and he's even gotten himself engaged to a lady of one of the finest families!"

He sank back in his desk chair, feeling very tired, but got

up again immediately and hurried into the sitting room to his wife.

"Charlotte," he said, with a gloomy mien, "sit down, Charlotte, and be completely calm. I have a very unpleasant piece of news to tell you: It has now been established that Karl Erik—that Count Oldendorp lives with the woman they call *Black Mira!* I see it sounds incredible to you, and that I can understand. But it has been established that it is so. Debes, you know. We are spreading our nets."

The bailiff laughed bitterly: "But this is going to be the drop that makes the cup overflow. We are through with that Oldendorp!"

Mrs. Kronfeldt rose from her chair, with folded hands, and sighed: "The good Lord help us! The good Lord help us!"

"Yes! This nerve-racking comedy just has to come to an end. He's going to be punished. He's going to be exposed. Placed in the stocks, that scoundrel!"

"But what do you intend to do?" his wife whispered nervously.

The bailiff's face once again took on that helpless expression, and he began to walk back and forth: "Yes, that is exactly the problem. What do I intend to do? There, there, stop your crying. *This* is nothing to cry about. It's going to get worse! Much, much worse!"

"I'm not crying," Mrs. Kronfeldt said, trying to look brave.

The bailiff continued: "Well, what should we do? It is not easy. It needs a lot of thought. But, don't start day-dreaming, now. Just rely on me. Right now I've got the fate of this miserable rogue in the palm of my hand!"

He returned to his office.

Now, then, to act on the case! The case of Count Oldendorp! How may a scandal be averted? *Can* it be averted? And even if that were possible: who can guarantee that he doesn't make new and even worse scandals? Is it possible to get rid of him without any one taking notice, and in what manner?

The bailiff placed himself slowly and carefully in a comfortable position in the leather-covered sofa and concentrated deeply on the matter.

This is how it was: At one time he had been genuinely happy over the prospect of having this *count* become a member of his family. There was something delightful and unique about the idea. Something really grand. Governor Effersöe had his Minister of Culture to brag about, Judge Pommerencke had his uncle, the professor of jurisprudence. This all had to be reckoned with when Oldendorp's pro's and con's were to be justly balanced. A count is and always will be a count. Yes, Kronfeldt unblushingly admitted to himself that he had become overjoyed the time he had received that letter from old Count Oldendorp of Krontoftegaard manor with a plea that—well, *plea?* Yes, it certainly must be called a plea. The letter could easily be located; the bailiff jumped to his feet and got it out of his well-ordered chest of file drawers:

"My dear Emanuel!

"I recently learned that you (I hope I can still be on a first-name basis with you) have become no less than a bailiff of a distant country. I wish you the best of luck, Emanuel, I am pleased to the bottom of my heart that you have gotten so far in life. Truthfully, I do not know what a bailiff is, but it sounds as if it is something like viceregent, but I always had an idea that you would become a Somebody in this vale of tears. How sad it is that your father, our lovable old gardener, who was such a trusty friend of us children (and your ditto ditto mother, the always-so-pleasant Gardener's Mette!), that the two old folks, whom I was truly so very fond of, should not live to see it!—I'm sitting here writing to you and thinking about the old days, when we played cops

206

and robbers and all that, and I was always the robber and you the cop, or *soldier* as we call it.

"All jesting aside, Emanuel, could you take note of this, as long as we are talking about robbers! My son, Karl Erik— he is the greatest sorrow of my life, he is not doing well at all —not because he basically is not a good-hearted fellow, but because he has taken to gambling and drinking and on the whole leads the kind of life that will be the death of me.

"Now I have hit upon the idea that if you, who are vice-regent at the very ends of the earth and are, I suppose, still a 'cop,'—that if Karl Erik came up to where you are and so to speak was to be alone for a while and could take stock of himself, in a place where there probably can't be any temptations of any great extent: that surely will have a beneficial effect on him. He will probably agree to it himself, for he is, as I mentioned above, basically a fine fellow and always filled with those good intentions with which the road to Hell is supposed to be paved, the Lord forgive me.

"Do write me and let me know what you think. I shall be waiting in great suspense. God will reward you, and so will I, of that you must not doubt. He is coming home from a most dubious visit to that lurid town Copenhagen tomorrow, the poor boy, I dread seeing him again, he will probably be a beautiful sight. But I will be waiting to hear from you in the very near future.

Yours very sincerely,
C. F. W. Oldendorp"

". . .Indeed a very touching letter." The bailiff folded it carefully and put it back in the drawer.

Well, he had swallowed the bait, and next came the arrival of this Karl Erik, that *lout*.

And in the beginning everything went off exceedingly well. He was amenability personified, and he was pleasant and charming, using the appellations "Uncle Kronfeldt" and

"Aunt Charlotte." It was a real pleasure to introduce him: the young Count Oldendorp, the son of my old friend, the Master of the Royal Hunt.

Yes, it actually seemed as if this dissolute fellow did see the error of his ways and would turn into a new and better man. He recovered quickly and was the picture of glowing health. That was due to that good soul Charlotte's efforts, she always took everything so seriously, she had fed him eggs and milk and all kinds of delicacies and had on the whole taken care of him in a manner that touches one's heart. And when on top of that he got engaged to Pastor Schmerling's daughter, a tall and quiet and competent girl, one was actually naive enough to think. . . !

And then. The first few times he let himself go and ended up in bad company—one just looked upon them as small relapses that would pass. Until the brute little by little began to show his true colors! Staggering dead drunk in among the worst drunkards on Skin Islet! Appearing in public in the meanest and lowest kind of company! And finally, to top it all: visiting by night that Mira, a common whore, daughter of the so-called Wailing Woman, illegitimate, of course. A count! Heaven help us! A man who had been introduced to the very best people in town, and of whom one had been genuinely proud. A formally engaged man!

And the end was not yet. The seamy side having been exposed, then . . . ! It was scandalous, scandalous!

The bailiff was writhing on the sofa. He rubbed his eyes with his fists, and his face for a moment took on a childish, sulking expression. Didn't he already seem to sense a rather frigid attitude on the part of the governor's wife? And wasn't there a trace of scathing sarcasm in the way Dr. Manicus said: "Your protégé, the ethnologist"?

Of course, it was a rather dubious invention, this story about Karl Erik's interest in ethnology. It had been meant to serve as a makeshift excuse. After all, one couldn't introduce this count as a poor deported slacker. It was only because of his love for a fellow human being that he had invented this business of ethnology, an idea which Karl Erik had most warmly approved.

The bailiff gave himself completely over to his sad reflections. He should have advised the Master of the Royal Hunt not to send his son up here. But he had acted in good faith.

But what would happen now? Get him shipped out of the country as fast as possible? Well and good, but what about the engagement? Could it be broken just like that? As regards Miss Schmerling, he could put the cards on the table and get that liaison terminated. In sum: he could expose the brute, just like that, and send him packing. There would be a scandal in such a case too, but at most a scandal of somewhat limited extent. . .

But it would still be a scandal of real dimensions!

Bailiff Kronfeldt's protégé, the count, the ethnologist— discovered in Black Mira's bed and sent on his way like a whipped dog!

But he did deserve it, the scoundrel! But then how would this affect his own reputation? People would poke their noses into what had happened, they would see through the entire comedy, and he would sink down to being the "son of the gardener at Krontoftegaard manor." And so on and on. . . ! Governor Effersöe, who was the son of a physician, Judge Pommerencke, whose father had been the proprietor of the well-known Pommerenckean factories—they would have themselves a quiet and enjoyable laugh at his expense. And so would the postmaster. And the apothecary and his wife. Dr. Manicus, too.

No, it seemed there was nothing else for it than to mend the confounded situation as far as could be done and to put the best face on it. It would be tough. *Tough.*

Or—why in hell can't a count born and bred, all things considered, allow himself extravagant habits? One could look at it in a big way and shrug one's shoulders: . . . something of a Don Juan, isn't he? And Black Mira is—just between us—not so bad at all, by God, right is right, and then she is the illegitimate daughter of a navy officer. And her mother, the so-called Wailing Woman, she is actually the daughter of no less a man than old Consul Sebastian Hansen! Thus one can understand the young rascal. And—as an aside—: the Master of the Royal Hunt was that way too in his young days, oh my! That's the way these counts and barons are made, gentlemen. Oh, I know it so well. And what haven't we even heard about members of the royal house? Oh, I beg your pardon! But let us rather keep quiet about young Oldendorp's escapades—for the sake of his sweetheart—that she fully deserves. And for the sake of Pastor Schmerling, too, that brilliant man.

Pastor Schmerling was the son of an admiral.

The bailiff got up from the sofa and rubbed his goatee. Yes, of course! And a man ought to be fully able to maneuver his boat around the skerries instead of navigating so badly that it would end up upside down!

The bailiff chuckled and went over to open the window. He had thought everything through. Everything was clear. Nothing is to be done. Karl Erik will be severely reprimanded in private, and if this thing about Black Mira becomes public knowledge, well, then one has to be something of a diplomat. And handle it like a man of the world.

The bailiff rubbed his hands and sighed, and began to hum. Then he walked into the sitting room to his wife.

"But, Charlotte, why such a flood of tears? There is no reason for that!"

"Oh, Emanuel, I'm so sad on your account."

"Rubbish." The bailiff patted her arm and said with a warm and tender smile: "Now, Charlotte? Don't you think *I* am able to handle that situation? You know better than that!"

He added in a serious tone: "Well, you see—it might be best that we continue to have patience with—with this fig tree that bears no fruit. It is our duty. After all, it is a human being who is involved. We can't give up on him just like that. I can't break my promise to the Master of the Royal Hunt. No, we'll have to overlook what he's done, Charlotte. For his own sake and for his father's. And for the sake of his future wife."

A trace of emotion could be detected in the bailiff's voice.

"No, Charlotte, we must—we must bear our cross. And we must hope for a happy outcome, in spite of everything. For he *is* a count and the son of a count!"

Part III

Which contains descriptions of a big and eventful—though somewhat confused—wedding feast, during which the beast Matte-Gok manages to feather his own nest

CHAPTER 1

Early preparations and the dress rehearsal

In our day it is rather rare that one actually *celebrates* a wedding. The customary thing is for the bridal couple to spend the evening in the bosom of their close family. At most, a glass of mulled claret is served and there is an insipid speech to which one listens without any feeling of joy. Gone are the days of the big weddings, the vigorous times of the real *wedding feasts*.

These old-time wedding feasts never went off according to a previously arranged plan, but unfolded, after the fashion of wild flowers, without any real regard for ecclesiastical or civil ritual—indeed quite often without any regard, so to speak, for the bridal couple itself. For at the really good old enormous wedding feasts the bride and groom really played a subordinate role. Shotguns were fired, toasts were drunk, and songs were sung for them when they returned from the church ceremony, but after the *bridal dance* had been danced, they quickly ceased to be the center of the festivities and could just as well have withdrawn to a peaceful family life without having attracted any attention.

This state of things was not due to a lack of tact or gratitude on the part of the wedding guests. They showed their gratitude in other ways than pestering and wearing out the bridal couple. People used to give substantial wedding presents: really magnanimous tokens of friendship. The most

215

prosperous ones gave money, and those who were less well off gave articles for everyday use, ranging from pieces of furniture and kitchen utensils to sheepskins or woolen stockings. Other gifts might consist of personal services: A shoemaker could thus offer to sole free of charge seven pairs of shoes whenever such work would become necessary, a glazier or a carpenter would bind himself to replace broken windows, without charge, following the end of the festivities, and so on. Of course, among the many guests there were some who would deceitfully participate in the joys of the feast without contributing anything in return, but such spongers were held in contempt by all the others, that is, if they were noticed at all in the general confusion.

On the whole, such a wedding feast would always yield a considerable surplus to the hosts, and it was therefore a party in which every one rightfully had a share and a part. And this is what gave rise to the sense of loyalty and fraternity that existed among the participants.

Such a wedding feast after the old fashion was held when Sirius Isaksen and Julia Janniksen were married.

The wedding was celebrated in several places and by many different groups. Thus, a part of the celebration took place in the premises of the Christian temperance society Ydun, another group gathered in blacksmith Janniksen's house, smithy, and garden, a third group celebrated in The Dolphin, a fourth in The Curious Duck, a fifth in the sail loft of the Höje warehouse, and so on.

In the late evening these various groups gradually merged with one another, with the exception of the first one, which stubbornly remained by itself. But—in time that group also began to merge with the others!

This first group had originally attempted to arrogate to itself a sort of monopoly as being the real and official one, owing to the persistent efforts and cooperation of savings-bank manager Ankersen and the mother of the bride. Their

216

plan of action was very simply to take possession of the bridal couple immediately after the wedding, bring them to the assembly hall of the Ydun Society, detain them there all night and to see to it that the Society's building be barred to undesirable elements. They were playing for high stakes, they incurred blacksmith Janniksen's wrath and exposed themselves to his revenge, but they did not care—as Ankersen expressed it: "For it is our task to do battle with the powers of darkness, and God helps him who helps himself."

The blacksmith, who very naturally assumed that his daughter's wedding would have her own home as its principal focus, had for several days been very busy with preparations resulting in much hullaballoo and ordering about. He had put many men to work; flags and pennants and colored lanterns, streamers and curlicues were obtained; Count Oldendorp had taken it upon himself to provide a full orchestra; men in high spirits were walking in and out of the smithy with drums and horns and peculiar-looking instruments; and level-headed neighbors, sitting behind potted plants and peeping out through their windows, saw eight men come after dusk dragging along something that looked like a cannon.

When the work finally had been completed—on the eve of the great day—the blacksmith gathered his friends and helpers inside the smithy, which had been converted into a sort of taproom; then he uncorked eight bottles and gave his last orders:

"Friends and relatives! We have now done a good job, as behooves men and comrades, and now this evening we will let ourselves go and as a sort of dress rehearsal celebrate a real wild evening! It will take place at The Dolphin. But before we completely lose sight of one another this evening I want to impress upon you what is to be done tomorrow, and woe to the dirty dog who does not remain at his post! To repeat: As soon as the church bells are ringing every one will stand ready—the count's orchestra and the choir at the entrance to the garden, the cannoneers on the other side of the smithy—in order not to frighten the wedding procession out of their wits, and make doubly sure that the cannon does not misfire, that would be an indelible stain on the honor of us all! Is that a promise? Well and good. *Skoal!*"

At the very moment when the joy-filled group made up of the blacksmith and his faithful comrades is on the way out to The Dolphin, a loathsome little episode takes place down by the beach, in the deep and dark shadows between two old boathouses, where Matte-Gok has asked Kornelius to meet him.

"Yes, tomorrow night between eleven and twelve," Matte-Gok says. "It's of course a bit unfortunate that it coincides with your brother's wedding. But nothing can be done about that, Kornelius, the calculation has been made, and it's now or never."

"As far as I'm concerned, it might as well be tomorrow night," Kornelius replies.

"Yes, isn't that right? For it's really something that one would like to have done and over with. You've been going around fooling with this treasure for so many years, Kornelius, and it would be a shame if you missed your big chance, now that it is here. You'll easily find an opportunity to go for a walk in the course of the evening, you're your own master."

"Of course," Kornelius answers. "But how will I get the treasure brought home?"

"You're not going to do that at all, Kornelius," Matte-Gok says, placing a firm hand on his shoulder. "When it's to be brought home, then I will come myself and help you. No, you're not even to dig it up tomorrow night. You are only to dig down to where it is, so that you can touch the copper. Then with your finger you are to draw three crosses on the lid. Three crosses, just like those on a bottle of poison. You

218

follow me? It's very important, this thing with the crosses, it is what is called the signification. I could have told you all this before, but it couldn't be done, it is to be told at the very last moment. If the treasure has been marked, then it will remain where it is, and we can later, as I said, both of us haul it up and take it away."

"But—that really makes it a different thing entirely!" Kornelius says, relieved. "I've been worrying so much that I would have to struggle with that heavy chest all by myself."

"See this," Matte-Gok says, pressing a small, hard object into the palm of his hand. "Take this, it is an iron ring, a ring for your finger, but you're not to wear it on your finger, just keep it on you, in your pocket, for example. It's my lucky ring. When you have it with you, you'll be infallible. And every time you're in doubt, Kornelius, then hold the ring in your hand, clench your fist firmly around it and press hard, then everything will be all right. But now I have to leave; I'm joining Ankersen on some revival work."

"Wait a minute!" Kornelius says, eagerly. "The whole thing would be much easier for me, Matte-Gok, if you agreed that we at least divide the proceeds!"

"I really don't need it," Matte-Gok says with a smile. "But if it is of any help to you, then let us say that I get one fifth for having given you a hand. But in that case I'll help you to get the whole job finished, that I shall—And, good luck to you, Kornelius, the Lord bless you!"

That evening, the wild evening, became one of The Dolphin's big and memorable evenings. It opened the doors wide on a world that the pale generation of the years following Prohibition never had known, on a world that turned its back on the entire arid and snobbish malice and spite that usually characterize life in a small town.

Ah, you young people who have grown up in the anemic part of the city, with its mission house, temperance hotels, neat little shops, notices, and police regulations: you have never experienced the rumble of the tremendous wave of singing and thumping on tables, clinking of glasses and spontaneous paeans of praise rising from exhilarated spirits, friendship and love and fisticuffs and all-forgiving weeping and faithfulness, that welled forth from Captain Öström's tavern during one of its most so-called *famous evenings!*

You have not known Ole Brandy when he was in his prime, you have not seen the gleam from his earrings flash through the steam and tobacco smoke in the men's big basement, known as the "Kitchen." You have not seen the intoxicated glow of joy in his eyes and heard him recite the elegy about Olysses. Nor have you heard the wild and amazed shouts that cut right through the general tumult when blacksmith Janniksen trod the measure of his colossal solo dance. One just cannot fathom the superhuman power and passion with which this partaker of joy and pleasure twisted his giant body in the stuffy room, full of sensual elation, with unrestrained scraps of poems and songs and blasphemies welling up from his chest in unending waves.

A secret band of resolute men of the sea surrounded the rabid mammoth and saw to it that he did not wrench the building off its foundations, and when the performance at last was over, the blacksmith was carried into an adjacent room to amass new strength in peace and quiet for another burdensome day's work. Ole Brandy placed a glass filled to the rim next to his couch.

When Ole returned to the "Kitchen," something was on the point of happening that had been completely unforeseen and was not on the program: through the smoke and steam could be seen the outlines of savings-bank manager Ankersen and his son Matte-Gok.

"This is something for me to straighten out," Ole Brandy thought to himself. He forced the two uninvited guests to take a seat at the table and poured each one a glass of beer.

"I hope it's birch beer?" Ankersen asked; he did not wait for an answer but emptied the glass, for he was very thirsty. Matte-Gok did not touch his glass. Ankersen began to work on Ole, in a low and earnest voice, while he was wiping his glasses: ". . . And what will be the end of all of this, Ole? Can you tell me that?"

"It'll be the *milk cure*," Ole replied.

Ankersen placed the spectacles on his nose. He gurgled uncomprehendingly, but Ole, in full fettle, continued: "The milk cure? Yes, you see, that is when you have drunk yourself into a completely flat state like a flounder and sort of just *can't* do it anymore, but neither can you stop and you just stand there wobbling right in the middle of the mess. Then you get hold of a pitcher of milk and swill it down."

"Milk?" Ankersen asked suspiciously.

"Not pure, unadulterated milk, of course," Ole explained. "Is that what you think? Oh, go home and take a leak in your teapot! No, there has to be an extra fine shimmer on it, first-class stuff, as for example extra heavy white rum. But for some time after you'll be completely clean on the inside, like a newborn lamb, you don't think an evil thought, you don't talk twaddle and drivel, but act like an honorable man, you won't bellow or complain any more, you won't bury your poison fangs into honest people, you won't frighten young girls out of their wits any more, you insane ape! And you, Matte-Gok, whoever it is that you are the son of, at least it's not that tulip flower sitting there, and then I'll tell you a thing that'll make you. . . ."

Ankersen interrupted Ole Brandy's speech by noisily clearing his throat and rattling his chair. He made an imperious sign to Matte-Gok, they both got up and started to sing in a loud voice. Suddenly all was quiet in the "Kitchen"; every one was listening with open mouth to the singing. Matte-Gok had a fine, well-rounded voice, Ankersen was shouting rather than singing.

The blind man sees and the fearful has faith,
the deaf man listens to the word of the book,
the mute can sing from joy and mirth,
the lame man can leap across the brook. . .

Ole Brandy assumed a comfortable listening position. But when the long-winded revival hymn at last had come to an end and Matte-Gok at a sign from Ankersen stepped forward to deliver a sermon exhorting everyone to repent, it just got to be too much for Ole, being in the condition he was; he got up and gave the young scoundrel a well-directed punch on the jaw. It came as a complete surprise to Matte-Gok, he tumbled backwards, fell to the floor and lay there flat on his back.

"And *now* maybe you'll buzz off!" Ole Brandy bellowed, closing in on Ankersen with bloodshot eyes.

Ankersen bent down, whimpering over his son. "Did you hurt yourself, Mathias Georg? There, there, you'll be able to get up again I'm sure, you're a strong fellow! You just try to get up, and then we'll leave this place, my boy. Hold your head high, young fellow! No, no, take it easy, we'll concede this first round. This was only a little foretaste. Come now! We'll go home and get new strength!"

"Get some speed on!" Ole Brandy bellowed. "Good! And make sure you lock that door, Jeremias, and let's have an extra strong drink that we can wash down the deck with!"

CHAPTER 2

Other storm warnings

The morning of the wedding day breaks with the most beautiful late summer weather, with sunshine and a deep-blue sky, with lovely fleecy clouds here and there, dainty and delicate as the wrinkled creamy film that forms on top of a bowl of cultured milk.

Mrs. Midiord, Ankersen's old housekeeper, is standing on the stoop of the savings-bank manager's house and is tying the ribbon of her black bonnet under her chin, while her mind dwells on all this heavenly purity. Alas, her eyesight is not so sharp any more, that is noticeable on a day like this, everything immediately begins to shimmer, the air is filled with small figures gliding up and down, sharp and clear like filigree work, ever moving about, and the most curious shapes: hairpins, music notes, hooks and eyes . . . perhaps it all has some meaning—Mrs. Midiord is of a nervous disposition and she has had bad dreams during the night. And this morning she has received an urgent message from the hospital to come out and visit her half-sister Ura. What could it be that Ura wants to talk to her about? Usually she is not that anxious to have visitors.

But, of course, Ura has lately become more peculiar and unbalanced than ever before, that is, since the time she fell down and was disabled. Yes, Ura is terrible in her unreasonableness and pigheadedness. Just imagine—she has not even been willing to see her own son Matte-Gok! He has paid her a visit many times, alone and also accompanied by Ankersen, but every time she has just lain there with her back turned on them, played deaf and blind, and hidden under the bedcover. She won't even mention her son's name; he doesn't exist as far as she is concerned. And no one knows better than Mrs. Midiord how this has upset the young fellow.

Mrs. Midiord had comforted him to the best of her ability: "My dear friend, your mother is not quite all there, and, as you know, she has not been that for a long time, and I also know when it started, it was already when she was in the hospital the first time for an operation for a tumor in the stomach; you see, that business she just wouldn't go along with, the obstinate woman that she is, but there was no way around it, and since then she has gotten the notion that Doctor Manicus took out her spleen, and that's a lot of nonsense, of course. But this time it's much worse, now she is raving mad, but don't you take it to heart, you're a strong and fine-looking young man, and your conscience is clear. . ."

Ura smiles grimly, her eyes are very small, her cheeks are aflame, she is almost unrecognizable.

"Do you have a fever?" her sister asks anxiously. Ura shakes her head. She looks around with displeasure in the fully occupied hospital room; there is a crowd of visitors. "Sylvia!" she whispers excitedly, grasping her sister's hand. "Sylvia! What *is* it that is going to happen?"

"Nothing," Mrs. Midiord says reassuringly. "Nothing, Ura. You just take it easy."

"Nonsense!" Ura says. She pulls at her sister's hand and then pushes it away. "Then tell me what is going on today? Why do you keep it secret from me?"

"You're referring to Sirius Isaksen's wedding? But that is no secret."

"No, *that's* not it," Ura snaps at her. "That is not the *whole thing*, Sylvia!"

She grasps her sister's hand and whispers: "What is *he* up to, that beast, that dirty dog? You watch out for him, Sylvia! He's planning something. There's something that Ankersen is up to! They are doing some kind of mischief, I just know it! Tell everybody that they have to watch out! Tell Kornelius especially, tell him not to get mixed up in anything, ask him to come out here tomorrow! It's all true, what I'm saying, Sylvia! That scoundrel has something evil in mind! And many people will suffer for it, Sylvia, as true as I'm lying here! If only I were my old self! Oh, if I at least could get up on my feet. . . !"

Ura makes a grimace of despair and suddenly bursts into tears; her sister has to kneel down by her bed and comfort her as well as she can.

Mrs. Midiord does have a suspicion about what Ura refers to, she herself dreads the thought of the very same thing; it is the possibility of impending warfare between the Ydun Society and blacksmith Janniksen, yes, it may develop into something awful, and certainly it is a daring notion on the part of Ankersen to want to hold back the bridal couple, since he so easily does get out of hand, and perhaps it will be Matte-Gok who will suffer for it, already last night he was almost knocked unconscious by that nasty old rowdy Ole Brandy. . .

Mrs. Midiord is herself on the verge of tears, but she braces herself and says: "You must have a fever, my dear. You'll get an antipyretic, and then you'll feel better."

Fragments of a certain musical composition continue to resound in Magister Mortensen's ear. A strange, intense music, rushing, storming, energetic, devil-may-care . . . what *can* it actually be? It is the curious, savage figures that introduce the march in Tchaikovsky's *Symphonie pathétique!*

225

Magister Mortensen is carrying a briefcase under his arm. And in this so ordinary-looking briefcase there are two large yellow envelopes, each of which contains fifty thousand crowns in big bills. He is on his way to attorney Wenning-stedt, in whose office he will deposit one of the envelopes, intended for Atlanta. In vain he has tried to find the girl's address. But sooner or later she will probably turn up, and she is to receive this gift, even though she at one time spurned his money. Or—just because of that. Eliana is to have the other envelope.

The attorney is not at home. Well, no matter, the thing just has to wait. There's plenty of time for everything these days. Then one can amble back and see if Eliana has come home. She is out for a walk with her four daughters, the two that are her real daughters and the two new ones, the Corpse Crower's Rita and Vibeke. Eliana is incomparable. Women like her somehow take center stage in this world. Their warmth radiates in all directions and reaches as far as the arctic regions. They represent in a way the meaning and the goal of human life. They are nothing but *action*. . .

And now she's going to be rewarded. She and Moritz are not only going to be able to afford a new and better apart-ment, but there will be lots left over, among other things money for their son's musical education. The little boy is indeed quite a marvel, he simply has to become a great musician. And poor Vibeke, she has it better now than ever before, she is in the best possible hands.

The rest of the money will go to Sirius and Kornelius, the two fellow musicians, ten thousand for each; it is meant to be a sort of thank-you for the music. And then the Corpse Crower is to get a little something, and Lindenskov, and then Boman is to get an impressive tombstone.

This is the final, unshakable decision, following fourteen days of deliberation, following fourteen days of lonely struggles . . . fourteen days of unraveling of oneself and damned play-acting and backbreaking warfare with trolls in the head and in the heart, in Ibsen's words. Some of those tireless small devils have not been completely silenced yet, they scurry about and pick at him, with their poisonous pointed nails: ... Ha, ha, Kristen Mortensen, you are a man who knows how to point your "good deeds" to a secret address, to your very own door. Both as far as Atlanta and Eliana are concerned! In the former case it is a sentimental declaration of love, a heavily underlined *that much I love you*! A heavily gilt forget-me-not on the breast of the loved one. And as far as the second case is concerned, it means: *and take good care of Vibeke.*

And that way you hope that your soul will have peace for the time being. Peace to return back to itself, to work, to solitude, to the *great work*!

Faugh! Self-deception, that's all it is.

Magister Mortensen stands still for a moment, gnashing his teeth. At that very moment he could commit murder. At any rate, commit suicide. The only result, he coolly admits to himself, the only result of your painful deliberations is and will ever remain that you recognize your own irremediable wretchedness. But at least that is some kind of result. You are unable to help yourself to escape from your dilemma. And that's the way you've always been. The peasant's primitive hunger for life is struggling in your sadly warped soul with the brooding intellectual's melancholy tendency toward sacrifice and asceticism. It is impossible for you to achieve any kind of liberation. You were born unfree . . . a wretched offspring of the thick and viscous Christianity of many generations . . . never, never will you succeed in liberating yourself from the old and mouldy moral obsessions . . . you reek from them just like a piece of clothing from perspiration, clothing that is never changed. Old, inherited, dirty underwear. . . !

"Yes, but what in blazes do you want me to do?" he mumbles half-aloud to himself, turning to face the laughing band of devils. "The money is in my way, it ruins my peace of mind, it must be converted—converted into action, into good deeds, *that* at least is certain. And can it be wrong, then, that I give it to fellow human beings who are in need of it and have deserved it? Should I perhaps have given the money to Pastor Fruelund or to Ankersen?

"But—enough of that. You have now been racking your brains a sufficiently long time trying to find out how plain and simple goodness is to be put into practice. You've played cops and robbers long enough with yourself. You had to go out and get some fresh air, no matter what's going to happen. . ."

"The decision is irrevocable!" he says imperatively, and the little devils flee every which way and lie down pretending to be dead, just as if they were spiders at which one blows tobacco smoke.

The girls have returned home, but Eliana is still away; she is over at blacksmith Janniksen's helping with something or other.

Well, then this has to wait, too. But he is not rushed for time. He can walk upstairs and sit down a while or fling himself down on the sofa while he is waiting.

Mortensen calls Vibeke, who is running about and playing with the daughters of the ferryman. She does not hear him. Yes, she probably hears him but doesn't want to come over.

"Come to Daddy, Vibeke!" he shouts to her, feeling very sad.

The girl shakes her head energetically: "Not to Daddy, no! Not to Daddy!"

"Hello, Mortensen!" says a cheerful voice behind him; it is Ole Brandy, he is accompanied by Moritz, the Corpse Crower, and Jakob Siff, they are on their way to the Höje warehouse to say hello to Olivarius. "Come with us, Morten, and have a little bitter . . . that is, if you haven't become

228

too stuck-up from all your money? What do you say, old boy? Do like the rich man, who said: eat, drink and be merry!"

Mortensen says with a friendly nod: "Yes, of course I'd like to."

But what about the briefcase? It has to be put in a locked desk drawer for the time being.

It is so done. And the apartment gets securely locked. Everything is all set. Magister Mortensen has been up in Olivarius's sail loft a few times before, one can have a wonderful time together with the old boys. The weather is lovely. The devilish figures from the Russian march float about in empty air. God in heaven knows that one needs some self-forgetfulness. Not the theoretical kind, that demands constant Herculean labors, but the practical absolution through Bacchus, the talk of doughty men and soothing chatter about stuff and nonsense.

"Wait a while, Mortensen!" A loud voice resounds up through the stairway. "Just wait a while, I must speak with you alone!"

It is Oldendorp. What can he want?

The count grasps Magister Mortensen's coat-collar and says in a low voice: "Mortensen, can you lend me five hundred crowns?"

"That I can, if it can be done in a hurry, for there are some fellows waiting for me downstairs."

Once again he opens the door and the desk drawer.

"Just five hundred?" he asks and flashes a bank note.

"Yes, thank you." The count shakes his hand. "Perhaps you'll never get them back, Mortensen, will you ever forgive me for *that*? If not, you'll get them back, for I do have a sense of shame. Incidentally, can you keep a secret, old fellow? Yes, of course you can!"

The count puts his mouth close to Mortensen's ear and whispers: "And then I'll say good-by to you now, Mortensen.

For I'm leaving early tomorrow morning on board the *Mjöl-ner*. Running away, just like that. Together with Mira! It's a deep dark secret. For I can't *stand* them any longer. There's going to be a whole lot of fuss, but it can't be helped. So, my old friend, good-by and live well, no matter where in the world you'll be, for I suppose you'll be leaving soon, too? And then see to it that you finish your book, so that they can really have something shocking to read, those nitwits! Well, let's walk down again and make believe nothing's happened, and then I'll say 'See you again soon' in order to make sure that we'll throw any possible spies off the scent. Constable Debes walks around eavesdropping everywhere!"

"Good-by, Mortensen, and see you soon again!" The count waves to him and disappears around the corner, with a merry expression on his face. A bit preoccupied, Mortensen joins Moritz and the others.

"Well, well, there he is, Matte-Gok!" Ole Brandy remarks and nudges Mortensen in the ribs. "He got a real brain-cruncher right in the mouth last night."

Ole Brandy hoots at him and shouts: "There's more to be had here, young fellow, you just come over here to Daddy!"

Matte-Gok stops and walks over to them, the ninny that he is. Ole Brandy looks embarrassed because of the other's simple-mindedness and says in a friendly manner: "You'll come along and have a drink with us, Matte-Gok?" But Matte-Gok smiles and shakes his head. He is a temperance man. But thanks just the same.

"Stand up straight when you're talking to your superior, you jerk," Ole snarls, turning his back on him to show his contempt.

Matte-Gok exchanges friendly glances with the others and ambles along, being in no hurry. Just when he walks past the Bastille he has great difficulty checking himself from running up to Mortensen's apartment to see how everything

230

looks when he is not home. But, damn it all, it is too risky in bright daylight, it must wait. But such an opportunity is not to be missed. He has a sneaking suspicion that, no, he actually *knows* how it looks up there. A decrepit old desk with the kind of lock that one can almost pick with one's fingers, and all the money'll be right in the palm of one's hand, if you please. Thoughtless and disturbed fools of Mortensen's caliber always keep their filthy lucre within reach.

With a winning smile he greets midwife Nillegaard who is rushing past with her bag.

CHAPTER 3

How the battle developed. The flight of the bridal couple.
Speeches and processions. The bridegroom's strange dream.
The bride's loneliness and consolation

Savings-bank manager Ankersen had anticipated that his
plan of battle might meet with resistance—even considerable resistance—for blacksmith Janniksen was a tough cus-
tomer. But that it should go awry at the very beginning was
something that he had not reckoned with.

From the very first, everything went according to the
program: the carriole, which he had borrowed from apothecary Fähse after strenuous haggling, looked nice indeed
standing in front of the church. Happily the bridal couple
stepped into the carriage, and the coal-black horse very
elegantly set off at a trot. But when the bride noticed the
direction in which they were going, she got to her feet and
ordered the coachman to stop, which he did, with much
surprise. Then she got down and motioned to the bridegroom that he should do the same. Hesitantly, Sirius followed his wife, who already had disappeared in one of the
alleys behind the nearest houses. He found her in Sexton
Alley, where she had hidden herself behind an open cellar
door to wait for him.

"Just what is all this?" Sirius asked nervously.

She took his arm and made him come along: "This way!
We don't want to stand there and confess our sins over at

232

Ankersen's club! It's all some mumbo-jumbo that Mother has come up with. Now they can just sit there, all of them!"

Ankersen, who had followed the two-wheeled carriole on foot together with the mother of the bride, the Nillegaards, and other friends and fellow members, was completely beside himself when he was told what had happened. He brandished his stick so wildly that the horse shied and set off at a gallop with the empty carriage.

"Yes, go, go—to the devil!" Ankersen cried, hurling his stick like a spear after the departing carriage. Then he raised his empty hands and turned imploringly towards the small group of people: "Go after them! Capture them! Yes, that's right, Mathias Georg, my boy: go and get them! We must not lose out in this cause! It's a good cause! We must give our all to this cause, every one of us!"

"Yes, that's what I think, too!" Mrs. Janniksen chimed in.

"But—h'm—no, no." Adjunct teacher Nillegaard cleared his throat and shook his head. "No, no, it is all in vain, Ankersen. We've got the worst of it, Ankersen! We'll be the laughing-stock of everybody."

With threatening gestures Ankersen stepped closer to the rebellious one. Nillegaard ducked but held to his opinion: "We must not act rashly, Ankersen! We have to think it over! They're waiting for us over at the Ydun Society!"

Ankersen was too angry to reply. A faint whining sound emanated from his dilated nostrils.

Suddenly there was heard a booming shot from a cannon. And then several gunshots.

Nillegaard was shaking all over his body. He was so frightened that he grasped Ankersen by the arm.

The cannon thundered once more. Nillegaard made a grimace and squeezed Ankersen's arm. Then another shot, and another one—nine in all. A murderous smell of gunpowder smoke filled the air. They heard bugle calls and an awful battle din. Nillegaard moaned and closed his eyes.

"Well, if—" said Ankersen.

Choral singing was heard from afar. Nillegaard opened his eyes and saw that he was alone with Ankersen.

"That was a terrible thing!" he said.

Ankersen seized his hand and said with great warmth, "But at least you and I remained at our post, Nillegaard. All the others fled. But let us now walk calmly over to Ydun and in close concord lay our plan of battle. We'll stick together, Nillegaard, we won't desert each other in the hour of need! Shall we agree on that?"

The two men set out for the Ydun Society, arm in arm.

Matte-Gok had returned, and he could report that the bridal couple had ended up in the smithy, where there were songs and speeches.

"Wait a minute," Ankersen said. He grasped Matte-Gok by the lapel: "It's best that you keep an eye on what they're doing. It may be of the utmost importance to us. You've nothing against that, have you? On your way once more, my dear boy, and keep us informed as to every detail!"

"We are going to win this battle!" Ankersen shouted, lifting both arms toward heaven. "We *are* going to reap the victory, no matter what the cost!"

In Janniksen's smithy things were already in full swing. The male choir had sung "At the Wondrous Moment of Dawn," and Oldendorp's fantastic band of lid-and-saucepan musicians was now playing a march that seemed as if it would never end; and finally the count had to stop the music with a firm hand, for now the time had come for the speeches to begin. He was going to make the introductory one himself.

The count spoke about the fraternity of mankind. He also quoted a passage from Schiller's Ode to Joy, well known as a part of Beethoven's immortal symphony. He lifted his glass: "And tonight we especially wish to pay tribute to blacksmith Janniksen, the father of the bride, this veritable

234

Hercules, this Vulcan, in whose smithy we are gathered. We will therefore lift our glasses and. . ."

It was at this very moment that the count interrupted himself, and with the hand holding his glass made a threatening gesture in the direction of the door, shouting: "I can see you very well, constable Debes! You temperance spy! But I'll advise you to call a retreat as soon as possible, unless you want us to get the dogs after you! Skoal!"

Everyone turned in surprise toward the door, but constable Debes had apprised the situation correctly and had already made himself scarce.

"To hell with him!" the blacksmith said with a thin smile. He got up; now it was his turn to make a speech.

This was something that happened very rarely—indeed it was now perhaps taking place for the first and last time in history. The blacksmith looked magnificent, dressed in a tight-fitting frock coat that emphasized his muscular body, with a full-blown poppy in the button-hole.

"We have in our midst a *count*," he said, "a real, blue-blooded count, a man whose forefathers used to ride on gold-caparisoned horses and dig the points of their spears into the diaphragms of their enemies, who also were counts and barons and doughty knights, something that we can read about in the old writings and also hear about in the famous and glorious folk ballads."

The blacksmith worked himself up, gesticulating with his large, scarred fists and staring majestically into space. He spoke in grandiose phrases and used words that no one would have believed this plain fellow even knew.

"Thus they rode forth, facing each other, dressed in armor and cuirass, beating their untarnished shields. And then! Spears flew in among the sections of the coats of mail, and the opponents toppled off their horses and writhed helplessly in the dirt, while the bloodstained horses returned from the field of honor. Those were the days! Those people didn't swallow down a mean insult the way people do today. No, it was the law of the fist that held sway, and with pomp and circumstance, the victor would return home to his beloved, who was gazing down from the lofty towers. Now then, as I said before, we have a descendant from those days among us, and what is more: he's coming to us with his own orchestra, the biggest, the only one, the best that he can provide, and thereby he's doing us all a great honor, for which he deserves our most worthy thanks. And now we'll let the corks fly and we'll say 'skoal' and shout a three-times-three hurrah for the count!"

The glasses were emptied, and the force of the hurrahs made the iron and the tin in the smithy vibrate, boom, and reverberate. Then the blacksmith took hold of the count's arm, and with the orchestra and the male choir in the lead every one walked in procession out into the illuminated garden.

Sirius had remained behind in the smithy. He was sitting on the grating over by the cold forge looking pale and depressed.

"I don't know quite what to make of it," he said, attempting a smile.

"You're always spoiling everything!" Julia snorted. "Just what is it that's wrong with you?"

"Oh, I don't know, I feel so out of sorts and tired, Julia." Sirius looked genuinely contrite. "Perhaps it will pass. Let's take a breather for a while."

"Breather!" mimicked Julia. "Breather! *Now,* even before we have really got started!"

Julia had an annoyed look in her eyes; she resembled her sourpuss of a mother, in a way that pained Sirius. He sighed: "But dear Julia, why don't *you* go on out to The Dolphin, and then I'll come later."

"That would really be a fine sight!" Julia laughed deri-

236

sively but on the verge of tears. Then suddenly she changed her tune, and she began to resemble her father in an attractive way: "But you look awful, Sirius! Have you had too much to drink? Do you feel sick?"

"No, no, it isn't that. But you just go, Julia, as I said. No one will notice that I stay away for a few moments. And I can go upstairs and lie down for a while."

"Then I'll go with you," Julia said, giving him a tender and uncertain glance. It was Julia's own, reflecting her innermost self. That's the way she is, he thought to himself.

They walked up to the little room in the attic. Completely worn out, Sirius flung himself on the bed, and Julia sat by his side. "You'll see it will go away," she comforted him, stroking his pale, clean-shaven cheeks.

In a little while Sirius had fallen asleep. Julia shrugged her shoulders and walked over to the mirror to fix her hair. A little while later she was on her way out to The Dolphin.

Sirius slept for about half an hour, dreaming all the while, but then suddenly he was wide awake and remembered so very clearly a dream that he had had.

. . . He was walking on the shore of a lake, upon the dark surface of which some curious bluish-white birds were floating, and all about, as far as the eye could see, there was a multitude of strange-looking birds: rosy-red flamingoes, daintily strutting about and emitting deep, harmonious sounds, birds of paradise, with glittering colors as clear as diamonds, slowly hovering birds of pure, luminous webs of mist. He turned around to face Julia and said triumphantly: "What do you say now?" But now it wasn't Julia who was standing next to him—it was Leonora!

"Leonora!" he said. "Are *you* here?"

She smiled: "Yes, of course, I'm here!" And then she suddenly began to sing, with a superhumanly warm and clear voice . . . a song with many beautiful stanzas, each of which ended with the words: "Your wedding night."

237

Sirius recognized the verses, they were his own; he listened enraptured and was completely lost in the melodiousness of it all, a polyphonous and blissful melodiousness, in which also the curious birds had a part, just like voices with a swelling orchestra.

". . . Your wedding night."

Leonora. Good God!

Sirius got up. Everything went black, and he had a prolonged coughing spell, but when it ended he felt much better. He went over and opened the window. The soft wind of evening sighed in the trees and bushes in the blacksmith's garden, and the colored lanterns flickered, ghostly and unreal.

". . . Your wedding night."

Sirius was strongly seized by the wonder of it all and also by an inexpressible gratitude toward Leonora, who in this way had come to him in his dreams and had sung for him. The firm and intimate ring of her words: "Yes, of course I'm here!" kept surging through his head.

Singing and loud voices could be heard from the smithy, dull and nonsensical drunken chatter that seemed to rip and scratch into his divinely bright and memory-filled solitude. He closed the window.

What's to be done now?

He felt no desire to be with the others, not even with Julia. He only wished to be alone as long as possible.

He stretched out on the bed and through his weariness he enjoyed that unbounded sense of well-being that comes from being alone—alone with the dream, with the song, with Leonora.

Julia walked aimlessly about. First she walked into the smithy, where the guests were eating and drinking, enveloped by a heavy aroma of food and liquor which was disagreeable to her and gave her a great distaste for food.

Then she went down to the improvised dance-hall, where they already had begun to dance. She stopped there a short while and wished that she, like any other young girl, could abandon herself to the music and the dancing.

From there she walked back up to the house. But there Sirius was still sleeping.

Off again.

There is in the whole wide world nothing as forlorn as a bride who has been deserted by her bridegroom. Every one she meets assumes that for one reason or another she is waiting for her groom, and that she is by herself only temporarily. Those who are sober enough give her a friendly nod of recognition and good wishes, but most people hardly notice her, especially since twilight has set in. She ambles about haphazardly.

She is alone, alone.

The colored lanterns in the garden are put out, one after the other. One of them is on fire. She stands there watching how it is being eaten up, and she lets it burn up until there is no more left of it than a few whitish shreds that float away in the darkness.

Then that too has come to an end.

She walks back to Sirius, who is lying there with eyes closed, looking very pale. She is seized by a sudden fear: is he breathing, or—? Yes, he is breathing, he opens his eyes and gives her a friendly look, strokes her hand, and she sits down beside him for a moment on the edge of the bed. But again he dozes off, and she is drawn away once more, out into the teeming and festively noisy night, which has nothing but loneliness to offer a wandering bride.

But at last she is overwhelmed by lonesomeness; feeling sad and cold she sits down on an old rotten bench in a hidden corner of the garden and falls into a reverie with strange and hopeless thoughts.

Then it is that Matte-Gok appears in the twilight.

239

"You're sitting here all by yourself?" he asks.

Julia doesn't know what to answer. She remains silent.

"Where's your husband, Julia?" he asks in a friendly tone of voice.

She remains silent.

"You mustn't be afraid of me," says Matte-Gok and without further ado sits down on the bench next to her. He grasps her chilly hand and says in a low and intimate voice: "You two should not have run away like that, Julia. Do you understand what I mean? Now be a good girl and let's get hold of Sirius and come with me to the Ydun Society; it is both cosy and warm there, and we're all longing so much to have you with us."

He squeezes her hand and moves closer; she feels the warmth emanating from his body.

"But you're freezing, you poor girl!" he says and presses her protectively to him; she feels his breath against her face, tears herself loose and flees, but in the wrong direction, seeking refuge behind the bench, in the dense shrubbery. He runs after her. They collide, it develops into a quiet and tender struggle that does not end until she gives up—but not until she has made him promise that for the love of everything that is holy it remain a secret. . .

Thus it happened that Matte-Gok that night succeeded in adding a new and rare item to his long and sinister catalogue of crimes. Violating a bride! That was one thing he had not attempted before. He would never have believed it, that one could experience such a thing—in this ludicrous, miserable hole of a town!

240

CHAPTER 4

Further as to the battle. The deliberations of the saintly ones

The gathering at the Ydun Society, which originally had been intended to be a wedding feast, had little by little developed into a kind of council of war.

Everyone was fully agreed that they should intervene against those leading a licentious life. But there were divided opinions as to the manner in which this was to be done. As usual, Ankersen represented the most extremist faction and maintained that the entire assembly after having their coffee should all leave together and seek out the bride and groom and try to bring them back with them. "We know that there will be resistance and we may have to go through horrible things together," he said, "but it just has to be that way."

"Yes, that's what I think too!" Mrs. Janniksen said eagerly.

Adjunct teacher Nillegaard, however, was strongly opposed to that plan.

"The idea is rather nice in and of itself," he said. "But the time is not right to undertake such a crusade. I shall be very glad to take part in a demonstration for the good cause, but let us wait! Let us just wait until the wedding feast has ebbed out in a few days, until reaction, fatigue, and remorse have set in. Then, and then only, is the fullness of time!"

The murmuring from the gathering indicated that Nillegaard's point of view met with general assent. But Ankersen stuck to his view.

"What Nillegaard says may quite possibly be true," he said. "But in a case like this I certainly don't think that cool calculation is the proper thing or is to be tolerated. On the contrary! The one who risks nothing, gains nothing, Nillegaard! I for my part have learned that it is *the holy fire,* and nothing but that, that will bring about the desired effect. When you encounter a mad bull, you can do one of two things: you can run away and let the bull rage on and do irreparable damage to your fellow men while you lock yourself up in your room, or with head held high you can face the intractable animal, look it in the eye and do whatever is in your power to subdue it!"

"No truer word was ever spoken!" Mrs. Janniksen affirmed.

Nillegaard shook his head and replied earnestly and with great emphasis: "I do not underestimate a sincere fighting spirit, Ankersen. I'm only of the opinion that we best serve the good cause by enlisting our good common sense in its service. A bull—yes, the metaphor is excellent! A bull is a bull, and no persuasion, no argument, no preaching will help one in the face of the blind rage of the forces of nature!"

Ankersen rose to his feet and made a sweeping motion with his arms. "The forces of nature!" he shouted scornfully. "Satan in Hell take the forces of nature!"

"No offence!" said Nillegaard, with an anxious smile on his face.

Ankersen laughed exultantly: "One can tell that you're a teacher of *arithmetic,* Nillegaard! But believe me—your calculations do not suffice in the face of the blind raging of sin! Arithmetic is arithmetic, but the holy fire is infallible! It is miraculous! Or—isn't it true that faith removes mountains?"

"Yes, indeed!" Mrs. Janniksen said triumphantly.

Nillegaard nodded his head wearily: "Yes, Ankersen, it's true in a way—in a certain way and at a certain time. And in a figurative sense. And I also understand very well your

242

—your unusual way of thinking. But I don't think that every ineffectual blow is a blow in the Lord's cause! We mustn't destroy ourselves because of our foolhardy courage and a too rash spirit of self-sacrifice! When the day comes that we have succeeded in putting *total prohibition* into effect by dint of our well-organized and tireless work, Ankersen, that day is our real day of victory. And we are not so far from the goal, either! Truly, the day of the sinners and profligates will soon come to an end. That which transpires in the gloom of this very night is the beginning of their last convulsions. Be therefore a wise commander, Ankersen, do not fence in the dark, do not make a sally in the wrong direction! You know that we have confidence in you, you know that we follow you, when. . ."

"When there are no more risks to be taken!" Ankersen cut him short. "When no one has to risk his own life! Thank you, Nillegaard, I'm telling you, and I'm telling this whole assembly, that I disagree with you! For the fact of the matter, Nillegaard, is that you are *afraid!* You're not only a cautious and calculating fellow, you are a troubled human being, a man of little faith! In truth, it is not going to be said of us that we lost a battle and then gave up, that we hurried up to get back home and hoped that we would have better luck the next time! We don't want to have that stain on our scutcheon!"

"No, we don't want that stain on our scutcheon!" echoed the blacksmith's wife with much elation.

Ankersen made an all-embracing motion with his arms: "Therefore I implore you for the last time, all of you: *follow me!* Follow me in this very hour! And if you do not come along with me—well, then I'll go into the battle *all by myself!*"

"No, you shan't go by yourself, Ankersen!" Mrs. Janniksen cried, sending the savings-bank manager a determined look.

Nillegaard blew his nose and said in a dry, complaining

voice: "Yes, yes, but what is it really that you want us to do, Ankersen? You certainly owe us an explanation!"

"No!" shouted Ankersen. His voice quivered: "We don't need any explanation, gentlemen! That which has to be, that will be!"

Nillegaard had turned pale. He said in a low but uncommonly clear voice: "The only thing you achieve, Ankersen, with this brainless course of action, is to sow dissension among us, who otherwise could have been a united and harmonious bloc of people, a formidable bloc that no one could circumvent!"

"Circumvent!" bellowed Ankersen and raised his fists. "Circumvent! Yes, that's how it is! Yes, that's just what you are doing, Nillegaard, afraid for your hide and for your good position and your reputation! That's the nub of it!"

Nillegaard smiled, trying to restrain himself, although feeling indignant to the bottom of his soul. He replied in a shrill tone: "You think you're some kind of prophet, Ankersen. But I just want to tell you that you're about the only one who thinks so, my dear man! You just go ahead and do as you please! All you will achieve at best is that tomorrow people will shrug their shoulders and say: 'Well, that fellow, Ankersen, that *crazy fool*, he was on the warpath again last night!' And the only thing you will achieve is merely doing harm to our cause. And all this to enable you to give in to your confounded penchant for *showing off!*"

Ankersen burst out in a loud, groaning laughter: "Thank you, Nillegaard. Thank you! Now I think that we all know you to the very bottom of your rattling doe's heart! You coward! You slacker! I . . . I have only contempt for you! How you shook and trembled the time that the cannon went off!"

He turned to face the gathering and said in a plaintive, hollow and somber voice: "Then choose, brothers and sisters! Choose between *this one and me!* If you choose him, well, then I'll understand your message. Then I'll leave and set my own course!"

"No! Ankersen must not leave us!" some one suddenly shouted.

It was not Mrs. Janniksen's voice. It was Mrs. Nillegaard who had spoken. She had risen from her chair and was wringing a handkerchief between the palms of her hands: "Ankersen must stay with us! Ankersen mustn't leave us!"

Mrs. Nillegaard's appeal had a powerful and immediate effect. There was a great commotion among the assembled people, many got to their feet, one woman wept loudly and provocatively. Nillegaard's face had taken on a curiously doltish expression; his lower lip sagged.

"Yes!" Mrs. Nillegaard continued in a fanatically loud, sing-song voice which could have melted a stone: "I disagree with my husband! I believe in Ankersen! He is right. For *the letter of the law killeth, but the spirit giveth life.*"

She almost howled out the last few words and at the same time shook her head rapidly.

Ankersen, too, stood there for a time unable to say anything. But then he suddenly started to speak, in a deep and gentle voice, like some one who is deeply moved and contented: "Thank you, Mrs. Nillegaard, thank you, my sister and friend. Thank you for those good words. But now listen to another word, you, my dear friends and fellow believers . . . . a word that concerns our brother Nillegaard. I wish to apologize to Nillegaard for my harsh words. I've known his kind heart, his clear mind, his tireless energy. We can't afford to do without him."

Ankersen then turned to address Nillegaard directly: "I want to take this opportunity to offer you, too, my most heartfelt thanks! Let all bitter feelings be forgotten. I believe that it's best that we give in to each other, in the name of

245

the Lord. *You* are right in saying that we should not lose sight of our final goal. *I* am right in saying that we should not yield in individual instances."

Ankersen once more turned to face the audience: "I therefore propose, dear friends, that we march in a body through the town this very evening—without attracting much attention, without interfering with any one, merely quietly singing. We'll walk once around the town, and then we'll return home each to his own. I think it is best this way!"

The assemblage rose, calmly. All the faces reflected great relief, a sense of gentle and happy contentment.

CHAPTER 5

*Further events in the course of the battle. Nillegaard's bitter
thoughts and misgivings during the procession. Ole Brandy's
seductive singing. The great clash. The victory of the
saintly ones*

Their voices muffled, the members of the Ydun Society
march along the shore toward the old section of town.
Ankersen is in the lead, he is on his guard and looks back or
to the side out of the corners of his eyes, scrutinizing everything at the same time.

"What an idiotic thing to do!" Nillegaard thinks to himself.
"What silly nonsense! In the name of heaven, what good
will it do? It's the result of a stupid compromise. Well,
Nillegaard, you could have refrained from participating! But
the thing is that once again you are a victim of one of
Ankersen's *coups*—and goodness knows how often this has
happened!"

Nillegaard gets more and more indignant at the thought
that once again he is dancing to Ankersen's music and sub-
mitting to his brainless dictates. For the good of the *cause?*
What rot! Their cause would have gained immensely if
Ankersen, in the presence of the entire membership, had
been put in his place once for all. Which actually had been
on the point of happening and would have happened if Ida
hadn't had her attack of hysteria! Crazy people and hysterical women, ugh! If you had any sense, you would just

247

get away from it all. And still you're shuffling along with them. Against your better knowledge. Old fool!

If only the whole thing had passed off without such complications! But it is useless to think that one can play with fire without being burned, especially when a detonator like Ankersen leads the way.

Nillegaard clenched his fists in his pockets and murmured to himself, his mind filled with dark intentions: "You just wait. You just wait."

In the sail loft of the Höje warehouse the bottle has been passed steadily from one to the other. There have been songs and speeches, Ole Brandy and Olivarius have vied with each other in telling ghost stories and hair-raising reminiscences from the stormy life of the sailor, and Moritz has several times on request sung the grand old wedding song "At the Wondrous Moment of Dawn." During all this the guests have several times agreed to go home, they have gotten up, they have begun stirring, pushing hither and yon coils of rope and other kinds of rubbish that are in their way, and have drunk the irrevocably final skoal—indeed, they have at one point gotten so far as to look for the trap-door leading downstairs.

But under the heavy burden of drink, the men had gradually lost that certain intimate contact with one another, had become reserved and sparing of words, victims of that peculiar aloofness from the world which is always lying in wait for the excessively joyful man, and they had finally arrived at that immense loneliness which is the final state of all living organisms.

That was not the case with Ole Brandy, however.

Sitting astride a gear wheel, he fought his way through this fatefully threatening sense of loneliness. He then obstinately forced his way through sleep and fog and a mess of different pieces of furniture and other things, and managed

248

to push open one of the hatches. The fresh air made him feel as if he had retrieved his balance, he took a drink from his hip flask, became once again aware of the stirrings of life in his soul and felt an irresistible urge to burst out in disconsolate but powerful song.

> Mourning measures, darkest dirges
> I must make my harp to play
> On my melancholy way.
> And by Babylonian waters. . . .

The Christian temperance procession, which was then just about turning the corner by the Höje warehouse, stopped and listened to this plaintive song that welled forth into the dark night. Ankersen stopped short, looking up and sniffing, wondering where the hidden source of the music might be.

"But it is a hymn!" he said as if transported. "Who might it be that stands on high singing hymns?"

"It's a drunk," Nillegaard informed him, with malicious pleasure tinging his voice. "And it's no hymn, Ankersen, it's 'Olysses'!"

Ankersen poked him with his elbow: "Hush! In truth, a drunken man can't sing like that. So heart-stirring! Only a soul in distress can sing like that!"

Nillegaard laughed to himself, a dry and bitter laugh. Ole Brandy kept on singing, his deep bass booming on, filled with lamentation and emotion.

> Fare thee well, my sweetest darling,
> Thou hast now thy blessing found.
> I must bear a mourning garland,
> All with crepe my body wound.

> Though thy flesh hath met a sea-doom,
> God thy soul keeps at his side.

Thou who wert to be my bridegroom
Hast become my Jesu bride!

"What did I tell you?" Ankersen turned around triumphantly. "Wasn't that a hymn, adjunct Nillegaard?"

"No," said Nillegaard, wearily. A feeling of powerlessness and despair welled up within him, he was on the point of weeping. For it *was* indeed "Olysses," an awful, sentimental old sailor song. But he didn't have the strength to argue any more with Ankersen.

The savings-bank manager made a funnel with his hands and shouted in an unctious tone of voice: "Who's the one singing up there?"

No answer. The singing ceased. Slowly, people continued their march.

Nillegaard, of course, was right, his forebodings proved to be the precursors of something dreadful and unavoidable.

An awful uproar, singing and shouting, a stamping as of wild animals, the clanking of iron, the clatter of bottles, trumpet signals, and loud squeals of laughter emanate from Janniksen's smithy.

Perhaps the worst may still be averted. Greatly agitated, Nillegaard pulls at Ankersen's sleeve and says excitedly: "Listen, there *is* no real reason why we should walk right by the smithy, is there? We made an agreement, that we— that we—"

"Of course," Ankersen nods in agreement. He turns around, looks out over the procession and proclaims in a threatening voice: "Here you can hear for yourselves! Verily, Sodom and Gomorrha cannot have sounded worse! Let us stop here a minute, gather around me!"

Nillegaard is shaking from the suspense of it all. He steals a glance at Mrs. Janniksen. The expression in her face

250

beggars description. Like a wounded wild animal she is staring at the entrance to the smithy.

Ridiculous as well as terrifying. And all of it Ankersen's fault. In his fright Nillegaard stares into vacant space, as if he had second sight and feels that a ghastly vision is about to appear.

And then it happens!

A few staggering torchbearers appear in the doorway of the smithy, twisting and squirming to the accompaniment of gasping roars of laughter. Then a man in shirt sleeves comes out. He carries a flag on a pole. It is Count Oldendorp! It isn't any regular flag that waves from the pole. It is a signal flag, yellow with a black ball in the middle. A strangely sinister banner of destruction.

Then come more torchbearers. Then a bugler, tooting with all his might. Then comes a man who knocks two bottles against each other, and then another one who is engaged in the same occupation. Then a man with an iron bar, from which he draws long, sickly sounds with the aid of a hammer. And another man with an iron bar, which does not seem able to produce any sounds. Then a new group of torchbearers. Following them a man with a pair of bellows to be worked by hand; he doesn't say anything either. But after him comes a man emitting an earsplitting horse's neigh, followed by a young lout who makes a piercing flute-like sound in a bottle. And at last, three or four men who drum away on tin pots and buckets.

Then come several torchbearers and a few fellows who are roaring with laughter and pulling at some ropes. What is it that they are pulling? The cannon! *The cannon,* of course! And now blacksmith Janniksen himself appears, illuminated from all sides by sputtering torches and *dressed in a red lady's gown!* God almighty! Of course, nothing less than that would do for him! Almost choking, he belches

251

out commands, his rough voice breaks from the inconceivable jollity of it all, he howls and screams like a young girl who is being tickled!

"Quiet, for God's sake, and remain where you are, all of you!" Nillegaard shouts.

But it is too late. Mrs. Janniksen has already moved forward. She is approaching her husband. Collision! Indescribable confusion, during which Ankersen is of course already involved. Mrs. Janniksen tears and pulls at the blacksmith's dress. Ankersen roars. No, he is *singing!*

Nillegaard turns away, lurching and staggering.

"Ida!" he shouts. "Ida! We must get away from here! All of us must get away from here! Quick!"

And he starts running. He can hear footsteps all around, and is not certain whether they are pursuers or fellow escapees; he expects to hear the crash of the cannon at any moment. . . .

Not until he is over on the other side of Skin Islet, at the foot of the hill that leads down to the Höje warehouse, does he stop and look back, and he sees that he is alone.

He can hear shouts and crashes, singing, bestial roars of laughter, squeals, and infernal noises. The battle is going on full blast. Mrs. Janniksen has succeeded in tearing the dress off her husband. Mrs. Nillegaard, too, has thrown herself into the battle and in a shrill voice demands that the bridal couple be delivered up.

"Julia! Julia!" Her voice cuts right through the din of battle. And Mrs. Janniksen chimes in: "Julia! Julia!" Ankersen follows suit, and soon the entire membership of the Ydun Society are shouting in chorus: "Julia! Sirius! Julia! Sirius!"

Sirius is awakened by the loud shouts, he walks over to the window, just in time to see Ankersen being lifted up on strong arms and carried around in triumph! An incredible, dreamlike sight! Ankersen does not offer any resistance at all, on the contrary he helps them along, on his face there is an expression of a certain grim and expectant joy. And just when the bearers, yelling and screeching, go forward, he looks back and shouts with all his might: "Cheer up! Don't give up! We will win out for sure!"

"Sirius! Julia!" the shouts continue. And now Julia walks in through the door, she is out of breath and bathed in tears. "Come!" she says. "Come, Sirius! Mother is here!"

To be sure—Mrs. Janniksen appears in the doorway to the bedroom, and behind her is Mrs. Nillegaard. They are both weeping. Mrs. Janniksen is holding a short iron bar in her hand and carries a crinkled bundle of red cloth under one arm. She flings the bundle right in Julia's face and lifts the spear threateningly, shouting, her face distorted by frenzy: "Come now, Julia! You're both coming with me, at once, right this minute!"

Mrs. Nillegaard tries to calm her down by putting her hand on her arm, pleading: "But, but—Mrs. Janniksen! There's no reason to threaten the two young people, they're not making any fuss about coming with us—are you now?"

Sirius sighs and says gently: "No, as far as I'm concerned, it's OK with me. What do you think, Julia?"

Julia steps up to him and, sobbing torrentially, clings to his arm.

Sirius is trembling as he puts on his jacket and his shoes. Mrs. Nillegaard walks over to the window and announces in a loud voice: "Quiet! Everything is all right now! We'll be down immediately!"

"Everything all right?" Mrs. Janniksen groans. She has sat down on the bed and is near collapse. "Everything all right, you say? But what about Ankersen?"

"*He'll* be able to take care of himself!" Mrs. Nillegaard answers with firm assurance. "Besides, he's not alone, Mrs. Janniksen. His son is with him! I saw him! He's fighting like a lion!"

She bends over Mrs. Janniksen, tugs at her and shouts

ecstatically: "This thing is *great*, Mrs. Janniksen. It's a *great thing!* This is *victory!*"

A little while later the temperance procession was on its way back with the bride and groom at its head, flanked by Mrs. Nillegaard and Mrs. Janniksen, and singing loudly and cheerfully.

Nillegaard was hiding in an alleyway and was watching the procession pass by. Alas, in spite of all it had ended with a victory for Ankersen!

Nillegaard gnashed his teeth. Unjust! Ridiculous!

But where was Ankersen, anyway? Nillegaard felt himself impelled by a curiosity that he could not keep under control. When the procession was out of sight, he stole out from his hiding-place and cautiously walked up to the smithy. It was empty. There was no one about. But yes—the Crab King. The dwarf was standing inside the half-dark smithy and staring at him in the light coming from pitch burning in the sputtering forge.

Nillegaard came over to him and said courteously: "You haven't seen Ankersen around?"

The dwarf did not reply.

Thereupon constable Debes and two deputy policemen came running, their sabres rattling.

"Do you perhaps know where Ankersen is?" Nillegaard asked them.

"No!" was the sullen reply.

Nillegaard joined the policemen. He thought to himself: "Maybe they have killed Ankersen." The thought affected him like some strange spicy taste on the tip of his tongue.

"Oh—oh!" A hollow sound of moaning was heard in the dark.

They stopped short and listened.

"O—oh!" they could hear once more, dully and half-choked. And then, muffled, but clearly: "Here! Help! I can't —I can't. . !"

The policemen walked in the direction of the sound, Nillegaard followed, hesitantly, trembling from excitement. He thought it was Ankersen's voice and in his mind's eye he saw the savings-bank manager lying in a ditch, bathed in his own blood. But no, it wasn't Ankersen. It was Matte-Gok! He was lying on the ground, alone in the darkness, in a bent-over position.

"Are you hurt?" asked the constable.

Matte-Gok had difficulty speaking, but otherwise he seemed to be calm and composed, he mumbled something about his back, about an iron bar coming down across his back. "I had the breath knocked out of me. But it is already a bit better now, I think. No, don't get a doctor. I'll be all right."

The policemen helped him get up. He had difficulty in standing up on his legs. "Thank you, many thanks," he said. "And then if you would be kind enough to help me get home. No, it's a little better, it'll probably pass off when I get to bed. I'm only so terribly dizzy and bruised. I fainted!"

"There!" said Debes. "Carry him home and put him to bed. Careful, now!"

The two men left with Matte-Gok between them. The constable and Nillegaard hurried on out to The Dolphin. "Ankersen," thought Nillegaard, "Ankersen, what about him?" And suddenly he felt quite certain that Ankersen had been killed. Dead. Fallen in battle. He had not wanted to listen to the voice of reason. Stubborn and filled with rage, he had gone to his destruction in this terrible night of tragedy.

But no—Ankersen was not dead at all. On the contrary he was at the top of his form. He was standing on a table in the crowded and stuffy room, speaking to the people!

It was not a doomsday sermon, as might have been expected, no, reconciliation and gentleness tinged his voice:

255

". . . It is never too late, dear friends, *never!* The door stands ajar even at the twelfth hour, yes, even when the twelfth hour has struck. . . !"

"Yes, Ankersen is a good fellow!" boomed a voice from somewhere. It was Count Oldendorp.

"Long live Ankersen!" smith Janniksen bellowed, and the entire assemblage shouted: "Hip, hip, hurrah!"

Stealing away, Nillegaard involuntarily ducked his head. He felt an urge to have a good cry all by himself.

CHAPTER 6

Concerning the fate of Magister Mortensen

Alas, still another dear musician friend of ours is wandering out of our story. But no, he is not wandering—he is actually running! He is running up the stairway of eternity, for even though he is both wounded and weary, he is not a glum and clammy soul, but to the very end a firebrand with a huge appetite for life!

Worlds come to an end and rise again and perish once more, values are reappraised and rejected, all things are subject to the inscrutable laws of transitoriness and regeneration, but tar and pitch retain for all time their penetrating, rugged smell of harbors and ships, of persevering maintenance and an irrefutable workaday existence.

Magister Mortensen is lying down, inhaling this smell, for a moment it completely dominates his consciousness: all that exists is this safe and dependable smell and otherwise there is nothing at all. Yes, he feels a dryness in mouth and throat and for that reason a craving for something to drink. And then there are the odd figures in that march, what was it called again—the March of Death.

Then he slowly becomes aware, as in a dream, of a sail draped in such a way that its excessively pronounced folds make one think of an extensive, bird's-eye view of a mountainous landscape over which dawn is breaking. The next

257

earthly thing to come before his awakening consciousness is the rusty funnel which has belonged to a discarded ship's siren. He involuntarily expects it to bring forth a sound, but it emits only silence and darkness.

Then the silence is broken by some piercing sea gulls' cries nearby, and his ear, which thereby suddenly has been made to function intensely, now registers other sounds: a deep, polyphonic snoring, muffled and stifling, which mingles with the refreshing murmur of waves against a shore.

He lifts his head and looks about him. It's Olivarius's sail loft, to be sure. He gets up, shivering from cold and thirst. Over by a pile of leftover sail-cloth the Corpse Crower lies sleeping. The expression on his face reminds one of that of the man frozen to death in the well-known painting *All Quiet in the Shipka Pass*. A bit farther away lies the harmless little merchant Jakob Siff, with an unruly mustache and a sweet and devoted smile on his face. And still farther over is Moritz the ferryman; he too is sleeping, but in a sitting position leaning against a coil of rope, and his lean face retains even in sleep its cheerful and honest expression. And over by the wide-open trap-door is Ole Brandy! He reminds one of something on the order of a Stone Age man who has been resurrected from the grave; he doesn't actually seem to be sleeping but is, on the other hand, not in a state that one would venture to call wide awake. Stupefied but indomitable, he stares into thin air. Now he lifts an arm and beckons with a finger, and Mortensen walks over to him.

Ole nods deeply satisfied and says in a thick voice: "There's a fask, a lask, in my bapocket."

"A flask in your back pocket." Magister Mortensen gets hold of the bottle and takes a swig. The lukewarm liquid makes him feel sick all through his body, as if he had swallowed a live fish.

"Me one—me one—!" Ole Brandy babbles, but then sinks

back fully asleep, with the hip flask pressed close to his vest, which is full of nap from the coils of rope. Mortensen drags him over to the pile of sail-cloth and covers him with the soft old foresail in which he himself has been sleeping.

The empty bottles standing over by the coils of rope give out a green glow in the twilight. A really stiff drink is left in one of them. Magister Mortensen takes another swig and heaves a deep sigh of relief. All the feeling of nausea seems to have radiated out of his body—it feels as if a bright and beautiful candle had been lit within him.

He lets his thoughts drift freely about in the huge loft. You're free! You're free, free as Satan himself. *Flieh! Aus! Hinaus ins weite Land!* No more of that damned private tutoring or of that dank library. No one to be responsible to, no need to slink around. No women's talk and nonsense any more, no more sentimentality. No crying need and urge for money. All of that is so far away and irrelevant. Over with. At last you've been able to rub off the damned old skin. The cocoon has burst! You're not walking around any more festering with that small-town infection. You don't hate any one, not even principal Berg. Not Östermann either. You are completely independent. As long as it lasts, you're independent. So, enjoy your freedom, fellow!

Mortensen gets to his feet. He walks over to the open trap-door. The seagulls are gliding past on wings made rosy-tipped by the rising sun. How grand! Like one of Homer's epics! It's incredible how long a seagull can soar without moving its wings. Paradoxical. It is indeed the symbol of unencumbered, complete freedom. Of how to live life to the full!

You're free, old fellow! You can afford to buy the fastest motor boat in the whole wide world.

The *"Hell Hound"* is to be its name!

The two fastest motor boats in the world: the *"Hell Hound"* and *"Satan Himself."*

The three fastest and most recklessly driven racing boats in the world: the *"Hell Hound," "Satan Himself,"* and *"The Devil's Master!"*

People are standing open-mouthed on shore. Whee! In less than a second one will disappear into infinity . . . with the ocean on all sides and drifting clouds. And whee! Back again to the gaping crowd. And whee! Out of sight again!

Beat that one, schoolteacher Berg with your checkered suit and your big behind and your sour-sweet tea-cosy of a wife, and with your not-so-young daughter! You're welcome to it all! And you, too, Östermann, expert on authorized mediocrity. Enjoy yourself and just stagnate in insipid and conceited idyll. Best regards from the *Hell Hound.* P.S. *Satan Himself* also sends his best regards. P.P.S. *The Devil's Master* sends his heartiest congratulations on the occasion of your silver wedding!

The rays of the sun light up the western half of the harbor. An exceptionally beautiful morning! The little, dust-covered and musty-looking windows of the warehouse are fighting a losing battle in trying to keep the sunlight out. But it is much too strong for them. It contains all the victorious power of goodness, it thaws them out together with their green mold and theological cobwebs, just as the good deed destroys the schemes and villainies of small men.

Unrestricted, the light throws elongated, proud wedges into the untidy loft and infuses the litter with a new and hope-filled life. It is reflected in the nap of golden and durable manila hemp, it casts light and shadow on mountains of sail cloth and conjures up formations that make one think of the most distant and inaccessible mountain areas, such as the Rocky Mountains, the Himalayas . . . or even of more distant, higher and more insurmountable crests and peaks. Or of that madness of the heavens that is known as Saturn! Morning on Saturn four hundred years ago! Or in three hundred and thirty-one million years!

260

This is certainly a wonderful place to live and to die! Here is joy, real joy!

> What joy I feel with every breath
> Each hour of life in this world!

Mortensen hums. The old hymn has always reminded him of extensive journeys throughout the world, about Sinbad the Sailor's mad voyages in fine and foul weather.

Yes, this is a good place. Here one can at last be oneself, be full of life, without any chains.

It's only too bad that the bottles are empty. And a pity that the sleeping fellows are to wake up to nothing but empty glasses!

But there is a remedy for that. There are still a few bottles back in the house. And now they can be put to good use.

Mortensen opens the trap-door and walks down the many steps of the steep stairway. It is only a little after four o'clock. But the town is far from quiet. The air is filled with song and with never-ceasing whirlwinds of many kinds of sound. He can hear that people are dancing out at The Dolphin. Two fellows, drunk to the gills, stagger by, arm-in-arm, loose-jointed from their feelings of friendliness and happiness.

The key! Good God, he hasn't lost it? No, it's still in the door, isn't it, and he just forgot to take it with him yesterday. . . ?

And if any one—?

Yes, of course. Mortensen finds that the lock of the desk drawer has been picked. And the folder and the envelopes are gone. Also the thirty or forty thousand placed by itself furthest back in the drawer. Of course. Of course.

Well, that takes care of that.

"It doesn't really matter," he says, trying to persuade him-

self that it really is so. "At least the bottles are still here."
He opens one of them and pours some into a dusty glass.
"Skoal to that. That was probably the best solution to it all.
And you won't have to suffer that internal hocus-pocus. . ."

He notices how a shameful paroxysm of rage is welling
forth in his breast. *My money!*

"Hush!" He tries to pacify himself. "What do you want
to use that money for? You were almost on the point of going
to rack and ruin when you did have it. You were not suited
for it. Is it now to be *lamented,* on top of it all?"

But the devil within his breast grumbles and is not satisfied. My money! He hisses and stamps his foot. My gifts!
And then suddenly the devil lapses into sentimentality and
begins to snivel: "My heart is so sorrowful. . ."

He gets up, rummages feverishly in his inner pocket and
gets out Atlanta's letter, places it flat on the table and with
his finger spells out the words in the girlish handwriting
until he finds the ominous sentence: "My heart is so sorrowful." Yes, here it is, here she writes: "My heart is so sorrowful."

He smooths out the sheet of paper, folds it carefully
and holds it several times close to his face before he puts
it back in his inner pocket.

And he has the feeling that the most important thing has
been saved after all.

Carefully, he puts the two bottles into the pockets of his
overcoat. And then back to the blessed cosmic spot where
freedom reigns, where all suffering and sorrow have been
silenced and forgotten.

> . . . to the land where never in sorrow
> souls will depart from others.

Up in the sail loft the Corpse Crower had awakened and
was sitting up, staring into thin air like a mortally sick dog.

"Cheer up!" Magister Mortensen said and pulled the bottles out of his pockets. "It's an extra fine three-star cognac! It's just been brought down from Orion's Belt!"

"This all seems so stronge!" the Corpse Crower said, looking dejected.

"Skoal!" Mortensen said, as if giving a command.

It wasn't long before the Corpse Crower recovered his spirits. Magister Mortensen took his arm, and they took a quiet walk around the room in the morning light.

It was in the course of this promenade that Magister Mortensen discovered the stairway to eternity. In appearance this stairway did not seem any different at all from the usual, roughly knocked-together stairs that one can see in all warehouses. It reached from the floor to the ceiling in the southwest corner of the room. But since there was no space or room above it, except the so-called outer space, this stairway served no purpose at all—it just stood there like a sort of mysterious new growth in nature, or like some work of art representing a unique and deep symbolism.

Magister Mortensen attempted to convey to the Corpse Crower that indescribable enchantment he felt because of the circumstances that the stairs did not lead anywhere. And in this he succeeded—seemingly contrary to all that he reasonably could have expected: a light of rapture shone in Josef's pale eyes, they emitted reddish sparks and his entire ghostlike and transparent face gleamed: "Exactly! Exactly so!"

"Yes, isn't that so!" said Magister Mortensen, he felt tears almost welling forth in his eyes from meeting with such a high degree of understanding, and so promptly.

"For it's just like my *stand!*" the Corpse Crower said and rubbed his hands in childish delight. "My stand—it's not going to be used for anything either, it's just supposed to be there, yes, just like a—stand of eternity!"

He laughed bashfully, a tender expression appearing at the corners of his mouth.

"It's going to be a fine stand," he continued. "I can already see it in my thoughts. It's going to be the world's best stand, Mortensen!"

Into his eyes there came a serious, resolute, almost fanatical expression, and he added, nodding his head vehemently: "And no living soul is going to come here and say: 'But it's just a plain old stand, Josef, it can be used for both this and that purpose!' No one is going to tell me that!"

The Corpse Crower extended his thin hand, and the two men shook hands. The Corpse Crower said with a glance at the stairs: "Of course, it's going to be quite a lot better than an old stairway like that!"

He kicked at the stairs, with a show of disdain.

"But why does it have to be?" Magister Mortensen asked.

The Corpse Crower turned up his nose: "Well, because that stairway can be used for something."

"Yes, but how?" Magister Mortensen asked with a show of concern.

"To get up on the roof, of course!" The Corpse Crower regarded the stairs with very obvious disdain.

Magister Mortensen's face took on an expression of disappointment. "Yes—but what would one do up there?" he objected, obstinately.

"We-ell, what would one do up there?" It was quite evident that the Corpse Crower had no immediate reply.

"There you see!" said Magister Mortensen and nodded his head.

The two men quickly ascended the stairs, as if acting on the same impulse. It led up to a kind of small room with a roof in which there was a shutter-like opening. Magister Mortensen opened the shutter and they looked out over the huge, gleaming tiled roof, which sloped steeply down and ended abruptly in nothing, fading into blue in the distance, just like the road to the end of the earth.

"What the devil can one do on a roof like this?" asked Magister Mortensen.

"Yes, what can one do?" echoed the Corpse Crower.

"Actually, it's not too bad up here," Mortensen said. "Just look how the sun is shining! And if you fall down you'll end up in the brine and sink to the bottom like a rock! It'll feel about like being shot out of a cannon, don't you think? Brrrrr! Let's go down again and drink a toast to that!"

They walked slowly down the stairs. They left the shutter open. Magister Mortensen quickly emptied his glass and poured himself another one, and then still one more.

But then something horrible happens: Mortensen once again ascends the stairs, hurriedly, almost as if he were running, climbs out through the shutter and disappears! The Corpse Crower can hear how he slides down the slippery tiles. Then the sound ceases.

The Corpse Crower opens his mouth to shout in alarm, but cannot utter a sound. He staggers across the floor, stumbles and remains lying there with his face buried in a heap of sail-cloth rags.

CHAPTER 7

*General confusion, sprinkled with additional harrowing
events. Bailiff Kronfeldt nearly collapses, and the
Crab King utters human speech for the first
and last time in his life*

There are times when a person gets so indignant that he
does not react at all. Shuts himself up, as in a shell. Tries
to laugh it off. Gnashes his teeth. Hums a little. Grabs a
newspaper and yawns over an advertisement: "Experienced
and reliable girl wanted—light work and good salary."

Imagine that, just imagine that.

Such was the state in which Bailiff Kronfeldt found himself on the forenoon that he received the threefold tragic
news about the count's flight with Black Mira, the burglary
in the savings bank, and Magister Mortensen's suicide.

The first items are connected, of course. For Karl Erik
had no money at all to pay for his passage. It's all too clear.
All one has to do is to break in some place and steal forty-
nine thousand crowns.

"And now it's our turn, Charlotte," says the bailiff, in a
calm and ordinary tone of voice. "Now it's our turn. We'll
just pack our things. We're through. I'm through as a government official. But we'll get along somehow, Charlotte.
You are so good at *knitting*. You can knit for people. And I
can get some kind of job in an office. Actually, both of us
might benefit from a little change. We've been too gullible.

266

We have to take the consequences. There's no reason to cry because of that. Actually, things could have turned out much worse for us. He might, for instance, have killed us both."

Constable Debes returns from the savings bank with very important news. The thief has left behind him his jacket and his cap in addition to a crowbar and a pair of pliers. In one of the coat pockets they have found a perpetual calendar that belongs to the savings bank.

"Cap?" asks the bailiff with a thin, venomous smile. "You mean *hat?* For he used a hat, not a cap."

"No, cap," says the patrolman, surprised. "The usual type of cap with a shiny visor."

The bailiff sits down at his desk. He chuckles a bit to himself. "No, of course not," he says, and suddenly turns rosy red all over his head and neck. "Of course. It's a man with a cap that's been up to his tricks. Not a man who wears a hat. Not a hat-man."

He gets up. "Well! Then we'll have to find the owner of the jacket and the cap. Is there any one in particular that you suspect, Debes?"

The constable sadly shakes his head.

The bailiff looks at his watch. His head seems to be swimming. For a moment he feels very happy.

"We'll no doubt get to the bottom of this, just as we've managed to solve everything in the past," he says to the constable, brimming over with friendliness. "Please do your best, Debes."

"Yes, bailiff." The constable withdraws with a little bow.

The bailiff walks back into his apartment. "Charlotte!" he says with warmth. "Charlotte! I'm afraid we were wrong. It wasn't *he.* It was a cap-man."

"So, but hasn't *he* left?" Mrs. Kronfeldt asks in a whisper.

"Of course, of course. Thank God for that. That's something that we both have been looking forward to for a long time, isn't it? Ever since Miss Schmerling broke the engagement. We have reason to be happy about this, Charlotte. Our most fervent wishes, so to say, have been fulfilled."

"I just can't forget how calmly you took it. . . !" Mrs. Kronfeldt says. She sits down, wipes her eyes, and heaves a long sigh.

"What else did you expect?" the bailiff says with a smile. He suddenly feels as if his knees would give way. The reaction to it all! He feels very dizzy. He pulls himself together and walks back to his office. Exhausted, he lies down on the sofa. Fireflies are dancing in the air right before his eyes.

The police begin the search for the owner of the jacket and the cap. But early in the forenoon the owner comes and gives himself up.

It is Kornelius.

"Yes, it's my jacket and my cap," he says. "But I don't know anything about the crowbar and the pliers, and not the perpetual calendar either."

Constable Debes can't hide his surprise: "Well, but . . . then it's you, Kornelius. . . ?"

"No, I'm not the one who committed the burglary, if that's what you mean," Kornelius replies, looking him straight in the eye. "I don't know who it might be. I've had nothing to do with it."

"What a terrible thing that happened to Magister Mortensen!" he adds with a sigh, shaking his head.

"But you did go up to the savings bank last night and . . . and. . . ?" asks Debes.

"No."

Kornelius does not wish to hide anything but wants to tell everything as it was.

"Yes, but wait a minute," Debes says, "and then the bailiff will be here himself."

Bailiff Kronfeldt is now very excited. His calm has

268

vanished completely, his hands are shaking and he has hectic red splotches on his face. He gives Kornelius a look filled with loathing and devoid of mercy.

"Hurry up, young man!" he says in a flat voice.

Kornelius gives an account of his doings and does not conceal anything. He is calm, he speaks almost without a stutter. The bailiff squirms in his chair: "A divining rod? A buried treasure? . . . You're certainly an optimist if you think you can make *me* believe that! And then you were *attacked?* By whom, honored sir?"

"By a . . . person, or what should I call him, it was so dark, and I thought his face was all black. And when he grabbed me and sort of wanted to choke me, then I got very frightened. Of course, I don't actually believe in ghosts. But I thought he sort of reminded me of Satan himself, or something like that! Then I tore myself loose and ran home. And the jacket and the cap. . . they were just left behind. It wasn't until later that I discovered I had lost them."

The bailiff snorts and says in a harsh voice: "Well, well, that's what you did, is it? Yes, I think this will do. But the money, where is that?"

"I don't know anything about any money," Kornelius replies, looking squarely at the bailiff. "There *wasn't* any money! There *wasn't* any treasure!"

"You'll be better off if you hand over the money right away and without any beating around the bush!" the bailiff says with an impatient little jump in his chair.

"But, it *isn't* me. . .!" Kornelius objects, feeling greatly disheartened.

The bailiff gets up from his chair, but sits down again and waves his hands; his face is completely distorted: "For heaven's sake, my good man! Whom do you think you're talking to? Do you actually believe that you'll get anywhere with such idiotic evasions?"

The bailiff is now in a towering rage, he is on the verge

of tears and sobs when he talks. Kornelius gives him a frank and open look and squarely meets his hate-filled glance. "For I *am* innocent," he reiterates.

Now it gets to be too much for the bailiff, he gives himself over to a sort of hysterical laughter, gets up and waltzes out on the floor with outstretched arms.

"Listen to me now! Will the honorable gentleman do the right thing?" he snarls. "Will he try to do it, now? Will he tell me where he has hidden the money? Isn't he going to? Well, then he will have to take the consequences! Debes! Debes! Great God! *Debes!* So, you *are* still here? I'm happy to see that! I thought you perhaps had gone home to play solitaire! Then we will place this obstinate fellow under lock and key! And then you *search his house!* Do you understand?"

"Yes, I'll immediately. . . !" Debes says, looking very unhappy and irresolute.

"You're supposed to say 'Yes, sir!' " Kronfeldt snarls at him.

Debes takes Kornelius by the arm.

"What are you supposed to say, Debes?" the bailiff shouts at him.

"Yes, sir!"

"It's a good thing you could remember it."

Out of breath, the bailiff tugs at his collar. He has begun to perspire profusely. His heart beats fast and he feels a pain in his chest. He walks over and opens a window: "Great God in heaven! Great God in heaven!"

But thanks be to God. Thank God Almighty. At least the burglary has not been committed by Oldendorp. And his flight with this Mira—well, it must be charged, then, to the unbelievably extravagant actions of counts and barons. It's not going to be easy, but it can be done, as long as one takes it in one's stride and doesn't lose face. "Yes, it was awful, good heavens! And actually done with tremendous verve, incredible daring! Almost the way it's done in an opera, ha,

270

ha! The abduction from the seraglio! He was really incorrigible, the young man. But we did our best. We did not let the old Master of the Royal Hunt down. My poor old friend. But the fellow was a bit too wild for us." And so on. One knows one's own business. One just takes things slowly and steadily. One uses diplomacy. . .

The bailiff calmly sits down at his desk and notices with unutterable satisfaction how everything gradually begins to get set aright, to come together and be seen from a pleasant perspective. The storm dies down. The sea is calm again.

Until a new wave wells up, a new breaker, if possible even worse than the first one. . .

For it is found that Magister Mortensen's money too has disappeared without a trace! Where can the money be? And who says that his death actually was an accident or a suicide? Couldn't it have been murder? A premeditated murder with intent to rob?

The interrogation and the testimony of witnesses lead one to suspect the worst. It really looks as if there had been a conspiracy. Some one has enticed Magister Mortensen to come up on the warehouse roof and has got him drunk, robbed him of his money, and then very cleverly pushed him off the roof and into the great beyond.

The big question now is: Was the *count* a part of the conspiracy?

"About that there can be no doubt at all, Charlotte," the bailiff says, making his voice sound dry and matter-of-fact as a pencil-sharpener. "For he associated with that rabble. He was best friends with that scum. And—to top it all—he was seen in the company of Magister Mortensen that very afternoon."

Kronfeldt is once again quite calm and collected, just as he had been that morning. He has muted all strong feelings. He whistles a bit, sits down, grabs the newspaper, and reads

271

an advertisement about coal and coke. He yawns, tapping himself lightly on the mouth.

"It's no use crying about it, my friend," he says in a casual manner. "We'll have to get used to the idea that he not only has behaved like an ass as far as *we* are concerned but that he is a first-class bandit. Murderer and robber! Ha, ha, ha! It's a degenerate beast, a murderer and robber, that you've been coddling, my dear Charlotte. It's a *serpent* that you've reared at your breast!"

"A serpent?" he repeats. "No, a Midgard Serpent,* Charlotte. Nothing less will do! *A Midgard Serpent!*"

He withdraws to his office, walking slowly and humming to himself. His voice is shaking with suppressed laughter: "A Midgard Serpent!" And then in a whimpering tone of voice, as if he were talking to a little baby: "A Midgard Serpent! A sweet little Midgard Serpent. . ."

Matte-Gok has played his cards with dazzling adroitness. His alibi is in complete order. He is still staying in bed following the feigned assault; he has even had the nerve to send for Doctor Manicus, and has had him examine his chest and give him some pain-relieving medicine. And both Ankersen and Mrs. Midiord are coddling him with good food and words of cheer.

"One must stand the gaff for one's beliefs, one must have the courage of one's convictions," says Ankersen, "and one must be willing to risk one's own hide. Then you'll receive an award that is worth more than gold, namely the wonderful bliss that is eternal life! Yes, even if your back had been broken in the scuffle, Mathias Georg, that would have been much preferable to your hanging back with your tail between your legs, like poor Nillegaard. You have shown that you're man enough to risk your hide, and if you keep that up,

* The Midgard Serpent, in Norse mythology, was the evil serpent that encircled the entire earth. Tr. note.

I can foresee a splendid future for you, my son! Oh, if I were only young like you, then I know what *I* would do! I wouldn't stay in a small place like this, I would set out for the lands of the heathens and become a great preacher!"

Matte-Gok becomes lost in thought. Slowly a gleam comes into his eye. He has seen this kind of trick done in numerous motion pictures. And gradually both he and Ankersen go into a veritable frenzy. It is such an easy thing to do, actually it proceeds so smoothly that Matte-Gok has to hold back a little, he must get a relapse and a feeling of fear and make believe that he lies awake the whole night in prayer and doubts.

But at last the decision has been made. The decision to go to darkest Africa as a missionary to the heathens.

And with the decision made his impatience grows, the *call* is insistent and will not leave him in peace. Whatever will happen, let it happen soon!

Matte-Gok is, as the reader knows by now, very much of a swindler, an unconscionable hypocrite and bandit, and every one may, if he likes, wish him all kinds of bad luck because of his evil deeds. But we must also say in his defense that he is a crook on merely a modest scale. He will have no trouble at all in finding his match among the climbers and careerists in the world; three out of four lawyers, for instance, can beat him as far as smartness is concerned, even without overstepping the boundaries of the law. And compared with the arms manufacturers, the diplomats, generals, and ministers of the church, who just in those very same years made everything ready for the mass slaughter of 1914–1918, the figure of Matte-Gok becomes almost completely indistinguishable—a tiny pale worm among the tigers, lions, and poisonous snakes of the jungle. . .

The search of the apartment in the Bastille has brought to light a new and significant factor in the case: the door between Magister Mortensen's parlor and Kornelius Isaksen's kitchen, which had been locked and wallpapered, proves to have been broken open, and it has happened quite recently, to judge from the freshly made tears in the wallpaper. The thief has very evidently entered this way, and as far as that goes Kornelius may have done it all alone. It fits in well with the fact that his wife keeps a complete and obstinate silence. She has evidently been instructed by him.

On the other hand, it is peculiar that Magister Mortensen on that very night was kept away from his apartment, and there is no reason to discard the hypothesis involving a plot or to cancel the order for the arrest of the men who spent the night in the sail loft together with the victim. All four deny their guilt, but there are signs of an incipient breakdown as far as both master carpenter Josef Simonsen and grocer Jakob Siff are concerned.

With regard to Count Oldendorp, no one has as yet mentioned his name. But Bailiff Kronfeldt becomes ever more firmly convinced that the count is the chief culprit and that this will become evident within a short while. He shudders and almost weeps when he visualizes the moment when the first one among the conspirators breaks down and throws the count to the wolves.

That horrible day comes to an end at last and an even more dreadful night begins.

The bailiff takes a potent sleeping powder and dozes off, but has nightmares and emits gruesome howls, as if he were dying. Mrs. Kronfeldt can't sleep at all. She tries to wake up her husband by giving him strong coffee, but it is all in vain. She tries with cognac, but that is also to no avail. Then she puts cold bandages on his forehead, but that doesn't help either. And the situation becomes downright terrible when the bailiff suddenly sits up, gets out of bed, and with eyes closed and mouth wide open begins to waltz around the room in his long ghostlike night shirt. Constable Debes has

274

to be sent for to help Mrs. Kronfeldt shoo the sleepwalker back into bed.

At last, he falls into a trance-like sleep.

His wife looks at him in pain. Even in sleep his face wears an expression of suffering, and his mouth hangs open vacantly.

Everything considered, it is a night of horror and fear. The town lies shrouded in a thick fog, in both a figurative and literal sense, an insidious and oppressive fog, in which the apprehensive lamplight from sleepless windows looks as ghostlike as luminous electric rays on the bottom of the ocean.

Even though the wedding has not come completely to an end, the guests have nevertheless become so subdued that they are almost unrecognizable. A small group of brooding men are sitting at The Dolphin with their beer steins, talking in low voices, as if they were attending a wake. They do not toast one another, for there is no reason to make a toast, they do not shout for the waiter but absentmindedly and with suffering expressions merely lift up their empty glasses when they want them filled.

Even blacksmith Janniksen has become meek and talks in a subdued voice. His eyes stare straight ahead, his puffed, reddish face is full of infinitely sorrowful creases, time and again he shrugs his shoulders, for the whole thing is so inconceivable.

"I can't believe it is the count," he says. "And about Kornelius and Moritz we *know* that they are innocent, yes, I'll even wager my head, right here and now, that they are as innocent as newborn babies. Then there is Ole Brandy and Olivarius—dear friends, dear friends, it can't possibly be them, can it? Of course, we know that Ole walks about grumbling and hitting people over the head when the spirit moves him, but *dishonest?* No, in the name of God, it's more likely that the moon would fall down from heaven. And then we have the Corpse Crower and that little weakling Jakob Siff—out of the question. No, it can't be any one of those that we have just mentioned, that's as sure as the Devil was under the church floor. Then it *has* to be the count after all!"

The blacksmith motions with a finger to the waiter, Jeremias, and makes a mute motion with his shoulder—it means a complete round of aquavit. "For it is damnably sad the whole thing," he murmurs. They drink in silence, and the blacksmith continues in a whisper: "If that damned slimy monster Matte-Gok was not flat on his back because of his misdeeds, just as he fully deserves, I would say without a moment's hesitation that it's him!"

The blacksmith breathes heavily and squints sideways thoughtfully: "But couldn't it have been him anyway? Can't he have pulled the thing off with a helper?"

"I've been thinking the same thing," says master painter Mac Bett.

"But who could have helped him?" says the blacksmith with a smile that fades into nothing.

That is just the point.

"Then there is this thing with the divining rod," says Mac Bett. "That's a strange story. For Matte-Gok maintains that it is all a bunch of nonsense that Kornelius has made up, all that business about the divining rod and the hidden treasure. And it may just be that he is right. For Kornelius *does* have a screw loose, I believe we all agree on that. We know that very well."

"What do we know very well? What do we know?" editor Jacobsen says, having just entered the room. He is in high spirits and seats himself at the table, and the blacksmith makes a sign with his elbow that he too is to be served a drink.

"That much we know," Jacobsen continues, in top form,

"that much we know, that it is Matte-Gok and Ankersen who are behind it all!"

Full of hope and in breathless suspense every one stares at the editor.

"Do you know anything for certain, or is it just the usual type of dumb newspaper talk that you're serving us?" Mac Bett asks sternly.

"It's Ankersen and his loathsome followers!" Jacobsen replies excitedly. "Prove it? No. Of course I can't. But. . ."

"Then you'd better shut up!" Mac Bett bites him off. "Keep in mind that you're not sitting around with a bunch of coffee-drinking old women. We're serious men, those of us sitting here. We take things seriously."

Jacobsen scratches his ear and seems to have given up on that idea of his.

With suppressed anger the blacksmith says: "The fact that we *wish* to see Matte-Gok and Ankersen ride to hottest hell on black skunks, that's another matter, Jacobsen."

"Tonight there'll be a prayer meeting at the Ydun Society," Jacobsen informs them. "Now they're going to celebrate the defeat of the hereditary enemy, of course. 'The old enemy odious' they were singing when I passed by a while ago. 'The old enemy odious is now in earnest furious.' "

But what is it that suddenly comes over blacksmith Janniksen? He gets up, his face all distorted; he pushes his chair away from him so that it scoots across the floor, he throws off his jacket and turns up his sleeves, he is completely beside himself and hisses: "Just bring them to me— the dogs! . . . I'll . . ! I'll . . !"

"Janniksen! Control yourself!" Mac Bett says peremptorily.

The blacksmith looks at him, as if in astonishment. Slowly he sits down again at the table. But his face is still distorted, and he has tears in his eyes.

From where he lies on the wall settee in the dark studio,

Orfeus can look into the kitchen where the light is on. His mother sits in there. She merely sits and stares straight ahead. Behind her sits her shadow; it is huge and gentle, like a benevolent spirit.

The boy feels a strong urge to get up and rush over to his mother, to console her, take her hand, comfort her with a thousand kisses. But he remains lying there, he steels himself. When he lowers his eyelids a bit, his mother's face looks different, it becomes hard and marble-like, just like the face of the figure-head Tarira. Weeping, he turns his face against the wall, he weeps so that his pillow becomes all wet, but at last he falls asleep, and now he dreams a strange dream that is at the same time full of suffering and of inexpressible joy.

He dreams that both he and his mother are dead, but live on as two shadows—two rushing and gently swishing shadows that hold each other by the hand and move about unseen, wherever they want to go. In the silent night and in the manner of ghosts they go to familiar places, as far out as Stake Spit, where the spray is swept up into the air from the sea, then out across the harbor inlet, with its soughing of waters and taut sails, and then farther on, low above the roofs of Skin Islet, lying there in a bleak and pale light.

But then suddenly it is no longer his mother that he is fleeing with, it is Tarira; she stares at him with her pale eyes; shuddering, he follows her up into the church tower and farther into the great cloudy abyss where the spirits of the dead float about. He keeps close to Tarira, he yearns for her to show him some tenderness, but she merely stares blankly at him.

Then, suddenly she is gone, and he sinks slowly down among the graves in the churchyard. Graves and still more graves . . . some are green, others have black frames around them or bluish-white frames made of zinc. Or recently covered graves, heaped over with dead leaves that hiss drily in the wind as if in silent fright. White figures rise from the graves with long waving draperies. Other specters come forth as naked skeletons, they dance in among the graves and wave to him to come dance with them. They look fierce and ferocious, they make long, slow jumps across graves and pathways, pull tufts of faded turf out of the ground and throw them to the winds. Some of them play on violins, white and yellowed bone violins that produce howling music in a minor key, descending harmonic minor scales.

There are entire orchestras of ghost musicians. They sit there rocking back and forth with their bald craniums, playing the while. They wave to him: "Where are you going, boy? Come over here and play with us, for you are musical just like your father!"

"No, for I'm not dead!" Orfeus shouts in great fear and hurries on his way.

But then he at last reaches the family grave, where his mother sits expecting him, silent and pale, but secretly happy over seeing him again and having him with her. "Here," it says on the gravestone, "rests the dust of Eliana and Orfeus Isaksen, mother and son."

But up above on a tall gravestone, on a very high mountain peak, Tarira sits waiting for him. She sits there, just waiting, with her huge wings poised, and he realizes with great sorrow that she is stronger than his mother and that now he must follow her and leave his mother alone and grieving in the grave.

He wakes up and notices a hand stroking his hair. It is his mother.

"Why do you cry like that, my boy?" she asks him gently. "Everything will be straightened out, you just wait. For there is still justice in this world."

He takes her hand and presses it against his cheek. A little while later he dozes off again.

Eliana goes back to the kitchen. She is sleepy and tired, but she doesn't want to go to bed. She sits there, nodding and half dozing. Suddenly she hears the hollow sound of some-one slowly clearing his throat, and she starts up. Right in front of her, in the middle of the kitchen, stands a small, black figure of a man. It is the Crab King. "Good heavens!" she exclaims. "How you frightened me, Poul Peter! You didn't make a sound when you came in! But sit down, Poul Peter. I'll make you a cup of tea."

The Crab King doesn't sit down but remains standing, he traipses about on his little crooked legs. He is silent, as usual. His face is indescribably sad, his eyes burn like coal, like black gleaming chips of coal. Suddenly he opens his mouth, as if he wants to speak, but nothing comes of it. And yet . . . something comes of it after all . . . a few deep, hoarse sounds, as if emitted from the throat of some curious sea-bird. And the strange thing comes about, that the Crab King begins to talk, almost like any other human being.

It sounds incredible. Eliana gives a start, it makes her heart beat faster and she gets shivers all over her body, it is so strange. The Crab King can speak. He is a human being.

"Things aren't going so well for Kornelius," he says.

"No, Poul Peter," she replies, "things aren't going well."

"But it was Matte-Gok who was in the savings bank."

Eliana looks at him, stunned and speechless.

"It's Matte-Gok," the Crab King repeats. "For I saw it myself. I saw it myself."

"Good heavens!" Eliana exclaims. "If that's true, what you are now saying, Poul Peter, then you can save Kornelius if you go up to the bailiff and tell him what you've seen. That you can do, Poul Peter! I'll gladly go with you up there, if you want me to. Do you, Poul Peter?"

The Crab King stares at her for a moment, but then he suddenly turns around and waddles over to the door.

"No, you mustn't leave now, Poul Peter!" Eliana says imploringly. "Listen to me! You must help us! Won't you? You will help Kornelius?"

But the Crab King is already outside the house. But he's not completely gone yet, for now he is standing there peering in through the window. He looks as if he is thinking things over. He leans his big head against the sash, just stands there staring straight ahead. Eliana is in an agony of suspense, she doesn't dare go out and try to entice him to come in again, she is afraid of spoiling it all. She fetches two cups and puts them on the table next to the window. Then she hurriedly butters a few pieces of bread and puts them next to the cups. She puts jam on the bread. It looks very inviting. The Crab King loves jam. And then she fetches the steaming tea kettle. Her hand shakes and she is on the verge of tears. The Crab King remains standing in the same position. She doesn't dare wave for him to come, but behaves as if nothing has happened.

A little while later he comes back in again. He begins to eat, in silence, as is his wont. But he nods to himself several times, and at last he begins to speak once again. He tells slowly about the time he saw Matte-Gok. Slowly, so slowly that she can hardly stand it. He listens, as it were, nervously to his own words. But what he does say hangs together.

He had been standing outside Ankersen's house, and at first he saw a window being opened and a man who crept out through the window and then sat in the little garden for a long time, well hidden. As for himself, the Crab King had been standing where no one could see him. It was dark, but he had seen enough to know that the figure emerging through the window was not Ankersen, it was no one but Matte-Gok. But when Matte-Gok reappeared, his face was black and he walked like an old man. But it was he just the same.

The Crab King makes a long, long pause. She pours him another cup of tea. She doesn't dare question him, merely hopes in a terrible suspense that he will resume his account.

And that he does. But he does not say whether he

281

followed Matte-Gok or how—suddenly we are at the savings bank and Matte-Gok has a key and lets himself in. Then a long time passes, while Poul Peter stands outside waiting. Then Matte-Gok comes back out through the door and hides in the garden. But before he disappears, he goes over and smashes one of the window panes. . .

"And then I walked away," the Crab King concluded, "for it was none of my business. But then they came and seized Kornelius and said that he was the one. But that he wasn't. It was Matte-Gok."

Eliana cried from joy, quite literally. She could not remember ever having felt so happy and relieved, and bubbling over with gratitude she grasped Poul Peter's hand. It was thoughtlessly done, she had completely forgotten how the Crab King felt about such things, that no one must touch him except perhaps Kornelius. He puffed out his cheeks, angrily blew the air in her face and quickly tripped out of the room. In despair she called after him, she pleaded and coaxed, but he would not let himself be mollified and did not return.

Nevertheless, the Crab King did let himself be mollified in a way. He came back in the early morning hours and was given another cup of tea, which he only dared enjoy while standing in the doorway. But he had completely stopped speaking. Not a sound passed his lips. And he would not at all agree to coming along to the bailiff, not even when Eliana said that Kornelius's life might be at stake. He was not to be persuaded. It was only Kornelius himself who might have been able to persuade the Crab King. It was a heart-breaking situation.

Eliana went off to the bailiff's office. She acquainted constable Debes with the situation.

"Oh my, did he really *speak?*" Constable Debes has to sit down and pause a while, so great is his amazement that the Crab King has talked.

"But it's too bad, though, it's too bad!" he says at last. "The Crab King is not the kind of man that one can rely on. For he's a bit insane."

"He's far from insane!" Eliana retorted, but she already felt that her efforts would turn out to be in vain.

"*I* would be the last one to try to stop Kornelius from being acquitted," Debes added. "*I* don't believe that he is the culprit. And in order to be on the safe side, I shall be very glad to report to the bailiff what you've told me and to get his opinion. But there's not much hope, Eliana, I can tell you that right now. There's not much hope, as long as it's *only* the Crab King who can be used as a witness."

"It won't do, then, to use him as a witness," Eliana said, heartbroken.

"But he will confirm what he's told you, won't he?"

Eliana shook her head and hid her face in her apron.

"But *then* it looks hopeless!" the constable said with a trace of relief in his voice. "Then there's nothing that can be done, Eliana. But let's just wait and bide our time. Justice will win out."

But Eliana returned in the afternoon, and this time she had the Crab King with her. Constable Debes was not present; Hansen, the chief clerk, who was a bespectacled young man and had just been appointed to the post, stared as if struck dumb at the curious-looking doll of a man and was unable to keep back a confused little laugh, and Eliana already felt convinced that everything would fail. Poul Peter was puffing out his cheeks and shivering, looking all around out of the corners of his eyes.

"We'll save Kornelius!" Eliana whispered to him encouragingly. He gave her a look filled with fear and dread.

Thereupon occurred that which had to happen. That which she could have told herself would happen.

Bailiff Kronfeldt came into the room with a great hustle and bustle.

"What kind of a comedy *is* this?" he says with an angry laugh. "Are you going to poke fun at me?"

He waves his hands, his face takes on a vacant and foolish expression, he turns his eyes heavenward. Then he suddenly stands straight and shouts while pointing at the door: "Get out! That dwarf is crazy!"

"No, he *isn't!*" Eliana has the courage to retort. She gets up and stamps her feet. She stares in impotent rage at the indignant pink-faced man with the goatee and the false teeth. She hates him. But nothing is of any use, for now the Crab King begins to howl! He howls in spasms, just like a little baby, but in a coarse and rough voice . . . it sounds frightful, they have never heard anything like it in their lives. And suddenly the Crab King begins to move and waddles like a mechanical toy out the door.

"Yes, there you can see for yourself!" the bailiff says, his voice turning gentler. For a moment he almost looks like a human being. "There, there, don't cry, little lady! You did it, I'm sure, with the best of intentions, but—running up here with some one who is nothing but an idiot, no, things are bad enough without that. Damn bad enough. Damn bad enough."

Breathing heavily, Kronfeldt retired to his rooms in the rear.

And the Crab King had once again become hopelessly silent. He had withdrawn into himself like a hermit crab in a sea shell. He was never heard to speak again.

But perhaps the battle was not lost after all?

In the meantime, however, there followed a number of days during which nothing new happened.

CHAPTER 8

In which matters take an unexpected turn

Yes, time passes. Count Oldendorp and Black Mira have crossed the ocean a long time ago, and on a foggy day poor Magister Mortensen has been brought to his final resting place in the cemetery in the presence of many people; "I Go away, and I Know where the Journey Will Take Me" was played at the funeral.

But Matte-Gok has been seized with great visions and inspirations. Ankersen has made much of the fact that the previously prodigal son has decided to become a missionary to the heathens, and all right-thinking people rally round the two of them, the father and the son. Also, in all those who have been lukewarm, something has caught fire, for the violent happenings of recent days have indicated that Ankersen is right, that the general licentiousness was, if possible, much worse than he had pictured it.

The big criminal case proceeds apace. Slowly, slowly. Much too slowly. The tension is unbearable. Now it is Justice Pommerencke, the *judge*, who will take the lead. All eyes are turned toward this one man. People shudder respectfully when they pass his big gray house, where they know that the tall gray-haired man with the friendly and observant look sits reflecting on the case.

But has he completely ceased to function, that Pommerencke?

No, that he has not, not by far. But the judge is a thought-ful man, and the case is an extremely complicated and un-usual one.

In Pommerencke's opinion, the suspect, former typesetter Kornelius Isaksen, was not the kind of cunning simulator that Kronfeldt wanted to make him out. There was much to indicate that he was really a naive and gullible dreamer. That he of his own free will should have been a partner in a *conspiracy* was not very probable. He was not the bandit type. He might, on the other hand, have acted as a tool for the others involved in the plot.

That is, if there really had been a plot. There was much to indicate that the other suspects also were innocent. They weren't bandits either, even though there were some black sheep among them, such as the blathering drunkard Ole Olsen.

The judge did not believe that there was any connection between the fact that Magister Mortensen was present in the sail loft in the Höje warehouse and the disappearance of his money. He did not believe in any murder with intent to rob. What was at issue here was either an accident or a suicide. Neither was there any reason to believe that Count Oldendorp was implicated. A man of Oldendorp's type, in spite of his otherwise many unfortunate qualities, was not a bandit either.

But was there actually a bandit involved in this at all? If so, it had to be this fellow Matte-Gok, who according to the testimony given by typesetter Isaksen had helped him to search for that so-called *treasure*. But the fellow did have an alibi. He even had the police itself as witness. The "attack" on Kornelius had occurred *after* this Matte-Gok had been brought home battered and bruised. But the judge was keeping his eye on this mysterious fellow—savings-bank manager Ankersen's so-called prodigal son, a man with an unknown and according to some reports checkered past.

286

If it had been he who had perpetrated the two burglaries during the tumultuous wedding of the blacksmith's daughter and had made the circumstantial evidence point to Kornelius, in that case one had to do with a very dangerous man, an almost unbelievably sly and crafty fellow, a master thief. One should certainly not hesitate to consider fantastic hypotheses. But this hypothesis was almost too fantastic. And yet, and yet. . .

But Judge Pommerencke was working with another fantastic hypothesis. To wit: typesetter Isaksen, the "treasure hunter," was the victim of a kind of autosuggestion and might have acted in a sort of somnambulistic state.

When a man for years has been going around talking wildly about a treasure that at one stroke will transform a poor devil into a veritable Croesus! When he exposes himself day after day to such mental *tension,* will it not simply lead him into a criminal career?

The judge consulted with Doctor Manicus on this question; the latter had a great deal of experience relative to pathological phenomena, and he agreed on the whole with his theory.

The judge also brought up his other hypothesis, the one regarding Matte-Gok's duplicity.

"Are you able to confirm, doctor, that that fellow really hurt his back during the night of the wedding, and that he isn't making up a story?"

"Oh, yes," says the doctor with a thin smile. "His back is black and blue like a thunderstorm, and he also has bruises on his upper arm."

"But wouldn't he still have been able to walk by himself that night?"

The doctor thought a bit. "Perhaps so," he said. "Yes, that he probably could have. But a man who gets the wind knocked out of him after being hit in the back, becomes a little bewildered in the beginning and is almost convinced in his own mind that he has been practically beaten to death."

"Is it possible that he has inflicted such punches and blows on himself, Manicus?"

"Yes, if he is something of a fakir," said the doctor with a smile.

"If this hypothesis holds true, then he *is* something of a fakir. He is something entirely out of the ordinary."

The doctor silently shook his head, and the tiny velvety wrinkles about his eyes contracted as if in a smile.

"My personal impression," he said slowly, "my personal impression of the man does not point in that direction. He does *not* give the impression of being very cunning. He is unreasonable, spoiled, a little childish, quick-tempered, slow-witted, just like Ankersen. He certainly resembles Ankersen a whole lot!"

"Only provided that too isn't play-acting," said the judge.

Something new has entered the case: Pieces of two scorched hundred-crown bills have been found among the ruins of the tumbled-down smithy. A close examination shows that a quantity of paper has recently been burned there. The ashes, which also contain the corner of a bank note, have been hidden underneath a couple of half-rotten burlap bags.

This gives rise to further mystification, further ponderings.

Such was the approximate state of things the day that Kornelius *confessed.*

Yes, the end of it was that Kornelius confessed his guilt in regard to both burglaries. It sounds amazing. But it is not too hard to understand, when all is said and done, that it had to end that way with a treasure hunter of Kornelius's type.

. . . Here you go for many years all wrapped up in a pet idea which you carefully keep all to yourself, and which after a while so to speak becomes a part of your inner self. It forces you into a curiously distorted relationship to reality.

But you get used to this distortion, you adapt yourself to the strange dual existence that you have slipped into, yes, you enjoy it, you feel comfortable in its darkling mood with its glimmering hopes, in which you can give your imagination free rein in solitude, at the same time making music—activities which you gradually have fully mastered. Just as your father in his day was a master on the aeolian harps in the lonely church tower.

Meanwhile you build up internally a curious resilience, not unlike the one that enables a deep-sea fish to live its life under the immense pressure caused by the volume of water in the ocean. This resilience comes to be exceedingly important to you, yes, who knows, without this power of resistance you would perhaps have become a useless wretch, a sort of Crab King, and not a man who is known and appreciated for his lighthearted, cheerful, and obliging ways.

And everything goes very well as long as mere figments of the imagination and alluring future possibilities are involved. Yes, you are downright in love with these possibilities. Way down deep you wish that they won't become reality, any more so than an artist has a desire to be confronted with the products of his imagination as palpable reality. On the contrary, he wants to transform reality into art and exerts himself to do so, thus putting it at a proper distance, since he is so very sensitive and thin-skinned.

Then one fine day the possibility gives a sign of becoming reality. It sets your nerves on edge and is far from a pleasant feeling. You are almost beside yourself. You lack the ability to reorient yourself under the new circumstances. Just like the deep-sea fish, which following a natural catastrophe is forced into a natural element which it is not used to. It wants to get back down to the bottom of the deep.

And then it is that you suddenly find yourself removed to a third world, with the existence of which you had not reckoned at all. You find yourself indicted for misdeeds of an extent that you cannot fathom, misdeeds of which you are not guilty, but in which you nevertheless cannot deny all complicity. It concerns money, large sums of money. And just at that time you have been abroad in the gloom of night with your spade in search of a huge treasure, which it was your intention to appropriate to yourself, even though you deep down felt that you were doing something shady.

Well, in the beginning you are at any rate fully convinced that you have not perpetrated these unheard-of misdeeds. You feel that should be self-evident and cannot understand that other people can look upon it in a different way. Of course, you are not blind to the possibility that the creature who attacked you and stole your jacket and your cap may have been Matte-Gok, he being the only one who knew what you planned to do that night. But even though you are convinced of the existence of justice and of the fact that the truth sooner or later will out, you just cannot rid yourself of the bad conscience that lurks inside you, for you are, in spite of all your curious ways, a decent and honest man.

Your dream of treasure is little by little transformed in a curious manner, deep down it gleams, fateful and sinister, it is fertilized under the influence of unpredictable forces which together with hard reality have penetrated it. It breeds shapeless and muffled self-accusations.

This is more or less what happened to our poor Kornelius.

It did not make things better that when he was interrogated he was asked the most fantastic questions, questions of the kind that would cast additional dark and ambiguous shadows in his mind, a mind that already was greatly troubled.

Do you walk in your sleep? Do you have very vivid dreams? Have you ever suffered from delirium? Do you think a lot about treasure hunts when you are under the influence of stimulants? Do you have visions? Is it possible that you got the money from some other source, in case there was no treasure?

And Doctor Manicus shows up, as if they supposed you were suffering from some kind of disease. He talks to you as if you were a child, he looks at you in such a gentle way that you get goose pimples all over your body.

Thereupon, you are left to yourself and your worries. You're brooding. You're longing to escape from all this. You feel terribly sorry for your wife, and it hurts more than words can tell that they have arrested your brother Moritz, your good friend Ole Brandy, and poor one-legged Olivarius. And you worry about the fate of the Corpse Crower and of Jakob Siff. In your mind's eye you see the little merchant's empty store, the sound of emptiness rings in your ears. And emptiness resounds in the big parlor in the basement of the Bastille, where all that beautiful music used to be heard and where you have enjoyed the happiest moments of your life. And emptiness broods inside Ole Brandy's little hut. And emptiness rings out horribly in Magister Mortensen's deserted apartment. The despairing violins of loneliness are playing in a poignant and heart-rending way, the hollow cello pizzicato is thumping as in a fever. You are tormented by nightmares and horrible dreams. At times you are overpowered by an icy fear. And during all this your feeling of guilt shoots new buds, curious and sickly aberrant shoots.

And Ankersen comes.

Yes, one is ignorant or unthinking or cynical enough to permit him to stop by. He sits by Kornelius like a father, sings comfortingly for him, reads from the Book of Books, impresses on him that all that is now happening is for his own good.

"Yours has been a mis-spent life," he says. "Drinking and fooling around with your so-called friends, who in reality were your enemies, playing dance music for that loathsome captain at The Dolphin, you've been in the clutches of evil powers.

"But all that is of the past now, Kornelius. The time of renewal has come, you're now facing a cleansing and re-

291

juvenation of the soul. You will soon confess your guilt. You know what is at stake. If you've done these misdeeds all by yourself, Kornelius, then like a Christian you will not leave your poor innocent brothers and your other acquaintances in the lurch. And if they are part of the plot, then you can also save them by confessing: you can give them an opportunity, Kornelius, an opportunity through confession, repentance, and penance, to rise again with cleansed souls in the great beyond and join in the joyful paean of praise:

> The blind sees and the frightened has faith,
> the deaf man listens to the words of the book,
> the mute man sings in his joy so great,
> the lame one cavorts by the brook!"

The sickly verse has a cooling effect on Kornelius, who, as we know, is a very musical fellow. But the thought of being able to save Moritz and the others—it ignites and breeds in his mind, for the only bulwark that does not collapse within him in this night of trial and desperation is his good heart. Kornelius's is not a great mind, he is merely a poor dilettante in life as in art, but his heart harbors the magnanimity of a frank and sincere human being.

With the passage of the days Kornelius gradually reaches the great watershed of his troubled thoughts and he is restored to a certain mental equilibrium. His ponderings reach their very limits and run around in circles like fish in an aquarium. In the end he feels dizzy and fed up with just thinking one thing. His only thought is: Moritz, cleared of any guilt, returning to Eliana, and they will take care of Kornelia. Moritz will play for her. For he too can play the cello. And when she hears cello music she feels so happy. For it is the cello that she loves. And Ole Brandy will go back to his hut, and Olivarius to his nice big attic, and Jakob Siff will return to his little store, and the Corpse Crower to his carpentry shop. And then everything will be all right again.

And the *treasure*—it is no longer of any concern to you at all. If everything having to do with Matte-Gok and the divining rod were lies, that would be a good thing. If the money has been consumed by fire, well and good. If it is never found, that is good too. You want nothing to do with it. Now a new day is dawning. Now you can rest from it all.

This is what happens to Kornelius, he sleeps an abnormally long time, he eats his meals, lies listening to the music welling forth in his mind, in short, he begins to enjoy the new existence and gathers strength to resist its pressures. Slowly he resumes his old place in the order of things.

On Bailiff Kronfeldt, Kornelius's confession had the effect of a cool shower on an unbearably hot and sultry summer day. To tell the truth, Kronfeldt had lately begun to fear that one of Pommerencke's subtle hypotheses might prove true against all expectations and put to shame his own plain and natural interpretation. But thanks be to God, once again he had received confirmation of the fact that a straight line is the shortest distance between two points. The little wretch had confessed everything. Naturally. The fellow couldn't have had an easier time perpetrating his deed. The late Magister Mortensen's irresponsible putting away of his money was a glaring stupidity which would attract any thief that came along, yes, it was not only tempting for his close neighbor to misappropriate this money without an owner, it was so to speak quite inevitable, he, he. And the carelessness with which they handled money in the savings bank had almost been equal to that of Mortensen. That Ankersen would now get a real hazing, perhaps he might lose his job—and that he thoroughly deserved. He should have been watching out for the money in the savings bank instead of running around making a fool of himself. After all, one didn't live in the old, peaceful days of yore.

The bailiff rubbed his hands and clucked loudly.

"Claret, Charlotte! *Claret!*"

293

The judge, on the other hand, had some misgivings about the little typesetter's unqualified confession. It is true that on the whole it had served to confirm the pathological hypothesis that he and Doctor Manicus had thought up between them. But just the same—. Deep down he could not completely accept the confession, could not see that it fit into the picture. But the strange court case had to take its course. He collected the papers having to do with it and commented carefully on every detail. He attached a statement from Manicus pointing out that it would be desirable to have Kornelius Isaksen undergo a thorough mental examination.

And then one fine day Kornelius was sent out of the country, leaving the town of his birth in a state of general puzzlement.

Those who saw him off were surprised that he was so calm and unchanged. The friendly, somewhat absentminded smile, the protruding jaw, the lorgnette, everything was the same. Yes, Kornelius was exactly the way he had always been. He was his old self.

A few days later Ura on the Cliff was discharged from the hospital. She was able to walk only with the aid of crutches. For the time being Ura moved into Kornelius's apartment in the Bastille. The first thing she did following her return was to send for Moritz and Ole Brandy.

"Kornelius has been sent away like a damned criminal," she said. "But who is the real criminal?"

"Matte-Gok!" Ole Brandy said. "But can *you* prove it?"

That Ura could not do. She just sat there squirming.

"I believe that justice will triumph in the end," said Moritz.

"Not at all," said Ura. "Not unless some one helps it get moving!"

Ura gesticulated with one finger, shook her head and said

with her eyes closed: "I have begged and implored my sister to rummage through Matte-Gok's belongings, to open his drawers, look in his bed, behind the wallpaper, all over! I *know* that the money is there! I have seen it in my own mind and dreamt about it time after time. But she doesn't *want* to. She's infatuated with him, the old goose that she is. She thinks I'm the one that's crazy. She talks to me as if I were a child."

Ura pointed at Moritz: "But now you, Moritz, you are going to clear up this case! Do you understand? In some way or other, you will have to get into his room!"

"Is he going to break into the house?" Ole Brandy asked derisively. "You'll never be able to make Moritz do that! But, I'll be damned—!"

Ole slapped his thigh: "I know what should be done, Ura! I know!"

Ura suddenly burst out laughing. She was seized by one of her old noisy laughing fits, she slapped her hands together, and the new hope suddenly infused her face with a youthful and bashful expression. "Ole knows what should be done!" she said. "Of course, he knows!"

Right off Ole Brandy had thought of Peter, the son of the gravedigger. If any one knew how to break into a house, it would be he. In truth, the boy did not do anything but that. And since he always committed burglaries anyway, causing injury to the interests of the townspeople and disgrace to himself, why not just for once make a useful burglary in a good cause?

"I'll be standing here right behind you," he said to the boy. "If any of us gets in the clink, it will be me. And I'll be able to tell them why we did it. And even if you don't find a penny, you'll get five crowns for your trouble."

The burglary took place that very evening. It was easily done. The house was empty. Ankersen, Matte-Gok, and Mrs. Midiord were all attending a meeting of the Ydun Society.

The front door was locked, but it was possible to get in through the basement. But the door into Matte-Gok's room was locked. An attempt would have to be made from another direction. His window was half open. Peter climbed up the rowan espalier. Ole Brandy stood watch and gave the boy warning signals through different ways of coughing and clearing his throat.

Peter remained so long in Matte-Gok's room that Ole had to walk all the way up to the window and get him out by loudly coughing and clearing his throat, for now it was close to the time that the saintly ones would be returning from the Ydun Society.

At last the boy appeared in the window. Ole ducked and disappeared.

They met again a little later down in Ole's boathouse. Peter brought with him a small brown leather handbag. "I looked all over," he said. "There was only one drawer, the drawer in the washstand, and the money wasn't there. Then I looked underneath the bed and in the bed and among his clothes that were hanging in the clothes closet, and over and under the closet and behind it, and behind the washstand and underneath the rug, and in the seat of the chair and in among the curtains, and felt with my fingers whether there were any bulges behind the wallpaper, but there was nothing there, only this little bag, I couldn't open it, and then. . ."

Ole Brandy couldn't get the bag wrenched open either. He got hold of a knife and cut a large gash in the leather. Lots of papers! Great scott!

But no money. Only religious brochures, tracts, copies of *The Messenger*.

Ole Brandy threw the bag away, kicked it, stepped on it. He poured gasoline on it and put fire to it. His eyes and his earrings gleamed in the light from the flames, and his broken nose was shining brightly. At that moment he could have burned Ankersen and Matte-Gok to death. He wished with all his heart that something terrible would happen to them.

When the fire had been put out, he turned toward the boy who was standing there waiting in the dark, exhausted and almost on the point of collapse, and suddenly he was overwhelmed by a feeling of regret and tenderness. He laid his hand on the boy's shoulder and asked him to come home with him to his cabin. Here he opened a drawer in his old chest and took out a shaggy, gray purse.

"Look here," he said in a friendly voice and gave the boy two gold pieces. "All told, they are worth twenty crowns. They are yours. And promise me that you'll be an honest fellow in the future. Come to me if you need money, or if there is something that you are in doubt about. Frankly, I think you ought to go to sea and embark on real man's work, just as I did myself when I was your age. And if you agree to that, then I promise I'll get you a job with a very fine and decent skipper, so that you won't be sorry for anything!"

With a little sigh he then shook hands with Peter.

Human charity and the spirit of sacrifice often manifest themselves in the most beautiful manner when it is a case of something toward which the public is favorably inclined. There was almost no end to the interest showered on Kornelia and her old foster mother after they had lost their provider under such dramatic circumstances. Hardly a day went by without some one visiting them, not only friends and acquaintances, but also people with whom they never even had spoken, and they received eggs and milk, cakes, bread, and coffee. Consul Hansen sent them eight sacks of coal. Pastor Fruelund came and gave them a word of comfort.

And the Christian temperance society Ydun's welfare committee, with Ankersen at its head, came and offered

297

them room and board. The conditions were: joining the society, this to be followed by confession, repentance and penance, joint prayers, and so forth. And the town council also showed up with a similar offer, their conditions, however, being somewhat different. Greatly moved, Ura thanked them but could also inform them that Ole Brandy already had been so kind as to put his home at their disposal, and in addition he—together with Olivarius, Janniksen, Mac Bett, and other friends—had taken it upon themselves to provide for their daily needs.

So much charity all at once tends to become a burden to the one who is its object. Ura was hard of hearing, old and disabled, and secretly wished that the whole fuss would soon come to an end. It seemed almost like a refreshing occurrence when one day there arrived a man who did not bring anything with him except an ordinary, old-fashioned bill. This man was attorney Wenningstedt. He looked around the room as if he were studying it and, nodding, he sat down on the sofa.

"Well—you see, it's a matter of the rent for three months," he said in a friendly tone. "What can we do about that? And then there's another thing! I have, of course, had several offers from people interested in this apartment, and I just learned today that the town council. . . ? So—you're going to move down to Ole Olsen? Well, that's really splendid. The day after tomorrow? Thank you. Then Olsen will also take care of this little account,—right, quite so—I'll talk to him about it."

Wenningstedt made another friendly nod, his ears slightly moving, while he secretly studied the blind Kornelia, whom he had never, despite repeated efforts, succeeded in seeing at close range. So this was the way she looked. Not bad at all. Far from it. And what people were saying—that she was in a family way—was a lot of nonsense. No sign of that. As skinny as a rail.

The attorney shook hands with her when he said good-by. He thought some more about the matter as he walked down the stairs; Ole Brandy is indeed generous to make such an offer. Very generous of him. H'm. Ulterior motives perhaps? The girl is far from repulsive-looking. And the old woman is hard of hearing and dullwitted. But—a blind woman! That would be shameful indeed. Downright shameful. But for that very reason, perhaps, it would have a peculiar attraction for some people—who knows?

The two ladies moved down to Ole Brandy's house a few days later. He had seen to it that the parlor and the kitchen were fixed up and cleaned, and he had moved his own bed up to the attic. The parlor was unrecognizable when he came home that evening. There were curtains in the windows, and all of Boman's composers had been put on the wall. The two old pictures of Vesuvius by day and Vesuvius by night that up to now had been the only ones adorning the house were still hanging above the chest, though. There would have been hell to pay if they hadn't.

Ole Brandy was no angel, of course, and in the evening when he had gone to bed in the narrow attic, where there was just enough space to squeeze into bed, and as he lay there listening to the women potter about in the room downstairs, he felt like a man who has to acknowledge that though his golden freedom may not exactly have vanished altogether, it at least has been drastically limited. But that's the way it had to be. There was no sense in regretting what he had done. He had felt it to be his duty to take care of Kornelius's dependents, so that they would be spared the shame of becoming a burden on the community. His conscience would have no reason to bother him.

And on shipboard one still remained, thank God, one's own self.

Whatever was stirring in Kornelia's mind will remain a

secret for all time. Outwardly one could not notice a thing. One might get the impression that she was completely unaffected by the whole business. Even in court she was surprisingly calm and did not bat an eyelid. Many people wondered at it, some even felt indignant over it and were of the opinion that the young lady was a hard-boiled one, without any deeper emotions. Others claimed that she hid her reactions behind a mask of studied calm. Others, again, were of the opinion that the poor girl, just like Kornelius himself, was completely subject to Ura's magic power. Doctor Manicus leaned toward the view that Kornelius Isaksen's wife was infantile, mentally as well as physically, and that her intellectual range was like that of a five-year-old child. But that, too, was merely conjecture.

But this much is certain, Kornelia endured everything that befell her with a patience that ordinary people can hardly fathom.

Part IV

*Which brings with it a sad ending, but at the same time a
hope for something new and better*

CHAPTER 1

New and mysterious excesses take place in the Ydun Society,
such as speaking in tongues and ritual dancing, and at last
occurs that which we all have wished for: the fall of the
beast Matte-Gok

There is something unreal about Matte-Gok; in a way he has
no face, no human soul. He merely exists as a cold and
irrefutable force. His profile is like a hawk's and he resembles
the god Ra, the god who had a nonhuman head, that of a
bird. A beast he is, a lonely bird of ill omen, a low-flying,
insidious bird of prey.

Granted that in comparison with other birds of prey and
with vultures he is merely a poor sparrow hawk. Still, in his
own way he represents a widespread evil of our time, the
cynical beastly instinct to prey, the dark and demonic
powers that suck one dry, that with their tremendous octo-
pus tentacles envelop our human life and feed on our
stupidity and foolish patience.

But as far as Matte-Gok is concerned, our patience has
come to an end. His days are numbered.

A marked change has lately come over Moritz. He has become pale and thin-lipped, his hair has even turned gray at
the temples and there are deep lines by his mouth. He has
become restless and absent-minded, he never touches his
violin, and his singing, always done with so much gusto in
the past, has also completely ceased.

He is not even pleasant to be with any longer, either at home or with others, he is turning into an ill-tempered and sulky person and a pessimist; at times he is so irascible that his wife and children don't believe their own eyes and ears.

And he has become a teetotaler. That certainly wouldn't have been a bad thing if he hadn't at the same time become such an old crab.

"He'll get over it soon," Ole Brandy tries to comfort Eliana. "He'll be all right, you'll see. It's what happened to Kornelius that's made him that way. It's Matte-Gok that he is furious about. Matte-Gok and Ankersen are the ones we're all so damned annoyed about. But you just wait, you just wait."

Ole Brandy, Olivarius, Lindenskov, Mac Bett, and Janniksen are putting their heads together out at The Dolphin. They agree that something ought to be done to cheer Moritz up a bit. But how? They are down at the mouth themselves. Truth to tell, everything's going to rack and ruin.

"Yes, to rack and ruin," editor Jacobsen agrees. He too feels debased by what has happened, his face looks old and grimy, and he has a straggly beard. "Injustice sits in the place of honor," he says, "the sectarian stupidity spreads like an epidemic. In a short while total abstinence will be introduced here. Then we won't even be able to buy a bottle of beer."

"As long as they can't prohibit ships from sailing the ocean," Ole Brandy says, darkly, "an honest sailor can always get any kind of drink he wants, as long as he takes the trouble."

Ole Brandy empties his glass, taking his time. He empties many glasses, and the others do likewise. But there is no pleasure in it any more, no singing and no music, no glamor, merely sweat and heavy thoughts. Ole Brandy staggers home, dead drunk and angry, his mind clouded by sorrow and shapeless thoughts of vengeance. He keeps on drinking heavily for eight days.

304

Then he suddenly disappears from the scene entirely. Once again he has ended up in the clink. He has attacked Matte-Gok. On a dark evening he has assaulted him brutally and stupidly in Sexton Alley, where he had been lying in wait for Matte-Gok and Ankersen as they were walking home from a devotional meeting. Matte-Gok did not resist at all. He was struck right in the face and was bleeding like a pig. He might even have been killed if Ankersen hadn't started to shout and call for help while doing his utmost to impale the perfidious assailant with the tip of his umbrella.

Matte-Gok wanted the case settled amicably. "The man is mentally deranged," he said. He even behaved as if he were his attorney for the defense: "For Ole and I have known each other a long time," he said. "Ole is not a bad fellow at all; it's just that he can't stand that awful drinking. But now, thank God, heavy drinking will be coming to an end around here!"

But the authorities looked at it in a different light. They wanted to be severe in order to warn others. Ole Brandy was sentenced to fourteen days in jail and was put on bread and water.

It is now, however, getting close to Matte-Gok's departure. The mood among the saintly ones alternates between sadness and an excitement flushed with victory.

The last evening he was present at the Ydun Society turned into a sectarian orgy along completely apocalyptic lines.

Ankersen had gotten the idea that Matte-Gok ought to be *anointed*. Teacher Nillegaard was strongly opposed to this, maintaining that it was a reversion to heathen barbarism, but, contrariwise, Ankersen could triumphantly cite a multitude of Bible verses. "It's an old Christian custom," he maintained, "a splendid custom, one that has far too long been disregarded."

The crowds that converged on the hall that night broke

all records. Inside, every square inch was taken up, both in the assembly hall itself and in the entrance hall, and outside there was a Babylonian confusion and crush of curious people, who desperately tried to force their way to a place by one of the open doors or in front of one of the windows. The evening was raw and cold, and those who were standing outside in the dark were shivering from the cold, from the excitement of it all, and from their misgivings. From inside they could hear ecstatic singing, which after a while dissolved into shouts of joy and exultation. Strange things happened in the Ydun Society that evening, unheard of things, miracles pure and simple, according to what some people claimed later. Mrs. Midiord, Ankersen's housekeeper, who until then had always remained in the background, stepped forward and spoke in tongues. She had brought with her a palm branch from Ankersen's living room, and waved it back and forth while speaking. Mrs. Ida Nillegaard, the midwife, responded to what she said in the same harebrained language. It was such a harrowing experience to listen to all this that several people fainted and the Wailing Woman burst out laughing.

While all this was in full swing, a piercing blast of a steamer's whistle was heard. It was *Mjölner,* the ship on which Matte-Gok was to leave. The steamer had arrived earlier than expected and a message was sent ashore to the effect that the ship would continue south immediately. There was only one hour to go. Moritz made his boat ready in a hurry. Only four passengers were supposed to leave, and three of them he notified in a hurry and brought onboard, but then there was number four—Matte-Gok. How would he get hold of him? It was almost impossible to force one's way through the crowd of people by the entrance to the assembly hall. But it had to and would be done. Moritz elbowed his way through, nothing could hold him back.

"Take it easy!" some people told him and used their elbows on him; others thought there was a fire somewhere, and here and there were signs of incipient panic.

When Moritz at last had fought his way into the main hall and had succeeded in making himself heard and announcing the ship's departure, Ankersen shouted back at the top of his lungs: *"There is no ship!"*

Ankersen's face was more flushed and puffed up than ever before; his eyes downright milled around in his head. He repeated: "Here we can't speak of any ship! Here it's only the living word that speaks!"

But Matte-Gok looked at things a bit differently. He got busy. He managed to impose some quiet and shouted, his voice calm and right-from-the-liver: "Friends! The hour of parting has come! But don't mind too much that I'm leaving! It's only my outer skin that's leaving, just my mortal frame! As spirit I shall remain in your hearts!"

There were many who didn't want to accept that interpretation, but Matte-Gok was adamant, he had to leave them. "My heart's bleeding," he said. "But you won't be able to tear me away from my call! My call is the stronger! One's call is the strongest part of a human life!"

"That's right!" Ankersen shouted. "One's call is strongest. One's call is strongest!"

"Yes, one's call is strongest!" Mrs. Janniksen shrieked.

"Medofigis epa abetesda!" Mrs. Midiord shouted joyfully, and Mrs. Nillegaard responded with eyes closed and almost without moving her lips: *"Esse eh! Esse eh!"*

All of it was so unprecedented, so bizarre, so appalling, such a completely unusual occurrence. But the strangest, the most horrible thing of all did not occur until Matte-Gok, following a brief final prayer, had started to leave.

It ought never to have happened, of course; it brought with it confusion and destruction, yes, it had an effect similar to that made by an evil, black water jet from a fire extin-

307

guisher right in the middle of a living bonfire of wild joy and childish faith.

At first it was thought to be an unfortunate accident, but one of those that sometimes will happen. It was believed that Mrs. Midiord's blouse had been torn to pieces in the crush of all the people. But when she began to tear her skirt into shreds, it was clear that something was wrong; those standing closest to her tried to intervene, but the old lady was completely out of her mind; she tore herself loose and began to dance, dressed only in her black half-length cotton bloomers! In and of itself, this dance was not shameful, on the contrary, it was not executed without a certain grace, and the older spectators could recall that Mrs. Midiord in her youth had had a small and nimble figure and had been a rather sought-after dancing partner at the balls of those days. She was a strange sight, but it was not carried off without decorum, and the whole thing might not have been so bad if only Mrs. Nillegaard had behaved herself. But suddenly she too had thrown herself into the dance, and she was almost completely naked. Due to the confusion it was never determined just how naked she was, for the whole episode lasted only a few seconds, until her husband lunged at her and covered her with his jacket. Others attended to Mrs. Midiord. The old lady smiled wearily and affably. But she kept on speaking in tongues. And she continued to do that for the rest of her life.

When Matte-Gok at last had managed to tear himself loose from Ankersen's embrace and had gotten into the ferryboat with his two suitcases, the ship's whistle signified imminent departure.

"Hurry up!" he said excitedly, poking Moritz in the ribs. He was perspiring. His tousled hair fell down over his forehead. He looked ferocious and forgot to play his usual role. "Hurry up for all the satans in h—!"

"We'll get there in good time," Moritz said to make him feel at ease. "First it has to heave anchor. That takes at least fifteen minutes. It's very often that others arrive just as late!"

The boat moved into the darkness. It was a cold but calm evening, with clouds and stars. Matte-Gok was dressed in a new ulster of mixed-gray color, he looked like an ordinary traveling salesman.

"You'll have fine weather," Moritz said. Matte-Gok nodded.

They drew near to the steamer, which was ablaze with lights. Matte-Gok was already rummaging in his pockets for the fare, but then suddenly Moritz changed course . . . Matte-Gok immediately suspected some mischief and rose to his feet. "What in holy hell. . . ?" he said, gnashing his teeth.

Moritz seemed unaffected. The boat moved farther and farther away.

"Well, is *that* the way it is!" Matte-Gok muttered between his teeth. "You won't get away with it, you big lout!"

With raised hands he staggered over towards Moritz, but suddenly the boat made a sharp turn, he lost his balance and had to sit down and lean back.

"You scoundrel!" he hissed.

Moritz waited until he had gotten up again, then he made the boat take another sharp turn and at the same time made it rock up and down. Matte-Gok had to bend forward and grab hold of the thwart. But at that very moment Moritz rose to his full height, grasped the handle of the club-shaped bailer and struck him a powerful blow over the head. Then another blow, and still another one.

Matte-Gok collapsed without a sound. The boat continued on its course at full speed into the darkness. The noise from the steamer's windlass resounded in the dark. Then everything became quiet. Moritz sat down. His heart hammered as fast as the motor. He was not able to collect his thoughts.

309

For a moment he wished that Matte-Gok would get up, or at least stir a little.

But Matte-Gok remained lying there. Moritz was horrified to see blood trickle out from the bruises in his skull and make two dark streaks down his coat. So—the thing had really happened after all.

Lurching, Moritz got to his feet. He got loose the lantern in the boat's stem, put it down on the floorboard and covered it with his jacket. Then he sat down again by the tiller, and there he remained while the boat sailed on into the darkness.

It had happened.

Ahead a bright star was shining. The Dog Star. It twinkled and changed color. The steamer gave out three short blasts and began to move out. Soon it had passed them. Its lights slowly disappeared in the distance. Moritz perspired all over his body, in spite of the fact that he was sitting in his shirt-sleeves. They passed the northern point of Seal Island, they were going out to sea, to sea. There was no way back.

A faint, bubbling sound emanated from the figure lying spread out on the thwart—a faint sign of life. Moritz began to tremble, he doubled up from loathing and fright, he had difficulty in suppressing an urge to moan out loud. Suddenly he got up, racked with anguish. He lifted the limp body and with some effort managed to push it overboard. There was a plop. It was done. This too had happened.

There were only the two suitcases left. He got out his knife and ripped open one of them and feverishly rummaged through it. Only clothing. A bottle. A new pair of shoes. Sobbing loudly he tore open the other one. *The money—* it just had to be in that one. Or was it all a lie, perhaps?

Yes! There it was! The bills were all bundled together, in a leather pouch at the bottom of the suitcase. He uncovered the lantern for a minute and could see the yellow-brown and grayish-green notes. He put out the light. The boat was racing out to sea in the cloudy night. The bright

310

star reappeared for a moment. It twinkled and changed color, now it was ruby red, now bluish-white, now icy green as death itself.

Moritz remained sitting at the tiller all through the night, frozen stiff, his mind completely vacant.

At dawn he got up with difficulty and got hold of the can with the extra gasoline. Now there had to be an end to it all. That too would have to happen.

The thought cheered him up and almost felt good, as crushing as it was.

He recalled the time that he had saved seven men from the *Karelia.* He recalled the dark night when he had been hurled ashore on Stake Spit and had felt the hands of death clutching at his throat, and the strange afternoon of the church concert when he had drifted out to sea together with the count's currant wine. And the rescue and the festive return. But now it was all gone and over with.

It was not any easy matter to pronounce those words: It is over. They stuck in his throat like broken glass impossible to swallow, they pained and burned, they drove him to unworthy deeds, he cried and howled frantically into the dark morning in order to gulp down a breath of air, he turned the boat around and steered back to shore, but it was in vain, it couldn't be done . . . he became his old self, concentrated once more on his decision to make an end of it. But first he wanted to send a greeting to Eliana. Here was a bottle, and he had a stub of a pencil in his pocket, there was some paper here too, there were, for instance, the bank notes. He opened the bottle, it was old rum, but that didn't make any difference, he didn't care to taste it, he emptied the bottle over the side of the boat. Then there was the question what he should write. . .

Hours passed before Moritz was able to decide what he should write on the piece of paper. The sky was light gray, bursting into light, and the sun emerged among the gray clouds like a veiled moon. At long last he managed to write the difficult words: "To Eliana, regards from your Moritz, we'll meet again."

He put the cork back in the bottle, threw it overboard and looked at it with a vacant stare until, bobbing up and down, it had disappeared among the waves.

Then once again he got hold of the can with the extra gasoline. With shaking hands he poured the clear liquid over the entire boat and lighted it with a match. He waited until the fire had spread so far that the heat became unbearable and his clothes began to smoke. Then, with a loud cry, he jumped overboard.

CHAPTER 2

The Mangling House

Thus Moritz, too,—musically the most gifted of our poor, lost music-makers, has made his exit from our story. The details about his disappearance never became known. A thorough and long-lasting search was made for the ferryboat, but to no avail.

Actually this would not have been surprising if there had been bad weather on the evening in question. It had happened before that the motor had failed and the boat had drifted off course. But in calm weather? The boat must have sunk for some reason or other. But how? Had the motor exploded? Fire on board? But a thing like that would inevitably have been observed by people on shore.

There was something completely mysterious about the whole thing. And the mystery was heightened when it was established some time later that Matte-Gok hadn't been a passenger on the *Mjölner* at all.

So it was evident that, for some reason or other, the boat carrying the two men had never gotten as far as the ship.

Now the guesswork starts in earnest. The whole town once again buzzes and bubbles. Another gruesome and mysterious event has occurred. But just what has happened?

"It's quite clear," Ole Brandy says to constable Debes. "Moritz has killed Matte-Gok. It's as plain and simple as that. And then he has set out to sea. It's just like him. And then he's been hauled up by some ship passing by. And then he hasn't told them who he is, of course, for he doesn't want to be beheaded just for doing his duty. You'll just see that he'll come back some day, when the whole thing is forgotten! I know him!"

"Yes, but the boat, it had a name and a registered number!" Debes objects.

"True, but he naturally tore off those number plates in good time," Ole says. "It's easily done. It may be that you, if you'd been in his place, would have forgotten all about that, Ludvig, but Moritz was not such a fool. But he was a wonderful fellow, and he consequently had to kill Matte-Gok, and God bless him for *that*."

"You had better keep quiet!" the constable admonished him. "You had better just watch your mouth."

But Ole Brandy did not keep quiet about what he regarded as truth and justice. As soon as he had gotten out of the brig he went straight to the Bastille to reassure Eliana and her children.

"He's not dead! He'll be back! As sure as my name is Ole Olsen, called Brandy, and my father's name was also Ole Olsen, known as Ole Jib, and my grandfather's name was also Ole Olsen, called Strong Ole!"

Eliana opened her red-rimmed eyes wide and just stared vacantly at him. He could see that his words did her some good. He thought to himself: "Eliana belongs to the hope-people. To those human beings who hope. Who are always hoping. People who hope never become completely unhappy, for they have their hope, which they hope for. One can buck up such people by pouring more oil on their hope."

"I don't dare believe it," Eliana said.

"Well, what do you believe then?" Ole Brandy asked scornfully. "Do you think that they've left the country and have divided the loot between them? Now, there you see!"

"They may have killed each other," Eliana sighed, shuddering. She wiped her eyes with a corner of her apron.

314

"And then scuttled the boat?" Ole laughed derisively. "Or where could it be? Can you think of a better explanation? Of course not, there you see once again!"

"The ocean is so big," Eliana sighed.

"Before long you'll get a letter from him," Ole said, unimpressed by the bigness of the ocean. "You want to bet? A letter without the sender's address, of course, for he knows what he's doing. He'll write that he is well and is living off Matte-Gok's money. For he has richly deserved it for all his trouble. And then it might even be that he ransoms Kornelius. Things like that have happened before. You know the old songs, Eliana."

Eliana took Ole's hand and patted it gratefully. "I know that you wish the best for me, Ole."

"She's been hoping," Ole thought, "she's one of the hope-people." He turned his face away. He was deeply moved. He withdrew his hand, making believe that he wanted to cut himself a piece of chewing tobacco.

On the very same afternoon Eliana had a visit from attorney Wenningstedt. He came, as he said himself, in order to talk about the future.

Wenningstedt had not displayed any lack of tact, he had postponed the visit until he thought it probable that the initial shock had worn off and the sorrow had gradually merged into the more pensive stage of sadness. He not only liked Eliana, he really felt a great deal of sympathy for her, in actuality he was very fond of her. For this woman knew how to work and apply herself. The only worthwhile person in the whole caboodle. And besides, she was still a charming woman. He had quite often felt it was a dirty shame that this really marvelous girl should have sunk so far down into the mire—she who so easily could have found security if she had acted sensibly in the past and had taken the advice of well-meaning people.

There were always prospects, of course, for girls with

315

looks like hers—even glorious prospects. But a woman's mind is imprudent. Imprudent to a revolting degree, indeed, stupidly so.

And still, when thoughtless girls have been married for a number of years or have become widows, their good sense will usually awaken. Especially when they have become a bit down at the heels. That, however, Eliana certainly was not, even though thirteen years had passed since this . . . well, nothing unfavorable is to be said about this *ferryman*. Indeed, there were many favorable things one could say about this man. Impetuous, somewhat slow-witted, but a fine fellow. A good-looking fellow. But—thirteen years, good Lord, is it really that long ago! Well, time flies, and one gets to be an old man before one knows it.

The attorney had seated himself and just sat there, staring ahead, his memories infusing his face with a kindly expression. He had a very good and positive suggestion to make to the young widow. But one couldn't come bursting out with it just like that. First there had to be a few words of sympathy, by way of introduction, and silent pauses and sad expressions.

At the time when this ferryman had disappeared out on the ocean with Count Oldendorp—at that time, it had for a moment seemed quite self-evident to Wenningstedt: she will be yours. It's certain, she'll fall to your lot. It can't be otherwise. It seemed to be in the air. And it was the same way now. It was in a way quite obvious that it had to happen.

After a while and with the application of due tact and prudence, attorney Wenningstedt touched on his plan. It was to the effect that Eliana and her children leave the Bastille and move into the late Mangling-Marie's little house by the brook, which was for sale at a very low price. He himself had been over to look at the house. It wasn't a bad idea at all, buying the Mangling House. And then it would not only provide a roof over their heads, but also offer a steady livelihood for the one who would take over the mangle and perhaps even wash and iron a bit for would-be customers.

Gratefully, Eliana immediately agreed to the suggestion.

"To tell the truth, it *is* almost impossible to stay here in the winter!" she said. "The Mangling House, of course, has a much more cozy and sheltered location, even though it is very small."

"But it's for sale and not for rent," the attorney said and made a pause. "It costs almost seven hundred crowns," he added. "Which one has to admit is rather high for that house. But that amount of money *has* been offered, so it won't be sold for less."

Another pause.

"Yes, that's a lot of money," Eliana said, trying to sound noncommittal.

"But I'm going to buy it," the attorney continued, eagerly rocking back and forth in his chair. "Is that all right then, Eliana? I'll buy it."

His voice almost trembled with emotion. He would have liked to add: "And then I thought you could have it rent free until we see how the business turns out. And if it isn't so good, then we'll just have to make the best of things."

But Eliana was too quick for him: "And then you can lease it to me, Wenningstedt! Oh, that would be nice of you! We can make a success of the laundry, for we are five women here, and both Franziska and Amadea and Rita are very handy and they will soon be grown women. And then we'll be able to make a living while we—while we're waiting."

Eliana blushed, which made her look especially pretty, yes, at that moment she looked the way she did when she was a young girl and was a waitress at The Dolphin and he used to visit the shabby restaurant for *her* sake and for none other.

She added with a smile, at the same time bending her

317

head forward and giving the attorney an oblique look: "Well, now you are perhaps thinking that I'm a little—a little too optimistic, Wenningstedt! But I've made up my mind to wait."

"Oh—wait?" said Wenningstedt open-mouthed. "How? Oh, yes."

"Yes, wait for Moritz to come home," Eliana explained, tossing her head in an obstinate manner.

"Well, of course," the attorney said and cleared his throat repeatedly as if something were lodged in his windpipe. "Well, yes, of course."

"*Or*," Eliana added with determination, "or until we know for certain that he's no longer alive."

"Well, yes, but, of course." The attorney once more cleared his throat.

Eliana grasped his hand and said, filled with gratitude, "I shall never forget your kindness to us, Wenningstedt! Many, many thanks!"

While walking slowly home, up through the bumpy alley, he thought to himself: "Such optimism! Good gracious! It's rather stupid the whole thing. Rather idiotic. Rather idiotic."

A few weeks later, Eliana moved into the Mangling House with her children and her foster children. The weather became gloomy, it rained persistently, and the rock-filled brook rushed noisily outside the windowpanes covered with raindrops, and inside, in the unpainted parlor, the mangle was thundering. It was a large, professional mangle, so heavy to work that it didn't really get rolling until all the children helped, but they managed—Orfeus, who had become a big boy, was a great help, and Ole Brandy, the Wailing Woman, and other friends and acquaintances often stopped in and gave a hand.

One day the Crab King stopped by. For several hours he

318

stood there, just staring at the large, shiny brook stones lying on top of the mangle and exuding a curious subterranean air of coziness, but it did not occur to him to help Eliana and the little girls, who were struggling and pushing the heavy carriage back and forth over the rollers.

"Now you just try for the fun of it, Poul Peter, and see how strong you are!" Eliana suggested with a smile.

Immediately the Crab King walked out through the door. But he came back a little while later, thin-lipped, with a strained expression in his face, and he seized hold of the mangle and showed what strength resided in his big chest and shoulders.

The Crab King returned the following day, and the end of it was that he got a permanent job with Eliana's mangle. Attorney Wenningstedt, who arrived one day to look at the enterprise, was taken aback by the strange sight that met his eyes. Eliana was not at home, but the mangle was going full blast. By one end stood the Crab King on a platform of wooden crates, Ole Brandy was at the other end, and on top of the mangle sat Magister Mortensen's retarded daughter and two other girls and applied themselves to the mangling with every indication that they enjoyed it immensely. And over by the window stood the boy Orfeus, scraping away on his violin with all his might.

Ole Brandy stopped the mangle for a moment, blew a few pungent and inhospitable clouds of smoke right in the attorney's face and said: "Was there anything you wanted?"

Wenningstedt shook his head and retreated, and the mangle began to roll again.

"That's what one gets for one's kindness," he thought to himself.

That is—kindness and kindness! Attorney Wenningstedt was no hypocrite, no matter what unfavorable things might otherwise be said about him. He had lived long all by himself and had benefited from deep reflection. He was a prac-

319

tical man, a rationalist, who had used the better part of his nearly sixty years in judiciously raking other people's chestnuts out of the fire for a suitable honorarium, and since he was frugal by nature he had gradually become an affluent and relatively happy man. But at times, and with increasing frequency, he was haunted by the troublesome thought that he had been cheated out of one of the most essential things in life. He would not be sentimental and call it *love*, that would sound too much à la Ankersen! But *woman* at any rate.

He appreciated woman, in a typically masculine way— namely, in the same fashion that a collector is fond of butterflies: they are lovely, they must be caught. To do that it is needful to use circumspection and to act resolutely. Wenningstedt had never lacked prudence and common sense, but on the few occasions he had displayed resolution the results had not been happy ones, and now his time was indeed getting short if he ever hoped to get a butterfly in his net.

He cannot be criticized for having selected Eliana, for she was the kind of woman that no one can be ashamed of having on his mind.

Wenningstedt admitted to himself without any pettimindedness that he had gotten Eliana on the brain. The young widow had an electric effect on him in his loneliness. Even though she wasn't very young any more, but about thirty-three or thirty-four, she was nevertheless the beautiful girl from The Dolphin, the girl one could never forget. And that this woman now would somehow fall to his lot—that was not unreasonable, it was no more than right. It was his turn. And a good beginning had been made. He had helped her, had been attentive to her, and had given her positive and real assistance, and she had been sweet and grateful.

Perhaps she would even have come around if it weren't for the fact that she was entertaining these foolish and vain hopes that her husband would come back. If one could only convince her in some guarded manner that it was impossible! But just be patient. The future will take care of itself.

But in this attorney Wenningstedt was sadly mistaken, for fate once again pulled a mean trick on him. What actually came to pass was nothing less than that attorney Wenningstedt was the one who found Moritz's bottle and his message!

This occurred during one of the attorney's frequent lonely, meditative walks along the beach, on a raw and blustery forenoon in February. There is a shining black bottle, casually bobbing up and down among the stones in the inlet, and he is suddenly seized with the boyish desire to destroy this solitary bottle; he lifts his stick in order to break it but then he notices that it is a corked bottle, one that possibly may contain a message.

True enough, there is a piece of paper inside the bottle. A five-hundred-crown bank note! Good Heavens! And across the bill in a clumsy blue handwriting it says: *To Eliana, regards from your Moritz, we'll meet again.*.

Deep in thought, attorney Wenningstedt folded the green bank note and put it in his pocketbook.

"We'll meet again," he thought. "Well . . . we'll meet again. But under what conditions, dear sir? It's best perhaps to keep quiet about that."

He kept quiet about it. But it must be said in his favor that to some extent he suffered from this silence and found it difficult to convince himself that he was keeping quiet for humanitarian reasons.

Attorney Wenningstedt kept quiet for three long months. Then at last his better nature won out, and he decided to sacrifice his own possible happiness and bring the note to Eliana. But before that was done, he suddenly died one day from heart failure.

Wenningstedt left behind him a sizable fortune, amounting to over one hundred thousand crowns. It was inherited by his only heir, his sister Alvilda, who was married to young Consul Hansen. But the Mangling House, with the mangle and laundry boiler, he had willed to Eliana—just in case.

The two women showed their gratitude in the most beautiful manner—his sister by erecting in memory of her brother a tall basalt stone with the inscription "Blessed are the pure of heart." Eliana planted a wild rose bush at the foot of the stone. As the years passed, the thorn bush with the wild roses grew up around the stone so luxuriantly that it completely covered the inscription.

And days and nights roll on, the mangle rolls on, the mill of time grinds on. It grinds out new events, or sometimes merely the gray dust of which humdrum existence is composed. Today is mercilessly ground into yesterday, yesterday into the day before yesterday, and the day before yesterday into the gray mass of the past; this in the course of time can be condensed and take on historical perspective but just as often it dissipates into darkness and myth, bits and pieces of songs and ballads, and mysteries that will never be solved.

CHAPTER 3

The poet and the moon

Sirius is lying in bed, looking at the full moon.

Once more he has moved over to master painter Mac Bett and again lives in the little attic room above the former schoolroom.

Sirius had been coughing and ailing for a long time; at last he had gone to the doctor, who had examined his chest and found that it was in pretty bad shape. This made it necessary for him to stay in bed, and it was on the whole a fairly alarming matter. But Sirius, on the other hand, was actually quite satisfied to be all by himself again. The brief period of married life with Julia had been nothing but trouble, partly because it had become ever more evident that they were not suited for each other, partly also for the reason that the blacksmith's wife always showed her feeling of contempt for him.

As far as Janniksen himself was concerned, he had always been Sirius's friend and protector, and the same could indeed be said about master painter Mac Bett. When Julia had given birth to a healthy baby girl in November and the doctor had given the family to understand that Sirius's presence in the home was undesirable, since he must be regarded as being infectious, the two men, after a brief discussion, had made the decision that had led to the present arrangement.

So now Sirius is lying in his old room and can on the whole live and do as he pleases. The blacksmith sees to it that he gets what he needs, with the exception of paper to write on. But in this respect Mac Bett has come to his aid and has turned over to the poet numerous scraps of wallpaper, which he has trimmed and bound together in small booklets.

These booklets are now to be filled with poems. They are lying there, thirsting to be put to use. It doesn't matter that they are not made up of glossy, white paper. On the contrary, there is a certain charm attached to these flowers and spirals on the back of each sheet of paper. It is almost like writing one's way through a bewitched forest. And the moon is shining so brightly tonight that it alone provides sufficient light to write by.

The moon, yes! A little while ago it rose above the blacksmith's garden, heavy and red, as if it were out of breath from the climb. Or as if it weren't the dead moon at all, but a newborn, living earth on the first day of creation. But gradually it has cooled off, and now it has become its real self, the lonesome but happy and carefree moon, the eternal sailer of the night.

What is there that cannot be said about the moon, the indestructible, old, and precious-looking object that every child on this earth has dreamed about capturing and making its toy. And still, there is no distance on earth that can compare with the distance to the moon.

Sirius is lying there staring into the moon's old, blurred, and inscrutable face. Tonight the face is placid and strangely blank, like an inviting sheet of paper. But at other times it is constantly changing its expression. No other face is as changeable and full of surprises as that one is. Now it is attentive and slyly observant, now sleepy and indifferent. At times a warm smile will pass over it, but it can also be sulky—indeed, the moon can become angry too and indulge

324

in a fit of subdued and somewhat ludicrous rage, especially when it is windy, when the clouds constantly flutter in front of its nose.

But it can also be solemn, not least when it is ringed in by a huge rainbow-colored halo. Then it wears an expression of distance and majestic gravity. And then the very same moon can at other times descend into the coarsest kind of indifference and become a sleepy old idler and sour-puss, whose only wish is to be left alone underneath his blankets.

He recalls the time when he first realized that the moon is not a creature on the order of a human being, but a globe just like the earth. At that time it was said to be a swampy and miasmal world, filled with endless and impassable morasses, here and there crossed by sluggish watercourses which lose themselves in stagnant lakes and oceans. During adolescence Sirius had been living in this dripping and seething moon world and in his thoughts sailed across its hidden waters: The Sea of Vapors, The Sea of Fertility, The Sea of Moisture, The Lake of Dreams, and whatever else they are called.

Later on he learned that the moon was a dried-out and ice-cold desert, a bleak ruin in the unfathomable solitude of space.

Yet, the moon is, of course, something more than a dead object, and even though its light contains no warmth it does have a living, spellbound soul of its own. It carries on its eternal sorcery in the nocturnal waters of earth, it plays in the shining treetops of the seaweed, conjures life into grass and gravel, flashes magically in windowpanes, fills children's eyes with joy and wonder, lights hot sparks of longing and dreams in young people in love.

Yes, the moon, the mischievous old fox—it knows everything, it is aware of the reverse side of the coin, no one can fool *it*. It knows, by heart, the entire past of this world, it

325

is the silent and secret confidant of the future and of its infinite possibilities.

Yes, how much there is that can be said about the moon! Sirius takes out his pencil and gets hold of one of Mac Bett's wallpaper booklets.

For the moon is a mirror that reflects the depths of space and the infinity of the universe, but at times is bedewed by the sighs of the human heart. Thou who art ancient and ever young, everything that is transient breathes its silent woe up to thee. Thou keepest vigil by cradles and by death-beds, thou hummest thy never-ceasing lullabies for those who are tired and weary. Thou keepest faith with the dead and thou knowest where even the best-hidden graves are to be found.

Thou art the friend of the poet who is ill, thou coolest his fevered brow and generously fillest his lonely heart with an intense feeling that this world is his home.

CHAPTER 4

The phantom Tarira assumes a kind of material form, but causes great complications and bloody strife

We are now approaching at a fast pace the conclusion of this tale about the lost musicians. It was on the whole a sad story, it may be said, but still, like everything else in this world, it did have its lighter side, for even if it turned out badly for our friends in the end, their young lives were filled by joy and trust in life, music and love, as well as comradeship and concord, in short, everything that makes of life a beautiful experience. It was no mere tale of broken illusions or of the victory of injustice. And something really great did come of it all in the end, something that later, when the time was ripe, was to be greatly appreciated by the wise and the well, and create confusion, if nothing else, among sour and sluggish people: Sirius's poems and Orfeus's violin playing.

As is well known, Sirius never experienced the joy of being recognized as a great poet. But he harbored within him, on the other hand, another kind of happiness, namely, the formidable joy that the power of poetry grants its votaries.

Sirius was not a very sagacious man, he was not calculatingly clever; on the contrary, for the most part he conducted himself in a rather foolish manner, and it was therefore to be expected that he incurred the impatient contempt of petty and pedestrian persons. But in return it fell to his lot to help give objects a soul, to awaken dead nature from its sleep of millions of years and give it the voice that all unredeemed objects are thirsting and longing for: the voice of art.

This is the strange process that transpires in the little room in the attic, where Sirius is in bed writing between the flowers in Mac Bett's wallpaper booklets. And a similar miracle unfolds at the very same time in dancing instructor Lindenskov's storage room, where Orfeus is practicing on his father's violin.

The violin mania came over this boy like a raging winter storm, at the very same time that his voice began to change, his facial features became large and desperate-looking, and he got painful religious scruples. It is quite clear that the latter, if not exactly awakened by Ankersen, were at least to a criminal degree nurtured by him; after the demise of Moritz he had descended like a raging epidemic upon the little family in the Mangling House, and it is hard to tell what the result would have been if Ole Brandy with his scornful talk hadn't always come to their aid like an unconquerable healing and cleansing antidote.

In this connection it is also fair to pay tribute to the name of dancing instructor Lindenskov. He placed his splendid and large storage room at the disposal of the young violinist and on the whole poured all the oil that could be pressed forth on the musical fire raging within the boy.

In this connection we should not forget Orfeus's friend Peter and his phonograph. The early origins of this phonograph are shrouded in a shady and dark past—one day it suddenly *was* there, and one day later on a furious bookstore owner came running and took it back together with some records that had been played so much that they were unrecognizable. But during the three or four months that the phonograph was in Peter's possession it was of incalcula-

328

ble benefit. The old deserted mill, where Peter hid his music machine, was in those days a very temple of art, thanks to the first movement of the Kreutzer Sonata, the Romance of Schumann's Fourth Symphony, as well as the irresistibly gay song for flute, "When I Wake in the Morning at Ten o'clock." These three records made up the entire repertoire; with no thought of stopping they played them time and again every night without ever changing the needle; the records were indeed fast plowed into pulp, but by then Orfeus had learned a part of the violin sonata by heart, not to speak of Schumann's catchy Romance, while Peter almost as if by magic imitated the flutist's playing and melodious singing.

Ever since they had attended Sirius's school, Orfeus and Peter had been friends. There were times when they would become distant toward each other, but then there was always something that would bring them together again; most often the reason would be that Peter was going to do something exceptionally unusual and exciting. But then one day something occurred that was to leave the boys suddenly the bitterest of enemies.

It all started in mysterious and oppressive circumstances, as so often when Peter had something planned. It started during the greenish dusk of a spring evening by Peter confiding in Orfeus that he had seen *Tarira*.

Of course, Orfeus did not believe that right off; one could never do that when Peter related something, but there would nevertheless be something to it, and that was also true in this case: "Up there! Can you see her now?" asked Peter. "Can't you? It's *almost* Tarira!"

They were standing down in Sexton Alley staring up at a gable lit by the evening sun, and there stood, lost in thought by the open window—yes, there indeed stood Tarira, the ship's figurehead and the dream vision, a young girl, blond and pale and with staring eyes. There stood Tarira, staring out into the pale evening.

329

Orfeus knew full well that it was *not* Tarira, but nevertheless he turned cold as ice from the emotion he felt. His throat constricted. His chest muscles twitched.

"Ha-ha," Peter laughed triumphantly. "It's only watchmaker Olsen's daughter Kitty! Did you really believe—?"

No, of course not. Orfeus smiled weakly and was still completely spellbound. He continued to stare, until the girl at last closed the window.

Following this episode, Orfeus would make secret pilgrimages over to Sexton Alley and stand hidden in an out-of-the-way nook, from which he had a view of the watchmaker's gable window. He came at dusk and often remained standing there a long time. It was only seldom that he could see something in Tarira's window, and it wouldn't be Tarira herself but her redheaded sister, who would whistle in a stupid way and wasn't anything to look at. Tarira herself never again appeared. But when lights were lit inside, Tarira's shadow would at times be silhouetted against the curtain. At least he imagined it was Tarira, and at the same time he connected this notion with Schumann's Romance. And when he had gone to bed at night in his little three-cornered attic room in the Mangling House, he would listen to the fervent sighs of the Romance, filled as it is with dusk and gloaming, in which a mysterious and warm light is lit—the loveliest sigh of longing in the entire realm of music, the tale of a budding love.

One evening he accidentally met the watchmaker's Kitty in Sexton Alley; she brushed past him at such close range that he could feel her breath, and inadvertently their arms touched.

"Look where you're going, you clumsy fool!" Kitty said.

Orfeus felt greatly humiliated, and several evenings he refrained from walking over to Sexton Alley. He sneaked the kitchen mirror with him up to the little cubicle where he slept, and in deep sorrow looked at his own face, which

330

seemed to him extremely ugly, large and colorless and full of red spots and blotches and soft down. Look where you're going, you clumsy fool! Yes, that's simply the way one had to talk to a face like that, that was easily understood.

But *Tarira herself*—she is not that way. She doesn't speak. She remains silent. She comes to him in his dreams and takes him along out into the dawn. She looks at him with a distant smile in her eyes and brushes past him, so close that he feels her breath.

There follow many nights without any dreams, and he feels a deep longing for Tarira. He lies there whispering her name; it sounds so smooth and gentle, almost like a sigh.

Other nights and days come and go, passing over the ocean and the winter-ravaged land, and in the distant cloudy chasm in the north the first anemic light of spring finally appears. For every day that dawns this spring light, so full of promise, increases in strength.

"Kitty has a crush on you!" Peter says one evening. "Shall I remember you to her?"

It appears that Peter knows Kitty very well.

"She would like to meet you," he continues. "She's been standing in Lindenskov's garden listening to your playing. She says that you'll undoubtedly become a second Pakkenini!"

Orfeus listens with only half an ear to Peter's entrancing words. But one day he encounters Kitty in Sexton Alley once again, and now she smiles at him, just as if she were saying: "Everything that Peter has told you is true!"

And from this moment on a fire is raging in Orfeus's heart, it spreads and consumes him completely; for weeks and months he cannot think of anything or any one else than Kitty. He avoids meeting her, for the same reason that he avoids Peter, he doesn't dare meet either one, he blushes and turns pale and begins to perspire and feels a blissful

331

ache when thinking about Kitty. Even his violin playing is almost put on the shelf. He is completely gone, he answers in confused syllables when he is spoken to, he becomes ever more pale and thin and walks around with a sickly smile and a lost look in his eyes.

His mother forces him to go to the doctor. But there is nothing particularly wrong with him. "Adolescence," says the doctor. "He'll soon be all right again."

It was in the old mill on a light evening at the end of April, with the fragrance of grass filling the air, that Peter confided to Orfeus that he had become engaged to Kitty. "For I'm the one that she's crazy about, not you at all," he said spitefully. "She says that you look like a bowl full of burned porridge!"

"We meet up here in the mill almost every night, she and I," he added. "We play the phonograph. I kiss her and everything. Now just go ahead and get mad, you dope! There's nothing to you—she says that too! Your grandfather was crazy, and your father was a murderer!"

With a loud and scornful laugh Peter jumped out of the doorway. Orfeus followed, blinded by tears and rage. Peter stopped in the middle of the hill and suddenly faced him: "Well, come on, you little worm, if you dare!" he shouted, rolling up his shirt sleeves. "I'll show you—!"

Orfeus rushed at him, they tumbled about in the new-grown grass, they rolled a short distance down the hill, bodies intertwined, and continued the fight farther down the hill. Orfeus was smaller and more delicately built than Peter, but he had the raging elemental force of jealousy on his side, and he won decisively; he pressed Peter's neck into the mud and placed his knee on his chest. Peter cried and spat furiously, but he had been vanquished. Both of them were bleeding from nose and gums and they were staring emptily and stupidly at each other.

"That's the way!" some one with a sharp and cheery voice

suddenly said right behind Orfeus's back. It belonged to master painter Mac Bett. The old painter was out for an evening walk, he had his best clothes on, with embroidered vest and a blue starched cap that looked like a royal crown on his well-shaped head. He was twirling his white ivory cane.

"Let him go now, and wash yourselves both of you in the brook before you go home, you really look like sin!"

Orfeus let Peter go, and the latter immediately began to run down the hill.

"I was watching you," Mac Bett said with a tight little smile. "I saw that it was you, Orfeus, and I thought to myself: Let's see how he'll manage that one! For your father would most probably have been able to handle such a situation, that I'll say for him, even though he wasn't a rowdy. But not your uncle, Orfeus! That poor weak-kneed Sirius would have allowed himself to be skinned and killed, that's for certain, and the other one, Kornelius, well, he *was* practically skinned and killed. He didn't resist either. He didn't have any backbone either."

The painter smiled sadly. "There's nothing at all that can be done with that kind of people. They have no staying power in life."

"And for that reason, my boy!" Mac Bett bent forward and fiercely looked Orfeus right in the eye. "And for that reason, my boy, for that reason it gladdened this old heart to see Moritz's son beat up that rascal! To see that you're made of sterner stuff than your uncles. That you can fight back. Yes, fight back, my boy, fight back when some one insults you or will cheat you or tries to knock you down. Don't forget, my friend, don't forget what old Mac Bett told you: Always hold your head high and don't let injustice get you down!"

The painter made a graceful slash with his cane, laughed a little, and smiling continued on his way.

That, approximately, was what master painter Mac Bett

said. It was said in praise even though it sounded strict, and it was meant as comfort and encouragement, but Orfeus did not feel encouraged at all, on the contrary, he staggered back to the mill, and there he threw himself down on the dirty floor, beside himself with the pain and the shame of it all.

CHAPTER 5

*Bygone days, broken dreams of happiness, and painful
longing, together with mysterious music in a
storage room and great bliss*

A great many of the more or less neglected small gardens,
spread throughout the old part of town, have reached quite
an old age. In his poem "The Green Oblivion," Sirius has
given expression to the peculiar combination of age and
dim memories that characterize these old gardens where
generations now dead have walked and have had their joys
and sorrows; the fragrance of the flowers or the soughing
of the wind or the dripping of the rain may at times bring
back memories of them and infuse the past generation with
a sort of ghost-like semblance of life.

Dancing instructor Lindenskov's house was surrounded on
all four sides by one of these old, overgrown gardens. It had
at one time belonged to the well-known Trade Commissioner
Trampe, who loved flowers with a passion, and here and
there between grass and weeds one could still encounter
small indomitable clusters of stately and luxurious flowers
from Trampe's time. Similarly, the impenetrable wall of wild
raspberry and rose bushes that lined the entire garden, together with the lush rowan espaliers, had been planted by
Trampe.

The constant greenish twilight in Trampe's garden as
well as in the large and dilapidated house owned by the

335

Lindenskovs, had a depressing and at the same time sooth-ing and healing effect on Orfeus's agitated spirit. It was a mysteriously closed world, a hidden and very moist world, inside of which something or other was always *swarming*. In the rooms of the house there was always a swarm of clothes, pieces of cloth and remnants, pincushions, rolls of thread, and thimbles. In addition, there was a multitude of bric-à-brac of all kinds, vases with perennial flowers, small terracotta figurines and statuettes, porcelain dogs, center-pieces, and old mouldy photograph albums bound in velvet. In dancing instructor Lindenskov's little room there was a swarm of pipes of every sort, from short sooty pipes to enormously long pipes with faience bowls. In his daughters' rooms in the attic there were swarms of colored greeting cards, which together with faded old flowers from past balls and dances had been placed like fans around on the sloping walls, and in the basement there were swarms of spiders, wood-lice, centipedes, and earwigs.

But in no other place were there such swarms as in the storage room, where Orfeus spent most of his time these days. It was absolutely incredible how many odds and ends of every possible shape and form had been stowed together.

Actually, this storage room was the brightest and nicest room in the whole house. There was a very special reason why no one lived in it: It was in this room that Trade Com-missioner Trampe, at that time an old man, had committed suicide by hanging himself.

In the beginning Orfeus had not felt very safe whenever he was alone in Trampe's parlor. But now, plunged in sorrow, he no longer felt any fear of ghosts; on the contrary, there was something almost comforting about being in the deserted and bright storage room with its many curious objects.

And as the days go by, Orfeus is immersed in a fecund state of dull and sad yearning. He makes believe that Tarira also has deserted him. She is flying all by herself now. He is just sitting there with his yearning, infinitely ugly and poor, despised and abandoned. That is the fate of all good men, he thinks. That's what happened to Sirius, he too was deserted and abandoned. But there is a sweet feeling attached to being among the abandoned, they live in their own world of sorrow and disappointment and longing.

With tears in his eyes, Orfeus plays Schumann's Romance. There's comfort to be derived from that piece. A green twilight sky and lighted windows in black gables. And behind closed doors and windows smoulders the world of love and joy that never will be yours.

The sewing machines whirr in Lindenskov's overcrowded parlor; the seven not-so-young daughters, the so-called "aunts," are all industrious seamstresses. At times the aunts will sing, and Orfeus will listen to the sad words of the song about a time that is past, flowers that are wilted, and birds that flew past and are gone.

> There flew a bird o'er the spruce-clad hill,
> that sings forgotten songs.

Old Lindenskov likes to join in and sing these forgotten songs, and his face will take on the same yearning and lost expression as his daughters.

There is so much that has gone by and will never return, no matter how much one yearns for it. The aunts are yearning, they often have tears in their eyes and just sit there, lost in their yearning. The trees in the garden are also yearning, and so does the wind on its eternal path.

And the junk in the storage room is yearning. And indeed, there's nothing that is so full of desperate yearning as Trampe's parlor. The large moisture stains on the faded wallpaper—they are nothing but yearning that breaks out in pale and puffy blotches.

And the brook that rushes past the Mangling House and fills the night with its somber murmuring, that too is filled with a ravenous and raging yearning. And the stones in the mangle lie there waiting, in a hopeless and ridiculous yearning that someone will come and plop them back into the water again.

One night Orfeus dreams that he is sitting in the basement of the Bastille listening to music just as in the old days. But it is not the warm, red music that he used to hear, it is strangely rushing, restless music, filled with sorrow and yearning. And there is only one person present in the big, dimly lit room. It is his mother. She sits staring into thin air, yearning, lonesome and abandoned . . . but suddenly it isn't she after all, but Tarira!

And now Tarira gets up and steps over to him, gliding along soundlessly, and then he must follow her, follow her with a boundless, sorrowful, almost despairing feeling of happiness.

They float out into the night and linger a moment in the church tower, where the old dried-up wrecks of aeolian harps quiver sadly, abandoned in the pitch-dark loft. And he follows her further on her eternal journey through the regions of dreams, where the sounds are lonely and immense. They both listen, and their eyes meet in silent terror.

This Tarira, this dream vision—why is she so tireless in her pursuit? Is she one of the demons who don't give up until they have led their victim to perdition? Is she a benevolent spirit—even though not a friendly angel, then at least a guardian spirit, unfailing and strong?

Later in life he often asked himself these questions, but the answer was never an outright yes or no: Tarira was a gift to you, in which something of the most profound within you found expression.

She was a personification of sorrow, longing, and love, sprung from the restless yearning of the spirit of an artist.

The days pass, and one evening Orfeus and Peter meet again, and things revert by and large to the way they had been before. "What I said about Kitty and me, that was a lie," Peter says, "it was something I said because I was so angry that Kitty is running around with that Kaj, apothecary Fähse's delivery boy. She doesn't care about me either. That was why I wanted revenge and told you the story about me and her. And that was why I lost the time we fought, because when you lie there's nothing that makes you stand up. But you thought it was the truth, and that was why you were so strong."

Orfeus, preoccupied, starts the phonograph. He is not angry with Peter. And not with Kitty either. He rather feels a bit disappointed that he has learned the truth. It adds a sense of disturbance to his yearning.

"She is certainly no Tarira!" Peter says scornfully.

"No!" Orfeus agrees, and they look at each other in a common feeling of contempt and loyalty.

"She's just a tramp," Peter says.

The summer season is on the wane, it gets to be autumn again with its lazy, wet and dark days, filled with yearning. From time to time one of the aunts will celebrate her birthday, then the rooms will be straightened out, and the Misses Schibbye and other elderly ladies pay a visit and drink chocolate from tiny gold-rimmed cups, and there's a lot of conversing—a lot of noise and chatter as if there were many busy birds around.

One afternoon, on a windy day with a pale sun in the sky, Orfeus had an unforgettable experience in the storage room. He had just put his violin away and was standing over by the window, when he heard behind him wonderful music, an inexpressibly deep and friendly sound, a chord slowly dying into nothingness. He turned around and stood a long time filled with great wonder. Where did this music come from, this strange ethereal music?

Ghosts? He felt a bit frightened, but wished that he would hear more.

He didn't hear more, however. But a little while later the head of a cat appeared in the middle of a junk pile. It stared at him, with eyes that seemed as deep as an abyss, steadily and for a long time. Then it disappeared just as silently as it had come.

Orfeus had a very uncanny feeling. The silence began to resound about him, and ghostlike shadows darted like elongated groping hands across the faded walls of the room. He felt as if he had been caught in a strange web of witchcraft and thought for a moment that he was dreaming.

But then suddenly there is rustling noise, and in a one, two, three, a big cat appears and jumps up on the window sill.

Well, there was a real cat in the room, then. Orfeus let it out. He calmed down and began to think things over. Perhaps the music also had a natural cause. It might be, for instance, that in one place or other in the piles of junk there lay a stringed instrument which the cat inadvertently had strummed. He became more and more obsessed with thinking about this instrument and began to rummage in the pile in which the cat's head had appeared. But the fear of ghosts still welled up within him, and suddenly he was seized by panic—he shuddered, pulled back, and opened the door with a fearful cry.

In the stairway he met Aunt Lucie, the oldest of Lindenskov's daughters, and almost knocked her down.

"Did you see something in there?" Aunt Lucie asked quickly.

Orfeus had to tell about the music that he had heard and about the cat that had jumped out of the window.

"Oh, was that all!" Aunt Lucie laughed and looked relieved. "Why, I thought that it was Trampe—! But it must have been only my old zither that you heard. It's lying some place in there. Come and I'll show it to you!"

340

Aunt Lucie found the zither after a bit of searching. "Alas!" she sighed as she strummed it. "It still sounds pretty good, but how rusty it is, and all that dust!"

She sat down on a backless chair, placed the zither in her lap and continued, while staring into the bright light of the afternoon: "Yes, time flies."

She slowly plucked the strings and sighed again: "This zither, my boy, was once given to me by my *sweetheart*. For I was engaged once. But then he left me, for he was a scoundrel. All men are like that. But now it's all so long ago, and he himself is dead and gone. It was such a sad thing, but now it's all over, thank God."

Aunt Lucie began to sing in a cracked voice, while her thin, veined hand groped over the rusty strings of the zither:

> I'm a stranger,
> I'm a pilgrim;
> Just one evening,
> Just one eve I tarry here . . .

But suddenly she got up with a little start and began to plant a lot of light kisses on his cheek, so that it tickled in his ear: "Bub-bub-bub-bub-bub! The world is faithless, but don't you mind *that*, for that is something that you'll get over. Well! But now you can have the zither and have some fun with it, if you want it. Then it will be of some use after all."

"Thank you very much," Orfeus said, flushed with joy.

As soon as Aunt Lucie had left, he grabbed the instrument, and the entire afternoon, until after dusk, he lay on the floor and strummed away. The long, drawn-out, singing tones threw him into a state of happiness almost on the verge of tears. One could strike chords and make it sound like an entire orchestra.

That night he had a wonderful dream.

He dreamt that he was standing in a huge empty room,

whose bare walls were bathed in a flood of afternoon sunshine. But at the end of the room was a platform with steps leading up to it, and on the stairs there was a multitude of musical instruments: big, reddish-brown and dark-brown cellos, sparkling violins, gleaming French horns and flutes, on top of the stairs a whole row of shining copper kettledrums. And all at once this tremendous orchestra began to play all by itself, without any one touching the instruments —a rushing windstorm of music that almost blew him down.

He awoke and for a long time he lay there twisting in quiet ecstasy.

CHAPTER 6

A new phase is marked in Ankersen's development by his quite unexpectedly turning his back on the Ydun Society during its great celebration

On the day that total prohibition, after much toil and struggle, was finally introduced by law, the Ydun Society held a meeting of solemn thanksgiving. As a sort of rounding-out of savings-bank manager Ankersen's portrait, we will here in conclusion give a brief account of the harrowing events that took place during this strange celebration.

"Of course, every one of you present here knows the reason why this hall is festooned and decorated with flags and why we've all put on our Sunday best."

It is Mrs. Nillegaard, the energetic vice-chairman of the society, who is speaking. Mrs. Nillegaard is deeply moved and in addition she is hungry and has a heavy cold. She blows her nose forcefully and in the process loses her lorgnette, which falls to the floor and breaks into many pieces; but this is no time to pay attention to trifles, she puckers her forehead and continues in a loud voice: "Yes! Total prohibition is now a happy fact. As we all know, it has been passed, first by a general plebiscite and then by law. So there's no way for any one to get around it."

Mrs. Nillegaard's face takes on an expression as if she suddenly is going to burst into laughter, but the reason is that she is about to sneeze. The fit comes and the hand-kerchief is again produced. She continues: "As I said, there's no way of getting around it!"

Mrs. Nillegaard once again looks as if she were being tickled, and another violent paroxysm occurs.

She continues: "It is under the leadership of savings-bank manager Ankersen that we've reached this goal that we have been desiring such a long time. We've all been infected with his enthusiasm. Like no one else he has risked his hide and gone through hell and high water. His example has steeled our will and under his leadership even the most spineless have been able to stand up straight.

"Thus it has at last fallen to our lot to place the crown of victory on our head. Yes, dear friends! The race is over. We've reached our goal. With King Solomon we can exclaim. . . !"

Mrs. Nillegaard is fighting a new attack of sneezing.

"Exclaim. . ."

Violent sneezing.

"Yes, exclaim with King Solomon. . ."

Still another fit of sneezing. Mrs. Nillegaard makes a pause. Her nostrils quiver. There is a suspicion of laughter over by the tables in the back of the hall. There is another attack of sneezing which she suffers with good grace. But then the road is clear again, and she continues: "Thus we can exclaim with King Solomon: 'And I saw that there is nothing better than that a man is fond of his deeds, for that is his part.'"

Another attack of sneezing is already coming up, and in order to get in first Mrs. Nillegaard delivers herself of the last part of her speech at a tremendous rate of speed: "And now, dear friends, now we will rejoice together, and I trust you will not disdain the wonderful rib roast that is gracing our table this evening! I hope you'll enjoy it!"

With a sneeze of final relief Mrs. Nillegaard steps down from the speaker's stand and places herself at the table between her husband and the savings-bank manager.

Teacher Nillegaard has been squirming during his wife's speech. Since the recent memorable events Ida has been in a disturbingly overwrought state, and besides that she has overexerted herself during the preparations for this celebration, the arrangements for which had been assigned to her. But thank God, the speech has gone off exceptionally well, and now it's all over. Without any speaking in tongues! Without any obscene incidents! Thus the worst is now happily over with. There is an aroma of a delicious rib roast, knives and forks start their pleasurable activity, and there rises a great buzz-buzz from the happy and secure people sitting at the large horseshoe-shaped table.

But Ankersen's plate is empty.

What does that mean?

"Aren't you going to have anything to eat, Ankersen?" Mrs. Nillegaard inquires anxiously.

Ankersen doesn't answer. He sits stock still.

The Nillegaards exchange glances. Mrs. Nillegaard wrinkles her forehead and demonstratively starts in on the roast. But suddenly Nillegaard has no appetite. A peculiar chill exudes from the brooding Ankersen and his empty plate.

Mrs. Nillegaard irascibly pokes her husband in the ribs. "Well, don't you like the food, Jens Enok?" she asks, chewing energetically. Nillegaard involuntarily gives a start: "Yes, oh yes, it is a splendid roast!"

"In that case, I think you ought to eat it!"

Mrs. Nillegaard pushes the meat dish closer to Ankersen's plate and thereby makes the gravy boat take a list and give some of its superfluity to the tablecloth: "Please help yourself, Ankersen, don't let it stand there and get cold!"

But Ankersen sits there as if he doesn't hear her at all.

Then he gets up, pushes his chair back with a great deal of noise and walks slowly and heavily up towards the speaker's platform.

Ankersen is going to speak! Hush! Every one becomes quiet.

Ankersen looks out over the gathering. He breathes heavily, looks preoccupied, and takes his time. At last he begins to speak. His voice sounds strangely sad and plaintive.

"I had imagined," he says, "I had imagined that this meeting would have borne the impress of seriousness. I had imagined it as a quiet and devout thanksgiving coming from our hearts. And not as a—an occasion to gorge ourselves!"

"Now, just a minute—!" Mrs. Nillegaard puts her knife and fork down.

"Quiet!" Nillegaard says, a note of warning in his voice. "Let Ankersen explain what he means."

Ankersen says in a louder voice: "I will be honest with you and say outright that when I stepped into this room this evening and noticed this smell of much food, then my heart was greatly astounded."

"That I can't understand at all, Ankersen!" Mrs. Nillegaard shouts from her place at the table. "For it was agreed that food would be served!"

Ankersen nods dejectedly. "It's true that there would be food, Mrs. Nillegaard! But not that the eating, if I may say so, should go ahead of everything else!"

Mrs. Nillegaard blows her nose violently. Her face, already flushed from her cold, turns scarlet, and her glance wanders all around; she's sorely in need of her lorgnette. Ankersen sends her a penetrating look, his expression is grave without actually being reproachful: "As I said, Mrs. Nillegaard, I had imagined that the food would be secondary. But—it just couldn't be postponed."

"No, of course not, it couldn't be postponed!" answers

346

Mrs. Nillegaard, her voice almost sounding mirthful from sneezing and indignation. "Of course, Ankersen! The food shouldn't just stand there and get cold, should it? Use your head, man!"

A bit of hilarity may be noticed here and there.

"Very well," says Ankersen. "Very well. In that case, I think I can understand it."

The hilarity grows.

"I'm glad to hear it!" Mrs. Nillegaard answers, pursuing her victory.

Ankersen gets a tired and greatly worried expression in his face. He nods and says: "Oh, well. I shall be brief."

Suddenly he lifts his head and raises his voice: "Yes, indeed, I have been noticing it for a long time! I've seen which way it would all go. It is the sad truth that the Ydun Society to an ever increasing degree has become a worldly-minded and empty-headed society! A society without any spiritual content! And now, when this our earthly goal has been reached, what remains of the spirit in which we began our work? It was not at all our intention that we should stop here! But well and good. Perhaps the mission of this society has been fulfilled. Perhaps we can't possibly go further at the present time."

Ankersen emits a deep sigh. The audience looks at him with rapt attention.

"But to repeat, that is the way I had imagined it. And now, dear friends, for that reason I will now resign from it all. From now on I don't want to have anything to do with this society. I want to set my own course. My place is not at the table of the voracious ones. My place is not in the circle of those who have eaten their fill. My place is right in the middle of the struggle! Wherever people do battle and bleed, that's where I want to be. And therefore. . ."

Ankersen is filled with emotion. His voice breaks: "For

347

that reason, dear friends! For that reason I now want to bid you farewell. Please don't let me disturb you. Eat with a good appetite. But I just want you to know that I feel superfluous here."

"No, no, Ankersen!" Nillegaard protests.

Mrs. Nillegaard pokes her husband violently in the ribs, shakes her head, and begins to speak: "Listen! May *I* be permitted to make a remark! First of all, I want to repeat that Ankersen himself was party to the decision that the menu was to consist of rib roast! I don't care what you say, Ankersen! You yourself mentioned rib roast! And when you now come here and spoil everything for us, then I say that it is a shameful thing to do! Shameful! That's what I said! Your desire always to assert yourself certainly knows no limits!"

Nillegaard: "Now, now, Ida!"

Mrs. Nillegaard holds a crumpled, soaked handkerchief in her hand and makes a threatening gesture toward the rostrum: "Tonight I want to say what I mean! It is a shameful thing for Ankersen to come here and interrupt our meal, just so that people should pay attention to him! He just can't stand that we're eating and that we're happy! Let me tell you, Ankersen, that we see through you! You could have withdrawn quietly, if you disapprove of the arrangements! But now it's too late! Now you've spoiled it all! We can't possibly go on with it!"

Mrs. Nillegaard is now tremendously excited and agitated. She turns toward the gathering: "The Lord knows that no one has admired Ankersen the way I have! I have been fond of him, yes, I have loved him! Yes, I have *loved* you, Ankersen! But now I *hate* you! For you're not a human being! You're a heartless, detestable tyrant! And I will now propose that we all just get up from the table and go home and leave Ankersen to that ice-cold loneliness. . . ! Then. . . !"

General confusion. Some of the celebrants get up from the table, others remain seated, a few indignantly begin to eat again.

"Scandalous! Scandalous!" Nillegaard moans. He clutches his head. But way inside his very being a small, long-suppressed flame begins to crackle and sputter.

"Ankersen!" he shouts triumphantly. "Ankersen! In all decency you can't leave now! You can't! Do you hear?"

But Ankersen, thanks be to heaven, is already out by the entrance. He is putting on his galoshes.

"Listen to me!" Nillegaard says. "Do you realize that you've almost been acting like a *boor*, Ankersen? You're a boor, that's what you are! Do you hear?"

Ankersen neither sees nor hears. His expression is that of one who is far away, in another world. He is not angry, he is only far away.

The flame grows inside Nillegaard, it is sooty and is belching smoke. He hisses and laughs scornfully: "But then you're through here, Ankersen! You've disqualified yourself in every way! You're a nasty boor, that's what you are, a real heartless scoundrel, between you and me, a demagogue and a hooligan, a narrow-minded fool, a spiteful old woman. . . !"

Ankersen stares at him. He remains silent. He does not look angry. He is merely far away. As if preoccupied, he shakes Nillegaard's hand and says: "Farewell, Nillegaard. I must go. Don't hold me back."

Disconsolate, Nillegaard turns his head away and looks for something among the overclothes in the empty cloak room. He just stands there for a moment, moaning.

Then a single, solitary sound emanates from the otherwise deathly quiet in the assembly hall—a horrible sound—like crows of lamentation from a rooster whose head has not been completely cut off—a loud idiotic wailing.

He rushes feverishly back into the hall and encounters

precisely the sight that he had expected, the sight of Ida leaning back in her chair and in vain trying to stifle her hysterical sobbing with the aid of her handkerchief.

Those crestfallen members of the Ydun Society who pass by the Shoemaker Flats on their way home from the interrupted thanksgiving feast can dimly see the contours of a small group of persons in the moonlit night gathered around a man who is singing.

It is Ankersen who has started all over again.

CHAPTER 7

The poet and death

Tonight the sky has a yellow, sickly color, something that every one knows means bad weather, and this is confirmed by the barometric pressure.

For some reason or other, there is going to be a storm.

Relative to the weather, human beings are just like children who observe the life and work of the adults without really understanding what actually goes on. Tonight the weather has made up its mind to be bad weather. A storm is brewing, and no one knows why. There is nothing any one can do about it but to put up with it. Put up with it, just as one does with fate.

Sirius is lying on his lonely bed meditating. He is in high spirits and actually looks forward with great pleasure to the impending storm. He has just had a visit from Ole Brandy and Olivarius. They are the ones who have told him about the unusually low barometric reading.

Where were we? To accept one's fate. There is also talk about revolting against one's fate. That was what Beethoven did, so they say. But isn't that at bottom a lot of nonsense? If a man surmounts his fate, as the saying goes, then his fate has decreed that it is to be surmounted. Fate is that which happens. How can it be otherwise?

Sirius is both tired and restless. He is staring into the dazzling square of the window, into the yellow abysmal

351

light of the late afternoon that now has a touch of red, reminding him of a distant trumpet call. Mountain-like formations of clouds glide forth, silver gray and ash gray. For a moment the entire sky takes on the color of dirty bedclothes. But it would be pleasant to be able to lie on top of one of the folds of this tremendous heavenly quilt and from such a dizzy height to look down into the abyss and observe the greedy broom of the storm as it sweeps the darkling ocean.

Ha! The storm seems to have set in already; there is a long-drawn-out and alarming whine around the gable of Mac Bett's house, and the bare trees in the blacksmith's garden clatter gently, just like skeletons arising from the dead. And suddenly a dark shadow envelopes the rushing clouds in blackness—it looks like the shadow of a high, uneasy mountain jammed in among others. Sirius recalls the adage about the mountain that was going to bear a child. The squalls and the darkness fill him with pleasure, he feels very happy and comfortable lying there in his bed.

Meanwhile the great storm is growing in intensity. Whirlwinds are waltzing around, lonely and desperately powerful, out on the surface of the ocean. Meaningless and enormous. Giant waves roll toward the northwest, as if they had to reach a certain goal; but as every one knows, no storm has ever had any goal but this single one—to storm.

In his inner eye he sees how the storm rushes along and makes the sea boil around the steep and lonely coasts. Columns of surf rise slowly and indolently in the sallow twilight, then unfold, stand there swaying for a moment, and sink quietly down into the depths, where darkness blossoms out like flowers of greenish foam. Some of the foam flowers are immense and passionately spread their pearly tentacles in the semi-darkness. The entire coastline turns into a living garden of luxuriant, fiery, ruthless foamy flowers.

There is a seething and a growing everywhere out there in the unreal doomsday light of the evening, roaring giant forests of darkness rise out of the abyss, heaven and ocean are joined together. In the end all is darkness. An overwhelming, foaming, storm-filled darkness.

Then comes a raging squall, it makes a wild and thousand-voiced din against the windowpanes and fills the grooves on the metal roof with purling ice-cold fresh water. Sirius is thirsting to feel the cool purling water against his hot forehead, he yearns for it, takes delight in giving himself over to the thick, the wet, the storm-filled darkness. . .

When blacksmith Janniksen the next morning stopped in to see his son-in-law, he found him dead.

Perplexed, the blacksmith scratched his neck and his eyes became round and staring.

"Oh my Lord, poor little fellow!" he murmured to himself.

CHAPTER 8

How it eventually fell to the lot of the resolute Ole Brandy to become the one who rescued Orfeus out of the underworld

Orfeus had begun as an apprentice with master painter Mac Bett. He was almost fifteen years old. His schooling had been completed, and he had to get himself a real job of some kind.

The Scottish impetuosity of the old painter had far from abated over the years; in the overgrown and introverted boy he suspected another Sirius, and one day when Orfeus accidentally had spilled a bucket of newly mixed paint, his temper ran completely away with him; he hurled a roll of gilt-leather wallpaper at the boy; it hit him right in the face, and he received a long cut in his forehead and a big black eye.

"The Lord preserve me!" the master painter wailed. "Oh what a picture you make! Oh my! And you're not even crying. That's to your credit, you're a really fine fellow, even though you're a clumsy fool!"

Breathing hard, he sat down on the bottom rung of a stepladder, pulled the boy to him, and stroked his hair. "How is this going to end," he moaned darkly. "What's going to happen to us, my boy? One day I'll probably kill you and I'll end my days as a common murderer and a ruined man!

"And then you don't even say anything, but put up with it," Mac Bett continued. "And you'll probably tell your mother when you get home that you've fallen and hit yourself on something. For that's the way you are, you're a good and kind boy. But you're not going to get the opportunity to *lie* about it. Come with me, you little devil, and we'll go to your mother this very minute. For even though I'm a poor old bully, Orfeus, I've nevertheless always striven to be fair and just in all my dealings. And then I've been fond of you, of both Sirius and your parents and also poor Kornelius, and that was the reason that I wanted to have you as an apprentice. I wanted to teach you something useful, make you into a methodical fellow, so that you would make out well in life."

Mac Bett closed his eyes and bent his head back. He looked very old and worn.

"And then I had—let me say it now while I'm at it, for later on I might regret having said it. . ."

Mac Bett pulled out a big red handkerchief, wet it with his tongue, and very carefully began to wipe away some dried blood from the boy's forehead. "Yes, I've had in mind that you would continue working here and take over the business later on, when I'm gone. For I've no children or heirs. At one time I had the same thing in mind for Sirius, but that went phooey, for he was really impossible. It's not a nice thing to say it, for he's dead, but he was impossible, right through and through. He lay there writing on wallpaper, that he did, and all his writings I've saved, in case there should be anything to them. At first I wanted to burn all that rubbish, but then a voice inside me said: 'Suppose there is something to it after all?' Suppose one day a scholar should come to me and say: 'Look here, Mac Bett, you can sell and get a lot of money for that stuff there!' One's heard worse things before. But what's this really got to do with the case? As I said before, let's go down to your mother. Now you're feeling a bit better, aren't you? Your eye's closing, but that's what it's supposed to do. Everything'll be all right, you'll see."

355

Ole Brandy and the Crab King were home alone in the Mangling House. They were just about finishing their lunch. Ole Brandy lit his pipe. His eyes flashed through the thick billows of smoke.

"There's no need for you to say anything, Mac Bett!" he snarled contemptuously. "It's not the first time that you've demonstrated your murderous bent!"

"Take it easy!" the master painter said threateningly. "You're not the one I'm looking for. You're not the one I'm going to apologize to."

The two men looked hard at each other. With his good eye Orfeus looked anxiously from one to the other. They were both angry and each in his own way looked terrifying and gave cause for alarm—Ole with his broken nose and his sneer, Mac Bett with white sideburns and the piercing hard look in his eye. On the verge of tears, Orfeus had to admit to himself that at bottom he was fond of both of them, as if they were his grandfathers. He thought of Abraham and Isaac and the other eccentric old men in the Bible; they too could be hot-tempered and unreasonable, but at bottom they were capable and kind men. It tore his heart to hear how Ole Brandy now began to give Mac Bett a piece of his mind.

But it didn't turn into a mean and rough quarrel after all, even though Ole Brandy used some strong language.

"For half a century," he said, "for half a century you've been painting and gluing up wallpaper, Mac Bett, glued and blotted and pasted and patched and pinched and scraped; you're dried-up and faded, with your venomous eyes, and for no other purpose than just sitting by yourself in the evening and sinking your arms into your money way up to your elbows! And if a poor apprentice is unfortunate enough to dirty one of your wallpapers, then you try to kill him, you bury your fangs in him, and then you shed crocodile

356

tears, for then your conscience shakes you up, for there *is* something to shake up in you, oh boy, that *is* some dunghill to clean out!"

"Now, now!" Mac Bett cautioned him.

Trembling with anger, he looked around for something to sit on. The Crab King suddenly rose from his chair and wriggled out of the room. Mac Bett took his seat and, trying to repress his feelings, made himself comfortable.

"Yes, now I'm leaving too," Ole Brandy said, "for I don't want to be under the same roof with you. But before I leave I'll tell you this: that boy there, you're going to let him go! Do you understand? He deserves a better fate than having your inch rule stuck in the eye! And that he'll get! *I'll* see to that!"

Ole Brandy sent an angry cloud of smoke in the direction of Mac Bett and disappeared out through the door with a contemptuous grunt.

Ole Brandy knew that he had said a bit too much when he promised to see to it that Eliana's son would fare better than to be an apprentice with Mac Bett. What could one possibly do, being poor and without any standing in the community? That evening he discussed the matter with Olivarius and Lindenskov. Olivarius was of the opinion that being with Mac Bett, the boy, in spite of everything, was in good hands. Lindenskov at first had opposed the idea of letting the boy become an apprentice painter, for it was music that was his field. But there was no other way of getting him started in life. Perhaps things would straighten themselves out some day. . .

"Perhaps he'll become Mac Bett's heir," he said with a dreamy look. "And with the inheritance he can travel to other lands and study the violin and become a real musician. On the other hand, that may not be for a long time yet, for Mac

357

Bett is still a vigorous man. He can live till he's ninety, and by that time the boy will be almost forty—and *then* it's too late!"

Ole Brandy was racking his brain almost all through the night; after a while he got a little tired of thinking about Orfeus. He had his own worries, too. On the whole, everything seemed to have gone strangely wrong every way he looked. Kornelius had been locked up in an insane asylum. And the Corpse Crower had also gone crazy and had built himself a foolish-looking tower on the roof of his carpentry shop. It was a ridiculous tower, a degrading piece of work. It was only big enough for Josef to be able to stick his head up in it, but it was equipped with pipes and valves and cogwheels and chains and a corkscrew-like spire. And the big black dent that Janniksen had had in his forehead for such a long time had begun to swell up, so that he was now lying in the hospital with his entire head swathed in steam-towels.

And nothing was heard from Moritz, so he was probably dead after all. But Ole was ever trying to keep Eliana's hopes alive, for she was a hope-person, and one must never try to kill hope in such people, for then they will just fade away. Hope is a curious thing, Ole thought with a shake of his head, lying there in the dark by his lonesome self.

And now, following the introduction of prohibition, it wasn't even possible to get a bottle of beer at The Dolphin. Öström was raving about closing and selling the whole business and going to Sweden.

And he himself was getting old, he was not by any means the man that he used to be, and one didn't get any better from drinking that flat prohibition beer.

But there were always the ships, their world did not change. It never changed. The men of the sea do not allow themselves to be fooled. They remain the same, generation after generation. The men of the sea—they are like the firm floor underneath one's feet, like deck planks that never fail. They are solid.

358

And the next day the ocean presents Ole Brandy with a gift and makes him happy, gives him encouragement, and really cheers him up again. For what fine ship is that sailing into the harbor but the *Albatross,* that wonderful old bark! The *Albatross,* on which he has sailed fully nine years of his life! The *Albatross,* the good and happy ship of his youth. The *Albatross* with the white and gilt figurehead underneath the bowsprit. But the yardarms are gone and a motor has been installed together with other things. But never mind that.

The *Albatross* has been away a long time, six or seven years at least. And now it has come back.

But the greatest and the strangest thing is that the Moster Man, his uncle, is still sailing on the *Albatross!* It sounds incredible, but the Moster Man, seventy-four years of age, is still sailing on the old ship and has hardly changed at all, looking thin and dried-out like an Indian and with his cap askew. Nothing in the whole wide world has been able to subdue *him!*

The Moster Man is still no more than an able seaman, but he is highly regarded on board and can do whatever he pleases. When he wants to treat to a glass of rum, then everybody has a glass of rum, and the chief officer and the captain come and lift their glasses to the happy reunion of two old friends.

It is altogether a wonderful ship, friendliness and cordiality envelope the whole vessel just like shimmering sunlight. Actually, it's not being used for anything any more, the Moster Man explains, it's only cruising about. It's actually a marine research vessel, but now even that's finished, and unfortunately, it's due to be broken up for scrap.

Ole Brandy feels a wistful happiness that seldom has entered his life. One of the Moster Man's ears still has the white scar from the time that the half-caste girl Ubukoshara bit it to pieces, about half a century ago. "Yes, yes," he says and happily shakes his head and exposes a lone tooth, the very last survivor.

There are so many strange people on board the *Albatross,* one of them wears spectacles and just sits there writing in a book. He doesn't do anything but write, the Moster Man says. Another one lies snoring in a chair on the deck; he has on a heavy sweater and rubber boots and sports a beard and a tanned face. "Yes, just look at him," says the Moster Man, "he is the concertmaster."

"Do you arrange concerts on board here, too?" Ole asks and again cannot help chuckling at the whole thing.

"All the time!" the Moster Man says with animation. "When he isn't boozing or sleeping he's playing his violin, even in stormy weather. Aside from that he's of no use. He doesn't even do any studies of the ocean. But just the same he's been hired as an able seaman, just like me. Of course he doesn't get paid any wages. But he doesn't give a damn about that, for he has a very good job on shore."

Ole Brandy spends a wonderful evening on board the *Albatross,* one of the best that he can ever recall.

But the following day he can't recall very much. The only thing that he can clearly remember is having sung "Olysses" several times on request, and that there was some violin playing.

Violin!

All at once Ole Brandy is struck by the word: *violin!*

He nods to himself as he sits there bent forward in the low-beamed attic, shaving himself before the little mirror. Strange, wide-ranging, and grandiose thoughts pass through his mind. And as in a distant and benign vision he sees old Boman, and Moritz, and Kornelius, and Mortensen and the other doughty music-makers from the good old days, with their bows and violins. Now they are all dead and gone or out of the running. But he is left. Ole Olsen, known as Ole Brandy, he, the son of Ole Jib and Strong Ole, he the

360

experienced seaman, he who never in his long life has taken an insult lying down. He never achieved fame, or riches, that is true—never even learned to play the jew's harp—but wait, just wait. If you can get Moritz's and Eliana's son wrenched out of Mac Bett's clutches and get him music instruction from people who know . . . if you can get him made into an Ole Bull, honorable sir, then you'll certainly not get rich on that, far from it, but noble hearts will joyfully enshrine your name in all eternity, Amen.

Now you're just sitting here talking nonsense to yourself, Ole, almost as if your name were Ankersen. Besides, you're a bit drunk. But that's a good thing. But get going on this now! The devil take this damned attic where one can't even stand up straight!

Ole shakes his fist at his clean-shaven picture in the mirror.

Among the many curious tales that Concertmaster Andersen used to relate from his vacation trip up north with the *Albatross* during the summer of 1914, there was also the one about the old salt Ole Brandy with his earrings and his protégé Orfeus, the wonder on the violin.

It was not a run-of-the-mill story, it was too touching to be that, as Andersen said himself.

"At first the old man had come aboard by himself and had sung for us a few indescribably somber and tearful songs about Olysses and Pimpileja; and what a marvelous sight he was: he looked like a cross between a Chinese pirate and the late conductor Johan Svendsen!

"And the next day he came onboard again and told us with an expression as if it all concerned a horrible crime, that up on shore there lived a great genius on the violin who was held captive by a dangerous and evil man named Mac Bett, and whom we should use all our power to set free.

" 'Yes, of course,' I said, 'if what you're telling me is true, there's no time to waste.' And then we went ashore in that

361

strange little town where Ole Brandy lived and did our best to make our way up the narrow steep alleys without stepping on too many ducks or eiderducks. It was a beautiful Sunday forenoon, chickens and sheep and goats were grazing on every roof. And Ole Brandy then stops by the absolutely smallest house in the whole world and asks if Orfeus is in. No, Orfeus is not home, he's in the storage room, is the answer.

"Then farther up we go, up hills and through small flower gardens, until we come to a house that's completely hidden by leaves and grass and overhanging branches, and then up into the storage room, and there we find, all by himself, a young boy. His eyés are red from weeping, and they have purple and green rings around them, and there is a dark streak, as if from a whip, across his forehead. He's lying face down on the floor strumming a zither.

" 'Now you play your violin for this man, the very best you know how!' Ole Brandy orders him. And the boy obediently gets up, not at all surprised or frightened—he only looks so terribly fatigued, he tunes his violin and plays the Romance from Schumann's Fourth Symphony.

"It wasn't exactly that piece I'd expected to hear, and it gave me a sort of musical shock, for the boy played with simple and unaffected sensitivity . . . yes, it was all so child-like, for the Romance can't possibly be played as a violin solo, but I have rarely been as moved by music as I was that time in the store room; I almost behaved like an idiot, and tears came to my eyes, and Ole Brandy and I agreed that this boy was not going to languish and go to the dogs there in Mac Bett's bewitched hut.

" 'It would be best if he could leave immediately,' said Ole Brandy. 'Mac Bett's in church right now.'

"Well, then we had a talk with the boy's mother and with the captain of the *Albatross*, and later on with Mac Bett too,

362

who proved to be a fine fellow and a gentleman of the old school with embroidered vest and white whiskers à la Gladstone, and then we took the boy along, and as every one knows, we've never had any reason to regret it."

Thus, on a sunny afternoon Orfeus departs from his homeland, his black eye is much reduced in size, and there are large tears on his cheeks, and he has his father's violin case under his arm.

Many people had gathered on the quay, and they all wanted to shake the boy's hand and wish him luck and God's blessing on the journey across the sea and on through life, and his head swam from looking into so many faces all at the same time, even though most of them belonged to old acquaintances—Ole Brandy, Olivarius, Mac Bett, Lindenskov and his daughters, Gravedigger Peter and his mother, the Corpse Crower, and the rose-painter Pontus.

Many tears were shed, not only by the closest relatives and by the Wailing Woman, but also by others, such as Boman's old housekeeper and the youngest of the three Misses Schibbye, and Aunt Lucie was completely inconsolable but assured them it was from pure joy on Orfeus's behalf. Indeed, an immense number of people showed up, and some of the good wishes were underscored with nice, suitable gifts, such as one hundred crowns from Mac Bett, twenty-five from Olivarius, and an old, used, but still very good pocketwatch in a horn case from dancing instructor Lindenskov.

Orfeus felt quite overwhelmed and couldn't even manage to say thank you because the emotion of it all made it hard for him to breathe, but he kept his chin up until the very end, when he was going to say good-by to his mother; then he broke down completely and had to be gently forced down into the ship's boat by Ole Brandy, who accompanied him on board.

363

Just when the little boat passed under the *Albatross's* bowsprit, Orfeus saw through a rainbow-colored grille of tears the face of the figurehead Tarira. He had never before seen it at such close range. It was a dead face of painted wood, a bit cracked and damaged, but for a brief moment a reflection of light from the waves flickered across her face and made it seem alive, as if she gave him a smile of recognition.